CENTER ICE

Boston Rebels Series
Book 1

JULIA CONNORS

© 2024 Julia Connors
All Rights Reserved

Cover Design by Qamber Designs
Developmental Editing by Melissa McGovern of Memos In The Margins
Copy Editing and Proofreading by Nice Girl, Naughty Edits

No part of this book may be reproduced, stored, or transmitted in any form or by any means, electronic or mechanical—including photocopying, recording, or by any information storage or retrieval system—without written permission of the author. The only exception is for the use of brief quotations in a book review.

This is a work of fiction. Names, people, characters, places, corporations or business entities, and events are either the products of the author's imagination or used in an entirely fictitious manner. The author acknowledges the trademark status of various companies and products referenced in this work of fiction. The publication/use of these trademarks is not authorized, associated with, or sponsored by the trademark owners.

*For all the women who have shouldered
heavy burdens on their own...*

Chapter One

DREW

"Well, well, well," my oldest sister's voice rings out from the side door, where she pauses as part of her dramatic entrance. Caitlyn is a woman of extremes, who doesn't do anything halfway. "If it isn't the prodigal son returned."

I pause where I'm kneeling at my mom's feet, untying her shoes for her. It's not that she can't do it herself, it's just easier and less frustrating for her if I do it instead.

"I don't think you know what prodigal means," I say, barely refraining from rolling my eyes.

"Ignore her." My mom's words are low and intended only for me. I glance up and her lips quirk in a pleasant smile, which is an improvement over the vacant look she seems to wear more often these days. Spending the last month with her up at our lake house has made me better understand how her disease is slowly deteriorating her body's ability to function.

"Of course I do," Caitlyn says, her brash voice filling all the space in the room. "I went to Catholic school K through eight, just like you did."

I choose to ignore her, because if I didn't let her little snide comments go most of the time, we'd always be at each other's throats—and that's not good for Mom.

"Why are you taking her shoes off?" Caitlyn asks. "She needs them for balance."

"Actually, her specialist suggested these slippers"—I nod toward the pair sitting next to me on the floor—"that are supposed to be better for her to wear around the house. They're supportive without being as restrictive as sneakers, so it will help with the foot cramps."

Caitlyn has gone back to school to get her nurse practitioner degree, so I've taken over responsibility for my mom's care. But the nurse in her refuses to step back, even though she essentially demanded I move back to Boston and take on this role.

"I know what I'm doing, Caitlyn." I may not know as much about Parkinson's as she does, *yet*, but I'm committed to being here for my mom and learning as much as I can. Aside from hockey, it's my singular focus.

My sister lets out a dubious grunt of acknowledgement. "You're not exactly known for your dependability, Drew, so excuse me if I have questions."

Anger prickles down my spine as I consider her words and her tone, but I ignore the barb. *There's nothing to be gained from fighting with your sister*, I remind myself. Instead, I help my mom slip her feet into the new slippers and fasten the Velcro for her, making a mental note to check on the shipment status of the new sneakers I found made specifically for

Parkinson's patients. They're flexible and will be easy for her to slip in and out of on her own.

My mom is only sixty, but the disease is slowing her down fast. It wasn't as noticeable at first, but over the last year, mom's muscles have started to stiffen up and she's become less confident and independent. Given that she's a tough-as-nails Irish woman, who raised three kids on her own after my dad died, it's been hard to watch her deteriorate. Especially hard because, for the past five years, I've been living thousands of miles away, playing professional hockey first for Vancouver, and then for Colorado.

I'll still travel for a good amount of the year for hockey, but at least when I'm home in Boston, I can be here for her. And give my sisters a bit of a break, though apparently, it'd kill Caitlyn to be grateful for the help, even when she's the one who benefits the most from it.

"You're coming to Missy's for dinner, right?" Mom asks me when I smooth my hands over her ankles to let her know I'm done. Sunday dinner is a family tradition that Missy picked up once it became harder for Mom to handle cooking large meals.

"I can't tonight, remember? I have to go to that thing at my agent's house."

Mom nods, and behind me, Caitlyn releases an annoyed sigh. If I *was* coming, she'd be upset about that too, especially because Missy's boys idolize me. I can't win either way with her, so I just don't try anymore. It's not worth the mental energy.

I feel a little guilty as I leave her with Caitlyn, knowing that I don't actually *have* to go to Jameson's get-together tonight. It's just s'mores around the fire pit with his family and a few of their neighbors, but some of my new teammates are also going to be there, and getting to know them before getting on the ice with them this week seemed like a smart move for my career—especially after the way I fucked things up with my teammates in Colorado when I started there a couple of years back.

As I head from my family home in West Roxbury to my condo in the Back Bay, I'm thankful that the Sunday afternoon traffic isn't that bad. One of the only things I miss about Denver, besides the natural beauty surrounding it, is the infrastructure—not that traffic was never a problem there, but the roads here in Boston were built to handle horse-drawn carriages, not a million cars.

And when I walk through the back door of my building and up the five flights of stairs to the top floor, I find my condo full of the furniture and boxes that were just delivered this morning. I wouldn't say it's a disaster, but I do wish I'd had a little more time to organize things as the movers were bringing them in. At least most of the boxes appear to be in the right rooms, if the labels are any indication.

In my bedroom, I take a few minutes to find the box labeled 'bedding' and then I throw my sheets into the washing machine, relieved I remembered to add laundry detergent to the grocery order I had delivered earlier today. I absolutely hate moving, but this is my third team in the last six years, so I'm getting to be pretty good at it.

I need to make this my last move, which means I need this trade to the Rebels to turn into a longer contract when mine is up for renewal at the end of this season. Now that I'm back, there's no way I can leave. Spending this summer with my mom confirmed my worst fears about her health, how much my sisters can handle, and how much time I might have left with her before she's only a shell of her former self.

I move my bed into place against the wall opposite the bedroom door. On one side is a complete wall of windows overlooking the Esplanade and the Charles River, and on the opposite wall is the bathroom and a substantial closet. This is definitely the smallest place I've lived in since getting drafted into the NHL, but the full roof deck above and the view from my bedroom, not to mention the prime location on Beacon Street, are what I'm paying for.

On my salary, I could have gone bigger and nicer—a luxury condo in one of Boston's new high rises near the Seaport, or something grander in Beacon Hill—but given Mom's rising medical bills, it seemed smart to be more modest. And this three-bedroom top-floor condo in a brownstone in the Back Bay is nicer than anything I could have imagined living in while I was growing up.

I want to unpack the two suitcases I've been living out of at the lake house this summer, but I can't find the box with my hangers, so instead I unpack my toiletries into the bathroom and find something that's not too wrinkled to wear tonight. I'm able to move my dresser into place opposite the foot of my bed, and then get some of my clothes unpacked into that before it's time to leave.

Half an hour later, I'm showered, have eaten something quick, and am throwing my sheets into the dryer before walking out the door to head to my agent's house. I'll feel more settled once I come home tonight and can get more unpacking done, but for now, I'll go chill with my new teammates so I can start to feel settled with my team as well.

Chapter Two

AUDREY

"I feel like every time you cook, I gain ten pounds," Morgan says as she leans back in one of my kitchen chairs and rubs her belly. Morgan is looking at my sister Jules, who is the cook in our family—it's how she celebrates and also how she handles stress, so there's always a lot of food around. "I don't know how you two don't weigh three hundred pounds."

"Jules got our dad's genes," I say. My sister looks like Barbie. She's tall and thin like Dad, but curvy in all the right places, with long legs and beautiful, long ash blond hair. "I, on the other hand, just work hard at not letting my hips get any wider." I roll my eyes, because while I'm not unhappy with my body, I am a little self-conscious about it. I wish I didn't have to watch what I eat and force myself to exercise regularly in order to maintain anything resembling my pre-baby form.

My twenties should have been full of late nights at the

bars, followed by greasy pizza, then brunch and shopping the next day to burn off the hangover. I should have been traveling the world, like I'd planned to after graduating from college. Instead, I raised a child on my own. Well, not entirely on my own. I'm extremely blessed to have the best siblings in the world who've been there for us every step of the way.

There is absolutely nothing I would change about my son, Graham, or our life together. But now that Graham's entered kindergarten, and the days are less intense, I've had some time to reflect—to actually stop and realize what I missed out on while I was so busy parenting—and it's made me realize that I do wish Graham had come into my life a bit later than he did. Not that I'd *ever* admit that to anyone, not even to Jules or my brother, Jameson.

Morgan groans as she sweeps her strawberry blonde hair off her face and into an elastic. "Your body is just fine, but with a face like yours, no one is looking at your body anyway. Those freaking lips..." She sighs, honing in on one of my most prominent features. "If I weren't straight, I'd want to kiss them just to see what they felt like."

Jules bursts out laughing. "Oh my God, someone get Morgan another Moscow Mule. Oh wait, I'm the bartender as well as the chef. I'm on it."

"You guys are ridiculous," I tell them, but I can't hide my smile. When my brother's fiancée, Lauren, relocated to Boston from Park City last winter, her cousin Morgan moved back here with her too, and she's since become one of our closest friends. "You better slow down on those drinks, because we're not rolling into a family friendly backyard party drunk."

Morgan lets out an adorable snort. "*You're* not."

"Nope, I'm definitely not."

Jules gets up from the table and heads to the counter where she's got tonight's drink station set up. She won't have another, I know, because she's already had two, and that's her limit, just like it's mine. When you're the child of an alcoholic, you learn your limits and hold fast to them. Unless you're our brother, in which case you've never had more than one drink at a time.

"Hey, we're celebrating," Jules says. "We're about to start the demo on the Livingston project"—she references the most lucrative project our company, Our House, has taken on yet—"and Morgan is...what are you celebrating, Morgan?"

While Jules mixes her another drink, Morgan tells me a little about work. She's the personal assistant for one of Lauren's best friends, Petra Ivanova, who is not only a famous television personality in her own right, but she's also married to one of the best hockey players of our time, Alex Ivanov. "So anyway, we're heading out to Las Vegas on Thursday for the National Television Academy Awards show."

I note the barely perceptible stiffening of Jules's shoulders at the mention of that city. But she plasters on a huge smile and asks, "She was nominated for an NTA Award?"

"Yep. I'm not surprised, but she seems shocked as shit. It's like she's having some major imposter syndrome. She never expected the show to do this well. She really thought it was going to be a six-month stint getting to film something amazing, then she was going to go back to event planning."

"Well, it's not a surprise to anyone who's seen the show," I say. Petra is incredibly down to earth, but she's also a feminist icon. I've never wanted to be famous—I don't in any way enjoy being in the spotlight—but it's fun to know someone who is.

"Hey, have you thought any more about my offer to get you set up on some dating sites?" Morgan asks me.

I can't hold in the laugh. It's funny that Morgan's such an organization freak, because her brain is a little chaotic. Conversations with her are often peppered with non-sequiturs like that. "How did you get there from just talking about Petra's award nomination?"

"I was thinking about how fun it is now that I'm running Petra's social media account, and that led to me thinking about dating apps and the offer I made you a few weeks ago."

"Yeah, thanks, but no thanks." Dating apps are *not* my thing. Not that I've ever been on one. In college, I met guys in my classes or at parties or at bars. Then I got pregnant my senior year, and for the last six years, dating has not been a priority. Which is probably why my last boyfriend, Scott, broke up with me. That and, after dating for almost two years and basically being a surrogate dad to Graham, he conveniently decided he didn't want kids.

"You said you felt ready to get back out there, but it's not like you're going to meet people at work." And she's right, because most days I work out of our home office in our basement and Jules is the only person I see unless we have a meeting with clients. Morgan sighs and says, "Honestly, the whole working from home thing is awesome, and I almost always love it, but it really makes it hard to meet new people. If I weren't on any of these apps, I don't know how I'd ever meet a guy."

"I'll just meet a guy the old-fashioned way," I say.

"You almost never go out at night. How exactly are you going to meet someone unless you join a dating app?" Jules asks.

"Who knows?" I shrug. I met Scott in line at the deli down the street, so it's not like dating apps are the only way to find someone. "The right guy will probably come along when I least expect it."

"If only it worked that way," Jules sighs. My sister is fairly convinced she's cursed after a string of bad first dates. Guys always find her intimidating because she's gorgeous and a little brash, and has a job that they seem to think threatens their manhood. She's a structural engineer and the lead contractor for our renovation business, and I think the combination of her beauty and brains, combined with being better with power tools than any man, makes her formidable. But she doesn't see that for what it is, she just sees that date after date end badly.

"It can," I say. "But right now, I've got an amazing kid, great friends, and the best siblings. Our business is thriving. I've got my rooftop garden I built this summer, I'm taking that dance class on Wednesday nights, and I'm not looking to get my heart broken again any time soon." I think back to how confused and sad Graham had been when Scott suddenly disappeared out of his life. I can't let that happen to him again. "Besides, I've got a friends-with-benefits arrangement that suits me just fine. *I'm happy.*"

They both look at me like they've caught me in a lie, but I'm telling the truth. I *am* happy, because my sense of happiness and self-worth doesn't require validation from a man.

I'm about to explain as much, but from upstairs, Graham yells, "Mom?"

"Shit!" I say, glancing at my watch. "I forgot to set the timer, and he's been in the shower forever." The kid loves water and has no concept of how expensive or wasteful it is for a tiny human to take thirty-minute showers.

I rush up the stairs and cross the landing before coming to a stop and knocking on the bathroom door, because my five-year-old is suddenly aware that we're different genders and insists he needs his privacy. God forbid, I walk in without knocking, even though he does it to me all the time.

"What's up, Graham?" I call out.

"I'm out of shampoo," he says, and I'm thankful that his little voice still has the sing-song quality it always has. As much as I appreciate that he can do a lot of things independently these days, it still feels like he's growing up too fast.

I crack open the bathroom door and a blast of steam hits me in the face. Flicking on the switch for the ceiling fan, I grab a spare bottle of shampoo from below the sink and pass it to him between the shower curtain and the tile wall. "I forgot to set the timer, so I'm giving you two more minutes, and then you need to get out."

"But I just got in," he complains.

I hit the buttons on the countertop timer to give him an alert when his two minutes are up. "Yeah, like twenty minutes ago. Wash your hair fast. It's almost time to get ready to go to Jameson and Lauren's."

"Okay," he says eagerly. Lauren's twins, Iris and Ivy, have been such a welcome addition to our family. Before them, Graham had no cousins, and he's absolutely flourished in his role as the big cousin. I've loved watching their bond develop, and at the same time, it's always a tad bittersweet because I think he'd be an amazing big brother. However, I wouldn't want another child unless I was in a happy, committed relationship. Doing the single-parent thing once was unavoidable, but I'm not choosing that path a second time.

There's only one branch on our family tree. And I was just fine with that until his stupid kindergarten project came home on Friday. It's Sunday night and I still don't know what to do about it. I head back downstairs, and I must be deep in thought because Jules takes one look at me and says, "Uh oh, what's wrong?"

My head snaps up in surprise, and both my sister and Morgan are looking at me with concern lacing their expressions. "Nothing's wrong."

"Bullshit." Jules pulls out my seat. "Here, sit and tell us before Graham comes back down."

I sink into the chair. "Graham has a family tree project for school. I'm not sure how to help him fill out the planning sheet, and I feel like a total asshole about it."

"Why do *you* feel like an asshole about it?" Morgan asks, and I hear the statement within the question—it's not like I *chose* to be a single parent.

"Because they're doing this whole big unit on families, and to the school's credit, they are trying to be inclusive. They've read books about all different types of families, and now the kids are going to create family trees. They sent home several planning sheets so that people could pick out the one that best represents their family. And you know what type of family tree doesn't exist? Apparently, the one where you have only one parent, no siblings, and no grandparents."

Jules's and Morgan's lips both turn down at the corners. "Maybe you could talk to the teachers and see if Graham could draw his own family tree?" Jules suggests.

"Yeah, maybe. But I don't even know what that tree would look like. And every other kid in that class is going to come in with their planning sheets full of names and be able to fill out a normal family tree. My kid is—"

"Amazing," Morgan says. "And it doesn't matter if his family tree has one branch or one hundred, he's still a great kid. After all, who else can tell you that there are over 130 species of ducks on this planet, or that penguins are the only birds that can swim but not fly?"

I let a laugh bubble up, relieved that my friends and family are always around to ground me when the pressure feels like too much. "That's true. I doubt many other five-year-olds are as weirdly obsessed with birds."

"You have to prepare yourself, because this is going to keep happening," Jules says, as if I don't know that I'll be facing this reality indefinitely.

"I'm mostly worried about how the other kids in his class will treat him once they figure out he doesn't know who his dad is," I admit. Graham has been relatively insulated because he hasn't been in school yet, but kids can be so cruel —whether intentionally or unintentionally. I probably need to talk to his teachers and let them know the situation, but the lie I've always told—*I don't know who his dad is*—was easier when I was saying it to my college friends or perfect strangers...but telling my son's kindergarten teacher? I don't want Graham to be known throughout his *chichi* private school as the kid who doesn't know who his dad is.

"Hey, Mom," Graham calls as he runs down the stairs. He

looks at the table, which was full of food when he went up for his shower after dinner. "Oh, did you guys eat all the food?"

We can't help but laugh because Jules always cooks enough to feed an army. "No, we just put it in the fridge because we're going over to Lauren and Jameson's."

"But I'm hungry."

"Really? After everything you just ate?"

"I'm a growing boy," he says, flexing his non-existent biceps.

"How about if I make you half a sandwich to eat in the car on the way over?"

He nods vigorously, and then Morgan says, "Why don't you come over here and tell me more about ducks…"

Chapter Three

DREW

I turn to walk up the driveway toward the backyard and I'm pretty sure I see Mathieu Coltier, the Rebels star goalie, affectionately known by Boston fans as Colt, walk through the gate ahead of me. Colt is essentially a local Boston celebrity, so it's no surprise he has his baseball cap pulled low across his forehead. Boston can be kind of nuts about their professional athletes.

I pick up my pace, but when I get to the top of the driveway, I don't see him amid the small crowd of people in the backyard. I thought this was a smaller gathering than it is, apparently. I push the gate open and look around, trying to locate Colt or my agent, Jameson Flynn.

"Hey," a woman with long red hair says as she walks toward me, "I'm Lauren."

Oh, so this is Jameson's fiancée—the single mom who converted him from a confirmed bachelor to a family man.

"I'm Drew. Jameson has said lots of great things about you."

"Well, that's a relief to hear! Drew..." She pauses, like she's trying to place me, and then her face lights up. "Oh! You're Drew Jenkins." She slaps her forehead with her palm. "Of course. I work in marketing for the Rebels. Welcome to the team."

"Thanks." I didn't realize she worked for the team, but I don't mention that in case Jameson told me and I forgot. "I'm really excited to be back in Boston."

"Yeah, Jameson mentioned you have family here?"

"I grew up in West Roxbury," I tell her. "My whole family's still there. My sisters live on the same street as my mom."

"They must be very excited to have you back here. Where are you living?"

"My family has a cabin up on Lake Winnipesaukee, so I was up in New Hampshire for most of the summer, but I just bought a place in the Back Bay. Moved in earlier today."

"You'll be right in the thick of things, then," she says with a smile.

I start to tell her that I picked it because it's easy to get to the arena and the practice facility. But then I hear "Jenkins!" from across the yard, and when I glance over, Colt is motioning for me to join him and Jameson.

I glance back at Lauren, who says, "I think you're being summoned by your team elder."

"Oh my God," I laugh, "do people really call him that?"

Colt has been in the league for like fifteen years. He's an amazing goalie, and one of the most notorious playboys to ever walk this planet.

"Only if they want to piss him off. I wouldn't recommend

starting off that way… In fact," she says, grabbing my forearm, "definitely don't do that."

And suddenly, I *know* my reputation has preceded me. Either that, or Jameson's told her what I told him about getting off on the wrong foot with my former team. But more than likely, everyone knows. "I won't. It was nice to meet you, Lauren."

As I walk across the yard toward Jameson and Colt, I feel like I'm being watched. But when I glance over my shoulder, I don't notice anyone overly focused on me.

"Alright, Jenkins," Colt says when I approach. "We've got a problem."

Fuck, no. I haven't even been in town for twenty-four hours. I can't possibly have mis-stepped already. I hold in the groan, because I'm a grown-ass man working on self-control both on and off the ice, and instead say, "What's that?"

"Renaud broke two fingers in some sort of a bar fight last night."

David Renaud is a Boston winger who plays the unofficial role of an enforcer. He's a very physical player who some games spends as much time in the penalty box as he does on the ice. Boston fans love him, and he's one of those players other team's fans love to hate.

Colt looks at me expectantly, but I'm not sure what he wants me to say. "That sucks. How long is he out?"

"He's not out," Colt says, like I'm a moron. "They're fingers. Fucking tape them together and you're good. But he's sure as shit not going to be able to punch someone in the face."

I don't know how Colt thinks Renaud is getting his fingers in his glove when they're broken and taped together, much less how he'll grip his stick and control it with the finesse necessary to play at this level. Training camp starts this week, and pre-season games follow, but at least the season opener is still weeks away. Maybe he means Renaud will be healed enough by then?

"It means you're going to need to step it up out there, rookie," Colt says.

"He's not a fucking rookie," Jameson says as he elbows Colt.

"On this team he is," Colt says.

I'm so tempted to ask him if he's still pissed about the hat trick I scored on him last season, but we're not friendly enough for that yet. I know better than to piss off the most senior member of my new team.

"Literally one of the things Boston said when they signed me was that I needed to tone down the fighting," I tell Colt, then glance to Jameson for confirmation.

After a year in the AHL, and then playing for Vancouver for my first three years in the NHL, Colorado offered me a great contract. But then I got off to a bad start with the team and it affected my play. I found myself in too many fights with other teams on the ice, and even more with my teammates off the ice.

I never lived up to what Colorado was paying me, and when they traded me to Boston, I took it for what it was: a chance to start fresh. I have one year to prove to Boston that they should keep me after my contract ends.

This is my year to buckle down. Nothing can mess this up.

"That's right," Jameson says. "A well-timed fight is always going to pump up the fans, but AJ didn't take over his contract to have him spend all his time in the penalty box."

In fact, according to my conversations with Jameson during the negotiations, one of the things that AJ—Boston's general manager and the only female GM in the league—insisted on was that I clean up my act. Less partying, and less fighting. I've always been a bit of a wildcard, and she wants me to be a steady presence on the ice.

"AJ knows we need someone to step up for Renaud," Colt says.

"She told you that?" Jameson asks, and it's clear he already knows the answer.

Colt rolls his eyes. "She would have, if we'd talked about it."

"Well, I actually did talk to her about it, and you're wrong."

Colt's neck stiffens, and he turns toward Jameson. In addition to being former teammates and Jameson now being Colt's agent, I think they're also close friends. But while Jameson is so serious he comes off as aloof, Colt is flashy and a bit hot-headed.

I don't catch what Colt says to Jameson because the back of my neck prickles with the sensation that I'm being watched, again. Scanning the backyard once more, I don't notice anyone focused on me. That is, until I lift my eyes to the deck, where a woman with dark hair falling in loose waves well past her shoulders is staring at me with the most beautiful blue eyes rimmed in long, dark lashes. She's talking to Jameson's wife, and she looks a bit panicked as she looks away from me. She also looks...familiar?

I continue to stare at her, trying to place how I know her,

and then her eyes widen, and she spins on her heel and heads into the house. And that's when I remember. She had that same look one morning right after I'd graduated from college, when she rushed out of my apartment because she'd fallen asleep in my bed the night before and was worried about being late for the first day of some summer class she was taking.

Audrey. She was a year behind me at Boston University and super smart. She'd tutored me through calculus—the one math course I needed to take to graduate and had stupidly put off until second semester my senior year—and we'd slept together once. Then I was drafted, and we never talked again.

Is she pissed about it now, all these years later? And what is she doing here? I wonder how she knows Jameson and Lauren?

"Where's the bathroom?" I turn and ask Jameson after Audrey shuts the screen door behind her.

"Through that door." He nods his chin to the door Audrey just walked through. "Go through the kitchen, and it's down the hall on the right, before the stairs."

"Thanks," I say, and walk purposefully toward the house. Once I step through the screen door, I see Audrey. She's pacing and looks like she's about to crawl out of her own skin.

"Audrey, what's wrong?" I ask, and she spins toward me.

Her eyes are full of panic and what I might even describe as fear. "Drew." The word is not friendly, so I slow my steps, stopping when I'm still a good six feet from her. "I was just leaving."

"Don't go yet," I say, even though I have no right to make

demands like this. But now that she's standing here in front of me with those bright blue eyes, her skin creamy and her cheeks flushed, I remember how beautiful I always thought she was. I also remember being a bit intimidated by how serious she was and how things like math just seemed to come easily to her. I was initially also a tad embarrassed that she was a junior tutoring me because she'd taken calculus in high school. But the more time we'd spent together, the more I'd liked her—and not just because she was pretty. "I haven't seen you in, what...five years?"

"More like six. But anyway, I was just leaving."

She grabs her bag off a hook near the front door, but I can't stop myself from trying to keep her talking, hoping she'll stay a little longer. "How have you been?"

She swallows, the sound is audible in the silent house. "Goodbye, Drew," she says, but she doesn't make a move to leave.

The screen door slams open behind me, and I turn in time to see a little boy barreling straight toward us. "Mommy!" he says. "Are we going already?"

I glance at Audrey, then back at the boy. His hair is a lighter shade of brown than hers, and his eyes are familiar.

"Yes," she says definitively. "Sorry, Bud, but I don't feel good. We need to go home."

"What's *your* name?" the boy asks, looking up at me like he just noticed me standing here.

"I'm Drew," I say as I squat down next to him so we're eye to eye. "What's your name?"

"I'm Graham." He gives me a lopsided smile as he stares back at me with his big brown eyes. It's like looking into a mirror.

"How old are you, Graham?"

"I'm five and I'm in kindergarten."

Heart stuttering, I glance up at Audrey, and I'm sure there's confusion written across my face. Even I don't need a tutor to do this kind of math.

Her arms are folded across her chest, and her voice holds a certain level of finality when she says, "It was good seeing you again, Drew."

I'm being dismissed. *Fuck that.*

If there's a chance that Graham is my kid, then I deserve to know, and to know why the hell she didn't tell me.

"Wait," I bark out the demand as I stand quickly. It's only when I look down at her that I realize I'm much closer now, so I soften my voice. I don't want to spook her like before. "We need to talk."

"We really don't," she says as she squeezes Graham to her side.

"We do." My whole reality just shifted, and while I haven't even had time to process it yet, I'll be damned if we're not discussing this—that's non-negotiable. "And we can either do it here, now, or you can give me your number and we can talk later. But we will be talking."

"You can get my number from Lauren," she says. "We're leaving."

"I'll call you tonight," I promise. "Make sure you answer your phone."

A scoff bursts out of her so quickly it seems to surprise us both. "Oh, like you did all those times I called you when you moved to Vancouver?"

"Audrey..." I say, hoping I can placate her. I was a stupid twenty-two-year-old who'd just been drafted into the NHL.

"Don't 'Audrey' me," she says. "I will answer my phone if I can. And if not, I'll call you back. That's what people normally do when someone's left them a message. Or twenty." Now she sounds pissed off, and she spins on her heel and heads toward the front door with a blonde woman I hadn't even noticed hot on her heels.

"Who was that, Mommy?" Graham asks when they make it to the front door.

"He's no one," Audrey replies right before the door shuts behind them.

Ouch.

With my stomach in my throat, I turn around, and my eyes meet Lauren's. I hope she can't tell how upset I am right now.

What is Audrey talking about? What twenty messages? I vaguely remember that she called me a few times and left a couple of messages. But I had a lot going on that first year in Vancouver, and I ignored her calls because I needed to make a clean break from my life back in Boston—I couldn't handle anything else on my plate. But twenty messages? I don't remember that. I'm trying to wrack my brain and remember what happened six years ago...

"You want to help me carry the s'mores supplies out, please?" Lauren asks me, shaking me from my stupor.

"Yeah, sure."

I follow her to the kitchen island, where two large platters with graham crackers, chocolate bars, and marshmallows sit.

"So, how do you know Audrey?" I ask her as I pick up one of the platters.

She holds up her left hand so I can see her engagement ring. "Future sister-in-law."

"Wait...Audrey is..." I try to make sense of this in my head. "She's Jameson's sister?"

"You didn't know that?"

"I had no idea."

"Weren't you already working with Jameson when you were playing hockey in college, with plans of him becoming your agent after you were drafted?"

That's how it usually works with college players if they haven't already been drafted. "Yeah," I say, shaking my head in disbelief, "but I didn't know Audrey was his sister."

Getting a girl pregnant in college is bad enough, but my agent's little sister? How did I not know they were related? How did I not know she was pregnant?

Fuck...I've not even been back in Boston for a full day, and I've already seriously screwed up. Or I guess I screwed up years ago, but I just didn't know it.

"Did she know Jameson was going to be your agent?"

"I don't know. I can't remember if I ever mentioned it specifically, but it was definitely public knowledge."

"How did you and Audrey know each other, again?" she asks with curiosity.

She obviously knows we know each other from college, but maybe Audrey didn't tell her anything aside from that? "She tutored me." I'm tempted to ask her for more details about Audrey and Graham, but if I have a kid, it really feels like the type of thing I should talk to Audrey about directly.

Outside, Lauren and I set the platters down on the table nearest the fire pit, and then she gives me Audrey's number. I consider leaving right then, just driving back to my place and calling Audrey to figure out what the hell is going on. But then I notice Jameson and Colt watching us, and I figure I better go finish my conversation with them.

No matter what is going on in my personal life, I have to start off on the right foot with this team. Everything depends on it. And since Colt is the longest playing and most highly respected member of the Rebels, I can't just ditch. So I head back across the yard toward them, forcing myself to put what just happened aside for a bit. Getting the Boston Rebels to sign me to a new contract after this still year has to be my single greatest priority.

Chapter Four

AUDREY

As soon as our clients, the Livingstons, leave our office, I carry my coffee cup over to the row of glossy-front white cabinets hanging along the wall of exposed brick. With the long wooden shelves held in place by brass brackets that hang above, and the wood floors with shiny white tables pushed together in the center of the room, our office is a study in contrasts. But it works perfectly and is a great example of how we blend traditional and modern design for our clients.

I pop a coffee pod into the machine and set my cup below it, realizing I've already lost count of the number of cups I've had this morning.

"You doing okay?" Jules asks from behind me. Because she's normally saucy and sarcastic, the concern in her tone hits me hard.

I stare straight ahead at the brick wall, afraid that if I look at her and see the worry in her eyes, I'll crumble. "I've been better."

"Did you sleep at all?"

"I'm not sure. Maybe a little."

Drew called right after I'd gotten Graham to bed last night, but I let it go to voicemail. I meant what I said when I told him I'd answer if I could—and emotionally, I just couldn't.

Six years. It's been just over six years since I discovered that our one-night stand resulted in a pregnancy. I'm still not sure how it happened. We were so careful, but that condom must have leaked without us realizing.

Drew wasn't even my first call when I found out. Jameson was. And then Jules. And finally, a week later, I worked up the nerve to call Drew, and he didn't call me back. Not then, and not the next twenty times. Twenty voicemails, and never even got a call or a text in return. So no, I'm not feeling any sense of obligation to call him back until I'm damn good and ready.

Last night, I'd lain awake most of the night, rehashing everything I'd gone through when I found out I was pregnant and realized I'd be doing this parenting thing without his support. I was up until the early hours of the morning, debating the pros and the cons of him coming back into our lives, trying to figure out what it means, and imagining what he might want.

"You knew this was a possibility when you heard about the trade," Jules reminds me. She's the only person on the planet who knows Drew is Graham's father.

I couldn't tell Jameson—he was too much of a hot-head back then, too protective of his baby sisters, who he'd practically raised. The first thing he'd said to me when I'd told him I was pregnant but didn't think the guy would be interested in being involved was, "I'm going to kill him."

Jameson was already Drew's agent at that point. If I'd told him the truth, Jameson could have—and probably would have—ruined Drew's career. And even though Drew didn't deserve my protection like that, he deserved his chance in the NHL.

"I was afraid I'd run into him at a restaurant or something. I didn't expect to find him standing in my brother's backyard. I thought at least family spaces would be safe."

"Knowing Jameson, he was just trying to smooth Drew's transition to the team."

"I'm sure."

Colt was there, like always. And I know Patrick Walsh, one of the alternate captains on the team, was supposed to stop by with his kids at some point. Having Drew get to know them before training camp starts is probably Jameson's way of helping, especially because everyone knows Drew's performance in Colorado suffered, and I'm sure he needs to get off on the right foot with this team. If the rumors are true, this year will be a turning point in Drew's career. Either he'll end on a high note and Boston will re-sign him, or Boston won't want him for another contract, and he'll end up as an unsigned free agent.

Even while I've had to pretend I have no idea who Drew is, I've followed his career closely. It's been tumultuous the past few years, and I'm trying not to be pissed off at him about it. It was one thing when he was playing for Vancouver and I felt like protecting his career for him the way I did was worth it, because he was doing so well. But then he went to

Colorado and his career went to shit, and I was left feeling like I'd made huge sacrifices on his behalf—which, of course, he didn't even know about—and he wasn't holding up his end of the non-existent bargain by kicking ass out there in the NHL.

I have no right and every right to hold it against him, and I'm a mess as a result of this dichotomy.

"Did he call again, after that first time last night?" Jules asks. She'd headed to her room after our quick chat about how I wasn't ready to talk to him yet, and this morning I'd shown up in our design studio—in the basement of our brownstone in Boston's South End—after taking Graham to school, only seconds before our clients arrived. So until now, we haven't had a chance to talk about this.

I pull the now-full coffee cup out from the machine and glance over at her. "Yeah, he called two more times."

"Did he leave more messages?"

"Yeah. I haven't listened to them, though." I take a sip of my coffee, hoping against logic that it'll calm me down.

"Are you going to?"

"Eventually."

"What are you waiting for, exactly?" she asks.

"I don't know." I glance out the wall of glass that leads to the small front brick patio and the few granite steps leading up to the street level. Despite this being a basement office, we made sure it gets plenty of light. I glance back at my sister and say, "Maybe just until I feel strong enough to deal with this."

"You ARE strong enough," Jules insists, raising her eyebrows like she's reminding me of something I already know. "And you don't really have a choice but to deal with it now that he knows. Or at least, we think he does. But we won't know for sure until you listen to his messages."

I wrap both hands around the mug and bring it just under my nose, inhaling the sweet smell of the coffee mixed with the vanilla creamer and hoping the familiar scent calms me. And then I admit my fear—the thing that kept me up all night. "What if he wants to be involved in Graham's life?"

"What if he doesn't?" Jules counters.

"I don't know which is worse," I admit.

I think of all the moments he's already missed, from the sleepless nights when Graham was a baby, to his first steps, to his first day of kindergarten just over a month ago. So much has happened in the past five and a half years since he was born, and Drew missed it all.

"He obviously wanted nothing to do with *me* when I was calling him non-stop after I found out I was pregnant. So imagining myself co-parenting with him is just...a lot to consider, I guess."

"Unfortunately, what's best for you and what's best for Graham might be different in this case. I think the question you have to ask yourself is: would Graham benefit from having a father in his life?"

I hear everything Jules isn't saying about our own father and how he walked out on us. How Jameson stepped up and filled that role, even though he was only in his mid-twenties, and how he's had to fill that role for Graham too. How Graham's never truly had a dad. And I think about that damn family tree and how different it might look if Drew was a part of Graham's life.

"I don't know. I guess it depends on what kind of a dad

Drew wants to be. We had a father in our life, and we were better off when he left."

Jules gets a look that's hard to read, like she always does when our dad comes up. Hands down, she was his favorite. We used to call her his shadow. She was swinging a hammer when she was five and knew how to use every major power tool by the time she was ten, because she wanted to be just like him.

In the summers, she worked for his construction company—she loved being on job sites, and it probably explains why she's the structural engineer and lead contractor, while I'm the architect and business manager for our little company. Saving the construction company was the only thing I asked Jameson for when Dad left, because together it was the one thing we could give Jules to make up for how much Mom dying and then Dad leaving had fucked up our family.

"Drew isn't a co-dependent alcoholic," Jules says dryly.

"That we know of."

We look at each other and then burst out laughing. If we don't make light of our history, it would probably crush us like it almost did when we were teenagers.

"You don't even know if he wants to be involved," Jules says. "But he at least deserves to know what happened."

I don't want her to be right, but I know she is. As pissed as I am, I still realize that not returning my phone calls six years ago isn't a reason to not tell him what happened or to keep him from Graham.

"I'm worried about him being involved—he's so volatile. His hockey career has been all over the place, he's known for being unpredictable and unreliable on the ice, and his...

extra-curricular activities seem to involve a lot of alcohol and a lot of women."

"I didn't realize you'd followed him so closely," Jules says, brow lifting as her eyes meet mine.

"He's the father of my child. It's hard not to want to know what he's doing while I'm here raising our kid. And I don't know if I trust him to be involved in Graham's life if that's the energy he's going to bring to the relationship, you know?"

"Maybe we should listen to the messages and see if that's even what he wants? You know, before you go too far along the path of thinking of all the reasons you shouldn't trust him."

Yep, Jules may have ended up with the daddy issues after our father deserted us, but I no doubt ended up with the serious trust issues.

I carry my coffee back to the table, where I sit while Jules does laps around the room. Except for first thing in the morning, my sister is a constant ball of motion. Taking a deep breath, I open up the voicemail and hit play.

Audrey... Drew's voice fills the room and then there's a pause. It's impossible not to remember how he said my name that way—equal parts awe and ecstasy—six years ago as he climaxed inside me. The moment that changed the entire trajectory of my life, but didn't impact him at all. *I don't know what to say, except that I have a lot of questions, and I'm really hoping you'll answer them for me. Call me, please.*

I look at Jules and lift my shoulder in a shrug. It's hard to read much into that message except that he's looking for answers. No indication of whether he wants to be involved, but I guess how could he if he's not even sure if Graham is his?

I hit play on the next message.

Audrey, I'm going a bit crazy here with you not returning my call. I'm sorry, I know that's a shit thing to be upset about after I didn't return your calls years ago. But I didn't know why you were calling. I thought... Another long pause fills the space, and I almost think he's hung up until I hear, *...You know, it doesn't matter what I was thinking back then. I'm so sorry I didn't listen to your messages after the first one. Please, call me back.*

Jules and I exchange a look. Hers says, '*Hey, at least he's sorry now.*' I don't know what my face is saying, but I'm frustrated, sad, and mad that Graham had to miss out on having a dad because of Drew's commitment to being a one-night stand kind of guy. I knew that about him when I chose to sleep with him; I just never considered that I might end up pregnant after he moved to another country.

I hit play on the last message. It's an empty two seconds, as he must have hung up without saying anything.

I stare at Jules, trying not to let my nerves get the best of me. "You going to call him now?" she asks.

"Yeah," I say, glancing at the time. It's mid-morning, and I know today's the first day of training camp, but he's not a rookie so he won't have practice until tomorrow. He might be around. Of course, there's every possibility that Jameson is with him. My brother is the agent for about a third of the Boston Rebels. But thinking Jameson might be with him isn't really why I'm avoiding the call. I'm putting it off because I'm so torn about how I'm feeling—I'm nervous, but also upset with myself about that because why does he make me feel this way after all these years?

"I have to head to the house in Wellesley," Jules says with an eye roll. The house is a bit of an inside joke because she's pretty convinced that the newly married couple we are renovating it for is going to wind up divorced before it's done. Renovations are seriously stressful. "Do you want me to wait until after you've called him?"

"No, go ahead. I'll let you know how the conversation goes." I don't know what I'm going to say, but it's probably better that I talk to Drew privately, even if I am going to end up telling Jules everything afterward.

"Alright." Jules picks up a few of her things that are laying around. "Call me if you need anything at all."

"I will," I tell her. "And I'll get these revisions to the Livingston project done today so you have time to go over those with them one more time before you head to Maine this weekend."

"Thanks," she says as she heads upstairs into our house to grab her keys.

I stare at my phone for a few moments, knowing that once I make this call, things will change. How drastically, I have no idea. But Drew knowing about Graham is going to change things, for sure.

Chapter Five

DREW

"I hate this part," Zach Reid, the other new player for the Rebels, says as we sit in Alessandra Jones's office, waiting for our meeting with the team's general manager. He's a couple of years younger than I am and was traded from Philadelphia.

"What part?"

"Starting over. This is only the second team I've played for."

I know this about him because I've made sure I know everything there is to know about everyone I'll be playing with this year. Easier to avoid missteps this way.

"Starting over sucks," I agree. "But it's also an opportunity."

"True," he says with a nod. "What do you think she's like?"

"AJ? She's like any other GM—a hard-ass, but only because she's committed to doing what's best for her team."

"That's the fairest assessment I've ever heard." AJ's voice

comes from behind me, and I thank God that she sounds pleased with my assessment. We've had a few conversations leading up to my trade, and I already feel like I know her better than any other GM I've played for.

Zach and I both stand as AJ sweeps into the room, followed by our team captain, Ronan McCabe, one of the alternate captains, Patrick Walsh, and our goalie, Colt.

We all shake hands and do some brief introductions, and then we're dragging our chairs away from her desk and toward the seating area near the full wall of glass that overlooks the practice facility. AJ and Patrick sit on the cream couch against the glass while McCabe and Colt each take the cushioned armchairs on either side of the coffee table.

Before he sits, McCabe grumbles about the throw pillow on the chair, and ultimately sets it on the coffee table so it doesn't get in the way of his huge frame, which fills every inch of the seat. AJ's office is surprisingly feminine for someone who's staked her reputation in hockey as a total ball buster, and it feels like McCabe takes offense to the soft frills.

"We wanted to meet with you both while the rookies are practicing," AJ says, ignoring McCabe, "because you each come with significant experience and a little baggage." She glances at me, then at Zach. "It seemed like a good idea to chat about the culture of the club we've built here—"

Ronan clears his throat, and we all turn toward him. "I think AJ just wants to make sure you're not going to be dicks."

It's amusing to watch the effort it takes AJ not to roll her eyes. She looks over at Zach. "You have a reputation for avoiding fights," she says, but that's an oversimplification. Zach Reid doesn't just avoid fights, he goads his opponent into losing his temper, but skates away before a fight can start. The mind games he plays on ice are both brilliant and infuriating—I know because I've fallen victim to them before when we played on opposing teams. "But I need to know that if we needed you to, you could step in and defend your teammates."

"You don't want me to fight," Zach says. "Trust me."

"Why?" Patrick Walsh asks. "You can't throw a punch? Or you can't take one?"

Zach presses his lips together between his teeth and says, "Quite the opposite."

We all look at him, awaiting elaboration, but he says nothing else.

"So is that a yes?" AJ asks.

"If I need to defend someone, sure." Zach shrugs.

AJ turns her gaze on me. "You, on the other hand, could benefit from a little restraint on the ice."

"I'm working on that," I assure them. "It won't be like that here."

"Let's talk about Colorado."

It takes everything I have not to respond flippantly with, "Let's not." Instead, I keep my face in the most neutral expression possible, wishing she'd brought this shit up in one of the conversations we had before she signed me, rather than now, in front of my teammates.

"You weren't overly big on fighting when you played for Vancouver. What happened in Colorado?"

I glance at Colt, McCabe, and Walsh, who all look interested in my response. I see the question on their faces: how does a player who spent less than a year in the AHL before being brought up to the NHL, who then had three great seasons with Vancouver, get traded to Colorado and let it all go to shit?

"I got off on the wrong foot with one of my teammates and it messed up my relationship with the whole team."

"We're going to need more details than that," AJ says, folding her hands in her lap as she assesses me coolly with her dark eyes.

I exhale so suddenly it comes out like a grunt. The rumors have been out there for years; she's really only asking me to confirm or deny them.

"On one of the first nights I was in Colorado, I accidentally almost slept with my team captain's wife."

Walsh, one of the most happily married guys in the NHL, looks like his head's about to explode. "How do you *accidentally almost* sleep with your teammate's wife?" He grits the question out between clenched teeth.

"I didn't know who she was." I emphasize this truth because his wife sought me out, not the other way around. "I'd only been in town a night or two, and went to a restaurant to grab dinner. I was eating at the bar, this hot blonde started chatting me up, and things...kind of progressed..." I don't mention that we full-on made out at the bar until we were asked to leave. "We were leaving the bar together when Leland Alistair showed up and introduced me to his right hook."

"Maybe if you knew someone for more than fifteen minutes before you decided to sleep with them, that wouldn't have happened," Walsh says.

McCabe shoots Walsh a look, then asks, "Did she know who you were?"

"Yeah. She did it to piss him off. In the end, I don't think he ever quite believed that I was just a pawn in her games, even though they were already well on the road to divorce."

"What's that have to do with your hockey game?" Colt asks, and I just stare at him in return.

"Seriously?" I ask.

"Yeah." He crosses his arms across his chest.

"Leland was my captain," I say again, trying to keep my tone level. "And he made sure I always felt like an outsider. He turned most of the other veterans against me, and even though several of them eventually told me I didn't deserve that treatment, it still messed with my game—badly." I was beyond pissed off every time I was on the ice, and I couldn't take my aggression out on my teammates, who were the real culprits, so I took it out on my opponents instead. Hence all the time in the penalty box.

"That's a coaching and management fail, if you ask me," AJ says. "If your teammates are out there on the ice and not passing to you after the puck drop..." Clearly, she's watched enough footage of the game to see how my teammates treated me after each face-off. "Why didn't the coaches get involved?"

"They did, eventually, but it took way too many games for them to figure out what was happening, and by then, the damage was done."

"Idiots," AJ mumbles. "It was so fucking obvious."

"Yep. I guarantee it won't happen again."

"Good," AJ says. "Because we need our Center on the ice, not in the penalty box all the time." And that's that. She moves on to other more logistical conversations about things like equipment, practice schedules, and our upcoming pre-season games, and ten minutes later, she's asking

McCabe to stay, and dismissing the rest of us from her office. Patrick Walsh and Zach Reid strike up an easy conversation as they walk down the hallway. AJ asked Walsh and Colt to give us a quick tour of the practice facility, and Colt falls into step beside me as we follow the others.

"You left early last night," Colt says.

"Yeah, I had some unpacking to do."

"You sure it had nothing to do with Flynn's sister? I saw you follow her into the house. You're damn lucky he didn't notice." Goosebumps trickle down my spine. I was hoping no one noticed, but Colt's apparently more observant than I gave him credit for.

I'm not sure I'll ever get used to the idea that Audrey is Jameson's sister. Did I ever know her last name? Did I even know she was from Boston? Did I know she had a brother? Did I know any damn thing about her, other than she was smart enough to get me through calculus, immediately put me at ease every time I was around her, and was pretty terrific in bed?

Shit, I was such an asshole.

"I went inside to use the bathroom, not to chase after his sister."

"Hmmm."

After a nearly sleepless night, my mind is mush today. I don't know if I'm reading too much into Colt's noncommittal reply, or not enough, but it leaves me wondering what he thinks he knows.

"Flynn said you two went to college together?" Colt says.

"Yeah," I say, taken aback that Jameson knows this. Given that his fiancée clearly didn't know that I knew Audrey until last night, I'm guessing maybe she told him? I decide this is the most likely scenario, since how could Lauren have *not* mentioned that scene in the kitchen? Then again, if she suspects I'm Graham's father, she clearly hasn't told Jameson, because there's no way he knows or I would have already heard from him. "She was a year behind me at BU and tutored me in calculus."

"Calculus?" Colt lets out a laugh that's practically a snort. "So you're smart, then?"

"Not at math, hence needing a tutor."

Like my fellow new player Zach, I know that Colt didn't go to college. They both came to the NHL through the Canadian Hockey League when they were barely twenty. And while Zach's still in his mid-twenties, Colt's got at least a decade and a half in the league. There's a ton of speculation about him being close to retirement, but the guy doesn't seem ready to leave the crease any time soon.

Colt lets out another noncommittal noise, then says, "Yeah, math makes sense, given that she's an architect now."

"Is she?" I spend a second trying to remember if I knew she wanted to be an architect or not. It's shameful how little I remember about her—my memories are more like short clips from a movie: meeting her for the first time in the library, the way she always smelled like honey and citrus, us sitting cross-legged on my bed as we reviewed problems before my mid-term exam, the way she tasted with my face between her legs, how her name sounded rolling off my lips while she was coming with me buried inside her...

"Yeah, she and her sister run a construction company. Jules is the contractor, and Audrey is the architect. It's actually..." Colt pauses with a proud smile and a quick shake of his head. "It's amazing what they've accomplished in the last couple years. Who knew so many people wanted a company that only hires women?"

"You mean all the contractors they work with are women?"

"Yep. And they're one of the fastest growing construction companies in Boston. They keep making all these 'Best of' lists." He tells me how they were featured in a famous Boston magazine last year, and how things really took off from there. I don't even know how to process what she's accomplished while also raising our child, except that I'm not surprised. If anyone could do it, it would be her.

"Hey," Walsh says, turning back toward us, "let's check out the locker room so you know where to go tomorrow."

After a brief tour of the locker room and some of the other parts of the facility, we head out. I'm walking into the parking garage attached to the rink, when Colt calls out from behind me.

"Hey, I like you, so I'm going to give you some advice."

I can't help but notice that he waited to share his advice until we were in an empty parking garage with no one else around. I turn to face him. "Alright."

"Stay far away from Flynn's sister… That's a path you do not want to walk down. He's overly protective of those girls, and you'd have to be crazy to test him like that."

"Why's he so protective? They're adults, and they're his sisters, not his daughters."

"Same difference, really."

"I'm going to need you to explain that, because if they're his sisters *and* his daughters, that would mean—"

Colt punches me in the shoulder hard enough that it

actually hurts. "Dude, watch your fucking mouth. First of all, they're his half-sisters. And second, he pretty much raised them."

I can tell there's a lot more to the story, but if Colt wanted to tell me, he would. Jameson's always struck me as an intensely private person, so maybe he's sworn Colt to secrecy, or maybe Colt's just the kind of guy who knows when to keep his mouth shut.

"Do you know them well?"

Colt shrugs. "He's my best friend. I've spent my whole adult life around that family. Those girls are practically like my little sisters, too."

It's hard to imagine looking at Audrey and thinking of her like a sister. It's her eyes that get me every time—they're a crisp, bright blue, and I've always found them hard to look away from. Last night was no different.

"So I'm saying this not just on Jameson's behalf. If you know what's good for you"—he raises his eyebrows—"you'll stay away from them."

Well, fuck.

Chapter Six

AUDREY

I'm just coming down the stairs into my basement office, the newest episode of my favorite horror podcast blasting in my ears while I try to get the nerve up to call Drew back. When I step onto the bottom stair, there's a loud knock on the glass door. I'm not expecting anyone, so it takes me by surprise, and I fumble my lunch, spilling salad all over as the plate and fork go clattering to the floor. Maybe if I wasn't listening to a terrifying story unfolding, the knock wouldn't have scared me so much?

I tap the earbud to pause the podcast as I let out a guttural sound—the groan of frustration that's been building all day as I've struggled through exhaustion and the worry over Drew knowing about Graham.

Then I hop over the plate, take the turn around the corner of the coat closet, and come face to face with the man who couldn't be bothered to return any of my calls all those years ago.

He's standing on the other side of the door, his hand over his eyes as he practically presses his face up against the glass. When we lock eyes, his expression takes my breath away. It's pain, and confusion, and—if memory serves—longing.

"Are you going to let me in?" he calls out as a sheepish grin spreads across his face.

Do I have a choice?

I take my earbuds out as I take the few steps over to the entrance and slide the lock at the top of the door up, then turn the deadbolt. When I swing the door open, he just stands there, saying nothing.

"You could have just called." It's a ridiculous thing to say, since he's already called multiple times.

"So you could just keep ignoring me? Which I'll be the first to admit, I deserve. I'm sorry to show up like this"—his lips press together and his eyes scan my face—"but I was desperate."

I can feel my eyebrows scrunch together, and I hear Jules's voice in my head, teasing me about how I'm going to develop a permanent crease in the space between them for how often I'm scowling. "For?"

"Answers? Last night was…a lot to process."

"Yeah," I say, a heavy dose of sarcasm in my tone as I turn and head into my office.

I can tell he follows, because I hear the door shut behind me. Walking to the table that takes up the middle of the room, I sit on the far side and gesture for him to take a seat. But he passes the seat I'm motioning toward and takes the one opposite the corner where I've just sat. He's as close as he can be.

And that brings back all kinds of memories about Drew's

lack of respect for personal space—not because he's being a dick, but because he obviously came from a family where close physical proximity and constant touch were the norm. I noticed it when I tutored him—the way he'd easily swing his arm over me and rest it against the back of my chair as he leaned in to look at a problem I was showing him, how he insisted on walking me home at the end of each nighttime tutoring session and how he'd always reach out and squeeze my shoulder and thank me, how when we joked around, he'd punch my arm lightly or poke me in the ribs or reach over and swat my thigh.

It was so different from my own experience after my mom died. She was always touching us—smoothing her hand over our hair in passing, giving us hugs when we'd had a bad day, kissing our foreheads before we headed to bed. Her love language was physical touch, and that didn't stop, even when she got sick. But once she was gone, the lack of physical contact was almost overwhelming.

Maybe that's why I started craving his attention and his affection. He had an easy-going spirit that could not have been more different from my own serious nature. He was light and happy, easily pleased and seldom bothered—a stark contrast to the man who now sits across the corner of the table facing me.

"Can you tell me what happened?" he asks, his voice gentler than I'd expect for someone who just found out he has a five-year-old.

"Sure," I say lightly and give him a little shrug. "I got pregnant. I called you twenty times to try to tell you, and you never called me back. Not even when I broke down and told you I was pregnant in a voicemail." I cross my arms over my chest, raising my eyebrows and biting the corner of my lip like I always do when I'm nervous.

I notice his eyes focus on that, and I want to scream *Really?* I just confirmed that he had a kid, and he's looking at my lips like he wants to kiss them?

"You still do that, huh?"

I squeeze my arms tighter against me, like I can use them as a shield to protect myself from him. "Do what?" I'm scowling, and I know it, but it makes one corner of his lips turn up.

"Bite your lip when you're nervous."

"What would I possibly be nervous about, Drew?" I bluff.

"How I'm going to react to the news."

"I'm more concerned with your non-reaction. You don't seem shocked. Or apologetic. Or any of the other reactions I might have expected."

"I've had all night to come to terms with the fact that I'm a father. I've had all morning to regret not getting to see him as a baby, not being there for his birth or his first steps or his first words, or any of the other moments that should have become memories." As he looks at me, his eyes never wavering from mine, and I note the regret in his expression. "I wasn't ready to be a dad five years ago, and I'm sure you didn't feel ready to be a mom. But if I'd known, I'd have stepped up." He reaches across the table and wraps his fingers around my elbow, giving it a quick squeeze. "I'd have been there for you and Graham. And it kills me that it's my own fault that I didn't know. That you had to do this all yourself, and that I missed it all."

I tilt my chin as I stare at him with what I'm sure is wide-eyed disbelief. I don't know what I expected his reaction to be, but it wasn't this.

"I didn't have to do it all myself. I had Jameson and Jules."

"Yeah," he says, leaning in. "Can we talk about how I didn't know Jameson was your brother, and how he clearly doesn't know that I'm Graham's father?"

I let out a sigh and deflate a little.

"I didn't tell you Jameson was my brother because I didn't want that to be a factor in our...friendship. My whole life, people used me to get closer to my brother. College was the first time that no one knew who I was or that we were related."

"But he was already advising me, so it wasn't like I'd have used you to get closer to him. I'd already committed to him being my agent once I was drafted."

While everything I said was true, of course he'd have to go and notice that it wasn't true for *us*. I wasn't worried he'd use me to get to Jameson. I was worried that he'd use his professional relationship with Jameson as a reason *not* to get close to me. And I craved my time with him, even while I pretended that nothing about him impressed me.

"I wanted to keep Jameson as far away from my relationships—both friendships and romantic—as possible. He was always a little...overbearing."

I feel guilty saying it because my brother is amazing. He retired early from the NHL when our dad left so that he could make sure Jules and I had as normal of a high school experience as possible. Without him, I have no idea what my life would look like. But it certainly wouldn't have involved the elite private high school I attended in Boston, nor going to Boston University, nor having the help I needed when Graham was a baby so I could get my architecture degree. And Jules and I definitely wouldn't have been able to save our dad's construction company. My entire life—all my successes—are because Jameson stepped in and stepped up when we needed him to, at great personal expense.

"Is that why you never told him I'm Graham's father?" He asks the question so casually, and I don't understand how this news isn't flipping his world upside down.

How is he so calm?

"Why are you not freaking out about the fact that you have a kid you didn't know about? I mean, you're so unbothered about it, it's kind of freaking *me* out."

"Believe me," he says, leaning back in his chair, "I spent a good part of last night freaking out, especially when you didn't call me back. It's why I'm here now, in person. Would you rather if I wasn't handling this well?"

"No," I say slowly, considering my words. "I guess I'm just projecting how I'd be feeling if I were in your shoes." I don't mention that—having watched his life as closely as I could for these past six years, and determined he was an impulsive and unreliable guy—I'd expected him to run away from this news, not toward it.

Drew gives me a half-smile. "I can't imagine you ever being anything but calm and collected. In college, I'm pretty sure you were the most mature person I knew."

Yeah, well, I had to grow up quickly, I think to myself. But I don't say it out loud, because if there's one thing I excel at, it's holding in my feelings.

"So…" Drew continues when I don't say anything. "How exactly did you manage to keep my paternity a secret when your brother is my agent? And *why*? When I didn't call you back, why didn't you just tell Jameson and have him reach out to me?"

A laugh bursts out of me. "Are you serious?"

He nods. "Yeah. That's the thing I don't understand. You had a direct line of communication to me, through your brother, and you didn't use it."

"Drew, I called you twenty times." I feel like a broken record player with how often I'm emphasizing this fact. "And *you didn't even call me back*. How do you think Jameson would have responded to the news that you knocked up his baby sister and then refused to take responsibility for it?"

He draws back, his eyes boring into me as they rake over my face. "That wasn't me not taking responsibility. I didn't *know*."

I give him the same look I'd give Graham if he was telling me he'd eaten all his dinner when he'd clearly just shoved his food in his napkin and left it wadded up next to his plate.

"I only listened to the first message, and you didn't tell me you were pregnant in that one or I would have called you back." Drew has the good sense to look ashamed when he says this.

I hear exactly what he's saying, it's what I've known all along: *I* wasn't worth calling back. Maybe if he'd known why I was calling, then he'd have called. But he wasn't going to call just because it was me. I didn't matter enough to even return my call.

"It didn't feel like the kind of information you should leave someone in a voicemail. What should I have said? *Hi, remember our night together before you moved to Vancouver? Well, I'm pregnant. Call me back, thanks."*

"Yeah. That's exactly what you should have said. It was a dick move that I didn't call you back, and that's on me. But also—"

The door at the top of the stairs swings open, and Jameson's voice fills the space. "Hey, Audrey," he calls as he jogs down the stairs, "have you seen the… What the hell happened here?"

He's stopped on his way down the stairs and is looking at the plate and salad spread all over the floor. He hasn't noticed Drew yet, and my eyes slide over to him in a look of pure panic. Under the table, Drew squeezes my knee in what I'm sure is supposed to be a reassuring gesture, but instead sends a full-body shiver through me.

"Uh…a client knocked on the door as I was coming down the stairs and it shocked me. I dropped my salad. I'll pick it up later."

Jameson's head snaps over to me then, noticing Drew sitting there for the first time. Thankfully, his hand is already back in his own lap. "Drew? What are you doing here?"

"I have some work that needs to be done at my mom's place," he says without missing a beat. "Colt mentioned that your sisters run a construction company, and I stopped by to see if the project is something they might be able to squeeze in. Audrey was kind enough to see me on short notice."

Jameson's eyes flick between us. I recognize the look of suspicion because he used to do the same to me and Jules when we were teenagers and he was trying to catch us in a lie.

"It's lucky she happened to be around." Jameson's voice is flat, and I can tell he isn't quite buying what Drew's selling.

"Indeed," I say. "Jules would have flat out refused to even talk to you."

"Why's that?" Drew asks, relaxing back in his chair casually, like this isn't the most awkward possible moment for my big brother to have walked in. Like we're not in the middle of lying to him, as if we're children caught doing something wrong instead of grown-ass adults in the middle of an important conversation about our child.

"Because we're perpetually overbooked. But if the project is small, we might be able to fit it in," I say, then I glance over at Jameson. "What was it you were looking for?"

"The electric air pump. We ordered a bounce house for the backyard for the twins, and I thought it came with one, but it didn't."

"It's probably in the storage closet off the playroom," I tell him as I nod my chin toward the door that leads to the playroom Jules built for Graham so he'd have somewhere safe to hang out while we worked. She added a climbing wall with harnesses last year, once he was old enough to safely use it, and the slide into the ball pit is still in one corner. Lauren's twins love to play down here with Graham when she and Jameson are over.

As he moves into the playroom, I grab my iPad from where it sits on the table and say, louder than necessary, because I want Jameson to hear, "So tell me more about your project."

"My mom has Parkinson's." The statement is quiet but decisive, a nod to the reality of living through a terrible disease. "I don't know how much you know about the disease, but it doesn't shorten your lifespan; it just takes away your ability to live normally. She was diagnosed right before I graduated—"

"Drew." The word is practically whispered. "I'm so sorry."

He'd never mentioned anything about this, even though it means that he'd found out during the second semester of his senior year, when I was still tutoring him. He'd always seemed so carefree, and now I wonder if at least part of that was an act?

"It was really hard to leave her when I was drafted, but she was doing okay for the first few years. My older sisters both live on the same street, so they were there to help her. But it's become progressively worse lately, and they basically told me they needed me around more. Hence the trade to Boston."

He swallows, and it's a deep gulp. There must be so much more to the story that he's not sharing, but I hope that while he's out there upending his whole life to come home and help out more, he's got people around to support him, too.

"I'm sorry. That must be really hard." I know what it's like to watch someone's health fail due to a disease that deteriorates the quality of their life drastically. I watched my mom slowly die from cancer, and my dad succumb to his alcoholism.

"It is what it is," he says, oblivious to my own experience with sick parents. "I got to spend the whole summer with her..." He glances off across the office and doesn't say anything for so long that I think maybe he's not going to finish his sentence. "It was hard to see how much she's declined."

"I'm sure," I say, reaching over to give his arm a

supportive squeeze. I immediately wish I'd never touched him because every muscle in his forearm flexes in response to my touch, and I'd rather not know how cut he is under his long-sleeve shirt—especially because I have a thing for forearms. When I pull my hand back quickly, his eyes watch it travel back to my lap.

"So anyway, the Occupational Therapist suggested some changes to her home that might make it easier for her to get around now and in the future. Some are minor things, like changing the type of doorknobs, that I can probably take care of. But there are two bigger things. One is turning our first-floor family room into a bedroom, and the other is retrofitting the bathroom—"

"Found it!" Jameson yells from within the playroom. I let out a sigh of relief, and then he appears at the doorway. "Thanks for this. I'll give it back to you Sunday night when you come over for dinner."

"Alright. Hope the kids love the bounce house. See you this weekend."

He gives us a nod and heads out the front door of the office, turning and giving us a wave as he leaves.

"Holy shit!" I say, followed by a big sigh as I lean back in my chair. "That was a close call."

"I take it you still don't want him to know?" Drew asks as he glances at me sideways. I don't like how judgmental the question feels.

"Until we've figured this out together, why would we want Jameson involved?" I ask as I close my iPad and stand, taking my coffee cup to the sink built into the counters along the wall.

"You're right," he says, and I can hear his steps behind me.

"Sorry, I just didn't like the way it felt like I was some secret you were hiding."

I spin back to face him. "No offense, Drew. But that's been the case for the last six years. And you can thank me later, because my ability to keep a secret probably saved your NHL career."

Chapter Seven

DREW

"What do you mean by that?" I ask, trying to keep my tone curious. I don't want to be combative about this. I understand that I missed the last six years and don't know what those years have been like for her. But what the hell is she talking about?

"Per the conversation we were having before Jameson showed up, how do you think he would have taken the news that Graham was your child and you didn't want to take responsibility?"

I step closer so that I'm looking down at her, and I try not to focus on how flushed her cheeks are or the slender column of her neck as she tilts her head up to look at me. "Let's get absolutely clear on one thing. I wasn't refusing to take responsibility; *I didn't know* that we had a kid together. I fully accept responsibility for not listening to your voicemails. It's my own fault I didn't know. But I need you to understand that if I'd known about Graham, I absolutely would have been here for you and for him."

She nods, her lips pressed between her teeth, before she says, "I spent the last six years raising our kid without you while you were off living your NHL life...most of it was really fucking hard, but much of it was also undeniably amazing. And I hated you for missing out on both parts."

My stomach sinks. I can't imagine what that was like for her, and I wouldn't blame her if she hated me for it.

"I regret missing out on all of that. But the reason I didn't call you back was because I was a mess. I'd moved to a new country, was living away from my family the first time, and had just found out my mom had Parkinson's. I was just trying to survive."

She turns around and sets the coffee mug in the sink, then with her back to me, she says, "You sure it's not because us sleeping together was supposed to be a one-time thing, and you thought I was being needy and not respecting those boundaries?" Her voice is teasing, even though her words aren't.

This is exactly why she thinks I didn't call her back—she still believes I didn't think she was even worthy of a return phone call.

I put my hands on her shoulders and turn her so she's facing me. "Audrey, me not calling you back—that was about me, and what a mess I was as I was trying to adjust to everything. It wasn't about you."

"Hnuumm," the sound of disbelief rolls out of the back of her throat.

"So that's why you didn't contact me through Jameson? You thought I didn't want any part of having a kid with you?"

"Yeah," she breathes out. "And I knew that if Jameson found out, he'd sabotage your career."

"So you saved my career, but cost me my son's childhood."

"I didn't think you wanted any part of that childhood, Drew." She practically spits my name at me, her pretty eyes narrowing. "*You* cost yourself your son's childhood because *you* couldn't be bothered to listen to my messages or to call me back."

"You're right." The words are a quiet admission, and I deflate a little as I admit this. If I had called her back, everything would have been different.

"So are you," she tells me, and I watch her body relax as she lets out a deep sigh. "I could have tried harder to get a hold of you."

This feels like progress. "We were idiots."

"We were."

"What are we going to do about it now?" I ask.

She bites the corner of her lip, and I wish she'd stop doing that, because I don't need any more reasons to focus on that part of her face. We're talking about really serious stuff—important things that will be life-changing—and I can't stop thinking about the feelings I had for her back then.

God, I wanted so much more than one night with her, but it wasn't possible. I needed to focus on hockey, and hanging on to Audrey when she was back in Boston and I was in Vancouver would have only gotten in the way of my game. Not calling her back had seemed like the right choice at the time.

But clearly, I was only thinking about myself and what I needed, and I had no idea how much she needed me to be there for her, and then for Graham, this whole time. I've always felt unworthy of her, but never more than in this moment.

Finally, she says, "I guess that depends on what you want."

"I want to get to know Graham," I tell her without an ounce of hesitation.

Her swallow is practically a gulp. "Not having a dad has been hard enough on him. But having one who isn't around, or doesn't make time for him, would be even worse. I'm not opposed to you being part of his life, but it has to be an all-in situation, Drew. You can't be unreliable when there's a child depending on you."

"I understand." The reality that I have a son is still settling in. I missed the first five-plus years of his life. Which means I'd be coming into his life right when my own father left mine.

My mom is wonderful—I owe everything to her. She somehow raised three kids on her own, and made sure I was able to keep playing the sport I love, despite how expensive it was. But not having a dad was hard on me, especially when I was a teenager. I have the opportunity to be the dad I never had. The dad Graham has never had, either. "I want to be there for Graham," I say with conviction, "but I'm having a hard time picturing how this will all work out."

"Me too," she admits, then walks around me and back toward the tables in the center of the room. "Shit. I forgot that I left my salad still sitting all over the floor."

I turn and follow her gaze.

"I'll help you clean it up," I say. "And then, maybe we can grab lunch?"

She glances at her watch. "I have some architectural plans

that I need to finalize so I can send them to Jules, and she needs them as soon as possible. I have to finish them before I pick Graham up from school, which, at this point, only gives me a little over an hour before I have to leave to get him. I'm sorry, I just don't have time today."

I blink slowly, reminding myself I'm the one who barged into her day. She owes me this conversation, but not necessarily at this time. "When's a better time to talk?" I shove my hands into the pockets of my jeans and glance out the front wall of glass with *Our House* etched into it. Outside, it's the perfect fall day—blue sky with puffy white clouds and temperatures in the mid-seventies. I want to sit outside and eat lunch with her, catch up on everything I've missed, maybe see her smile. I adored that smile, and I've yet to see it again.

"Are you free tonight?" she asks.

I'm so relieved that she's not trying to put this conversation off for another day that I blurt out "Yes!" without even considering whether I have plans. "Wait, actually, I told my mom I'd come over for a while after my meeting with the team doctor this afternoon. But I could be back into the city by seven or eight."

"Let's say eight," she says. "That way, Graham will already be in bed. I just have to make sure Jules can stay with him, but I'm like ninety-nine percent sure she'll be home tonight packing. I'll make a reservation somewhere and text you the details, or I'll text you if anything changes."

"Alright," I agree, relieved that she's willing to see me again so soon. This has all been a lot of change for me, but I know it has for her too. And if I remember correctly, she's someone who really needs to be in control.

I turn to leave, and when I'm halfway across the room, she calls my name, so I turn back to her.

"Were you serious about wanting us to work on your mom's house?"

"Yeah. It's not why I came over, but I do want to have that work done. Maybe at some point, you can come take a look and see if it's feasible?"

She crosses her arms in front of her, and it's like she's already putting those walls back up. But her voice is soft when she says, "Why don't you send me a video of the space and explain exactly what you want done."

Not what I was hoping she'd say. I can feel her holding me at a distance, which is valid. I haven't given her any reason to believe that she can trust me…yet.

Chapter Eight

DREW

"You know the Rebels are my favorite team," my mom says as she looks down at the new sweatshirt I picked up at the practice rink's gift shop after my medical clearance appointment with the team doctor. "But if I get used to wearing this gear while cheering for you, I might not recover if you end up going elsewhere."

She's teasing, but it's a subtle reminder that I need to make this year the best year of my career.

"I'm working on making it permanent," I tell her. "But with only one year left on this contract, we have to be prepared for any possibility." I wish I could say, *'I'm not leaving Boston, no matter what.'* But that's not realistic.

Mom's disability money doesn't come close to covering what she'd be making from her teaching salary if this disease hadn't forced her to retire early, and her medical insurance doesn't cover as much of her therapy as I wish it did.

For years, I've been making up the difference, which is

easy to do on an NHL salary. But if I had to leave the league in order to stay in Boston, what would I do for work? I have no other skills or experience to speak of. I've been smart enough with my money that it's not like I'd be broke, but the medical bills add up quickly, and without new income, my savings would take a big hit.

"I'm not worried," Mom says, her tone filled with confidence. "I have a feeling this is going to be your best year yet."

Her unwavering support reminds me not to waste my time worrying about something that hasn't happened yet. I have an entire season ahead of me to prove myself. If I think about the future imagining that I will fail, that's exactly what will happen. Over the summer, I worked with a sports psychologist who liked to remind me that I've gotten in my head like that before, and the results weren't pretty. At least now I have strategies for how to handle those thoughts when they rear up.

"Tomorrow's our first pre-season practice."

"You're ready." She spent a good amount of time with me at the ice rink up north, near the lake, where I practiced several times a week all summer long. I've practiced and worked out more during this off-season than any other, and spent a good amount of time improving my mental state as well. I'm counting on that dedication paying off.

"I know. I feel good about this change. I think being back in Boston will be good for me."

Until today, my mom was the only person I've openly shared the details with about what went down in Colorado. She's equally pragmatic and supportive, so she's always been my sounding board when making decisions. I wish I could be honest with her about how much pressure

I'm under right now, but she'd feel terrible if she had any idea how much her care had cost me over my career, or how much my sisters, Caitlyn in particular, had pressured me to move back to Boston. I don't want her feeling guilty.

I also wish I could tell her about Graham, but I know I need to talk more about that with Audrey first. I don't even know yet what my relationship with my son will look like, or when it's appropriate to bring my family into his life. Mom will be absolutely thrilled at the prospect of having another grandchild while simultaneously devastated to have missed out on the first five years.

I already feel overwhelming guilt about missing those years myself, and I hate that my selfishness caused her to miss out on them too. Especially because she's declining and there's so much she *can't* do with him that she could have done earlier.

"It *will* be good for you," Mom insists. "It already has been. You're a lighter, happier person since you moved back at the beginning of the summer."

"It was the off-season," I say with a shrug. "I spent most days on the lake. I worked out and ran drills on the ice, all without the pressure of games or teammates. How could I have not been happy?"

"You weren't this happy in previous summers." My mom folds her arms across her chest.

"I was never home for the whole summer. Things are just…different here."

"Which is why it's perfect that you're back living here, and not just visiting." She gives me a small smile, and then there's a knock on the door and Missy is coming through with her boys hot on her heels. Am I a bad person for being thankful that Caitlyn has classes tonight? Probably.

"Uncle Drew!" Ryan shrieks as he runs right past my mom and wraps his whole body around my legs. If I wasn't expecting it, he'd probably have knocked me over—at four, he's unusually tall for his age.

"Hey, Ry," I say as I reach down and ruffle his hair.

"Look what I brought," Finn says, holding up a graphic novel that I recognize. It's part of the series I ordered for him a couple of weeks ago. The kid has been determined to read for a year, and first grade has already brought big gains in his ability. Graphic novels intended for his age have been perfect for capturing his attention without being too full of big words that frustrate him.

"Great! Are you going to read it to me?" I ask, and it makes me wonder how Graham feels about reading? Does he like Audrey to read him stories before bed at night?

"Yeah, if you want."

"Books are boring," Ryan complains.

"Not when you can read them yourself," his older brother tells him.

"Well, I can't read yet."

"But you'll learn," Missy says with the gentle, patient voice she always uses with her boys. Ryan, in particular, is very high energy, while Finn is quieter and more independent. "I bet Finn could teach you some words, if you'd sit still long enough to listen."

"I'd rather play," Ryan says, holding up two action figures I didn't even realize he was holding.

"That's fine," Missy says, "but don't try to interrupt your brother while he's reading to Uncle Drew, okay?"

Ryan groans. "Reading is *so* boring."

Missy looks at me, widening her eyes, and I immediately know what she wants from me. "I bet you haven't read enough books to really know what kinds of books you like yet," I tell Ryan, squatting down to his level. "Reading lets you go on adventures in your imagination, and it's awesome."

"I don't want adventures in my imagination. I want *real* adventures."

"Yeah, but when you read, you can go places that don't even exist—like a land with dragons, or an underwater castle, or a city where superheroes live."

"Like in the movies?" Ryan asks, his interest visibly growing.

"Exactly."

"This book has superheroes," Finn tells him.

Ryan's eyebrows raise and his lips press together in a suppressed smile that has all of us laughing. It's the perfect *I'm interested but pretending I'm not* look.

"Maaaaaaybe I'll listen when you read it," he says begrudgingly to Finn.

"First, though, are we going to eat this amazing-smelling food Uncle Drew brought, or what?" Missy asks, sending me a grateful look.

"Yes!" the boys yell as they run toward the table where aluminum containers full of BBQ are spread out.

"Thanks," Missy mouths silently.

"Rusty working tonight?" I ask as we head into the kitchen.

"Yeah, there was a call right before closing about a hot water tank that's not working."

"That couldn't wait until tomorrow? It's not like it's cold enough at night yet that they need it for heat."

"Apparently, dishes and showers couldn't wait, and you know how Rusty never says no to overtime."

It's true. He owns his own plumbing company, and has always set aside the overtime dispatch fees. He then used that money to buy their family boat, fittingly called *Overtime*, that they keep on Lake Winnipesaukee all summer long. This summer made me realize how much I love being out on the lake, and as long as things pan out with the Rebels and I'm still around, I fully plan on buying myself a boat next summer.

"Good thing he doesn't." I smirk. "You and the kids reap the rewards of that."

"Yeah," she says, but she sounds resigned.

"Hey." I elbow her. "What was that?"

"Just wish he was around a little bit more. Sometimes I feel like a single mom."

That term hits me like a barb stuck right under my skin, poking in a way that's annoyingly painful. What's life been like for Audrey? She said she didn't do it alone, that she had Jameson and Jules, but that can't have been the same as if I'd been around to share in the parenting. Could it? Though with my travel schedule for road games, she'd still have been doing a lot of it without me.

"I'm glad you're home now, though," she says. "The boys love you and are looking forward to spending more time with their fun uncle."

"Me too," I say, and even while it's true, I'm already doing the mental math, figuring out how I'm going to balance all these new draws on my time. It's just been me, on my own, for so long. Now I've got my mom, my sisters and nephews, and Audrey and Graham in my life.

I've never had to prioritize other people into my schedule, and I'm already worried about how I'm going to manage it all in addition to hockey.

Chapter Nine

AUDREY

"Why did I agree to this?" I ask Jules as I stand in our entryway, staring at the front doors. They're a narrow pair of old wooden doors that Jules recently found at a salvage yard and refinished for me. She knew I wanted to have the original side-by-side doors that were common when our South End row house was built in the mid-1800s.

"Because deep down, you know that you didn't try hard enough to get ahold of Drew before, or since, Graham was born."

Over my shoulder, I give my sister *the look*. It's the same one I've been giving her my whole life, and it basically equates to: *Develop a fucking filter, Jules*. She's a tell it-like-it-is girl who doesn't believe in sugar-coating things.

She blinks back at me, all wide blue eyes and flawless skin. With her hair piled up in the messy bun she often wears, she looks too young to be mad at. Sometimes I have to remind myself that she isn't the little girl Jameson and I coddled after our mom died, and even more so after Dad left a note under an empty scotch bottle on our kitchen table that said, *I can't do this anymore,* then disappeared from our lives. She's a full-grown adult who needs to develop some tact.

"What?" she asks, when I continue staring at her. "You know it's true. You could have contacted him through his publicist or even through his team, sent him DMs through social media, given Jameson some made-up reason to have Drew contact you, or looked up his family's address in Boston and contacted him that way."

"I know," I sigh. I was hurt, and I let my pride get in the way. "I get it, Jules."

"Good," she says decisively, then takes a few steps so she's standing next to me. She slings her arm around my shoulders and gives me a squeeze. "You've been a great mom, and so strong doing this on your own. But Drew *wants* to be involved."

"It's not that easy," I say. "We still have a lot to figure out."

"So go figure it out. And I'm here if you need to talk when you get back."

It only takes me about five minutes to walk from our place in the South End over to the Back Bay. I picked a small Italian restaurant tucked away on a side street off Newbury Street, and I asked for a very private table when I made the reservation.

And now, as I stand there looking at the painted black door beneath the ornate sign with the name of the restaurant, I want to turn and run away—go back home and change out of this dress and into the sweats and t-shirt I was wearing earlier, then cuddle up under a blanket on the couch and watch a mindless TV show with my little sister.

I'd made peace with being a single mom. Graham and I were doing just fine. I was comfortable with our life exactly how it was. It was maybe a little lonely, but it was safe. And welcoming Drew into our lives feels like it carries too many risks. So much could go wrong.

But what if everything goes right?

"You going to stand there, staring at that door until it opens itself?"

His voice comes from right behind me, but even though I was too lost in thought to notice his approach, I don't startle. His voice is like honey—smooth and sweet and rich. It flows around me slowly, until I feel it making my limbs heavy.

"For real, though," he says when I don't manage to respond. "What's going on?" He puts a hand on each of my shoulders.

"Just lost in thought, I guess," I say, my voice falsely bright to cover the reaction my body is having to what I'm sure is supposed to be a supportive, friendly squeeze.

This is why it's a bad idea to let him into your life. I push that thought right out of my head, because it doesn't matter whether his presence is good for me or not, as long as it's good for Graham. And I have no idea why, but I suspect that Drew will be a great dad—or at least, he'll be a fun dad. And my serious little boy could use that.

"You ready to go in, or you want to stand out here thinking some more?"

I sink my elbow into his ribs playfully, and he must not have expected it because he lets out a little grunt at the contact.

"Toughen up, Jenkins," I say, then reach forward to open the door. I step through it into the narrow, dim entryway, and right as I go to pull the interior glass door to the restaurant open, he reaches over my shoulder and plants his hand against the door. The exterior door shuts behind him, and it's just the two of us, pressed together in the tight space.

"You really think I need to toughen up?" His words are low and spoken directly in my ear as his body practically cradles mine. "Or was that a throwback to when you said that to me before?"

"Drew," I say, stepping away as I turn to face him, wishing I'd never opened my mouth. I definitely intended it as a little reminder of how often I'd said that to him when he'd whine or complain during our tutoring sessions. But I'd forgotten that I also said it right before we had sex when he'd looked at me and said, *"You're going to be my undoing."* And now, our eyes locked on each other in this tight space, I can clearly see that the last time I told him to "toughen up" was the one that stuck with him. "Let's forget I said that and go inside before we're late for our reservation."

"Yeah," he says, moving his hand down to the door handle, "wouldn't want to be late."

I ignore the undercurrent of sarcasm in his voice and sweep through the door he's holding open for me. The host directs us to a table in an alcove off a hallway. The brick walls are windowless, and the space is dimly lit by wall sconces and the candle in the center of the table. I asked for privacy and got romantic instead. Now I wish I'd just had him meet me at a bar so this felt more like friends getting a drink, rather than a date.

When he takes his seat across from me, he eyes me like he's trying not to laugh.

"What?" I say as soon as the host leaves. I'm frustrated at myself, because I can tell he's sensing my inner turmoil.

"You look horrified by the table choice. It's fine," he says, opening the drink menu. "It's not like I think this is a date."

It's funny how we're already falling into the same patterns as college—him trying to goad or annoy me to get a reaction, and me secretly loving the attention and the banter.

"Good. Because this is actually a business meeting."

He lifts one eyebrow, and I can tell how hard he's working to hold in a laugh. "A business meeting? Are we discussing our *mutual assets?*"

"In a way, yes."

"So you see our son as an asset?"

I groan, even though I know he's teasing. "You know that's not what I mean. But if you want to be involved in Graham's life, then we have to agree on some ground rules. I think it makes sense to look at this like a partnership."

"A partnership," he repeats, nodding slowly as it sinks in.

"Yeah. Where we both want what's best for Graham, and that's the basis for our decisions about how this goes."

"That's fair," he says, right as our waiter arrives to take our drink order. Once he leaves, Drew asks, "So how do you think this should work?"

I've actually given this a lot of thought over the last few hours.

"From my perspective, I think it would be ideal if you got to spend some time with Graham, get to know him a bit, before we tell him that you're his dad."

"You afraid I'm going to change my mind?"

I set my elbows on the table with my arms folded across the space in between. "I think it's a possibility." Pausing, I assess the look on his face. "Don't look at me like that. Right now, anything's possible, because you don't even know him yet. Maybe you two won't click."

"Whether we click right away or not doesn't change the fact that I'm his dad, Audrey." Drew's voice is a tad exasperated. Good, I appreciate seeing that he actually wants this. Even so, I need to proceed with caution.

"I know it doesn't. But if you change your mind, I don't want him to know what he's losing or missing out on."

"I'm *not* going to change my mind."

"You don't know that, Drew. You haven't been a dad before. And you're walking into this when he's five, not when he's a baby."

He raises his eyebrows at that, and instantly I feel the accusation, because whose fault is that? Mine.

"I see the guilt in your eyes, and I wish you wouldn't do that. Audrey," he says softly. I hate the way I love the sound of my name coming from him. "We both made mistakes. And now we need to get over that and move on. We can't keep rehashing the past. We need to move forward, thinking about the future. Can you do that?"

I'm surprised that he's not more upset. "Yeah. The only thing we need to think about moving forward is what's best for Graham. I have thoughts on the best way for you to meet him."

"Yeah?" There's an excitement in his eyes that almost has me smiling.

"Jameson coaches Graham's hockey team," I say. "Practices just started back up. I know athletes are always looking to do volunteer work in the community. Maybe you could tell him you're looking to do some community service, and ask him if he knows of any youth hockey programs you could work with. Hopefully, he'll volunteer his own team and you don't have to bring up that you know he coaches."

"Okay. I'm not sure how well I'll be able to get to know Graham in that circumstance, though."

"Maybe after practice, I can invite you to get donuts with us or something?"

"And that won't be suspicious?"

"We don't have to leave the rink together or anything. And we're friends from college, remember?"

"Friends, huh?" He winks at me.

"That's our story. We became friends when I tutored you, but we lost touch after you graduated."

"And what happens when everyone learns the truth?"

"Eventually, we'll need to come clean about the whole story, I guess. And when we get there, we'll figure out how to do that."

"Who are we hiding this from, exactly? Is there really no one who knows I'm Graham's dad?"

"Jules knows. That's it."

"I think Lauren suspects, too," he says.

"Because of our conversation at her house the other night?" I'd kind of forgotten Lauren witnessed that whole thing.

"Yeah. After you left, she was asking me how I knew you. You knew exactly what I meant when I asked Graham how old he is, and I'm pretty sure Lauren at least suspects why I was asking."

"She's become one of my closest friends," I say, then tell

him about how Lauren and her twins moved to Boston last winter, and how Jules and I became friends with her as we renovated her new house, and how she ended up dating my brother. "I want to tell her the truth, but I don't want *her* to have to lie to my brother in order to keep our secret."

Jameson finding out would add a whole other layer of complexity, and our situation is already complicated enough. Drew and I need time to figure this out ourselves before anyone else gets involved.

"Has she asked you about it?"

"Not yet. But if you show up to that hockey practice, she sure as shit will be asking questions." And if she starts asking questions, I don't know how I'll lie to her—so it's best if she's not asking them.

"She'll be there?"

"She and the girls usually come to watch the Saturday morning practices. A bunch of five-year-olds learning to play hockey is always highly entertaining, and her twins love being at the rink. Jameson is teaching them to skate, actually." I love seeing this side of my brother—the protective, nurturing side that he tried so hard to hide for so many years.

"We almost always have games Friday or Saturday, so the chances of me ever being at a Saturday morning practice are slim. But I'll follow your lead on whatever you want to do about telling Jameson and Lauren," Drew says.

"I guess for now I can ask Lauren not to ask any questions so that I don't have to lie to her, or ask her to lie to my brother?"

Drew half-laughs, half-snorts. "So you mean, you're going to tell her without telling her."

"I don't know what other choice I have." I sigh as the waiter sets our drinks and charcuterie tray on the table. Once he leaves, I continue. "Family is...complicated."

He stares at me with a look I can't decipher, and I can feel the heat creeping into my cheeks under his gaze. Finally, one corner of his lips turns up, but he's not looking at me with amusement. It looks more like...pride?

"Why are you looking at me like that?"

Chapter Ten

DREW

I don't know how I'm looking at her, so I'm not sure how to answer her question. Instead, I continue to stare at her as her cheeks get pinker until she looks like one of those 1940s pin-up girls with flawless porcelain skin and rosy cheeks and lips.

Finally, I admit, "I'm just taking it all in, and I'm impressed."

"Impressed?" She asks the question like she doesn't understand why I'm using the word in this situation.

"Yeah, you've just managed to accomplish so much in the past six years—your architecture degree, starting a business, raising our child. I'm in awe…like always."

"What do you mean, *like always*?" She sounds both confused and even a little defensive, then she looks down at the charcuterie tray and adds some meat, cheese, and olives to her plate, like she'd rather do anything other than meet my eye while asking me this question.

"I mean, even in college, you just kind of...had your shit together? You were smart and self-assured, and you didn't take any of my crap. I couldn't even flirt with you, because you shut me down every time. We both knew you were way too good for me."

A laugh bursts out of her, and it's a relief to see her smiling. I've always loved the way her defined cheekbones reveal dimples when she smiles.

"Drew," she says, after laughing for longer than I'd expect. "We did not *both* know that."

"What do you mean?" I ask, taking a sip of my beer and wishing I could sit here drinking and talking to her all night.

"I mean, you were freaking un-touch-able in college. A shameless flirt, sure. But I was not your type. At all. And we both knew *that*."

"You weren't my type," I admit. "Which is what I liked about you. Fake girls who were only interested in me because I played hockey got old after a while."

"I was only interested in you for the tutoring fees," she shoots back without even having to think about it, which makes me wonder if it's true. The school paid well for that service for its athletes, if I remember correctly.

"Ouch!" I say, and when she smirks at me, the resemblance between her and her brother is so strong, I don't know how I didn't see it sooner. "See, just like that. You never put me on a pedestal. Kicked it out from under me is more like it."

"You needed to be taken down a peg." In some ways, she's right. But I also knew her at the absolute most stressful and lowest time of my life, something I hid behind my life-of-the-party persona.

Senior year was a crossroads for me. College had been the best four years of my life. Hockey, interesting classes, living in the city, the parties, the girls...it was a dream for a guy in his late teens and early twenties.

But while I'd spent those four years working my ass off to develop into a strong enough player that I'd even have a hope of getting drafted, it was still far from a sure thing. If I didn't get drafted, I wasn't sure what I wanted to do. My degree in journalism felt like a placeholder—something I'd worked on to justify being at college, but really, in my mind anyway, I was there to play hockey.

My mom had just been diagnosed with Parkinson's. And Caitlyn, who'd just finished her nursing degree and worked for a few years in New York City, had moved home so she could help with Mom's care. She pressured me from the beginning to "get a real job" in Boston instead of pursuing my NHL dreams.

It felt like I was on the precipice of everything crashing down around me.

With the benefit of hindsight, I allow myself to consider how I would have reacted to the news of Audrey's pregnancy. I know I would have stepped up and done the right thing, but would I have had to give up hockey to stay in Boston and be a dad? Would I have resented her for it?

"Yeah, you're probably right." I agree with her because divulging all the shit I was going through has the potential to derail the pleasant walk down memory lane this has become. I'd rather spend this time on a positive note.

We order more appetizers and chat while we eat. She catches me up on Graham's life, showing me a few photos and telling me about the baby years, then moving on to his toddler years.

"This is beyond weird," I say when she shows me a picture of him on a step stool at the kitchen counter, wearing nothing but an apron while learning how to make pesto.

"Cleanup from messy food is a lot easier when they're naked," she says, sounding defensive.

"I mean learning about my kid's childhood through pictures…I missed so much." If you'd asked me a week ago how I would take the news that I have a five-year-old son, I'd have guessed that I'd feel overwhelmed or upset. Instead, sitting here seeing everything I missed, I just feel sad and disappointed. "Now," I tell her, "I just want to know my son."

"Drew," she says, her voice gentle and sympathetic, like she's about to break some bad news. "You can't just waltz into his life, tell him you're his dad, and see if you like playing that role. Because if you change your mind—"

"Why are we having this conversation again?" I think we already established that I'm not changing my mind.

"Because even guys who think they want to be a dad sometimes change their minds," she says, and looks off past me toward the main part of the restaurant.

I want to ask her whether she's speaking from personal experience, or in general, but I'm not sure we're in a place yet where she'd want to answer that. It feels too personal, which is a weird feeling to have about a person you made another human being with.

But right now, she only knows some past version of me, and maybe the current version the media portrays. She has no reason to trust me, but we'll get there.

"He's *my* kid, Audrey. That's not something I can change my mind about."

"What if you get traded again? You're only for-sure here for a year. Maybe it'll be longer, but maybe not."

I press my lips between my teeth as I consider that possibility. Because as much as I don't want it to be, there's a chance that I'll only be here for a year. "I'm doing everything I can to stay in Boston—hopefully, for the rest of my career."

"But it might not happen," she says. "You could do everything right and still get traded. Even if Boston is happy with you, there are salary caps that GMs have to consider, or they may still trade you because it's what's best for the team, especially if there's a chance to secure the Cup. There are a hundred different reasons it may not work out…"

"I know." I glance down into my empty beer glass, then back up at her big blue eyes. "But whether I get traded or not, that doesn't change the fact that I'm his dad, and I'll still want to be involved in his life. I know that maybe you can't believe that this is what I want yet, so I'll just have to show you."

"You do that," she says lightly, her eyebrows raised and a hint of a smile curling her lips, like she wants to believe it's possible but isn't quite sure.

"Oh, don't worry, I will."

She excuses herself to go to the bathroom, and I eat the last few truffle fries while I wait, even though after having dinner with my family and then having more food with Audrey, I'm not actually hungry. I'm about to pull out my own phone when hers lights up on the table in front of me, where she's kept it all night in case there were any issues with Graham. I glance down at the screen to make sure it's not Jules contacting her, and instead I see a message I wish I hadn't.

> **KARL**
> Hey, you around tonight? I could come to your place.

It's nearly ten at night, so who is this asshole contacting her for a booty call? Or, is this guy her boyfriend? I don't know which option is worse, honestly.

I glance up as Audrey approaches the table.

"What's wrong?" she asks the minute we lock eyes.

I have no business asking the question, but I ask anyway. "Who's Karl?"

Her eyebrows scrunch together. "What?"

"He just texted you—"

The phone lights up again with the second notification about the message, and she snatches it up so quickly I stop speaking. Her eyes scan the screen, then she narrows them at me. "Why are you reading my messages?"

"Your phone was just sitting there, so I glanced at it to make sure it wasn't Jules contacting you with some sort of an emergency."

"If there was an emergency, she'd have called." She doesn't slide into her seat, so I get the sense that she thinks we're done here. I'm thankful I paid the bill while she was in the bathroom, so I can stand and we can finish this conversation. Because even though I have no right to get involved, I'm determined that she's not going to rush home to meet whoever this asshole is.

"So, who's Karl?" I'm doing what I can to unclench my jaw, but even I can hear how terse my words are.

"It's none of your business." She folds her arms defensively, and even with my eyes focused on her face, I notice how it pushes her cleavage up into the V-neck of her sweater dress.

Keeping my movements slow and calm, I take a step toward her—I'm trying very hard to be careful and cautious with her, and with our whole situation. And even though I know she's right, and it's none of my business, there's an undercurrent of jealousy coursing through my veins that I can't stop myself from acting on, even while I tell myself to calm the hell down.

I don't want her to be with anyone else.

"Maybe it's not. Except that he's talking about coming over to your place, and Graham's there. Are you seeing someone? Is he part of Graham's life?"

She sighs, and it's like the movement physically deflates her. Her shoulders sag and she looks at the ground.

"Hey." I reach out and tilt her chin up, but I don't remove my hand. I love the way her jaw looks cupped in my palm and the way her smooth skin feels as my fingers slide along it. "I know I'm not even a part of Graham's life yet, so I'm just trying to understand the situation."

"No judgment?"

Thank goodness she didn't ask me to commit to not being jealous. "No judgment."

"It's just casual. He worked at the firm where I did my post-grad professional internship. He's recently divorced, I have a kid…neither of us is looking for anything serious."

"Has he met Graham?"

Her piercing blue eyes stare up at me from beneath her dark lashes, then she lifts her chin so I have no choice but to drop my hand. I let it land on her shoulder and pull her a bit closer to me. I can feel her breath on my neck as it comes out in short bursts.

Finally, she says, "No."

"Good. I'd really prefer if we kept it that way."

"We're keeping it that way because that's what *I* think is best for Graham." The rigid set of her jaw and the tense note of her words let me know that I am not a factor in this decision. *Yet.*

"I'm glad we're on the same page."

"Don't step into this situation thinking you have any control over *my* life, Drew." Audrey looks up at me as she speaks. She sounds breathless, exactly how I remember her sounding when I went to kiss her the first time and she stopped me to say it was probably a bad idea. As it turns out, everything had changed in that moment; I just didn't know it until last night.

"I'm not trying to control your life. I'm just trying to be part of it."

"Well, stop," she says, but there's no force behind it. "We are Graham's parents, but that doesn't mean we're part of each other's lives outside of our son."

"Agree to disagree," I say, then I drop my hand to her lower back and move her down the hallway toward the front door.

I can tell she's got a hundred excuses ready to throw at me, but I'm not hearing any of them. Because all it's taken is a couple of hours in her presence for me to remember how much I liked her when we were in college. If I hadn't moved to the other side of the continent, I would have wanted *all* her nights, and probably her days too.

And as I walk her home, the realization creeps over me slowly but surely: I want her, just like I did six years ago. Everything's more complicated now, and getting involved with her is probably a terrible idea. But I can't shake the sensation that even though I'm not what she wants, I might be exactly what she needs—and she might be what I need, too.

Chapter Eleven

AUDREY

"I'm so glad you called," I say after navigating through the lunch crowd and slipping into the seat across from Morgan. "I was going a little stir crazy in the office."

"Why were you going stir crazy?"

"I don't know," I shrug, even though I know exactly why. Thoughts of Drew have consumed my every waking moment, and it has me on edge. I used to be able to go weeks without him crossing my mind. It's only been two days since I first saw him again, and he's invaded my every thought.

"You sure about that?" she asks.

I narrow my eyes at her. What's that mean? For a minute, I worry that Lauren might have said something to her about Drew and me, but that really isn't Lauren's style. I still haven't talked to Lauren yet because she's been so busy between work and the kids, so I can't imagine that she'd go telling her cousin. And I know Jules, who has kept my secret since she was eighteen, wouldn't do that either. So Morgan can't know. Can she?

"I just have a lot on my mind."

I smooth my hair back from my face with both hands. It's a blustery October day and the threat of rain hung in the air as I walked from the South End over to the Back Bay to meet her. By the time I arrived, my hair was already a windblown mess. Twisting my hair up, I secure it with a claw clip, glad to have the static-y mess off my face.

I glance down at the menu in front of me, and when I glance up, Morgan has her phone out and is snapping a picture of me. She turns her phone so I can see it. My cheeks are pink from the wind, but my eyes are bright. There's steam rising up around me from the bowls of pho at the table behind me. "When being home too much finally gets to the homebody," Morgan says, like she's captioning the photo. It's true, I'm a total homebody. At first, it was out of necessity, but now I suppose it's out of habit.

"Will you send that to me?" I ask. It's rare that someone takes a photo of me that I truly like, and I do like that one.

"Of course," she says, and taps a few times on her screen before setting her phone down. "That would make the perfect profile picture on a dating app, you know."

I give her the look that normally shuts people up, but she continues anyway.

"Come on, Audrey. Like I said the other day, when you work from home, how would you ever meet a guy otherwise?"

"I guess you'd have to go to the bars on the weekend, and meet someone the old-fashioned way," I tease her. But even as I say it, I know that would never be doable for me because I have Graham at home. Which is why I was half-way considering her offer, until Drew walked back into my life. And now that he's in my head—even cuter than he was in college, and the father of my child—how am I supposed to think about anyone else?

"Meeting a guy at a bar feels so"—she twists her mouth into an adorable pout as she thinks—"impersonal. Like the only thing I can tell about a guy if I see him at the bar is whether I think he's cute or not. So, am I supposed to only go talk to him if he's cute?"

"I mean, that's normally how it works, isn't it?"

"Ugh. Like I want to know not only if he's cute, but if we have anything in common."

"Isn't that what talking to him is all about?"

"Oh yeah, because so much quality *talking* happens at a bar on a Saturday night."

I'm struck with a memory from the last night I saw Drew. It was a couple of days after finals ended, and the seniors had just graduated that day. The enormous ceremony took place in the football stadium, which was something of a joke because the school hadn't had a football team in over a decade.

I'd gotten a text from Drew telling me that he was at a bar close to campus called The Scarlett Letter, and that I should come celebrate him passing calculus and graduating.

It was the first time he'd suggested we see each other outside of our tutoring dates, though maybe I shouldn't have been surprised, because when I saw him right before his calculus final, he'd said, "We're going to have to figure out a reason to see each other now that I won't need you to tutor me anymore."

This text, a few days later, felt like him finding a reason.

I'd wasted at least five minutes reassuring myself I wasn't hallucinating and trying to calm down my racing heart. Then I'd convinced my roommate, Jasmine, to head out to the bar with me.

When we showed up, Drew and half the hockey team were taking up a massive booth in the corner. I was about to shrink back into the crowd and pull Jasmine with me, when the DJ changed the song and the crowd of people on the dance floor began jumping up and down, pushing us forward toward their table. When Drew looked up and saw me there, his whole face lit up.

We spent most of that night tucked away in that booth, talking while Jasmine busied herself flirting with half his friends. It had felt like I was seeing a totally different side of him, like maybe there was a depth to him that he didn't show everyone because he had this other persona that people expected to see. And when I gave myself to him that night, it felt right. It felt life changing. And it was, just not in the way I expected.

"Besides," Morgan continues, "I can chat with a guy and figure out if we click online, from my couch, in the comfort of my pajamas. I don't have to get all dressed up and drop a hundred dollars on a night out."

"Fair point," I say. Then I think back to how jealous Drew was about Karl, and I wonder how he'd feel about me dating someone. His opinions shouldn't matter—they *don't* matter—but it also feels like the wrong time to start dating. How would I even explain the situation with Graham and Drew to someone I'd just met, when I haven't even explained it to my own family? "I just don't think it's the right time for me right now."

"Okay, but don't think I'm not bringing this up again sometime in the near future. You're too young, smart, and beautiful to be sitting home alone every night. You deserve someone who makes you happy, Audrey. And not because you can't be happy on your own, but because you already are, and you deserve someone who will bring even more happiness to your life."

When she puts it like that, it does sound nice. But in my experience, relationships are rarely that uncomplicated. Even my brother and Lauren, who have the healthiest, happiest relationship I've seen, started out rocky and spent five years apart before they reconnected.

"Thank you," I say. "What about you? Any promising guys on the horizon?"

"Well," she says, a smile spreading across her face as she rolls her eyes, "there is a guy I was talking to last night. We ended up video chatting with each other, and he is really cute, and really sweet, and we're going to see each other next week after I get back from Las Vegas."

"Yes! That's awesome," I say, and then we're distracted as the waiter comes over to take our order.

Once he leaves, Morgan says, "So, I had an ulterior motive in asking if you wanted to grab lunch."

"Oh?"

"Yeah. Now that I'm managing Petra's social media for her, I'm looking to expand in that area a bit. Lauren already connected me with Sierra," she says, referring to another of Lauren's best friends who, along with Petra and their friend, Jackson, round out Lauren's tight-knit group of friends from when she lived in Park City. "She used to run the social media accounts for the National Ski Team, and now she co-runs one of the most popular travel accounts on Instagram with her husband, Beau. She's also talking about starting a Bookstagram account, because that girl is a diehard romance fan."

Even though I've met Sierra a few times and knew she was a photographer, I didn't realize the extent of her social media presence.

"So that's been really helpful," Morgan says. "Now I'm interested in taking on some more accounts, and I'm wondering if you'd be interested in me helping you manage and grow the Our House account?"

"Yes!" There's not a moment of hesitation. Our social media accounts fall under my purview, and it's one of my least favorite responsibilities, mostly because of my own lack of understanding about, or interest in, how social media can be used to help generate leads. "Please…can you just take the whole thing over?"

"We haven't even talked about compensation," Morgan says with a laugh. "What if my fee was ten thousand dollars a month?"

"Is it?"

"No."

"Okay, so I'm sure we can work something out, but I absolutely hate managing our accounts—"

"That's what Jules said, which is why I'm making this offer. But Audrey, you and Jules are the face of that company, and if you want your social media accounts to be successful, you're going to have to make an appearance once in a while."

"I *am* on there. I've posted pictures from the various articles that have been written about us. And the shots we had taken when we first launched the company."

"That's all completely scripted. People want to see more behind-the-scenes stuff, not just professional photos of completed projects or photos that appeared on other media outlets. You guys are selling Our House as the preeminent all-female construction company in Boston. But the thing people want to know when they hire a design and construction firm like yours is that they're not only going to like the end result of what you create, but they're going to like working with *you*. Show them who you are, let them get to know you, and you will have more business than you know what to do with."

"We already have more business than we know what to do with. Our waitlist is six months out."

"So you may need to grow." She says it like doubling the size of your business every year for the past few years isn't enough.

"We *are* growing. We're just trying to do it at a sustainable rate. And we're committed to only hiring extremely qualified people. You probably won't be surprised if I tell you there's a shortage of female subcontractors. Women are greatly outpacing men when it comes to going to college, but not when it comes to the trades."

"Maybe because not enough young women know that it's an option for them. What kind of relationship do you guys have with trade schools in the area?"

My jaw drops open. I had never considered creating the

kind of pipeline from trade schools into our business that she's suggesting. If we could help coordinate apprenticeships and then hire people full-time once they're licensed, instead of having to hire them as subcontractors, that would help a lot with scheduling and costs. It would also mean a lot of additional business expenses, but in the long run, it might be the best way to expand our company while also maintaining the quality we're committed to. "That's kind of genius."

"Thanks. I do have an MBA, you know?"

"You *what?*"

"Yeah. My undergrad is in business, and I had a job all lined up in Austin after graduating from NYU, but I was moving there with my college boyfriend, and he broke up with me. So rather than move there and be entirely on my own, Lauren hooked me up with a job as Petra's admin in Park City. I worked on my MBA part-time, and I just finished it last year before moving back to Boston."

"Holy shit, Morgan. That's amazing. And you're using it how?"

"Well, for starters, I'm setting up my own social media company. Eventually, I may also work with companies on other types of growth strategies, but for now, this is what I can handle while still working for Petra. So, are you in?"

"Only if you promise you'll also advise on some of these other types of growth strategies," I say. "And if we can afford you."

"We'll work it out," she says. "And my first post is going to be the picture I just took. I'm going to caption it, *'Quick lunch meeting to work out some exciting new business plans. Any guesses what's coming next?'* People love the opportunity to engage; you just have to invite them to do so."

"I trust you to handle this," I tell her. And I do, even if it might mean that she wants me to appear on there a bit more. I really do hate the spotlight, but if it's what's needed for our company to keep growing, that's what I'll do.

Chapter Twelve

DREW

"That was a lucky shot, Jenkins," Colt calls out to me after the puck sails right past his glove and into the net.

"Lucky, my ass," I call out as some of my new teammates clap me on the back.

Despite being tired from staying out later than I should have with Audrey, and then spending half the night thinking about her and Graham, I'm on fire this morning. I stole the puck straight off the defenseman's stick with what I'll admit was a lucky swipe from behind when he thought he was secure in a breakaway. Then I sent the puck to the corner along the boards, where one of the wingers was waiting for it, and he slapped it back to me as I was skating full force across the blue line. But right as I went to shoot, the opposing defenseman got in my personal space. I managed to drag the puck, but it got ahead of me as I lost my balance. Falling, I reached out, and my stick made just enough contact with the puck to push it forward as I landed on my butt. It felt like everything was going in slow motion as I slid across the ice, but I noticed that Colt had come far enough out of position to leave a large opening between him and the net. I knew he wouldn't have time to reach his stick out to stop a shot, so I grabbed the puck with the edge of my skate and kicked it toward my stick, then sent it toward the net with a one-handed backhand while sliding across the ice on my back, and scored. As I slid into the boards, Colt dropped to his knees in disbelief.

I glance over at Coach Wilcott, and he nods in acknowledgement of a job well done. Even though it was a once-in-a-lifetime shot, I don't let it go to my head. I just skate back to center ice and line up for the next puck drop.

Later on, when I'm showered and headed toward the locker room door, Wilcott calls me into his office. I have the distinct notion that he's been poised at his door, waiting for me to walk by.

"Close the door?"

I do as he asks, then take a seat in the chair he's gestured toward. "What's going on, Coach?"

"Wanted to talk about Colorado. Heard what happened there." The man's apparent inability to use pronouns is distracting me from what he's saying.

"From?"

"McCabe."

Why is Ronan McCabe talking about me to our coach?

"Before you get your balls in a twist, McCabe wanted to make sure nothing like that would happen here."

"With all due respect, sir, I've already made sure it won't happen here."

"How so?" he asks.

"I followed all my teammates on social media. It's easier to avoid their wives and girlfriends when you know their names and what they look like." I'm determined not to let ignorance derail my career like it almost did in Colorado. "Plus, the game is getting all my time and focus right now. There's no time for women."

Of course Audrey's face pops into my mind, but I don't allow myself to feel guilty because I'm not lying. She's determined this is going to be a co-parenting relationship, so it's not like we're dating.

"You sure?"

I almost say, *The only woman who will be taking up my time is my mom.* But no one here knows about that. I didn't want the team to think my reasons for coming to Boston were anything other than the team, or that my attention will be on anything other than hockey. I'll tell them eventually, once I'm more settled here, and my position is more secure.

"Positive. Hockey is my number one priority, and I'm not doing anything to risk my position on this team."

"Are you worried about your position?" he asks. I can tell it's a genuine question by the curiosity I hear in his voice, but I've known plenty of coaches who like to use the last year of a contract as leverage to get the most out of their players. Even little comments like "Show us you want to come back next year" can load unimaginable stress onto players.

"It's the last year of my contract and I'm new here. So yeah," I say, giving him a lazy half-smile that I think probably hides my true fear, "I'm a little worried."

"Don't be. AJ wouldn't have brought you on if she didn't think this was the right place and you were the right person."

That shocks the shit out of me.

"You have a lot of faith in her decision-making," I say.

"I've never known that woman to be wrong about hockey," he says. That's damn high praise for any GM, though you don't make it to the top in this industry without a cut-throat attitude, deep hockey knowledge, and a determination to be the best. I sense that AJ has that all in spades. "So don't worry too much."

When he asked me to close the door, I wasn't expecting a pep talk. "Thanks, Coach."

"Door's always open, Jenkins. You need something, or something's not going right, you let me know."

I almost don't know what to do with his offer. Having a coach who seems like he genuinely cares, after what I came from on my last team, will take some getting used to. "Will do, Coach."

When I head out of the office, Zach Reid is still in the locker room. He's showered and changed, but he's sitting there with his eyes closed and his head leaning back against his hockey pants where they hang from the hook above his seat.

"You good?" I ask.

He opens his eyes slowly. "I'm good."

"Why are you just sitting there?"

"Just soaking it all in. Trying to figure out the energy of this place, you know?"

"The energy?" Is this guy for real?

"Yeah. Every team has its own energy."

"Sounds a little woo-woo to me," I tell him.

"Everything is based on energy," he says. "From the smallest building blocks of atomic elements to intergalactic travel. It's all just energy." His words are lazy and slow. It's amazing to me how chill he is off the ice, given how fast and aggressive he is on it.

"So," I say, crossing my arms as I lean against the doorframe, "what's this team's energy then?"

"Too early to tell," he says decisively and stands. "You heading out?"

"Yeah," I say, and he grabs his bag and follows me out of the locker room.

"So, how's it feel playing for your hometown team?" he asks as we walk down the hallway that'll lead us to the parking garage.

"It hasn't really sunk in yet," I say, thinking about the giant Rebels symbol on the ceiling of our locker room. I remember touring this new practice facility with my club team when it was built—back when I was in high school—so it's a bit surreal to be playing here now. "Ask me when we play our home opener."

"I will," he says, and it occurs to me that this wasn't Zach making casual conversation. He actually cares about my answer.

"How's it feel to you, playing here?" I ask him.

"Little weird, not going to lie. I grew up in Canada, then spent the last seven years in Philadelphia."

"Philly's a pretty cool town," I tell him. "But Boston's better."

He lets out a low laugh. "Figures you'd think so."

"Because it's true." We chat about where he lives and what he's done in Boston since he moved here earlier this summer. He's an easy-going guy, and before I know it, I'm at my car.

"You going on Saturday night?" Zach asks me as I drop my bag into the trunk.

"Definitely." When Colt invites you to a party at his place, you go. End of story. "You?"

"Feel like I need to go, you know?"

"You don't want to?"

"The party scene just isn't really *my* scene. I'm a morning person, so staying up all night partying really impacts my day."

I shut my trunk and turn toward him. "Hey, you've played in the league longer than me, but as someone who's had to switch teams more often, here's a piece of advice. When the team is all going out, you go. Whether you want to or not."

If I'd been less intimidated by Leland and his cronies in Colorado and spent more time with the team off the ice, it might not have taken them a full year to realize I wasn't the douchebag they thought I was.

"Yeah," he says in defeat. "I know. I'll be there."

"Good," I tell him, then get in my car.

As I'm backing out of my space in the player's section of the garage, my phone rings, and Jameson's number flashes on my screen. I hit the button to answer it, and his deep voice fills the car.

"What are you doing Thursday night?"

"Uhhh…" I can't tell by his tone if he's upset, or if this is just his typical *I hate everyone* voice. "I don't think I have plans?"

"Good. I have practice for the hockey team I coach, and my assistant coach can't make it. Can you help out?"

This feels almost too easy, which makes me instantly suspicious. "Sure. It's funny that you called about this, because I was about to call you to see if you knew of any youth hockey teams in the area who might like to have me volunteer. You know, getting myself out in the community, and all that."

"Yeah. Audrey mentioned that and suggested you might want to help when I told her about my other coach bailing for Thursday night. I'm glad you can make it. It'll give us a chance to talk about how you know my little sister so well, and why you're going to stay away from her from here on out. I'll text you the details about the practice," he says, and the line goes dead.

Chapter Thirteen

AUDREY

Knowing that Drew's going to be at Graham's practice tonight, and actually seeing him on the ice interacting with our kid, are two totally different things. I thought I was prepared. I was dead wrong.

"What's wrong?" Jules asks. "You just winced."

Did I? "I'm just sore from dance class last night." It's not a lie. I am always sore on Thursdays.

I may have misled my family and friends into thinking I'm taking the type of dance I did all through high school and college—jazz and hip hop. Thank God no one's asked for specific details, because what I've really been doing for the last four months is taking pole dancing lessons. It's an amazing workout, and I leave every week feeling incredibly powerful, both physically and in terms of my sexuality.

Last night's class, however, we tried a new move and today my *serratus anterior* muscles—a back muscle that works with the trapezius for upward rotation of the shoulder blade

—are screaming in protest every time I move my arms or shoulders. I didn't even know the *serratus anterior* existed until I looked at an anatomical diagram this morning to figure out what was hurting so bad.

"Have you talked to Lauren yet?" Jules asks from her seat beside me, oblivious to my pain. We're snuggled down under a blanket together, and I'm trying to pretend like watching Drew on the ice with Graham isn't turning my whole world upside down.

"No. She sent me a text yesterday, saying she wants to talk about Sunday, but that she's been swamped at work, and then when she's home at night, Jameson is always there. She's planning to call me tonight while he's at practice," I say, nodding toward the rink where our brother skates around, barking orders.

Jules's big eyes widen. "You're going to take that call right here?"

"I mean, I'll probably head out to the lobby or something. But I can't ignore the call."

"Are you ready for more people to know?" Jules asks.

On the ice, Drew bends over and helps a kid reposition his hands on his stick and walks him through the motions of a slapshot. Then he calls Graham over and does the same thing. When he puts one hand on Graham's lower back to straighten him up a bit, I try to ignore the memory of the way he ushered me out of the restaurant on Monday night. His hand on the small of my back had my entire core quivering, and it was a relief when he dropped his hand outside the restaurant, because I cannot be having these feelings for him.

He's not the kind of guy you settle down with, and even if he was, getting involved with him would be too risky. If it didn't go well, it could ruin his relationship with Graham. Me and my stupid sex drive—which is inconveniently more super-charged than ever—are not going to be the reason Graham doesn't have a dad in his life.

"Eventually," I tell Jules, "everyone's going to know. But for now, while Drew gets to know Graham, I want to keep it as quiet as possible."

"So are you going to ask Lauren not to tell Jameson?"

"I can't ask her to lie to him. We'll see how it goes once I talk to her."

On the ice, Drew's hands are back on Graham's, and again, all I can think of is how his hand brushed mine multiple times on the short walk from the restaurant back to my place. By the time we reached the steps up to my front door, I felt near ready to combust, and then he leveled me with a look so perfectly laced with longing that I think it must have been rehearsed. He probably gives women that look and they start stripping their clothes off immediately.

It was a good reminder that he has his choice of women, and no shortage of them, so I remained strong. And by "remained strong," I mean I thanked him for the drinks, then turned and practically sprinted up the steps and through my front door. I couldn't even collapse against the closed door once I was safe inside, because Jules had gotten me the wooden doors with the big glass panels I'd wanted so badly and he would have seen me.

Instead, I headed straight to my room, and after getting ready for bed, I may or may not have crawled between the sheets completely naked and imagined that my hands were Drew's as they crept all over my body. And it definitely wasn't his name on my lips as I made myself come. Nope, because I'm *not* thinking about him like that. He's my kid's biological father, and that's it. That's all he can be, because anything happening between Drew and me is a disaster waiting to happen.

In my hand, my phone buzzes, and before I can even glance down, Jules says, "Well, speak of the devil." When my eyes land on my screen, Lauren's photo is lighting it up.

"I'll be right back," I tell Jules as I stand and start heading down the stairs of the bleachers. When I hit the rubber mats at the bottom, I answer the phone. "Hey," I say, "hold on one sec, I'm just going to find somewhere more private."

"Okay," Lauren's sweet voice carries through my phone.

I head through the glass doors, and luckily the lobby is empty like I hoped it would be. I take a seat on the bench along the far wall. "Alright, all good."

"Didn't want to have this conversation in the rink, in front of the other parents?" she teases.

"Definitely not. Especially with both Drew and Jameson there."

"Drew's there?" Lauren's interest is clearly piqued.

"Uhh...Jameson didn't mention that?"

Her voice takes on a sing-song quality as she chirps, "He sure didn't."

I tell her about the assistant coach canceling for tonight and that Drew was looking to do some volunteer work in the community.

Lauren's chuckle interrupts me. "Uh huh. I'm sure it has nothing to do with you and Graham being there."

"Listen, Lauren. I know you probably have questions about that conversation you witnessed Sunday night."

"You got that right," she says, and in the background, the

white noise fades. I can picture her walking farther from the baby monitor. She probably just got the girls down for bed a few minutes ago.

"Here's what I'm thinking. It would be great if you didn't ask those questions, so that I don't have to lie to you, or ask you to lie to my brother."

"Not ready to talk about it?" she asks.

"Trust me, I *want* to talk about it." I love that Lauren's in my life now—she's like a big sister who's now a good friend. "But I'm not ready to talk to Jameson about it. Drew and I have…things we need to figure out first."

"And if you talk to me about it, you think I'll tell Jameson?"

"No. I think that if he asks you about it, right now you have plausible deniability."

"Are you doing something illegal that I should be pretending I don't know about?" she teases.

"No, but you know what I mean. When Jameson asks if you know if anything's going on between us, or whatever, you can honestly say you don't know."

"Why? *Is* something going on between you guys now?" I can't tell if she sounds extra-curious or hopeful, but there's definite excitement in her voice.

"No, definitely not. So you can be honest about that."

"Do you want there to be?"

"No, and Lauren, we're *not* having this conversation, remember?"

"I can't help it!" She sighs. "I'm so freaking curious about what's going on."

"Well, once I figure that out, I'll let you know."

"Al-right." She drags the word out slowly, sounding an awful lot like Eeyore, which makes me laugh.

"I've got to get back to practice," I tell her. "I'll see you Sunday night for dinner."

"Okay. Come early, because we're supposed to have perfect fall weather this weekend, and Jameson inflated the bounce house the other day. The girls can't wait for Graham to go on it with them."

We say goodbye, and when I head back into the rink, the boys are coming off the ice. Graham is running toward me on his skates, and over his head, Drew and I lock eyes as he steps off the ice. He looks like he wants to devour me, and it has heat flashing through my whole body. I look away, hoping no one else noticed.

"Mom!" Graham says with a big smile, one that I instantly match. "There's a new player on the Boston Rebels and he's here helping Uncle Jameson."

"Yeah, Bud, I can see that." I glance from Graham over to Drew where he's chatting with Jameson, and the conversation looks a bit heated. Drew texted me Tuesday, letting me know about his phone call with Jameson, which is yet another reason it's best if Lauren can deny knowing anything at this point.

"I told him we were going to get cookies after practice tonight," Graham says, excitement making him speak so fast he's hard to understand. "And he said he loves cookies. Can I invite him to come too?"

Graham's got sweat dripping down his neck from his hair and is still in all his gear, and when I glance over at Drew again, Jameson locks eyes with me. *Shit.*

I squat down next to Graham, wondering when they had

this conversation—maybe while I was on the phone with Lauren? "You know what, he looks kind of busy with Uncle Jameson right now. Let's not bother him. We can always ask him next time."

Graham's face falls, but he says, "Okay," and sits on the bench to start taking off his skates and gear. As I bend over to untie his skates for him, I wonder if he isn't just a little too compliant for a five-year-old boy. I mean, I didn't want to raise a hellion or anything, but Graham's a really sweet kid, and I always worry that maybe he's not tough enough.

"I can do the rest," he tells me once the double-knots are out, and so I stand, glancing up at Jules where she sits a few rows behind us.

Even though my back's to the walkway, I can tell Drew's walking toward us by the way Jules's eyes track the movement, and the way Graham's head snaps up with a hopeful look on his face.

"Good job today, Graham." Drew's voice comes from behind me, and the smooth sound of it washes over me just like it did outside the restaurant the other night. Then he drops his voice so low that only I can hear him say, "Check your texts," and keeps walking.

"Hey." I hear my brother as he approaches. He must have been hot on Drew's heels.

"Hey." I try to keep my voice completely neutral. I don't want him to know the effect Drew's presence has on me, or how much it hurt that he didn't stop just now—even though I suspect Jameson's the reason for that.

"Good practice today, kid," Jameson says as he reaches over and ruffles Graham's hair.

"Thanks," my son replies. "Are we playing a game on

Saturday morning? Or just practice?"

"It's a scrimmage," Jameson says, and I know he's explained this to the boys, but Graham still doesn't quite understand the concept. "It's like a practice game. We're not going to keep score. It's just a good way to put into play all the things we've gone over in practice."

"But it's at the Rebels' practice rink?" Graham asks.

"Yep."

"Do you think any of the Rebels will be there?" His face and voice are so hopeful, you'd think the kid had never met a real-life NHL player, even though he's been surrounded by them his whole life.

"Maybe," Jameson says. "But if they are, they won't be in their jerseys or anything."

"Why not?" Graham asks.

"Because they won't be playing, you will be. Alright, gotta run. Lauren's got the twins in bed, and she ordered dinner for us," he says.

I laugh, because this man who swore up and down that he'd already raised me and Jules and was never getting married or having kids literally can't wait to get home to his future wife and kids.

As he leaves, I help Graham pack his gear into his bag, double-checking that there's nothing he's left behind. His whole bag already smells terrible, and we're only a few practices into the season. *Maybe Drew will have some tips for this?* I think to myself as I pull the zipper shut, and then remind myself that I can just ask my brother.

He picks up the bag now that he's finally—barely—big enough to carry it himself, and I pull out my phone to look at my texts as we walk outside.

Chapter Fourteen

AUDREY

DREW:

Sorry, couldn't stop and talk with Jameson right there. He just read me the riot act about not going near you. Anyway...I hear cookies are tonight's plan? Send me your and Graham's order and I'll meet you at the location on Boylston Street.

"Did you tell Drew where we were going for cookies?" I ask Graham.

"Yeah, he said that's his favorite place too."

Of course they both have the same expensive-ass taste in cookies.

"What kind do you want tonight?" I ask him as we leave the rink and head to the car.

"I think..."—he carefully ponders his options—"tonight feels like an M&M cookie kind of night."

> AUDREY:
> So sorry to have missed THAT conversation. Graham would like an M&M cookie, and I'd like a salted caramel, please.

I don't tell Graham that Drew is meeting us there. I try to convince myself it's because I don't want him to be disappointed if Drew doesn't show, but maybe it's also because I don't quite want to get my own hopes up and potentially be disappointed myself.

Drew seems like a different person, in a different place in his life now, but his reputation is unchanged. If anything, according to the media, he's even wilder now than when I knew him in college. And he let me down in the biggest way six years ago, so it's going to take a bit for me to trust him again.

Of course, we manage to find parking right in front of the store—benefits of going after the work crowd has left the city—and Graham practically shrieks, "Mom, Drew's in there! Do you think he came to see me?"

"I bet he did," I say, giving him a smile in the rearview mirror as I unbuckle.

"Can I go in?"

I glance across the wide expanse of sidewalk between the curb and the store, and there's almost no one around. "Sure, go ahead," I say as I open my door and step out. He zooms out, slamming the car door behind him, and makes a run for the door to the store, which he's barely able to pull open by himself. Through the large windows, I see him bouncing up and down in front of Drew, who looks nervously beyond him at the door.

When I walk in, Drew looks relieved. "I was worried you weren't coming," he says to me as I approach the table.

"Yeah, I just let my five-year-old run wild in the city by himself."

"You do *not*," Graham insists. "You don't even let me cross the street without holding your hand!"

"Good," Drew says definitively, and that has Graham's eyes snapping back to him. "I grew up in Boston too, and cities aren't safe places for kids to run around by themselves. So make sure you're always with your mom or a trusted adult, okay?"

Graham nods, then looks up at me. "Is Drew a trusted adult?"

"I don't know," I say, eyeing Drew. He bites his lower lip like he's trying not to smile and shakes his head at me—he thinks I'm teasing him, and in a way, I am. But I'm also serious. "I think we should probably get to know him better before we decide."

Next to me, Graham nods like I've said the wisest thing in the world. "Are those cookies?" he asks as he eyes the large box sitting on the table in front of Drew.

"Sure are. I thought maybe we could take them and eat outside since it's such a nice night. Copley Square?" he asks me.

"For a few minutes. It's getting close to bedtime."

Drew glances at his watch. "Alright, we'll take a quick walk down there, eat a cookie, and then get you home in time for bed."

I know he doesn't mean he's coming home with us, but it half-way sounds like that's his intention. And I don't hate that idea.

Yes, you do. It's a terrible idea.

My mind is at war with itself, reminding me why I can't be interested in Drew, while simultaneously reminding me that there's a distinct possibility he might be around more often if this all goes well. Which means I'm going to have to keep my fucking hormones at bay so I don't screw this up for Graham.

"Uhh, you ready?" Drew's looking at me like I'm a bit deranged, which is when I realize that he and Graham are ready to go, and I'm standing like a statue blocking their path to the door.

I turn to head out, ushering Graham in front of me, and there's Drew's hand again, on the small of my back, just like the other night. This time, he doesn't drop it when we get outside. Instead, his palm lies flat against my spine and his fingertips press into my sweater like five points of contact anchoring him to me.

As we walk, he traces his thumb along a muscle in my lower back and a chill ricochets up my spine as my body reacts. It's probably just because I'm getting my period soon, so my lower back is already stiff and sensitive. But a quick glance sideways tells me that he's noticed, and I don't want him to get the wrong idea, so I look down, holding out my hand to Graham, who takes it and falls into step with us.

We pass the Public Library and cross the street to where the grassy square, dotted with trees and benches, spreads out before us. At the far end of the grass, Trinity Church stands in all its Romanesque Revival glory. This US National Historic Landmark, with its heavy arches and huge towers built of granite and brownstone, spawned my love affair with architecture. I spent countless hours here as a teenager, in the shadow of the massive, mirrored Hancock Tower, sketching this building and drawing up my own designs.

"This is my mom's favorite building," Graham says as Drew sits on a park bench and opens the box of cookies in his lap.

"Is that so?" He hands Graham an M&M cookie, then glances up at me through his impossibly long lashes. The same ones that line Graham's eyes.

I nod as I sit down next to him.

His voice softens as he asks, "What do you love about it?"

The light is fading as sunset approaches, so when Graham hops up on the ledge lining the fountain across from us, I call out, "Be careful, please!"

Graham doesn't say anything, just keeps walking cautiously along the ledge as if his actions are his response.

"So? What is it that you love about Trinity?"

"How much time do you have?"

"For you, I've got all night."

I roll my eyes. "Do those kinds of cheesy lines usually work?"

"I was being serious." In the golden light, the line of his cheekbones stands out against the skin cast in shadows below them. His nose is perfectly straight, and his lower lip is a bit fuller than his upper lip. He's too good looking for his own good. "But also"—he gives me a sheepish grin—"yeah."

I shake my head. "We're not in college anymore, Drew. You're not going to win your way into my bed with cheesy pickup lines, followed by a cheeky grin."

He leans into me, knocking his shoulder against mine playfully. "*Should I be* trying to win my way into your bed?"

"No." I say the word firmly, even though my body is screaming, *Yes!* "Partnership, remember? Nothing more."

He presses his lips together, but nods. There's amusement in his voice when he says, "Right. Partnership."

"Drew," I say, like he's a child.

"Is that your *you're in trouble* voice, Audrey?" He leans in a little closer and raises an eyebrow. His breath ghosts across my lips when he says, "Because, just a warning...I like that quite a lot. Makes me wonder what else I should do to get a reaction out of you."

The heat creeps into my neck as the flush works its way toward my face. His words have me thinking about all the ways he could get a reaction out of me, but that line of thought needs to stop, so I change the subject.

"I got the video you sent of your mom's house. I showed it to Jules, and she felt like we could probably fit that in this winter. But we need to see it in person, and I need to take some measurements and draw up some plans. Think it's possible for us to stop by sometime?"

"Of course. I'd like to be there when you do, so it doesn't confuse my mom."

"Absolutely. We can coordinate something. When's your first road game?"

We talk a bit about scheduling and realize that because Jules is leaving tomorrow for Maine and will be gone all week, and then he's traveling, it'll be almost two weeks before we can make it work. "Alright, I'm putting it in my calendar right now," I say as I pull out my phone.

Just then, Graham gives a helpless squeal as water splashes out of the fountain in front of us. He stands there, one leg in the water and one leg on the ground, straddling the ledge he'd been walking on.

"Shit," I mutter, pissed at myself for letting him walk on there in the first place, and already anticipating having to get his sneakers dried out before school tomorrow.

Drew stands, setting the box of cookies on my lap, and is over to Graham in three steps. He lifts him up, setting him on the ground, then kneels down in front of him.

"You have a pretty wet leg, my friend," he says to our son.

From this profile view, I can see that Graham's eyes are filled with tears and his lower lip is trembling as he tries to hold it together. Mostly, I think he's embarrassed. He just nods back to Drew.

"Well, that would be an uncomfortable walk back to the car," he says. "How about I give you a piggyback ride instead?"

Graham looks at me, checking that it's okay, and I give him a little nod and smile. Drew looks over his shoulder, and says, "Climb on."

I watch Graham throw his arms around Drew's neck, and Drew hooks his arms under Graham's knees to anchor him in place. As I stand and carry the box of cookies over to them, I can't help but notice how easily Drew just diffused the situation. Where I might have reminded Graham that I told him to be careful or given him a little lecture as I made him walk back to the car with his dripping wet shoes and pant leg, Drew acknowledged that it happened, and moved on.

His place on Drew's back makes Graham a head taller than me, and he looks over at me and says, "I'll be more careful next time, Mom."

"Sounds like a good plan, Bud." And then, because I'm struck by how much they look alike as Graham sits there with his chin resting on Drew's shoulder, I ask them to pause for a picture together. I expect Drew to balk at the idea, but he doesn't. They both smile happily.

"Send me a copy?" Drew asks as we start walking again.

"Sure." I text him the photo, and when we arrive back at my parked car, Drew shuts the door after Graham climbs in the backseat, then turns toward me.

"Thanks for carrying him back," I say. He's big enough now that carrying him several city blocks would have been nearly impossible.

"I'm happy to help. Really," he says, then reaches out, tilting my chin up so I'm looking at him. Then his fingertips slide along my jaw and tuck my hair behind my ear. The wave of longing that runs through me is damn close to incinerating me. "If you ever need *anything*, just call."

"Thanks," I say, then move to hand him the box of cookies because I need to put some physical distance between us so I don't jump him.

"You didn't have yours yet," he says, nodding his chin at the box in my hands. "You should keep them."

"How many cookies are in here?" I ask, eying the box.

"Enough." He gives me a small smile and turns, walking down the street. He hangs a left at the intersection, moving out of view, and as I watch him walk away, it occurs to me that I'm not mad about him being back in my life. In fact, I'm kind of liking his presence a little too much.

Chapter Fifteen

DREW

The thumping music and press of the crowd have me practically yelling, "Your place is awesome!" in Colt's face. I've been here for an hour and just now found him, standing at the enormous two-story wall of glass at the far end of his living room. The view of the Seaport spreads before us, the lights of the buildings below glittering in the rain before the dark expanse of Boston Harbor begins. Through the rain, we can barely see East Boston on the other side of the Harbor.

"Thanks," he says. "Glad you made it."

"What are you doing over here all alone?" I ask.

"Just waiting for Jasmine to get back from the bathroom."

"Who's Jasmine?"

"Some hot friend of McCabe's girlfriend."

"McCabe has a girlfriend?" I don't know why, but the image of our captain with a girlfriend does not compute. He's so serious, and he's got an infant daughter that his ex just dropped off on his doorstep a few months ago. From what I can tell, it's been a huge adjustment and every minute he's not playing hockey, he's focused on her. I'm shocked he has the time to date, or that he'd be here tonight. Then again, team bonding—especially at the beginning of a season—is always a priority, and he's our captain.

"Yeah, it's a recent development. Her name's Annabelle."

I'm about to respond, when a pair of arms snake around Colt's waist from behind, and then a petite brunette with long hair, fake lashes, and a top so small it could pass for a bathing suit slides up next to him. "Hey, big guy," she says, and I try not to cringe, "sorry to keep you waiting."

"Jasmine, this is my new teammate, Drew." He nods his chin toward me.

She extends her hand toward me. "Nice to meet you, Drew." But when she shakes my hand, her thumb strokes the back of my hand, and her eyes sparkle at me with interest. *Ew, no.*

"You too, Jasmine," I say, and then in my peripheral vision, I see Zach Reid. He looks uncomfortable, like he doesn't want to be here. "Alright, I'll leave you two kids alone." I raise my eyebrows in Colt's direction, because I'm pretty sure there's only one reason he's interested in her, and it'll be easier to get her into his bed if I'm not hanging around.

I turn and walk over to Zach, where he stands on one of the two steps leading from Colt's dining room to the wide-open living room. "You good?" I ask as I approach.

"Yeah. Just counting down the minutes until I can leave."

"Dude, relax. Hang out with your teammates, enjoy the

fact that the women outnumber the men here by about three to one, and have a damn drink. Let's go."

I turn, and he follows me as we head toward the kitchen, where I get him a beer and grab another for myself. "Why are you so averse to fun, anyway?" I ask as we leave the kitchen and head through the dining room.

"I'm not. This just isn't my idea of fun."

"You need to get laid," I say, and the two girls who were walking toward us stop, their faces clearly showing their interest in Zach now that I've made that announcement.

"Asshole," he mutters under his breath as the women come to a complete stop.

I laugh under my breath, and then say, "Hey, ladies, have you met Zach Reid? He's new to the team this year."

"Hey, Zach," they both respond at the same time, in nearly identical voices, which is creepy as fuck. Or am I just comparing every woman here to Audrey, who would never throw herself at a guy the way these women are?

I keep moving, leaving him with the two women who are now plastered to his sides. His night's about to get a whole lot more interesting. But I'm only a few steps farther, just taking the stairs down into the packed living room, when I feel my phone vibrating in my front pocket.

I slip it out, and Audrey's name flashes on my screen. It's too loud in here to be able to hear her, so I reply with a text.

DREW:
I'll call you back in just a minute.

I look around, searching for some part of Colt's place that might be quieter. My eyes land on a door that leads out to a balcony. Because of the rain, no one is out there, even though the large space looks like it's covered. So I make my way across the living room that's turned into a dance floor, nodding at my teammates as I pass. When I open the door and step outside, I realize there are actually two people out here on the couch. They're full-on making out with her straddling him, and I don't want to interrupt, but there's no way I'm not calling Audrey, so I turn my back and hit the call button on my phone screen.

"Hey, what's going on?" I ask when she answers.

"I know when you said I could call you if I needed anything, you meant about Graham—"

"No, I meant what I said. If you need *anything*."

"What if I just need a quick delivery?"

"Of what?" I ask.

"Ibuprofen?"

"Are you sick?"

"In a manner of speaking."

Why is she being so vague? "What does that mean?"

"Well, I get sick like this once a month."

Ahhh, okay. As someone who grew up with two sisters, this is becoming very clear. "Understood. I'm coming from the Seaport, so give me, like, twenty minutes, maybe more if there's traffic."

"No, Drew," she says, "if you're out doing something, I don't want to take you away from that. I only asked because you live five minutes from me."

It hits me then: there's nothing I could be out doing that I wouldn't drop for her. But I can't tell her that without her thinking I'm crazy. Hell, I think I'm crazy. She's the mother of my child, and unless I want to screw things up with Graham, that's all she should be. I know this. I know that the responsible thing is to not get involved with her in any way. But when I'm around her, all that flies out the window, because I *want* her.

I want her just as much as I did my senior year of college, and possibly more. Because I thought she was amazing then, but the woman she's grown into—the patience she has with Graham, the sacrifices she's made to raise him, the business she's built...a woman like her needs a man who can commit. A man who is dependable, and around a hell of a lot more than I am. She deserves someone like that, and for the first time in my life, I want to be that person for someone else. Not because it benefits me, but because it's what she needs.

"I'm already on my way. See you soon." I hang up on her before she can object anymore. I know what it took for her to call me—she must not have any other options right now—and I'm not giving up my chance to see her, especially since I'm guessing this means Graham's in bed already, and she's alone. As much as I loved spending time with Graham the other night and am looking forward to seeing him again, the thought of having more time alone with Audrey doesn't feel like it'll ever lose its appeal.

I take the elevator down to the bottom of Colt's building and ask the doorman to point me in the direction of the closest pharmacy, which turns out to be just around the corner.

There, I grab some ibuprofen, some stick-on heating pads, and three pints of ice cream in a variety of flavors. And when the car drops me off at her doorstep, I practically run up the steps of her brownstone because I'm so damn eager to see her.

She answers the door in sweatpants and a fitted t-shirt,

under which she does not seem to be wearing a bra. But I force myself to focus my eyes up on her face, rather than on the stiff peaks of her nipples, because I'm trying not to be an asshole.

"Thank you so much," she sighs, leaning against the door frame like it's taking effort to stand.

"C'mon," I say, sweeping my hand forward like I'm gesturing her through the door, "let's get you patched up."

She furrows her brows. "Patched up?"

"Yeah, I got you some of those stick-on heating pads, because I hear heat works well for cramps," I say, thinking of all the times Missy would curl up with one of those microwavable heating pads to help with her cramps. "Between that, the ibuprofen, and the variety of Ben & Jerry's options I have in this bag, you'll be feeling much better."

"You want…to come in?"

Even though she'd asked about a "delivery," the idea that she just wants the supplies and not my company hits me right in my gut.

"You were just using me as a delivery service? Ouch."

"Actually, I thought you were busy and were just doing me a favor by dropping off some ibuprofen. I figured you'd want to go back to whatever you were doing."

Don't make any jokes about who *you want to be doing right now*, I have to remind myself. Every time I'm in her presence, all I can think about is the last time I saw her before the draft. The way her skin felt beneath my hands, the sound of my name rolling off her lips, her grunts of pleasure, the way her nails felt as they raked along my shoulders—all of it was better than I'd imagined, and I'd imagined it plenty.

"I'd rather hang out with you, if you're open to company."

She sighs, and I'm pretty sure she's going to send me away. "Well, I guess you did bring enough ice cream for two, so come on in." She turns and walks into the house, leaving me to shut the door. I almost forget to lock it, though, because I'm so focused on the way her ass looks in those sweats as she walks into her kitchen.

I follow her, taking in the terracotta patterned tile, the dark cabinets, and the stone countertops of the room, with its crisp walls and black-framed windows. "Your house looks like one of those *after* pictures you see on social media—you know, like when a designer posts them?"

"Well, since this is basically what Jules and I do for a living, it'd be sad if our house didn't represent our style, right?"

"Did you guys do this whole place?" I set the bag on the counter and start taking the contents out one at a time as I glance around the open first floor of their brownstone.

"This is our childhood home. Jameson did a barebones remodel while Jules and I were in college, just to freshen everything up," she says. "He made the third floor into a one-bedroom apartment that he lived in until he moved in with Lauren this past spring—there's a great roof deck up there that I turned into a garden once he moved out. There are two bedrooms and a bathroom on the second floor, which is where Graham and I ended up living after I graduated from college, and then there's another bedroom off the living room for Jules. So anyway, once we moved back here post-college, we worked on some redesign and redecorating."

"Colt said you guys were featured in some fancy Boston magazine recently."

"Did he?" She gives a small laugh. She holds her hand out

as I unpack the ibuprofen and then open the box to remove the pill bottle. "Yeah, that was a bit of a turning point. Our company is still really new, and all the attention is a lot to balance. We don't want to turn people away, but we also don't want to overbook ourselves and do a bad job. We're working on forcing ourselves to expand at a manageable speed because we're both kind of workaholics—but especially Jules."

Once again, I feel so damn proud of her for all she's accomplished, even though I had nothing to do with it. "Well, it's incredible. You've done so well already."

"We're trying." She shakes three pills out into her palm, then reaches for an acrylic tumbler sitting on the island and swallows them down. "Thanks so much for these, I really needed them. Normally, I'd have asked Jules, but she's in Maine for this whole next week, or Morgan, but she's in Las Vegas for the weekend."

"And Morgan is?"

She explains her relationship with Lauren and how she's become one of her and Jules's best friends over the past eight months.

"So, how did you not have any painkillers in your house?"

"I ran out and forgot to replace them." She shrugs. "I thought about just taking some kids ibuprofen that I have for Graham, but there wasn't enough left in the bottle to equal one adult-size dose, much less a dose and half, which is what I need when I feel like this."

I grab the box of heating pads off the counter and open it. "Let's get one of these on you and see if that helps too."

"Alright. Thank you for thinking of that, too." She pulls her shirt up as she turns toward the counter and plants her elbows there so she's bending forward with her lower back bared to me.

As I step up behind her, I make sure to keep my distance because the peach shape of her ass in those sweatpants has me growing hard just looking at it. It's all I can do not to step up against her and settle myself right between her ass cheeks so she can feel exactly what she does to me.

Instead, I peel off the backing of the sticky pad, ask her to point out where it hurts the most, and then gently press the pad against the offending muscles. "Do you need one for your abdomen too?"

"No, it's really my back that hurts the most. My belly is fine if I just curl up into a ball—that's how I spent the last hour on the couch."

"Let's move you back there. I'll bring the ice cream. Pick your poison," I say, gesturing to the three options. She points to one, then heads to the living room, so I pick one for myself, throw the other in the freezer, grab two spoons and follow her.

Chapter Sixteen

AUDREY

I'm trying so hard to focus on the movie, rather than the way the outside of Drew's thigh is pressing against my knee as we sit beside each other. My cramps are a little better, but I really want to curl into a ball, and I don't feel like I can do that with him here. Either I'd have my back to him, which feels rude, or my head would be in his lap.

"I'm going to get this ice cream in the freezer," I say as I reach past the two pints sitting on the coffee table and grab the remote, "before they're soup. Unless you want more."

Drew pats his stomach. "I always want more, but I'm trying to practice restraint…in all areas of my life."

"Oh yeah?" My voice takes on the teasing quality that I almost can't resist using when he's around. "Where else do you need to practice restraint, besides ice cream?"

"I've been told I need to do less fighting on the ice," he says. "And I'm trying really hard not to bite my sister's head off every time she opens her mouth—"

"You don't get along with your sister?"

"I have two. Missy's great. She's married and has two boys, one a year older than Graham, and one a year younger."

I gasp without meaning to, and he looks at me with concern. "I'm sorry, it didn't even occur to me that Graham might have cousins. I don't know why I never thought about that."

"Yeah. Someday, it would be great if they could meet. I bet they'll have a blast together."

I don't even know how I feel about this. Having Drew back in Graham's life is one thing, but he has a whole family, too. And, of course, they'll want to get to know Graham. It makes sense; it's just another layer I hadn't really thought much about yet.

"So yeah," he continues, "Missy's great. Caitlyn is another story. I think she's deeply unhappy, and her defense mechanism is to make others unhappy in return."

"That's pretty insightful," I say as I carry the pints of half-melted ice cream to the kitchen.

"Thanks," he calls over the back of the couch. "Took me decades of frustration to finally come to the realization. Knowing that her behavior stems from her own unhappiness helps me remember that I don't have to respond to every little insult she slings my way."

He's balancing a lot—a new team, relocating, helping with his mom, and now finding out he has a son. I wish his sister was more supportive. "So it's always been like this with you two?"

"Kind of." He shrugs. "Once my dad died, she always acted like she needed to be the second parent in our family. It was probably part of how she coped with his death, whereas I barely have any memories of him at all. But she's never done anything but make me feel guilty about it. Every little sacrifice she's made, she rubs in my face. And she treats hockey like it's some game I'm off playing so I can avoid real life, instead of it being my career."

"Sounds like she gives you lots of opportunities to practice restraint," I say, hoping to lighten the mood a bit.

He pauses, a thoughtful look on his face. In most ways, Drew is clearly older now, but the way his eyebrows raise when he's thinking and his hair flops forward a bit, makes him look almost the same as in college. And for a moment, I feel like I'm transported right back to his apartment, where I spent stupid amounts of my time and the school's money trying to get him to focus on calculus long enough to understand it.

"Yeah, I think you're right." He gives me a lopsided smile while brushing the hair back off his face, and my heart warms toward him. His boyish charm was nearly irresistible back in college, but seeing glimpses of it now amid the more mature pro hockey player makes him…maybe even harder to resist?

I return to the couch, but I can't get comfortable enough to restart *Sweet Home Alabama.*

"Hey," he says, putting his hand on my thigh to stop me from squirming. "What's wrong?"

"I just can't find a way to sit that doesn't hurt my lower back."

"What's normally most comfortable when you feel like this?"

"Curling up in a ball."

"Let's do that then," he says. "Obviously, I need to know if

Melanie ever signs those divorce papers, so we'll finish the movie that way."

Do I want to be lying down, curled up with Drew curled behind me while I re-watch a rom-com I've seen a hundred times? *Hell yes, I do!* But is it the responsible choice?

"Drew…" I leave his name hanging there like a warning. Neither of us is stupid enough to pretend it's a good idea to be cuddling on the couch, because we both know where that might lead. After all, we've been there before.

"You know it turns me on when you say my name like that, right?" His voice is teasing, but it's also dropped an octave and wraps around me like a caress. I don't know how his tone gives my body such a physical response, but it keeps happening.

Hearing him say that I turn him on has me afraid to reply. My logic and emotions are all over the place right now, so instead, I roll my eyes at him in response.

"You know what I hear *really* helps with period cramps?" he says.

"If you say sex, I'm going to punch you in the face."

His laugh is a quiet rumble, and I like the sound of it way more than I should. In fact, it's got those abdominal cramps subsiding in favor of a tingling pressure building throughout my core instead. "I didn't know sex helped with that," he says, his voice quiet, "but I mean, if that's a sacrifice you need me to make…"

I roll my eyes. "It's not." It's unfortunate how often I have to say the exact opposite of what I want to say when I'm around him, but someone has to be the adult here.

"I was going to suggest a massage, actually. Parkinson's causes muscle rigidity and massage can really relieve some of the stiffness, so I learned how to give them in order to help my mom. I could probably help your back muscles relax a bit, too."

"I'd say it can't hurt to try, but let's not forget what happened last time you had your hands on me."

"I won't touch anything but your back." He gives me that same lopsided smile, and it's so hard to say no to him, especially when we want the same thing. "Unless you ask me to."

"Fine," I sigh, as if I'm giving in to something I don't actually want—when, in fact, my body is literally aching for him to touch me. "And I'm not going to ask you to touch any part of me but my back."

He lets out a small grunt of disapproval. "Your loss."

Drew has me lay on my side, and then he snuggles in behind me. I turn the movie back on, enjoying the way his strong fingers dig into my muscles as we watch Reese Witherspoon and Josh Lucas banter about their failed marriage.

"Can you roll toward your stomach?" His breath warms the side of my face as he asks the question. I startle because he's made sure no part of his body is touching mine except for his hand on my back, so I hadn't realized quite how close he is.

"Sure," I say, and try not to groan as I move. The right side of my back, which he's been massaging, feels amazing, but the left side is still incredibly tight. Once I'm on my stomach with my head resting on my hands, I try to turn my attention back to the movie, but I can't. Because the warmth radiating off Drew, along with the way my muscles are finally starting to relax, makes it damn near impossible to keep my eyes open.

I wake up gradually in the silent, mostly dark room. The movie is over, and the TV is frozen on the screen, suggesting the next movies I might want to choose from.

My neck is crooked from having it turned so sharply while lying on my stomach, so I go to flip onto my right side and come face to face with Drew. I don't know why it surprises me that he's still here, but it does.

"Hey," he whispers, his eyes opening just enough to see me. A small smile plays across his lips, and his arm snakes around my back, pulling me flush against him. I want to close my eyes and go back to sleep, but with every part of my body touching his, I'm on fire. My nipples are pressed up against his chest and his fingers are gently massaging my lower back again.

Desire courses through my blood. My heart is pounding like it's going to explode and the muscles in my lower abdomen contract involuntarily as yearning pulses through my core. That motion has my body pushing right into Drew's dick, which is already getting hard, and he groans and pushes his knee forward, between mine.

"Don't do that," he says, a note of warning in his voice, "unless you want more than a back massage."

My brain is screaming at me to stop, to show him the door and go upstairs to my bed alone, like always. But the hard ridge of his thigh is settled right against my clit, and my hips move forward against it, giving in to the need. The friction as I rub myself against him like that has me stifling a moan of pleasure so that it almost sounds like I'm choking.

Drew looks down at me, the question written clearly across his face: *Is this really what you want?*

Yes. No. I don't even know. I feel so needy and out of control, but also like I'm tired of always having to maintain an iron grip on everything. I'm certain this is a terrible idea, but in this moment, I don't really care. I just want to feel good, and I *know* Drew can make me feel good.

I reach over, wrapping my hand behind his neck and intending to pull his face closer. He beats me to it, bringing his hand to the base of my skull and crashing his lips into mine. The kiss is needy and rough and passionate right at the first brush, and my lips part, inviting him in. He invades my mouth like he's intent on conquering me, his tongue tangling with mine, his teeth grazing my lower lip as I continue to grind myself into his thigh.

He trails his fingers down my neck, across my shoulder, down the side of my ribcage, and to my waist. There, his thumb strokes the strip of skin that's exposed between my t-shirt and my sweats. When he pulls back from the kiss, I want to push forward, chasing his mouth, but he looks at me and raises an eyebrow as he flattens his hand against my skin under my shirt and slides it up.

"May I?"

"Well, since you've asked so nicely…"

He pushes my shirt up at an achingly slow pace until my breasts are exposed, but I hate the feel of the shirt wadded up under my armpits, so I reach behind me and grab the shirt, lifting slightly as I pull it over my head and drop it on the arm of the couch.

Drew stares down at me with raw lust, and when he lifts his eyes to mine, his pupils are huge, making those brown eyes nearly black with need. I've never had anyone look at me with the longing I see reflected back at me right now.

His palm skims the underside of my breast, his thumb stroking across my nipple as I arch into his touch. He leans down to kiss me, gentler this time, his lips toying with mine like he's taking his time while his thumb continues to circle my nipple. This achingly slow pace is driving me crazy. I want more of everything. I want to lose myself in these feelings until there's nothing but pleasure racking my body.

Drew's hips move forward, pressing his hard length into my lower abdomen. Raising my knee to his side, I wrap my leg around his lower back and line myself up with him, sliding my center along the hard bulge in his pants. The way his thumb is stroking across the hardened peak of my nipple has me groaning into his mouth, which in turn seems to light him on fire. His kisses are more insistent, and his pace is faster, until it feels like he could make me come just from the intense pleasure of his kiss and the friction of his dick pressing into my clit through my sweats.

He rolls to his back, holding me so that I end up completely on top of him with my knees on either side of his hips. My hair has fallen forward over my shoulders, mostly covering my breasts, so he sweeps his hand behind my neck and twists my hair into a rope that he releases down my back. "My God, you're so fucking beautiful," he says as he gazes up at me in the darkness.

The way he's looking at me makes me *feel* beautiful, because there's more than just lust in his gaze. I don't know how to quantify it, but he's looking at me with some degree of affection and understanding and respect, which doesn't even make sense. I barely know this man now, and I never knew him that well in the first place.

"Audrey, I want you so badly. But you have to know that I'm not in a place in my life where I can be in a relationship. Not because I don't want that with you, but because hockey and my mom have to come first. And I need to prioritize getting to know Graham. I've thought about this a lot, actually." He sighs. "And you deserve more than to be fourth in line for someone's attention."

It's nothing I didn't know—it's what I've been telling myself about him all along—but him verbalizing it in this moment is enough to give me pause. I know that he means what he's saying. This isn't just sex. But it also can't be more than that right now.

"Are you not available for a relationship right now, or ever?"

His shoulders relax, and one corner of his lips turns up. "You're the only one I'd be interested in having a relationship with, when I am able."

I rest my forehead against his, reminding myself that it's okay to have this night with him, even if it can't be more. It's okay to let him make me feel good, and to make him feel good in return. We can do that for each other, without having to put a label on it.

"Okay."

"Okay?" He sounds surprised, but then his hands skim up my sides to cup my breasts, and I lean into his touch, eager to be closer to him. And just as he slides his thumbs across my nipples again, we hear Graham's voice, sleepy but laced with a little worry, from the top of the stairs. "Mom?"

My head snaps up, and Drew and I lock eyes, my

panicked expression meeting his amused gaze. And the way he's not taking this situation—the fact that our son might walk down those stairs and see this—seriously pisses me off.

I reach down and scoop my t-shirt off the arm of the couch, dragging it on as I call out, "I'll be right there, Graham." Then I'm climbing off Drew and rushing up the stairs to find out what's wrong.

"I didn't know where you were," Graham says when I hit the top of the stairs.

"I haven't gone to bed yet. Why are you up, anyway?" I ask as I run my hand across his head, smoothing the hair off his forehead, which is warmer than it should be.

"My head hurts," he says. "So does my throat."

I feel guilty that my first thought is *Of course*. Of course he gets sick when Jules leaves and I don't have anyone here to help me, when I have my period and feel like crap myself, and when I have a hot guy downstairs who was about to do unspeakable things to make my body feel better. *At least it wasn't the middle of the night*, I remind myself. I'm trash at dealing with things like this when I'm woken up from a deep sleep.

"Okay, let's get you back into bed and I'll go get you some medicine and something to drink." I walk him from the hallway back into his room, and tuck him into his bed. "I'll be right back," I say, giving him a kiss on top of his head.

Then I rush down the stairs and find Drew sitting on the couch, staring blankly at the TV. I explain the situation and tell him he needs to go.

He stands, and suddenly we're toe to toe. "Why?"

"Because I need to go focus on Graham and figure out

what's wrong, and I don't want to have to explain why you're here at 11 p.m."

"But I can take care of *you* once you're done taking care of him," he says, reaching out and running his hand along the side of my abdomen. The offer is distinctly sexual, and it frustrates me that this is where his mind is while our son is upstairs and sick.

"Drew, this isn't the time. Graham's sick."

"Yeah, but you feel like crap too. And once you've got him back to bed, I can still be here to take care of you."

Five minutes ago, taking care of me changed from ibuprofen, a heating pack, and a massage, into full-fledged foreplay. And as much as my body still wants that, that's not what I need to be thinking about or doing when Graham is sick.

"I have to go be a parent now. I have to put Graham's needs before my own. I'm here doing this all the time, even when it's not fun—even when I have a sick kid, or more laundry to fold than I know how I'll ever get through, or endless amounts of paperwork to fill out for school, or whatever real-life tasks await." I pause, about ready to burst into tears because I'm overwhelmed and frustrated. "Because this is what parenting is."

"Audrey..." Even though I think he's going to say more, and maybe his heart is even in the right place, I don't have the time to hear him out, because Graham is waiting for me.

So instead, I push him toward the entryway, hand him his shoes, then open the door. And once he's gone, I grab the children's ibuprofen, thankful that I didn't take it for my period cramps, and head back upstairs to Graham.

Chapter Seventeen

AUDREY

I hold my top arm straight against the pole and bend my bottom arm slightly as I take a few steps and use the momentum of my body to lift my feet off the ground. I'm supposed to spread my legs into a split as I spin gracefully around the bar, but my arms are shaking like I've never done this before, and I somehow feel weaker than when I started my pole dancing lessons four months ago. It's impossible that I've suddenly lost all the muscle I've built—I felt so strong last week.

Then, suddenly, my arms give out, and I go sliding down the pole. Luckily, my feet hit the wood floor first, but it's like my body has turned into silly putty and can't withstand my own weight. Crumbling to the floor, I lie there on my side. I close my eyes, and despite the thumping of the music and the pink and purple strobe lights, all I want to do is sleep.

"Girl, this ain't no sleepover. You better get your ass back on that pole," I hear from above me, and when I open my eyes, I'm greeted by the shiny white leather of Danika's platform lace-up heeled boots. I don't know how she walks in those things, much less dances, but on my first visit here, she assured me she'd have me in a pair within six months. That's never felt less likely than in this moment.

"I can't." The words come out like a pitiful croak.

She must squat down next to me, because suddenly her ass is perched on her heels, and across her thick brown thighs rests her leather whip—not that she'd ever actually use it on us, but she threatens us every class. Danika is big, and powerful, and so incredibly badass. I adore her no-nonsense, no-excuses approach. But right now, there's no amount of threatening that's going to give me the strength to get back up there.

"Again!" she barks at the rest of the class. Then she reaches out her hand and uses the backs of her fingers to push my damp hair off my forehead. Her fingers feel like icicles as they trail along my burning skin. "You sick?"

Is that concern I hear in her voice?

"I don't think so?" But even as I say it, I realize that there's no other reason I could be feeling this way. I must have caught what Graham had. Or maybe not strep—because my throat doesn't hurt—but some sort of virus.

"You need to get your skinny ass off this floor and get yourself home and in bed."

"I don't think anyone has *ever* referred to my ass as skinny," I mumble, and my lips curve up in the faintest hint of a smile.

"Yeah, sure." She lets out a throaty laugh. "Can you walk out of here, or do I have to call someone to carry you home?"

Who would I even have her call? Lauren's doing me a favor and watching Graham tonight since Jules is out of town. Jameson is at home with the twins, who are definitely asleep by now. Morgan's on a plane halfway to Las Vegas. A couple of years ago, I could have called Scott—he would have come and picked me up, although probably begrudgingly. I don't know why my mind immediately goes to Drew, and the way he dropped everything a few nights ago to come bring me ibuprofen. I can't call him to help me out again so soon, and I shouldn't be comparing him to Scott anyway. The situations are not the same.

"You got a boyfriend or something?" Danika asks, because apparently, I haven't bothered to respond.

"Nope."

"Any friends I can call?"

I push myself up onto one elbow. "No one who's free tonight. I can get myself home." I roll onto my hands and knees and muster up the energy to stand. The muscles in my legs protest, the tendons screaming at me as they stretch out. Why does every muscle ache? I hold on to the pole for balance.

"You sure?" Danika asks.

"Positive," I say. I've always taken care of myself, and usually everyone else around me too.

When I make it to my car, where it's wedged into the tiny lot with too-small spaces, I collapse into the seat. If Lauren wasn't at my house, waiting for me to return so she could go home to her own family, I'd probably lock the doors, close my eyes, and sleep. But I can't. Instead, I back out of the space, using all my strength to turn the steering wheel, and then head out onto the street.

I have my car call Lauren's cell, and when she answers, I tell her I'm on my way home. "Is Graham in bed yet?"

"No. Should he be?"

I glance at the clock on the dash, realizing that I'm thrown off because I've left dance early. There's still half an hour before his bedtime. "No." The word sounds like defeat rolling off my lips.

"What's wrong?" Lauren asks, and I can picture the look of concern on her face.

"I'm sick."

"Oh no. Think you have strep?"

"No idea."

"Want me to take Graham back to our house? Jameson can bring him to school in the morning. It's right by his office."

Tears leak out of the corner of my eyes. I'm so thankful for the offer that I almost can't respond. I don't get sick. I haven't felt this bad since I had the flu in college, and so I'd forgotten how much it sucks.

"Yes, please. His antibiotics are in the refrigerator. Will you bring them for him to take in the morning? I don't want him to miss a dose."

"Okay," she says, then I hear her call out to Graham, "Hey, Bud, your mom isn't feeling good. How about I bring you back to my house for a sleepover? You can wake Iris and Ivy up in the morning with donuts!"

The tears roll down my face, and I don't bother wiping them away. I have the best freaking family.

"Thank you." The words are a whisper, but she must hear them because she tells me that's what friends are for.

And when I get home, she's already left with Graham. I force myself to go up the back stairs and into my house, where I collapse on the couch and give in to the exhaustion.

Chapter Eighteen

DREW

"I wasn't expecting to see you here tonight," Jameson says as he comes to a quick stop in front of me. His words are casual, but his tone is laced with suspicion.

"Didn't we decide I was going to volunteer with the team when I wasn't traveling?"

"You know Audrey's not going to be here tonight, right?" he asks.

This feels a bit like a trap. "Why would I know that?"

"I thought you two talked."

"Not often enough that I know her whereabouts," I say right as Graham skates up, grabbing onto Jameson's leg with both arms.

"I had strep throat," he tells me.

I almost say, *I know*, but catch myself. Jameson doesn't need to know that Audrey texted me Sunday to thank me for the children's ibuprofen I'd left on her back steps that morning, and again as they left the doctor's office to tell me the diagnosis.

"Oh yeah? Are you feeling better now?" I ask.

"Yeah, I'm not con-tay-jus anymore." He struggles over the word. "But now Mom is sick. I'm staying with Uncle Jameson and Aunt Lauren again tonight so she can rest."

"Oh no. Does she have strep too?"

Graham shrugs right as Jameson mutters something about her being too stubborn to go to the doctor. I'm about to ask more questions, but Jameson picks that time to start practice. So instead, I spend the next hour working with the kids on some basic shooting skills while worrying about Audrey and why she hasn't gone to the doctor if she's sick.

And when it's time to leave, I drive straight to her place. I call her when I'm a couple of blocks away, but she doesn't answer. So I send her a text instead.

DREW:

I'll be at your house in a few minutes.

AUDREY:

I'm not feeling good and don't want company.

DREW:

I'm not company.

AUDREY:

Oh yeah, what would you call yourself then?

DREW:

A concerned friend? The father of your child?

AUDREY:

I feel like death.

> **DREW:**
> Which is exactly why I'm coming over.

When I knock on the back door, I see movement through the frosted glass. I'm surprised when she opens the door without me having to bang it down.

She stands in the doorframe as if she could block me from coming in. Her dark hair is greasy and held off her face in a messy ponytail, and she looks deathly pale. I reach out and place my hand on her forehead, and her lips turn down at the corners in response to my touch.

"You're burning up." I know she's an adult capable of taking care of herself, but I'm worried about her just the same. I hate seeing her sick and in pain.

"Thanks, Captain Obvious," she croaks, her voice hoarse, like she'd been screaming at a concert all night.

"Have you been to the doctor?" I ask, even though I know the answer.

She folds her arms across her chest in defiance, and her chin tilts up as she says, "No."

"Why not?"

She looks away, focusing on my Jeep sitting at the bottom of her back steps. "You found the parking space, I take it."

"Yes, and I'm about to throw you in my car and take you for a strep test."

"The doctor's office is closed."

"Yeah, but you can do a rapid strep test at almost any pharmacy. I checked the one two blocks away, and it's open for another half hour."

She leans against the door frame so quickly I'm afraid

she's about to collapse. "Drew, I don't even have the energy to get dressed."

"Which is exactly why you need to go take a test. If you got strep from Graham, you can get antibiotics and feel better in, like, twenty-four hours. *Why wouldn't you?*"

Looking away again, she clears her throat as she refuses to meet my gaze. Then she winces in pain, and I'm guessing that her throat hurts too much to respond.

"Audrey, when Graham had all the symptoms of strep, you took him to the doctor's, right?"

She looks over at me and nods.

"Your throat hurt too much to talk?"

She nods again.

"Where's your health insurance card?" I ask.

Reaching over, she grabs her purse off the kitchen counter right inside the door. I scoop her up in my arms—shocked she doesn't protest—then hold her tight against me while I reach out to shut the door and press the button on the keypad to lock it.

She rests her head against my chest as I take the few steps down to the back alley. The crisp fall air is cold tonight, and by the time we reach my Jeep, she's shivering even though I can feel the heat radiating off her.

"When's the last time you took something for this fever?" I ask as I pull the door open with one hand and maneuver her into the seat.

"Don't remember." The words are practically mumbled.

I don't understand why she's being so irresponsible about taking care of herself, but I'm also willing to bet there's a reason, because she's old enough and mature enough to know better.

When I climb into the driver's seat, I reach over and turn her seat warmer on, and by the time we've driven the few blocks to the pharmacy, she's half-asleep in the seat. "Think you can walk in, or should I carry you?"

Her eyes shoot open, and then a faint smile graces her full lips. "Why are there plastic ducks lined up on your dashboard?"

I glance at the row of plastic ducks that sit wedged between the dashboard and windshield. "It's a Jeep thing. So...are you walking, or am I carrying you?"

"I'll walk."

Forty-five minutes later, we're back at her place. I made her take ibuprofen and drink a bottle of water while we waited for the positive test results at the pharmacy, and now that we're home, she can eat something and take her antibiotics.

I get her seated at one of the barstools, refill her water bottle, and go about making her some toast.

"You want to tell me why you didn't go to the doctor when you started feeling sick?"

"Not really," she says. She lays her forearm across the counter and leans down to rest her forehead on it.

"Audrey, left untreated, strep can turn into scarlet fever. You're too smart to not take care of something like this."

"I just don't like going to the doctor."

"Why not?"

"Too many bad memories."

I consider how much to push her for information. She's not volunteering it, but I want to understand what the fear is. "Want to talk about it?"

She's silent for so long, I'm thinking maybe she fell asleep, but then she says, "My mom died of cancer when I was a teenager. There were a lot of doctor's visits. A lot of hospital stays. And eventually, a lot of hospice equipment in our house. There were also a few misdiagnoses, and I just don't trust doctors."

I come around the counter and set her plate with her toast in front of her, then pull out a seat for myself. I rest my hand on her back, wanting her to know I'm here for support. "I'm sorry you went through that."

"Me too," she says, then she sits up and pulls the plate with her toast closer. She takes small bites and washes them down with water, while I sit next to her, wishing there was something I could do to take her pain away. I'm not so worried about the strep, as that'll clear up quickly once she's got a couple of doses of the antibiotics in her. But I wish her past wasn't so painful for her.

"What did you do about doctors and hospitals when you were pregnant, and for Graham's birth?" The shame that I wasn't there for that, to support her and help her, feels almost overwhelming in this moment. I've already let her down so much in the past, but there's nothing I can do about it now, except be there for her moving forward.

"I had a nurse practitioner who worked with a doula, and I gave birth at a birthing center instead of a hospital."

"I'm so sorry I wasn't there for you then," I tell her, chest tight.

"We're not dwelling on that," she says softly. Her voice is scratchy in a way that I'm sure reflects how sore her throat is, but it's sexy, nonetheless. "Remember?"

I glance over at her and nod. Her big blue eyes now have sunken purple hollows beneath them, but even sick and without a dab of makeup, I'm still struck by her natural beauty.

"My dad died when I was Graham's age," I tell her. "I don't remember him, really. He was a linesman for the electric company and a car crashed into the truck holding his lift when he was up in the bucket working on an electrical pole." A shudder runs through my body as I picture the terrible scene of his death, and Audrey moves her hand to my forearm. "You know the state law about how there has to be a police detail now any time there's a public works project? My dad is one of the reasons that law exists."

She squeezes my arm, but doesn't say anything. Then she rests her head on my shoulder, but after only a minute, her hand on my arm goes limp and her head feels heavy. This is the second time she's fallen asleep in as many hours.

"Hey," I whisper, not wanting to startle her. She jolts awake anyway, her head flying up off my arm. She relaxes when she sees me sitting next to her, but I have to wonder if this reaction is left over from years of being woken up by Graham in the middle of the night when he was younger. "Let's get these antibiotics in you and then get you to bed."

I push two tabs out through the foil on the back of the plastic holder, and hand them to her with her water. She swallows them down with a little wince, and without thinking, I reach out and smooth the wrinkle across her brow.

"C'mon, I'm going to carry you upstairs."

"I can manage the stairs," she whispers.

"You couldn't even walk up the half flight of stairs to your back door when we got home twenty minutes ago"—I slide one arm under her knees and another behind her back, and lift her from her seat—"and now you think you're going to do a full flight of stairs on your own?"

"I could have done it if I had to," she says as she relaxes into my chest.

That sentence haunts me as I carry her through the entryway and up the stairs. How much of her life has been defined by that sentiment—*I could have done it if I had to*?

Her eyes are already closed when I lay her on her bed. As I set about taking off her shoes, unzipping her hoodie, and then lifting her enough to get her under her covers, I keep thinking the same thing: *I don't want her to have to do this all by herself anymore.*

But what does that even mean? What *can* it mean? I'm gone half the season for hockey, and I have this one year to prove to the Rebels that they should sign me to a new contract. There's never been a more important year in my career. Because I have to stay in Boston to help with my mom—she has to be my number one priority when I'm not playing hockey. It's what I committed to when I moved back. It's what I promised my sisters. It's what's right, after everything she's done and given up for me over the years.

And now there's Graham. I want to get to know my son. It's going to be enough of a struggle to find the time to spend with him. How could I throw Audrey, and any potential feelings I have for her, into the mix too? It wouldn't be fair to make her my fourth priority. Like I told her the other night, she deserves to be someone's first priority.

As much as I've tried to come up with a different solution, I arrive back at the same conclusion each time.

I reach over and turn out the bedside lamp I turned on when we came in, but then Audrey's arm flies out like she's grasping for something, and her hand lands on my stomach, only inches from the waistband of my sweats.

"Stay?" The word is so quiet I'm not sure if I heard it or imagined it.

"What?" I whisper, reaching down and smoothing her ponytail back away from her face.

"Will you stay for a minute? Rub my back until I fall asleep?" I don't know if it's because she's half asleep or sick, but she sounds so vulnerable. She could ask me for just about anything, and I'd say yes. She's the weak side I didn't know I had and am not sure I want to give her up. But what choice do I have? I can't be what she needs.

"Sure," I say as I sit on the edge of her bed.

She scoots toward the center of the bed and rolls on her side. "I'm making room so you can lay down."

I chuckle to myself when I consider what happened when we were lying next to each other on her couch the other night. But she's sick, so it's not like anything is going to happen tonight.

I lie on my side, facing her back, and let my hand stroke up and down her spine. She's not burning up like she was before, but she's still warm.

"Thank you," she says, her voice groggy as she's clearly on the edge of sleep. "I really hope I don't get you sick, though."

"My tonsils were removed when I was seven. I can't get strep."

"Good. Because it's been nice having someone take care of me for a change."

I rub my hand along the bumpy ridges of her spine, then sweep over her upper back like I'm tracing wings along each side. "Anytime, Audrey."

The orange light of early morning is streaming through the open curtains at the edge of her room as the sun rises just enough to light the sky, but not high enough to be visible above the three- and four-story brownstones of the South End.

Audrey's in the center of the bed, lying on her stomach with her arms folded so her elbows are out and her hands are beneath her cheek. Her face is turned away from me so I can't see if she's awake, but her low and steady breathing has me pretty convinced she's still sleeping.

Knowing she needs as much sleep as possible to recover, I get up as quietly as I can. I didn't mean to fall asleep here last night, but since I did, I'll make her some coffee before I head out.

In the kitchen, I get the coffee going and then look around for something I can use to write a note. There's a packet of papers sitting on the counter along the wall, so I head over to see if it can be written on. When my eyes land on the photocopy of a family tree, with the lines to write in the members of a family, my jaw drops.

The tree has a line drawn in pencil straight down the middle, from the top of the tree right through the trunk. The right side is completely shaded in, like Graham took his pencil and scribbled as hard as he could across the side meant to house the information about his dad's family. On the left side of the tree, Audrey Flynn is listed on the branch labeled *Mom* and small red hearts are drawn around her name. The small branches below it, meant for siblings, and large branches above it, meant for grandparents, are all blank.

My stomach flips over, the bile rising to the back of my throat, and I swallow it down, but it feels lodged there, burning away at my esophagus. I grip the edge of the counter and look up at the ceiling. "Fuck," I mumble under my breath as my fingertips press into the countertops so hard it makes my knuckles ache.

"Yeah." Audrey's soft voice fills the space, and I glance over at her standing in the opening to the kitchen. Her skin glistens with a thin sheen of sweat, like her fever broke in her sleep. Her tank top clings to her, and her sweatpants hang on her hips. She looks exhausted, but she walked down the stairs by herself and is leaning against the door frame without looking like it's holding her up—which is progress. "That was a tough kindergarten assignment to have sent home. I'd asked if he could draw his own family tree so he could include Jameson and Jules. But there was a note on it from his teacher that just said, 'Graham decided he didn't want to draw his own family tree.'"

A hundred questions run through my mind—about what Graham does and doesn't know, about why her parents aren't listed there, about whether she eventually wants to give him siblings...

"Audrey—" The angry buzzing of my phone stops me short, because when I glance down at where I must have left it on the counter next to my sweatshirt last night, Caitlyn's name is flashing on my screen.

And *I know*. Right in that split second, I know that I fucked up. I was so concerned about Audrey last night that I completely forgot I was supposed to be at my mom's house early this morning so I could bring her to an appointment at the hospital. "I'm so sorry," I tell her, "I have to answer this."

She nods and folds her arms under her chest, and I'm already grabbing my keys and my wallet and shoving them in my pocket. "I'm on my way," I say into the phone.

"Where the hell are you?! I've called you *four* times. You were supposed to be at Mom's *an hour ago*."

"I'm so sorry. I overslept. I can be there in, like, twenty minutes."

Caitlyn barks out a laugh. "You can't get anywhere in Boston in twenty minutes. It's rush hour. By the time you get out here, and then back into Longwood Medical Center, you'll miss the damn appointment, Drew." She spits out my name like I'm the world's biggest asshole. And in this moment, maybe I am. "This is kind of an important one, you know."

"I know, and I'm sorry."

"I have to leave for work. I'll bring Mom with me. You can meet us at my office and take her from there."

Even though the doctor's office Caitlyn works at is only two blocks from the hospital, we generally try not to do this type of hand-off with mom because it can be confusing for her. But right now, we don't have a choice.

Caitlyn hangs up on me, and I look at Audrey helplessly. We deserve to have this conversation about Graham, but I can't do it right now. "I'm so sorry, I have to go. I was supposed to take my mom to an appointment this morning."

"It's okay, Drew," she says, and she sounds resigned. "I get it. We'll talk later."

I'm angry at myself, and at this situation, and at the way I'm making her feel like she's not a priority. But isn't this what I was reminding myself about last night—that I already have too much on my plate? She deserves better than what I can offer her right now. She deserves someone who can give everything to a relationship, who can put their whole focus on loving her like she deserves to be loved.

She locks the door behind me, and I take the steps down to my Jeep, knowing that there were no good choices in this situation, but feeling like I somehow made the wrong decision, nonetheless.

Chapter Nineteen

AUDREY

"Tell me again why you've pulled that hat down so far you probably can't even see?" Lauren teases as we walk down the steeply pitched steps inside Boston's Liberty Arena, where the Rebels play their home games.

"He's not going to see you, you know," Jules says from behind me.

"Oh?" Lauren says, her voice taking on the higher-pitched note of interest. "Are we talking about this now?"

I grip the railing in the center of the stairs so I can shoot a look at Jules over my shoulder and not go tumbling down headfirst. I really *can't* see much from under the brim of this hat. The players are already on the ice warming up, and the last thing I need is to make a scene and draw attention to myself.

I haven't talked to Drew since he left my house yesterday morning, and I'd really rather he not know that I'm here tonight.

"No," I say, my voice strong and certain. "We are *not* talking about this right now."

"We're going to have to eventually," Lauren says, pausing as she looks around for her fiancé. He and Graham went ahead while we stopped to grab some drinks and popcorn, but they're not in our usual row.

"Yes, but eventually is not *now*." A few rows up from the ice, I see Graham standing on a seat with Jameson holding on to his waist so he doesn't fall, and waving up at us.

Lauren laughs, but continues down the stairs until she gets to the row where Jameson sits with Graham. "Babe," she says, and it amuses me to no end when she and my grumpy brother, who absolutely melts for his future wife, use these terms of endearment for each other. "Are you just down here to watch warmups?"

"No, these are our seats."

"Our seats are up there," she says, hitching her thumb over her shoulder and motioning behind us.

"Remember, I said I was getting new seats this season?" he asks.

"I remember you saying you were getting *more* seats," she says, and that's how I remember it too.

Jameson previously had two season tickets for his former team, and they were eighteen rows behind the Rebels' bench, which would have put seventeen rows of fans between me and Drew. This set of six seats is only five rows back from the bench, and the knot of dread in my stomach curls its tendrils into my chest. Unless he never glances up, there's no way he's not going to see us here every time he comes off the ice, especially since right now there are only a few other people scattered amongst the seats between us and the glass.

"This was what was available if I wanted six seats together." He shrugs. "Why? You don't want to see the game up close and personal like this?"

A shiver runs across my shoulder blades. Back when Jameson played for the Rebels, our family had season tickets and we'd go together to watch him play. Dad always loved the brutality of hockey. If there was a dirty hit or a fight broke out on the ice, he'd be the first one out of his seat cheering. But that's the part I hate, and the part that worries me about Graham loving this sport so much. It's hard to imagine my sweet boy getting pummeled, and even harder to imagine him hurting someone on purpose.

"They're great seats," Lauren says as she scoots into the row and takes the seat next to Jameson's. "No complaints."

Jules sighs as she scoots into the row and sits. "Ugh. I feel like I can smell their sweat from here."

"They're not even warmed up yet," Jameson says. "Stop being so dramatic."

"I just hate hockey," Jules says.

"We know," all of us say in unison.

"Why did you come if you hate hockey?" Graham asks his aunt. It's an innocent question, though the answer is anything but. There was a time when Jules loved hockey, then a trip to Las Vegas ruined it all.

"Because I love *you*, Bud. And I wanted to see you watching your first professional hockey game."

When Jameson promised Graham he'd bring him to the first home game this season, I'd assumed he meant the home opener. Then yesterday, after I finally showered and was feeling a bit better, Jameson called to remind me about tonight's pre-season game.

I feel weird being here without having told Drew I was coming, but he hasn't reached out since he rushed out for his mom's appointment yesterday morning, and I felt awkward being the one to contact him. I rationalized coming tonight by assuring myself he'd have no idea I was here. But now...?

We need to talk. We need to figure out what we're going to tell Graham, and when. I need to know when he's planning on telling his family, and I want to talk about how we should tell Jameson. But we can't have that conversation, or at least not in person, because when this game is over, they're hopping on their plane and heading out for two pre-season road games. He won't be back until later this week.

From her seat next to me, Jules knocks my elbow with hers. When I glance up, she looks toward the ice. Drew's standing there talking to the Rebels captain, Ronan McCabe, who looks pissed off—but that's kind of his default. It's funny, though, because I can't quite get a read on Drew. He doesn't seem quite like himself.

Then McCabe skates away and Drew's gaze drops to the ice as he takes a deep breath, and then looks up, his eyes scanning the stands. He gives Jameson a nod, then his eyes widen. Graham is waving at him frantically, and Drew gives him a smile and a wave, and then his eyes move down the row. When he sees me, he quickly turns away, skating over toward the blue line where some of his teammates are congregated.

I know it's just because he doesn't want Jameson to notice him looking at me. But two nights ago, he took care of me while I was sick and he slept in my bed, and a week ago, he was halfway to making me come before Graham woke up sick. So him ignoring me now stings, and it's an important reminder that this is exactly why it's a mistake to get involved with Drew—there are too many complications.

If I want him to have a relationship with Graham, and I do, then I can't be a drain on his time. He knows what his priorities are—what they have to be—and I have to respect that. Besides, the absolute last thing I need in this world is another broken heart. And as I watch the women who are up at the glass for the warmups wearing his jersey and yelling his name to get his attention, I know that's what Drew is…a heartbreak waiting to happen.

"What's wrong?" Jules leans in toward me and whispers.

"Nothing." I rest my head on her shoulder, using her thick blond hair as a pillow. She'd come home yesterday—a full day early—because I'd texted her that I had strep, and I'd neglected to mention that Drew was there taking care of me. She'd found me asleep on the couch an hour or two after Drew left, and forced me to take a shower. By last night, I'd felt like I was on the mend, and I woke up this morning with barely a sore throat. Drew was right about getting the antibiotics and taking care of this, and I feel a bit ridiculous that I didn't go on my way home from pole dancing when I first felt sick.

"You're going to have to tell people soon." Her whispered words graze over my hair, and the knot of dread settles into the pit of my stomach. "Everyone's going to figure it out—not only because Graham looks so much like him, but also because he can't take his eyes off you."

My eyes are fixed on Drew, so I haven't missed the number of times his have flicked sideways to glance at me while he's on the ice stretching. Watching him, with his knees spread on the ice as he lightly bounces and shifts his weight to each side, stretching out his inner thighs and groin, has the desire snaking up through my core and winding its way around that pit in my stomach. I don't know which emotion—desire or dread—should win out.

From my other side, Lauren whispers, "See something you like?"

I jolt up, my head flying off Jules's shoulder as I sit ramrod straight and make sure I'm looking anywhere but at Drew. In my peripheral vision, I see Jameson turn to me. "You okay, Audrey?"

"Yeah," I say. "Jules just poked me in the side, is all."

From my other side, Jules's shoulders shake with laughter.

The players finish their warmup and head to the locker room. Hockey players are the most superstitious athletes you'll ever meet, and I wonder what Drew's doing right now. I imagine him quiet and focused on game day, the way he was when he was really trying to understand calculus. But he could have any number of things he does right before a game, and I'd have no idea—because I don't know him anymore, and probably never really did.

Instead of sitting there through the music and announcements and driving myself crazy trying to figure out who Drew is now, I excuse myself and head to the restroom. By the time I get back, the arena is dark and the blue and white lights are flashing to announce the Rebels. While the music blares and the players skate out through the mist at the entrance to the rink, fans are whipping around the white towels with the dark and light blue Rebels logo that they handed out at the entrance to tonight's game. The entire arena is filled with a palpable sense of excitement at having them back on the ice again for the first time this season.

And for the next two hours, it feels like I do nothing but focus on my own body. On making sure that I don't let my eyes track to Drew when he's on the bench, only a few rows in front of me. On reminding myself to breathe every minute he's on the ice, because I'm both elated to see him skating and also terrified something will happen to him. On how my fists clench with nerves each time he takes a face-off, and how quickly I jump out of my seat when he scores the second goal of the game.

By the time we're halfway through the third period, my whole body is exhausted from the tension. So I leave before the game is over, carrying a sleepy Graham down the escalator to the street, and catching a cab home.

And an hour later, with Graham fast asleep in Jameson's old Rebels jersey he didn't want to take off, I'm now sitting on my bed with a wholesome British baking show on the TV across the room, and a pile of clean laundry that needs folding spread out before me.

Next to me, my phone lights up with a new text.

DREW:
We're boarding the plane. I wish I could have had time to see you and to talk before I left on this trip.

AUDREY:
It's okay, we can talk when you get back.

I honestly don't want to wait to talk to him—there's so much to figure out—but I also think the conversation we need to have deserves to be in-person.

DREW:

What are you doing right now?

AUDREY:

I'm home, Graham is in bed, and I'm having a wild Saturday night folding laundry and watching a baking show.

DREW:

Wish I was there to help you.

I actually laugh out loud at how ridiculous that statement is.

AUDREY:

Yeah, sure you do. If you weren't on a plane right now, you'd be out celebrating with your team.

My brother was a professional hockey player, and I know all about the debauchery that goes on the night after a win. The VIP rooms in clubs, the women who flock to wherever the players will be, the alcohol that flows freely. If Drew was in town, he most definitely would not be sitting on my bed folding laundry with me.

DREW:

Not if you were home with Graham and needed my help.

AUDREY:

I don't need your help. I'm more than capable of folding my own laundry.

DREW:

I know you are, but it would be more fun if I was there. 😉

> AUDREY:
> I'm perfectly happy doing it myself. You'd just be in the way.

> DREW:
> Keep telling yourself that.

Even my thoughts feel like a broken record now: *I need to be the responsible one here.* Because having flirty text exchanges with Drew is not going to get us to the point where we can co-parent Graham.

If I let things happen between me and Drew, and then it didn't work out, I can't have him walking out of Graham's life like Scott did. I know Drew thinks he'd never do that, and it's probably not fair of me to assume he'd be anything like Scott in that situation. But at the same time, I have to consider the possibility. And it would be a hundred times worse for Graham this time around, because Drew actually *is* his dad. Plus, he was young enough when I was dating Scott that eventually he forgot about him, but that wouldn't be the case with Drew.

Which means this conversation needs to be shut down. Right now.

> AUDREY:
> Have a good flight. I'll talk to you when you get back.

I turn my phone over, screen down, so I won't be distracted by his texts. And then I sit on my bed, folding my laundry into neat piles while I watch people bake savory meat pies. And I try not to wonder what it would be like if Drew was here keeping me company.

Chapter Twenty

DREW

"What the hell's wrong with you?" Coach Wilcott yells while I go skidding across the ice on my stomach. I have no excuse to give him. We're doing our game-day practice skate, and I just reached for a fast-moving puck that should have been an easy grab, and instead I'm splayed out, ass up on the rink.

I finally come to a stop in the neutral zone, with the red laces of my coach's skates staring me in the face. I try to stand up, but my limbs don't seem to want to cooperate. I manage to push up to my hands and knees, and then I sit back on my heels.

This has been coming on gradually. We barely won our second pre-season game two nights ago, and I didn't play as well as I did in the first game. Then, when I woke up yesterday morning, I felt off. I chalked it up to the late-night flight after our game the night before. I got through practice yesterday, but I wasn't at my best, so I went to bed early thinking I just needed to sleep it off. Today, I woke up feeling like absolute ass.

"Something wrong?" Coach barks out. "Or did you just forget how to play hockey?"

My brain screams at me to get up and fucking do the job they're paying me millions to do. But my body just laughs at the idea that I could play hockey right now.

"Pretty sure something's wrong," I say, resting my hands on my knees. Several of my new teammates are now congregated around me, looks of concern on their faces. I was part of the starting lineup again tonight.

"You going to tell us what, or do we need to become fucking mind readers?" McCabe spits out.

"The other night I helped a friend who was sick with strep. I probably caught it from her."

Six pairs of skates glide backward, away from me.

"I'm not going to fucking kiss you," I mutter. "It's not like you're going to catch it."

"Ohhhh, lover boy here got strep kissing a girl," Colt says, his voice obnoxiously sing-song. "And now he's fucking up his career and our chances tonight because of it."

"I wasn't kissing her," I clarify. "I just gave her a ride to go get a strep test."

"So you shared space in a car with her, and since then, we've shared locker rooms, meals, and a plane with you. So fucking pardon us for thinking you might get us sick." I don't even know who says this, because I'm so focused on how I'm kneeling on the ice but still feel like I'm burning up.

I rise to my feet slowly.

"Go see the team doctor, Jenkins," Coach says.

I nod and push off toward the wall, letting myself glide along slowly until I get there, then I step through the doorway and walk down the hall to find the doctor.

It's getting dark when I wake up, disoriented about where I am and why I hear banging nearby. But as the room comes into focus, I realize the banging is at my hotel room door.

I roll out of bed and shuffle over to the entrance, thinking about how all I want to do is sleep. I'm still pissed off about missing the game, and annoyed at how the doctor actually laughed in my face when I said it couldn't be strep because I didn't have tonsils.

"Why would you think that meant you couldn't get strep?" she asked.

"The whole reason I got my tonsils out was because I got strep so frequently as a kid. And I haven't gotten it since. Why would they take my tonsils out if it wasn't to stop me from getting sick?"

"It greatly decreases the likelihood of you getting it, and it sounds like it worked. But if you sleep in the same bed and share the same pillow as someone who has it," she said, making me wish I hadn't told her that part, "of course you're going to get it."

I'd let out an annoyed growl when she told me I needed to wait another fifteen minutes for the result. As soon as the test showed I was positive, she made me take some painkillers, gave me some throat lozenges and antibiotics, and told me to isolate myself in my hotel room.

Now, as I swing open the door, I'm moderately surprised to find her standing there. She's not in the scrubs she was wearing earlier at practice, but is instead in slacks and a sweater, with a Rebels staff jacket hanging open. She must have just come from the game.

"Did we win?" I ask, using the heels of my palms to rub my eyes.

"The game doesn't start for another two hours," she says. "Just thought I'd check on you before I headed back to the arena."

I shake my head, hating how out of it I feel. "Oh, it's dark out, I thought..."

"Have you been asleep since you left practice earlier?"

"Yeah, I think so."

"Good." She reaches into her bag and pulls out two bottles of electrolyte water and hands them to me. "Drink these, and then go back to bed. Your body needs as much sleep as possible."

"God, you're bossy." I don't like being told what to do, and I'm too sick to consider that it's probably out of line for me to say this to the team doctor.

She lets out a laugh that's practically a snort. "You've heard of the phrase *doctor's orders*, right? It's almost like I spent seven years in med school and training to make sure I know what I'm talking about—"

"I wasn't questioning your knowledge. Sorry, I just feel shitty..."

"Go back to sleep, Jenkins. If you feel well enough in the

morning, you can fly home with the team. Just wear one of the masks I gave you so you don't get anyone else sick."

"If I don't feel well enough?" I ask.

"Just catch a flight home as soon as you do."

The thought of having to coordinate my own travel is more than my mind can handle right now. So before I crash back into my bed, I set an alarm for five in the morning, determined to make that flight.

Chapter Twenty-One

AUDREY

I'm washing dishes at the kitchen sink when I see Jameson pull up to the back door. He's out of his car and up the back steps so fast that I'm certain something is wrong, and when we lock eyes through the window, my stomach drops. He looks pissed.

Then the back door flies open, and he takes up the whole frame, blocking out what little light is left now that the sun sets by dinner time. The faint orange tinge to the sky is an ominous backdrop to his imposing size.

"What the hell's wrong?" I ask my brother.

"I'm going to ask you a question, and I need you to answer me honestly."

I try to swallow down the lump that rises in my throat and the result is an audible gulp. "Okay."

He shuts the door behind him and takes a step closer. He towers over me, but I don't shrink in his presence. It's not that he would ever use his size to intimidate me or anyone else, it's just that sometimes I think he forgets how big he is.

"Is something going on with you and Drew?"

I don't look away, but I don't give him what he wants, either. "What would make you ask that?"

"Because it's obvious he's interested in you, and he's out for tonight's game...with strep. How did he get strep, Audrey?"

Fuck. Drew didn't tell me he's sick, so I wasn't prepared for this. So much for not being able to get strep because he doesn't have tonsils!

"Yes, something's going on, but it's not what you think."

"What the hell does that mean?"

I obviously wasn't planning on saying anything to him until I'd talked to Drew about this once he's back. But now that Jameson is standing in my kitchen, demanding answers, I don't feel like I can keep lying to him.

"Hold on," I say, grabbing my phone off the counter and swiping to the photo I took of Drew and Graham together the night we got cookies—the photo I'd taken because of how much they looked alike at that moment. I hold the phone out and he takes it, his eyes narrowing as he studies the photo.

"Shit." The word is low, almost a whisper on a long exhale. Then he looks back to me, our eyes meeting, and neither of us says anything. Finally, he asks, "Why didn't you tell me?"

I explain about Drew not returning any of my calls or messages. "I was afraid that if I told you, you'd try to ruin his career. It wouldn't be the first time," I remind him, and our eyes lock over the situation our family never talks about.

Handing me my phone, he crosses his arms, then leans back against the kitchen counter. He bites the corner of his lip as he thinks—a classic Flynn trait that all three of us do when we're thinking. "You were probably right."

"Drew swears that if he'd known, he'd have been there for us."

"You don't sound like you believe him," Jameson notes.

"It's complicated. I don't know if twenty-two-year-old Drew would have been the father to Graham that I needed him to be."

"And twenty-eight-year-old Drew?" Jameson asks.

"He seems a lot more mature now—serious even. I know what his reputation is, but...I don't know how much of that is perception rather than reality. He says he wants to step up and be the father Graham deserves. But it's complicated. He's got a lot on his plate with the team and his family—"

"What's going on with his family?"

He hasn't told Jameson about his mom? With Drew requesting the trade, how is that even possible?

"That's not my story to tell. So anyway, he wants to be involved in Graham's life, but we haven't figured out yet what that looks like, or how we'll tell Graham. Which is why we haven't said anything to you or anyone else yet."

"What about you and Drew?" Just the mention of us in the same sentence has my heart responding with a flutter. One that I try very hard to ignore.

"There is no me and Drew."

"Why not? His interest in you is blatantly obvious. Even though I told him to stay away from you—"

"Asshole move, by the way. You aren't in charge of my love life."

"Just trying to protect you, Audrey."

"I don't need protecting. I need you to respect the fact that I'm an adult, and a mother, and completely capable of making my own decisions about who to get involved with. And I've already decided that nothing's going to happen between me and Drew."

"Why not?"

Is he for real? Didn't he just say I shouldn't get involved with Drew? "Because it's not what's best from Graham."

"Why?"

"Because what if it didn't work out? Need I remind you what happened when Scott and I broke up?"

"Just because Scott was an asshole, doesn't mean Drew would do the same thing."

"It's still not a chance I'm willing to take. Graham needs his dad in his life more than I need Drew."

"Okay, so if nothing is going on with you two, how did Drew get strep?"

"On Thursday night when you guys had practice and he found out how sick I was, he came over and took me to get a strep test. He carried me to his car, and then back into the house afterward, because I was too weak to do the stairs. He didn't think he could get strep because he'd had his tonsils out."

Jameson coughs out a laugh, like it's common knowledge that you don't need tonsils to get strep, but I didn't realize it was possible, either.

I push off the counter I'm leaning against, opposite him, and walk through the entryway to the bottom of the stairs. "Graham," I call up to him, "is your bag packed yet? Uncle Jameson's here."

"Almost!" he calls down.

I turn back toward my brother. "Thanks for taking him tonight."

"No problem."

"What are your plans with him and the twins?" I ask as I grab Graham's school folder off the kitchen table and put it in his backpack. Jameson is taking Graham back to his house, then Lauren will come meet me, Jules, Morgan, and Lauren's sister Paige, for a girls' night. Even though we're just grabbing dinner and drinks, Graham will spend the night at Jameson and Lauren's. Tomorrow morning, Jameson will drop Graham off at school on his way to his office.

"I made a big batch of homemade mac and cheese the other night, so we're going to have leftovers and watch a movie. Then after they're in bed, I'm going to watch the Rebels game."

I look at my brother, standing there in his custom-made suit with the top button of his shirt undone and no tie. His neatly trimmed facial hair is the same as ever, but his dark eyes don't look tired like they used to.

He's happy. The man who'd retired from the NHL to raise me and Jules, built a thriving sports agency where he represents the who's who of the NHL, and who swore up and down that he didn't want a wife or kids of his own, is engaged and happier than I've ever seen him. This realization never fails to shock me, no matter how many times I consider it. Eventually I'll get used to it.

"What?" he asks as I stare at him. Of the three of us, he and I look the most alike because of our fair skin and dark hair.

"I'm just happy to see you so happy," I say.

He rubs his palm along his jaw and gives me a sheepish smile that's so unlike him. "Yeah. I really am." He shakes his head slightly, as if he can't even believe it himself.

"Good."

"I want this for you and Jules, too," he says, his voice quiet. "But Audrey, I don't know if Drew is—"

"It's none of your business, Jameson," I remind him. "I'm not a kid anymore, and the over-protective big brother vibe is not necessary. He's getting to know Graham, and I want that relationship to develop. I already said I'm not going to fuck it up by getting involved with him."

Jameson looks like he's going to say something, but Graham comes barreling down the stairs, and so my brother gives me a succinct nod, like he agrees, then turns his attention to my son.

―――

"So," I say once we're all seated at the table and the waiter has taken our orders, "Jameson and I had…a moment…earlier tonight."

Lauren bursts out laughing. "What does that mean, exactly?"

"Yeah," Morgan says, "because that sounds…borderline inappropriate."

I don't have to imagine the look of horror on my face—I can tell it's there by the way my sister and friends laugh in response.

"No, like, we almost had a fight."

"Why's that?" Jules asks, sounding like she knows exactly why. Even though I didn't tell her when she got home, because I didn't feel like telling this story twice, she *does* know. She's been telling me Jameson was going to figure it out soon. And surprisingly, him knowing and me therefore being free to talk to Lauren, Morgan, and Paige about it, is freeing.

It was hard enough to keep Graham's paternity a secret for the last six years. But it's been infinitely harder since Drew has been back in Boston.

I shoot my sister a look, then turn my attention to the rest of the table. "Because I finally told him who Graham's father is."

"Oh my God," Lauren says, pressing her hands together like she's praying, "please tell me he took it okay?"

"Wait," Morgan says, looking at Lauren. "*You* know who Graham's father is? Did I miss out on some sort of news brief?"

"You and me both," Paige says. "Am I just traveling for work so much that you guys don't keep me in the loop about big news like this?"

Paige is a couple of years older than Lauren, who is a couple of years older than me. She has her own circle of friends—people she's known since college and others she's met at work. But I love it when she's around because she has a quick wit and a dry sense of humor. She actually reminds me a little of Lauren's friend Petra, all badass career woman, who takes no shit from men.

"No, I hadn't told anyone—ever—except for Jules—"

"You knew all this time!" Lauren says, her eyes wide. "And you didn't say anything? I didn't even think you were capable of keeping a secret, much less lying about it."

Jules just laughs as she tugs her loose boatneck sweater

back onto her shoulder. "Just because I call things like I see them doesn't mean I don't know how to keep my sister's biggest secret."

"Anyway," I say, facing Morgan and Paige, "Lauren kind of figured it out a couple weekends ago because I walked into her backyard and saw Graham's father standing there talking to my brother."

"Holy shit!" Paige says, and her face lights up. "I need the whole story, now!"

So I recount everything that's happened over the last two and a half weeks, ending with Drew getting diagnosed with strep today.

"Wait, so he's back in your life…you're attracted to him…he wants you…and you're not letting that hottie rail you every chance you get?" Morgan asks. "What the hell is wrong with you?"

"What part of 'doing what's best for Graham' wasn't clear?" I take a sip of my water. "And how do you know he's hot? You don't even follow hockey." Morgan's dad was Jameson's sports agent when he was in the NHL and gave him his first agenting job once he retired. While Morgan knows a ton about every professional sport by virtue of growing up with her dad as her sole caregiver while her mom was off running all over the world, marrying a new guy every few years, she doesn't really follow any sports as an adult.

"Uhh, I was there, remember? At Lauren's, the night you're talking about? We all were. And even though you and Jules left almost immediately after arriving—and now we know why—the rest of us stayed. I talked to Drew. He seemed like a pretty nice guy." She tilts her wineglass toward her lips, but before it makes contact, she lowers it again and says, "And he's hot. Like, let's not overlook that fact. Is *this* why you wouldn't let me set you up on any of the dating apps?" Her jaw drops, and her eyes widen like she's just made a huge discovery.

When my cheeks redden, Lauren slaps the table. "Oh my God! You're holding out for him, aren't you?"

"No," I try to laugh it off. "I'm holding him off, is more like it. Besides, I have Karl, and no-strings-attached sex is all I need or want right now."

"Right," Jules says the word slowly. "So, when was the last time you and Karl had sex, then?"

I bite my lip, realizing that I haven't seen Karl since before Drew and I had dinner.

"So not since Drew came back into your life, at least?" Paige asks.

"No. But I had my period, and then I got sick…and, like, this length of time isn't totally unusual."

"You have a guy waiting around to bang you whenever you want, and you go more than three weeks without sex?" Morgan asks. "Sounds like he's either not great in bed, or you've just been thinking about Drew."

Images of the night I woke up on my couch next to Drew flash through my head—a highlight reel of all the ways he touched me, how close I was to letting him get me off even though I was having my period—and my body reacts to the memories as if they were happening, sending a flash of heat and a full-body shudder through me.

Paige laughs. "Oh girl, you have it so, so bad for him."

I cross my arms under my chest, and as I glance down, I notice how it pushes my cleavage up into the V-neck of my sweater. Suddenly, I wish Drew was here. I wish his hands were on me. I wish so many things that should never be.

"I don't," I insist. "And even if I did, I wouldn't do anything about it because of Graham."

"If my dad has taught me one thing about hockey players," Morgan says, "it's that when they want something, they go after it a hundred and ten percent. So I hope you're prepared to resist him, because I have a feeling it's going to be harder than you realize."

But it won't be, because Drew is the one with other priorities. And he's too smart to let his focus wander in a way that could complicate his life even more than it already is. Who knows, we might be the right people for each other, but it is most definitely the wrong time.

Chapter Twenty-Two

DREW

It's still dark out when my alarm goes off, which I know because apparently, I never shut the curtains. Outside my hotel room window, the lights of the surrounding office buildings glow faintly. It's too early for people to be at work. I groan as I roll to my side, searching for my phone. My body still hurts, but my head feels better than it did before.

I snatch my phone off the nightstand, but when I go to touch the screen to turn off the alarm, my options are "Accept" or "Decline." That's when I realize it's not my alarm, it's a video call from Audrey. And according to my phone, it's almost midnight.

I accept the call before I really consider whether it's a good idea to talk to her when I'm in this feverish state. "Hey."

"I'm sorry I'm calling so late." Her room is dark, and her face is lit only by the phone screen. She's lying on her side, her head on her pillow and her dark hair falling along the side of her face and across her bare shoulder.

"Don't be. I'm glad you did."

"How are you feeling?" she asks.

"I don't know. I was dead asleep. Give me a minute and I'll let you know. Wait...how did you know I was sick?"

"Heard it from Jameson when he barged into my house, demanding to know how you got strep. A little warning would have been nice."

"Fuck, Audrey, I'm so sorry. I didn't even think about that possibility. I should have given you a heads up. I came back to the hotel room and fell asleep."

"When was that?" Her brows scrunch together, leaving an adorable crease between them. I want to reach over and smooth my thumb over that space, tell her she can relax because I'll be fine. But I can't because she's in Boston and I'm in Florida. And I've never hated road trips until right now.

"Around lunchtime. I woke up again when the team doctor stopped by to check on me. She said I can fly home tomorrow if I feel up to it and if I wear a mask on the plane."

"Your team doctor is a female who makes hotel room visits?"

"Don't be smartass," I say, even though the thought of her being jealous brings a sick sense of satisfaction. "She brought me some electrolyte water and checked on me before heading back to the arena for the game. Shit. I don't even know if we won or lost."

"Lost, sorry. It was 3-2."

"Fuck. I feel responsible." I press my palm against my forehead, wishing this headache would recede.

"Don't. Colt played like shit—you couldn't have stopped those goals."

"Maybe I could have stopped the puck from getting down to the crease."

"Maybe. Maybe not. But there were five other players on the ice who were meant to do just that."

"Fair point."

"So anyway, yeah, Jameson knows. I didn't want to tell him until we'd talked and figured out how to go about it. But he thought something was going on between us and you got it from hooking up with me—"

A low laugh rumbles out of me. "I wish."

"—so I had to tell him the truth. I hope you don't mind that we weren't able to talk about it first."

It makes me wonder how many other things there will be in Graham's life that we'll need to talk about first to make a decision. I hate the thought of us parenting Graham and it not being a true partnership. I always imagined I'd want a family eventually, but I never imagined I already had a child or that I'd be incapable of thinking about anything else but his mother twenty-four hours a day.

"I don't mind," I say. "He's your brother, and I trust that you know the best way to handle him. Is that why you called, to warn me that he knew?"

Her cheeks turn pink, and she bites her lip. "Maybe that should have been why I called. I just really wanted to talk to you. I tried to talk myself out of it—"

"Why?"

"Because you're sick, and it's late. You probably need your sleep."

"Not as much as I need to see you right now."

"Drew." She says my name the same way she always does, with a hint of warning. It gives me the same butterflies in my stomach that it always does. "You can't say things like that to me."

"Why? Would you rather I lie to you?" This is a path I shouldn't be going down and I damn well know it. But seeing her, even on a video call, has made me feel a hundred times better.

"No, I never want you to lie to me."

"Well, same. So tell me, why couldn't you stop yourself from calling?"

She huffs out a breath and gives me a little roll of her eyes.

"Audrey, you said you never wanted me to lie to you. Can you not even give me the truth right now?"

"You don't want the truth," she says. That has my attention.

"And why not?"

"Because I went to dinner with my sister, Lauren, Morgan, and Paige tonight. I was finally able to tell them what's going on now that I don't have to worry about Lauren having to lie to Jameson about it." She stops talking and her cheeks get even more pink. She brings her free hand to her throat, like she's trying to make herself stop talking, and the sight of her fingers pressing on her neck like that has my dick suddenly wanting in on this conversation.

"And?"

"And I told them about how we hooked up that night. It just got me…thinking."

"About us?" I ask, hoping I'm right.

"Yeah. It's probably just because it's been a long time since I've had sex."

"Oh yeah? How long?"

"Since before you were in the picture." She clears her throat, and the sound is loud in the silence of her bedroom.

"What about your little friends-with-benefits situation?" I ask the question as casually as I can, as though the thought hasn't been plaguing me since she told me about that asshole Karl. What kind of moron could fuck her and then walk away, not wanting a commitment? I mean, besides me when I was twenty-two.

"I haven't talked to him in weeks."

"Why not?" I know the answer, but I want to hear her say it.

"Why do you think, Drew?" The look on her face is one of exasperation.

"I think I want to hear your explanation."

"You're such a dick," she says, but she's smiling now.

"Go on."

"My life is complicated enough," she says. "Hooking up with Karl would just make things more of a mess."

"Why, because I'd be so insanely jealous I'd probably break his face?"

Her eyes widen.

"I guarantee you that whatever this is between us, it would be so much fucking better than what you had with him."

Now the blush is creeping up her neck and her face is full-on flushed. She looks away and doesn't say anything.

"And you know it too, don't you?" I ask, but she's still looking off into the distance. I say her name forcefully, and her eyes snap back to mine. What I see there is blatant desire. "If you gave me that look in person, I'd already have my face between your legs."

She lets out a strangled sound and her lips part. "Jesus Christ, Drew."

"You can pretend like you don't want me, if that's the lie you need to tell yourself. But don't think for a second that I don't know...or that I don't feel the same way." I haven't exactly tried to hide how much I want her, but it feels good to be so open about it—even if maybe it isn't the smartest decision I've ever made. In the darkness, though, with her practically panting on the other side of my phone screen, it seems like a phenomenal idea.

"This is a terrible idea," she says, but it seems like she's speaking more to herself.

"What, exactly, do you think is a terrible idea?"

"Letting our hormones get the best of us."

"What is it that you're afraid of, Audrey?"

"Everything." The word manages to break through the fog of desire that's clouding my judgement. I don't want her to have any fears about us at all. But until I know what she's afraid of, I can't help alleviate her concerns.

"Tell me more. What is *everything*?"

"In the most immediate sense," she says, her voice dropping so low I have to turn the volume up to hear her, "I'm concerned about something happening between us over the phone. I've never done that before."

"Me neither." My lips spread into a small smile at the thought of us being each other's "first" for something like this, and I can tell by the way she raises her eyebrows that she wasn't expecting this bit of information. "What else are you afraid of?"

"Starting to care for you? Wanting more than what you can offer? You getting bored of me quickly? Graham getting hurt as a result?" She lists off her fears rapid-fire, as questions. But they're not questions. She's thought these things through, and she still can't wrap her mind around the idea that this could actually work.

Until tonight, I wasn't sure it could. But now, I don't see how there's any other possibility than her being mine. She's going to fight me every step of the way—hell, that might be part of the appeal, if I'm being honest—but I'm going to convince her to give me another shot if it's the last thing I do.

"I want this to happen not just because you've got my dick so hard I feel like I'm going to explode, but because I want to see where things can go between us. Your concern about Graham getting hurt if things don't work out is valid, but everything else is nonsense. Yes, my time is limited during the season, especially with my mom needing my help. But what time I have left, I want to devote to you and to Graham. And there's no chance that I'm going to get bored, Audrey. I haven't so much as thought about, looked at, or talked to another woman since I saw you at Jameson's. You're always on my mind. Not just because I want to finish what we started that night on your couch, but also because you're you. I liked you way too much when we were in college—"

"You did?" she cuts me off, and I huff a laugh.

"God, yes. I made up excuses to see you all the time. Homework I understood just fine? I still asked if you could meet to tutor me on it. Happening to be near your dorm and asking if you wanted to fit in an extra tutoring session at the dining hall? Totally pre-meditated on every occasion. I thought about you all the time; I just didn't think you had any interest in me."

"I figured being interested in you was a lost cause," she

says, tilting her chin up in defiance. "You had girls all over you. And I knew exactly what hockey players were like, since I'd spent so much time around professional players."

I let out a low rumble of laughter. "I still can't believe I had no idea."

"Yeah, well, if you'd actually gotten to know me, maybe you would have."

"I want to know you *now*. I want to know everything about you and what your life is like. I want to celebrate your wins at work, support you when things go wrong, spend time with you and your family, meet your friends, see you as a mom, and give you everything you need. And, I also want to remember how you taste when you come on my tongue, and what you feel like when you're wild and needy, stuffed full of my cock."

"Fuck." The word is practically an exhale as a full-body shudder shakes her frame.

"You're needy for me right now, aren't you?" I slip my hand into my sweats, thankful I'm not wearing my briefs under them, and grip myself hard.

"Yes."

"Will you touch yourself for me?"

Chapter Twenty-Three

DREW

"Do you swear you won't take any screenshots or video of this, Drew?"

"I swear on my life. Here," I say, setting a pillow on the bed next to me and propping my phone against it. "I'm not even touching my phone."

I watch her eyes rake over my bare chest. "Okay," she says, and her body shifts as she reaches down.

"I want to see your hands on your tits first. I want you to imagine that it's my tongue circling those nipples. I want you to make yourself good and ready for me."

She lets out a humorless laugh. "Believe me, I'm already ready. I'm glad I'm not wearing any clothes, because my underwear would be soaked through."

Oh, she's into dirty talk. That's a pleasant surprise.

"Good, let's get you even more ready. I want you to show me what you like."

She props her phone up on the bed like I did, horizontally,

and then lies back down, facing the phone. Then she folds back the blanket that was covering her, and I take in the perfect form of her naked upper body. She's so fucking hot that I can't help but pump my hand over my cock, tugging slowly as I watch her bring her thumbs to her mouth and suck them in, then cup her breasts in her hands and slide them across her nipples. She tilts her head back so I'm looking at the creamy expanse of her neck, and I imagine running my tongue along her skin.

When she lets out a low groan of pleasure, I say, "I want to kiss you so fucking bad."

She looks back at the phone. "Alright, sicko. You just stay in your lane over there, because I have no desire to get strep again."

"God, that mouth," I say. "I can't wait until I'm there in person because I can think of all kinds of ways to shut you up."

"Instead, you're getting phone sex," she says with a smirk. "Beggars can't be choosers."

"I'll remind you of that sometime when you're begging me to fill you."

Another low groan escapes the back of her throat as I watch her roll her nipples between her fingers. "Fuck, Drew. I already want you so bad."

"Yeah?" I say as I tug on my cock, pulling harder, wanting to feel the tightness I remember feeling last time I was inside her. "Show me. Reach down there and swipe your fingers against your pussy so I can see if you're really as ready as you say you are."

She reaches her hand out of view, then holds two fingers close to the camera. They are glistening with the signs of her arousal. "Fuck me," I say. "I wish I was there with you right now."

"Why?" she asks, her voice suddenly teasing. "What would you do?"

"What *wouldn't* I do? First, I'd want to taste you," I tell her, and she reaches her hand down. The small movements of her arm make me think she's circling her clit. "Are you touching yourself?"

"Yes," she sighs, then brings her hand that's on her breast up to her mouth, circles the tip of her thumb with her tongue —which has me letting out a groan that's part frustration, part pleasure—and then brings it back to circle her nipple again.

"Good. But don't enter yourself yet. I'll tell you when we're at that point."

"It's cute that you think I need your permission to get myself off, Drew."

"Again, with that mouth, huh? I'd like to see it so full of my cock that you couldn't smart off at me."

"But since we're on the phone, I guess you'll just have to suffer through listening to me then."

My chest shakes with the quick laugh that erupts out of me. "Move your phone back. I clearly need to see what you're doing, since I can't trust you."

Her lips curl up on one side. "You first."

Reaching over, I push the phone, along with the pillow behind it, far enough away that she can see my dick jutting out of my hand. Her sharp intake of breath is proof that I've got the phone positioned in the right place, and I slide my hand up to the tip, circling it before sliding my hand back down. "This would feel so much better if you were drenching my cock right now."

I watch as she pushes her phone farther away and repositions it so I can see her. She's got her top leg bent with her foot resting on her opposite calf, and her fingers return to her clit, circling it a few times. Then she rubs her fingertips along her entrance and brings them back up to the camera. "Is this what you want? You want to be covered in this?"

Shit. I was not expecting the mouth on her, and I'm not sure I'm going to survive her. "Yes, and I will be. But for now, we'll make do. C'mon, circle that clit for me again. Let me see you get yourself worked up."

I spit in my hand, and then slide it up and down my shaft as I watch her pinching one nipple and circling her clit with her other hand. She increases the pace, and as her fingers continue working, her hips start thrusting forward.

"Now I want you to imagine yourself on your knees, doing this to yourself as I fill that filthy mouth with my cock."

Her eyes flutter shut as she groans and her hips jut forward. "I need you, or something, inside me," she mutters.

"Do you have a vibrator?"

Her eyes fly open. "No. I wish I did, though. Something shaped just like you that could be inside me right now. Watching you jerking yourself off like that has me about to come."

Well, fuck me. I tighten my grip, practically choking my cock as I glide my hand along myself from base to tip. "Put your fingers inside yourself, then."

She keeps playing with her clit, then reaches down with her other hand, and I watch her fingers disappear into her pussy, wishing the camera angle was different so I could see an up-close view. But I want to see her face, see her chest heaving with desire, see the way her abdominal muscles keep contracting as the need rolls through her. I can tell she's almost there.

Her hand moves slowly, her fingers dipping in and out of her body. "Harder," I growl as my own pace increases. "If I was there right now, I'd be fucking you harder and faster than that, because I can see how close you are."

Both of her hands move more quickly, and she's letting out soft grunts of pleasure. "It's not enough, Drew. I need it to be you."

"It will be, baby, but for now, you've got to make yourself come. Imagine it's my cock, filling you all the way up." She groans, and her eyes flutter closed as she listens to my words. "Imagine you're straddling me, and I'm as deep inside you as I can go. My mouth is on your nipple, licking and biting." Another deep groan leaves her as she squeezes her eyes shut, and I'm jerking off so hard I won't last long. "You're so close, then you reach down and press your fingers to your clit, and as you run your fingertips over yourself, you feel the first traces of your orgasm."

"Yesss," she hisses out. "I'm so close."

"Good, more pressure."

She rewards me with another groan of pleasure, followed by, "Oh shit." Then she stretches her head back, her hips bucking wildly as I watch her entire core contract.

"Yes, come for me, Audrey."

She opens her eyes then, focuses them on my face, and says, "You first."

"If I was there, I'd never let myself come before you did."

"But you're not. And seeing you come will tip me over the edge. I won't be able to hold back."

I sense that for her, this is an issue of trust. She wants me vulnerable in this way before she makes herself vulnerable, too. So I stop holding back. A few more pumps of my hand over my cock, and I'm rolling forward a bit to spray my release onto my t-shirt. And then my eyes meet hers, and I can tell she's incredibly close.

She's still working herself, but slower. "Alright, Audrey. Let's see you finish yourself off—hard and fast, like I'd do for you." Saying nothing, she gets onto her knees and turns the camera vertically, then sinks back onto her heels. She glances at the phone, then wraps one arm around her abdomen and her face falls. "What are you doing?"

"I just…" She glances down at her body self-consciously. "…my stomach is—"

"Perfect. Your whole body is fucking perfect, Audrey. Don't you dare try to hide yourself from me. I want to see every part of you."

"My body isn't the same as the last time you saw it." Now her other arm wraps around her stomach, like she's forgotten that I had her shirt off the other night and liked everything I saw.

"Because you had *our child*, Audrey. And your body is even more beautiful for it. Let me tell you what I see. The most beautiful woman I know has her knees spread with her pussy on display for me, her tits are gorgeous and the perfect size, and I can tell by her nipples how aroused she is. I'm so fucking turned on by this view that I can barely breathe, and I'm already getting hard again." I reach down and grip myself so she can see what she does to me, and in response, her lips part with a sigh. "I wish I was there to rain kisses over any part of your body that you see as a flaw, because from my perspective, you are fucking perfect."

"Drew." My name is just a whisper.

"Now let me see you finish yourself off, so I know how needy you are for me."

She nods, swiping her fingers through her slickness and moving them back to her clit, then bringing her other hand around behind her. I watch as she enters herself with two fingers. From this angle, I have the perfect view and it's the hottest fucking thing I've ever seen. The blood rushes to my dick so fast I feel lightheaded, or maybe it's because my body is reminding me that I am, in fact, quite sick. But there is *nothing* that's going to stop me from making sure Audrey gets this orgasm.

"Add another finger," I demand. There's no way two of her fingers are anywhere close to how I'd feel if I were inside her, and she does what I ask, but I can tell by the exquisite look of torture on her face that she still wants more, and I want to be the one to give it to her. I want her to be sinking back onto my cock, in front of a mirror, so she can watch as I enter her. I will make her see how beautiful she is.

"Tell me what you're picturing right now," I say.

"I'm imagining that I'm straddling you, like that night on the couch," she says. "Even after all these years, I haven't forgotten how good you felt inside me, and my fingers are not up to the task. I need you here, filling me completely."

Fuck. My balls tighten up in response.

"I have half a mind to charter a private plane…"

She gives me a small smile and rolls her eyes. "You're sick, and by the time you got here, Jules and I would already be working." She sinks onto her fingers harder and faster, and I watch her tits bounce as her speed increases. "So you're going to have to settle for the show instead."

"Nothing about you equates to settling, Audrey. I hope you know that."

Closing her eyes, a small, satisfied smile graces her lips. She tilts her hips forward, sliding her fingers into herself, and I am overcome with the realization that my whole world has shifted.

The second I think about forever with her, she's moaning my name, then her head tilts back and her jaw falls open, and I watch as her orgasm ripples through her entire body. The sexy-as-hell view has lightning running through my veins, and then I'm coming all over the sheets again.

"Holy shit," she says, and her eyes meet mine as she collapses onto her bed and picks up the phone. "Did we really just do that?"

"I hope so, because if I wake up tomorrow and find that this was all a fever dream, I'm going to be so fucking pissed."

She laughs softly, and her eyelids flutter closed. "Shouldn't you go back to sleep so you can get better?" Her voice is low, and her words are slow, like she might fall asleep any second.

"Probably. But Audrey..." I wait for her to open her eyes. "We're going to talk about this."

She sighs, her lips barely turning up at the corners as she closes her eyes again. "We don't have to talk about it, Drew. It doesn't have to mean anything."

"Like hell it doesn't. This means everything—stop pretending like it doesn't."

She sighs again but doesn't say anything or open her eyes

to look at me. I don't think she's pretending to sleep to get out of talking about this, but I can't really be sure. "We'll talk when I get back to Boston."

No response, and her breathing is now slow and deep. I disconnect the call and cancel my alarm for the morning. My whole body is spent. There's no way I'm getting up in four hours to make the flight home with the team. And this is the one rare instance when I'm sure that missing my flight was one thousand percent worth it.

Chapter Twenty-Four

AUDREY

"You can't keep showing up at my office like this," I say as Drew shuts and locks the door behind him.

"Do you actually mind?" He crosses the room in a few long strides, and I take a step back but run into the cabinet behind me. His fingers are already trailing beneath the hem of my dress, and he leans down and peppers kisses along the bridge of my nose. "Because I swear you sent me a text saying you hadn't stopped thinking about having sex with me since our phone call this past weekend. And it seemed like stopping by this afternoon, while Graham is at school and Jules is on a job site, meant we might have some privacy."

His hair is damp, and I assume he took a quick shower and headed here right after his post-practice workout. It was his first full practice since getting sick, and I wonder if he's exhausted. It definitely took me a few days to feel back to normal, and I wasn't trying to power through grueling workouts.

"I have to leave to pick up Graham in an hour," I tell him, wishing kindergarten didn't get out a full hour earlier than the rest of his elementary school. "I have so much work I was supposed to do between now and then."

He leans in, resting his hand against the wall behind me so that I'm completely wedged between him and the cabinet. His proximity has my nipples hardening, and the way they're pressing into my lace bra is sending heat shooting through me straight to my core. I press my thighs together to alleviate the ache between them.

"I don't have to stay if you don't want me to," he says.

Memories of our video call flood my senses and overwhelm all logic until I'm incapable of making good decisions. Or maybe having sex with Drew *is* a good decision?

He steps forward, his whole body pressed against mine so that my nipples drag along his rock-hard chest. "But if I leave now, I'm afraid you'll be so distracted imagining what could have happened if I'd stayed, that you probably wouldn't get any work done anyway." His voice is low and cajoling in my ear, and the fact that it's been three days since our call and since my last orgasm has me needing him badly. "So I'm probably doing you a favor by staying."

My chest shakes with laughter, but that only has my breasts heaving against him, and as a result, Drew's lips part as he hums his approval. Then he slides his hands along the backs of my thighs and lifts me onto the cabinet so I'm sitting with my legs spread on either side of him. He steps in closer and grips my ass, pulling me forward and lining my center up along his truly impressive dick, every inch of which I can feel through his gray sweatpants.

"You're probably right," I say, my voice teasing as I tip my weight back onto my tailbone so my center runs along the length of him. "How would I *ever* be able to focus after seeing you for five seconds?"

"Such a fucking smartass," he says, a smile playing on his lips. "I can leave if you'd prefer."

I wouldn't. But I should probably tell him to go, anyway. Nothing good is going to come of letting my hormones carry me away. *Except orgasms...they're good.*

"You're literally panting in my ear," he says, tilting his chin toward me and trailing hot kisses up the side of my neck. I can feel the way he smiles against my jaw when the resulting sigh escapes my lips. "So, you want me to stay?"

"Drew, I really do need to finish some changes to the plans I'm working on." I know that's the smart decision, the responsible thing to do. But my body doesn't seem to be listening, because my hand plants itself on the countertop behind me so that my back arches and my breasts run along his chest again.

The groan he releases into the crook of my neck before he pulls back lets me know that he disagrees. But he's respecting my boundaries, and that might be the biggest turn-on yet. It spurs me on even when I know I shouldn't let this go any further. But I ignore those doubts, instead linking my feet together behind his legs before he can step away, then lifting my free arm and wrapping it around his neck, pulling him back to me.

"It seems like maybe you should give me at least *one* orgasm, you know, for the inconvenience of interrupting my work."

He rests his forehead against mine. "For the inconvenience, of course."

"And maybe, if I'm feeling generous, I'll even return the favor."

"If you're feeling generous, you can let me fuck you like I've been literally dreaming about for the last three nights. I've been walking around with a perpetual hard-on since I watched you slip your fingers into yourself."

Heat flashes through my skin, thawing me completely. It seems I can only ice him out for so long before I become a complete puddle in his presence.

"That sounds like a *you* problem," I tease.

"I think it's actually a *you* problem," he says, "because I've never been this way around anyone else."

His lips meet mine gently, but this isn't the time for gentle. I stretch up into him, taking his lower lip between mine and nipping at it, which has him opening his mouth. Our tongues tangle and his hands roam down to the hem of my dress as he slides it up my legs. I'm so focused on the kiss, on the way that his fingertips are grazing the outside of my thighs, that the sound of leaf blowers on the street level outside the office barely registers—until a small rock comes flying at the glass. The loud crack has us jumping apart, and Drew looks like we just heard a gunshot.

"It's just a rock," I say, and nod my chin to where we can see the work boots and jeans of the men working for the landscaping company, who are doing their weekly maintenance on the small area along the front of our brownstone.

"I don't love that you work down here by yourself with an entire wall of glass," he says, looking back at me. "It doesn't seem safe."

"It's actually glass-clad polycarbonate," I tell him. "Otherwise known as bullet-proof glass. Trust me, I don't want anyone breaking in here, either."

"Alright," he says, stepping back between my legs. "Though I'd prefer if it were one-way glass so you could see out and no one could see in. I want you naked right here, right now. I want to spread you out on that table and feast on your pussy, then watch your body bounce as I fuck you like you want me to. But there are"—he glances back at the glass entryway—"at least three guys out there."

"From the sidewalk, you can only see the first foot or two into this room," I tell him. But right as I say it, one of the workers comes down three of the concrete steps toward the basement. We can only see the back of him as he blows leaves toward the street, but if he turned around, he'd be able to see pretty far into this space.

Drew follows my gaze, then raises his eyebrow. "Where can we go so I can get you naked?"

His words have me rubbing myself against his hard length because I'm desperate for how I know he can make me feel. I glance toward the door at the back of the office that leads to the playroom, thinking that although that would be completely out of view, it's probably not the best choice. Instead, I lead him across the room toward the stairs—the site of my dropped salad the last time he stopped by—because they're tucked behind the entry closet and you can't see the space from the front windows.

As we walk, he threads his fingers through mine and gives me a squeeze. "What if Jules comes back?"

"She's actually going to be late tonight. I was going to text you and ask if you minded if I bring Graham with me to your mom's later this afternoon when I come over to measure. Jules will have to see the space another time."

"Of course. I'd love for my mom to meet him."

I stop, and he runs into the back of me. "But…we're not going to say anything yet, right? I don't know if I'm ready for that."

"We can do this on your time frame, Audrey. I'm fine with her getting to know Graham, and then us telling her later, once you're ready."

I look up at him, and I'm sure he can see the relief in my eyes. "You sure?"

He kisses the top of my head. "Positive."

When we hit the landing of the stairs and are out of view of the street, he turns me so my back is against the wall and pushes up against me. "Alright, we're hidden. I'm going to need that dress off. Now." His voice is hard, but needy.

I raise an eyebrow. "Then maybe you should ask nicely."

He steps back and tilts his head down so he's looking me in the eye. "Audrey, please take your dress off before I rip it to fucking shreds. I'd hate to ruin it, but I will if I have to."

I bite my lower lip but can't keep my smile in. As I shake my head at him, I find the top button at the front of my dress. I'd chosen this one because I knew I was seeing him later and meeting his mom, and I get compliments every time I wear it.

"It really *would* be a shame to ruin this one, so I guess I'll just have to take it off."

"Good choice," he growls as he stands there, watching me make quick work of the buttons down the front of the dress. The crepe floral material slides to either side of my breasts as I undo the buttons near the waist, and Drew's sharp intake of breath as he sees my lace bralette is louder than the leaf blowers outside. I glance down at where his dick is straining against those sweatpants, making an enormous tent.

"Like what you see?" There's amusement in his voice, so I look back up at him.

"Eh." I shrug as I lower my arms and let the dress fall off my shoulders and down my arms, then I slide it over my hips and let it pool at my feet. "I guess it'll be sufficient."

He gives me a full-out smile. "Oh princess, this is going to be so much more than sufficient."

"We'll see." I wink so he knows I'm teasing, but it's possible he misses the gesture as he tears his Rebels hoodie and t-shirt over his head in one movement. His body is a chiseled work of perfection, and I try not to be self-conscious about my own body as I look at his.

He's an athlete. It's his job to be in the best shape he possibly can be. I'm a mom who hardly has time to take care of my own basic needs, much less spend the time it would take to get back into shape. Unless you count my weekly pole dancing class, which has definitely helped.

He reaches out and takes my chin in his hand, tilting my head back and locking his eyes on mine. "Don't do that."

"Don't do what?"

"That thing where you look at my body and then think yours is anything less than perfect."

"Are you a fucking mind reader?" I try to laugh it off.

"Your face said it all."

"Drew, you could have any girl you want and most of them would have much better bodies than mine. So you're just going to have to accept that I'm a little insecure about this."

"I'm not, actually, going to have to accept that. Because you're perfect exactly how you are, and like I told you on the phone, I haven't so much as looked at another woman since I saw you again. Nor do I plan on looking at another woman any time in the future." He tightens his grip on my chin when I try to look away, forcing me to meet his gaze. "Take my pants off."

"W-what?" I fumble the word.

"Take my pants off. I want you to see for yourself what you do to me."

I glance down at his sweats, and I can see exactly what I do to him. When I hook my thumbs in the waistband, Drew lets out a breath that sounds more like a hiss. I glance up at him, and he just raises his eyebrows like he's challenging me.

"What if I don't want to take your pants off?"

"Then we can stop this right here. We don't have to do this if you're not comfortable. In fact, I don't *want* to do this if you're not comfortable. But I love the way your body looks, and I want you to love it too."

"You can't make me love my body, Drew," I tell him. "My feelings and opinions about it are my own."

"True, but I can tell you what I love about it," he says, reaching out to cup my breasts in his hands. My nipples strain against the sheer fabric, and a moan rips from the back of my throat when he sweeps his thumbs across them. "I love the way your body is eager for mine. I love your absolutely perfect rack." He slides his hands down so his palms skim across my stomach as his fingertips grip the edge of my back possessively. "I love how soft your skin is, how your waist nips in here, but how your hips and ass are curvy in all the right ways. Men literally write songs about women with asses like yours."

I don't know what he's talking about—my hips and ass are not proportional to the rest of my body.

He drops down to his knees, running his fingertips down the length of my legs. "I love how strong your legs are. Why are your muscles so defined in your legs?" He trails his fingertips along the back of my legs, tracing the edges of my calf muscles.

"I dance once a week." I obviously don't think before saying this.

"What kind of dancing?" he asks, looking up at me, and I can feel the heat creeping from my chest up my neck.

"Oh, you know," I say, rolling my eyes and brushing off the question.

He stands quickly, stepping close enough that my breasts brush his chest. "No, I don't know. But you seem embarrassed that I asked, which has me even more curious."

I press my lips between my teeth, cursing myself for not just saying I was taking a ballet or a jazz class. Now I can't backtrack to one of those answers or he'll know I'm lying.

"Never mind about the dance classes, Drew," I say, and hook my thumbs back into the waist of his sweatpants, hoping I can distract him by taking his clothes off.

Instead, he presses each of his hands over mine. "Why won't you tell me?"

"Because it's embarrassing. Please, drop it."

"I have a feeling that whatever you think is embarrassing, I'll think is insanely hot. So you should probably test that theory out and see if I'm right."

If I ask him again to drop it, I know he will. Part of me

wants to know how he'd react, but I'm not sure I'm brave enough to find out.

"Right now"—I reach out to stroke him through his sweats, and his hips instinctually tilt up, thrusting him into my hand—"the only theory I *really* want to test is whether the sex will be as good as I remember."

Chapter Twenty-Five

DREW

I know she's distracting me from something she doesn't want to talk about, and I want to circle back to it, but I'm not strong enough to resist what she's offering. She'll tell me about her dance class when she's ready. In the meantime, she's gliding her hand along my shaft and then rolling her thumb over the head of my dick, and I can't help my body's reaction. I thrust right into her hand, needing the friction.

Instead of giving me what I want, she slides her hands along my abdomen, her fingertips dipping between my sweatpants and the elastic band of my boxers. And then, she's pushing my sweatpants down my hips and pulling them along my thighs. At my knees, she lets the material drop to my feet and stands back up, letting her entire body rub along mine until she snakes her arms around my neck.

"Have you forgotten why I asked you to take my pants off?" I ask as I reach up and slide my fingers along her cheeks, catching her long dark hair and tucking it behind both ears so I can see her whole face.

"Uhh…" She pauses and looks a little confused. "Kind of."

I take a small step back from her and glance down. She follows my gaze. "I want you to see exactly what you do to me. The other night on the phone, you completely rocked my world. Since then, I've taken two showers a day so I can jerk myself off and get rid of the constant hard-on every time I think of you. Every part of you," I tell her, looking into her eyes, "is flawless. Especially the parts you don't like." I reach out, making contact with her rib cage below her breasts and running my hands along the soft skin of her abdomen. It's not that I don't see the thin silvery stretch marks there, it's that they represent how she carried our child. They're evidence of her strength, and I want to trail kisses over each one to thank her for bringing Graham into this world when I was too immature to be there with her.

Then I pull at the tiny straps that rest across her hips, sliding her thong down her legs. She lifts each foot to step out of the underwear, and then I'm lifting one of her legs over my shoulder and holding her hips back against the wall behind her.

"You seem to like being on your knees for me," she says, looking down at me.

"I'll get on my knees for you whenever and wherever you want. I swear I spend half of every day thinking about how much I adore this pussy." I use my thumbs to spread her lips, baring her to me. Leaning forward, I run my tongue along her entire seam. "You taste…like heaven."

She laughs, and the husky sound spurs me on. "It's true," I tell her, glancing up before reaching my tongue forward and gliding it over the sensitive ball of nerves. She moans and presses her back into the wall, but her eyes are still locked on mine as I run one of my fingers along her seam, which is dripping with need. She groans out, "Yes," and drives her hips down toward my finger.

I'm happy to oblige, and I relish the silky feel of her as I imagine what it would feel like to slide into her bare. God, I've never wanted that with anyone else—never been willing to take that risk—but for Audrey, I feel like I'd risk anything. Maybe even everything.

"I feel so out of control around you," I say as I look up at her from my knees. "I want you so badly, I can't even see straight. I'm pretty sure there's nothing I wouldn't do for you."

"Drew!" she gasps, my name punctuated by a sharp intake of breath as I add a second finger and drive in deep. I curve my fingers forward, sliding them against her inner walls—I know I've found the right spot when she starts moving her hips in tune with my fingers. I love watching her, but I'll love making her scream my name even more, so I lean in and lap my tongue flat against her clit. The mewling sound that tears from her lips at that contact sends longing through my entire body, so that I have one singular thought: I need to be inside her.

I use my free hand to pull off my boxers, letting them drop down to my knees, and then I grip my aching cock, sliding my hand up and down and wanting it to be Audrey touching me. I can tell she's close by the short, panting breaths that punctuate the otherwise silent room, and I desperately want to hear the sound of her pleasure. When my lips circle her clit, enclosing it so I can suck gently, her mouth falls open.

"Oh my God," she says, repeating it over and over until finally she half-screams, "Yes! Drew, yes!"

Her eyes are screwed tightly shut as she rides out the waves of pleasure, and I don't stop stroking her until I can feel every last trace of her orgasm pass. She starts to slide down the wall, as though her legs can't hold her up anymore, but I catch her waist as I stand, lifting her and pinning her between my upper body and the wall. Her legs wrap around my waist, and I can feel her hook her feet together behind me as my hands cup her ass.

"You want to know the only thing that would be better than hearing my name roll off your lips?"

Her eyes are still closed, her lips parting as she tries to catch her breath. "Sure."

I lean my head down to trace the shell of her ear with my nose. "Hearing my name roll off your lips while you're coming all over my cock."

A full-body shudder moves through her, then she eyes me lazily. "Agreed."

"Tell me what you want me to do," I say. I don't want to assume that just because I can't wait to be inside her, that's what she wants at this moment, too.

"I want you inside me."

"Do you want me to get a condom?"

"Are you clean?" she asks, already tilting her hips up so her wet seam slides along my raging hard dick.

"Yep, I've never done this with anyone else, and I was just tested before training camp. You?"

"Same." She rubs herself along me again. "Plus, I'm on the

pill."

"Are you sure you're okay with this?" I ask, praying that she says yes, but willing to stop if she's uncertain.

"Drew," she pants, "fucking get inside me now."

"Yes, ma'am." I hold her hips and line myself up with her entrance. And as I slide into her, stretching her fully, I lean forward and our mouths crash together. This is no gentle kiss, it's the longing we've both felt for days coming to fruition. The sliding of her tongue against mine, the growl that rattles around in my throat, the way her breasts press against my chest as her pussy swallows me until I'm seated fully inside her, it feels like I'm being given a surprise gift.

And then I'm lost to the feeling, the emotions, as our bodies meet over and over. The way her ass flexes in my hands, the feel of her nails digging into my shoulders, the way her breasts bounce every time I enter her fully, the way her eyes roll back and her lips part when I hit deep inside her, the way her teeth sink into her lower lip.

I wrap one arm under her hips and push her back into the wall for leverage so I can use my other hand to pull the sheer lace of her bra down on both sides. The way the fabric cups her breasts from beneath, pushing them together, has my balls tightening. I lean down and capture one of her nipples in my mouth, sucking on it hard enough that she gasps, and then using my tongue to roll over her nipple gently, soothing it. But the contact also seems to stoke something inside her, because she slams her hips into me faster and harder than before.

"You like this?"

"Fuck yes," she says, and I love seeing this uninhibited side of her. She's all-business at work, and in total mom mode whenever Graham is around, so I feel like I'm seeing a whole other aspect of her personality that few other people have ever seen. I love how in touch she is with what she wants and needs.

I latch my mouth onto her other breast, and her hips thrust erratically. Moving my other hand back down, I hold her on both sides where her thighs meet her ass, and I slam into her until she's chanting "Yes!" repeatedly.

She clenches around me tightly, and the tingling starts at the base of my spine. I need her to come now, so that I don't finish before she does. I lift my head and look at her, at the way her cheeks are rosy and her lips are swollen and her eyes are glassy.

I lean back a bit so my upper body doesn't block her view. "Look at how beautiful you look, taking my cock so well," I say, my voice insistent as she looks down to where I'm entering her. "Now I want to feel you come like a good girl."

The groan that leaves her mouth is part pain, part pleasure. "I can't just come on demand—"

I swallow her protests with a kiss as my entire body presses hers against the wall, our chests scraping against each other and my body rubbing against her clit as I hold her hips in place and rail her into the wall. And in less time than it takes me to realize this is by far the best sex I've ever had with anyone, she's coming on my cock, her muscles squeezing me rhythmically so that there's no way I could hold back even if I wanted to. And as I pour everything I have into her, into this moment, I'm left absolutely dumbfounded. Because Audrey is everything I didn't know I wanted, and I'm not sure I can live without her now she's back in my life.

Chapter Twenty-Six

AUDREY

I follow Drew into his childhood home, trying not to think too hard about what *this* all means—the mind-bending sex we had earlier today, the way he came to school pickup with me and Graham's elated reaction to finding Drew in the passenger seat, the fact that Drew took Graham to the park and to get hot chocolate afterward so I could do the work I'd neglected while he gave me multiple orgasms, and the way he drove my SUV out here with me in the passenger seat and Graham in the back seat.

It all feels too...relationship-like. And Drew already made it clear that he can't be in a relationship right now. But then he told me that this physical aspect of our relationship means everything, and that there's no way he could ever grow tired of me. So now I'm just feeling confused—is this just a physical relationship, or is it more?

We clearly need to talk, and I'm hoping maybe we can do that tonight, after Graham goes to bed.

"Hey, Mom!" Drew calls out as he walks through the back door with me and Graham on his heels.

"Drew!" She sounds surprised that he's here.

We follow him through the kitchen and into the living room, where she's sitting on the couch watching a show. She's smaller than I'd have imagined, given Drew's imposing size, and her light brown hair that was probably the same shade as Drew's and Graham's is now streaked with grey. The fine lines around her eyes and mouth make me think she spent a lot of her life smiling, but her lips turn down at the corners now. When she notices us with Drew, her eyebrows shoot up, then she puts one frail hand on the couch next to her and one on the arm of it, and stands slowly.

"Mom, this is Audrey," he says, putting his hand on my lower back and guiding me in front of him. Her eyes fly to my hip, where he's rested his hand. "She's the architect that I told you I was bringing by to take some measurements so we can make some adjustments to help you get around better."

She looks at me with interest, which I'm guessing has more to do with the way her son's fingers are curled around my hip, rather than my profession. I'm tempted to swat his hand away, but I think that would make things more obvious.

"It's nice to meet you, Audrey," she says, and then looks down at Graham. "And who do we have here?"

"This is my son, Graham," I tell her.

"I'm five, and I'm in kindergarten," he says. It's impossible to forget how he said those exact words to Drew a few weeks ago. "How old are you?"

Drew's mom bursts out laughing, and it's a welcome

sight. Next to me, I feel Drew relax, even though he grips my hip even more possessively than before.

"I'm a lot older than five. But I love hanging out with five-year-olds. I used to be a kindergarten teacher."

"You did?" Graham asks, his voice full of the awe that kids reserve for situations when they see a teacher in the wild. I glance at Drew because I had no idea his mom had been a teacher. I know almost nothing about his family, and even though I've been curious at times, I never wanted to pry. But she seems open and friendly, so maybe it wouldn't be prying?

"I did. Do you like reading stories?" she asks.

"Yes, but I don't know how to read them myself yet. Except board books, I read those to my little cousins, Iris and Ivy."

I don't correct him, because even though he knows that reading is different than telling a story you've memorized, I love that he wants to read to Lauren's twins.

"How about you and I read a book together so my son can show your mom around?" She sends a small, conspiratorial smile our way.

Oh shit, is his mom trying to play matchmaker here?

"Okay," Graham says, and his voice lacks the dubious sound it sometimes carries when he isn't sure about something. I relax, knowing he's comfortable with her.

When Jules and I were kids, our father took us plenty of places we shouldn't have gone, and left us in the care of far too many sketchy adults, so he could go drink with his friends—especially once my mom got sick. I'd never want Graham to feel like I was off doing something else and leaving him in a situation where he didn't feel safe.

I wait while Graham kneels down at a basket Mrs.

Jenkins has pointed to and selects a book. When he climbs up on the couch and settles in next to where she's sitting, I say to Drew, "Alright, maybe you can point out what you'd like to do so I know which rooms to measure?"

He leads me down a hallway and shows me around the minimalist space. Like most houses built in the 1960s in the Boston area, the hallways are narrow, and the rooms are all divided up, completely enclosed with only a narrow doorway to move through. For someone with mobility issues who needed a walker, or eventually a wheelchair, I could see how it would be hard or even impossible to get around. There's no way, for example, that a wheelchair could make the turn from the hallway into the room Drew wants to convert into the primary bedroom—the angle you'd have to turn to fit through the doorway would be too tight.

We talk a bit about how we could move the door to the end of the hallway so it would be a straight shot in and out of the room, and then tuck the bathroom over on the side with a double-wide doorway to get in and out.

Luckily, his mom is not at the point where her mobility is severely impacted enough that she needs a walker or a wheelchair, but he speaks quietly about the possibility of a cane or a walker in the near future.

"I just want her to be able to stay in her home for as long as is humanly possible, you know?" His lips turn down at the corners and, without thinking, I reach up and cup his cheek in my hand, smoothing out his frown with my thumb. His eyes widen and, for a second, I'm afraid I've overstepped, and then he presses his hand over mine, holding my hand to his face. "Thank you."

"For what?"

"For being here. For considering this project, even when I know you and Jules are overbooked. For being you."

My stomach flips over, and I'm not sure how to respond, but then we hear Graham yell, "There's a cat in the yard! Can I go out and pet it?"

I can hear his feet running across the floor, presumably toward the door, and that's when Drew says, "I've got this. You good to start measuring?"

"Yeah. Thank you for keeping an eye on him."

I listen as Drew offers to take Graham out to see the cat and throw around a football, and as they walk out the door to the backyard, I hear Graham say, "I've never thrown a football. Will you show me how?"

"Of course, Bud," he says, already adopting the nickname that my whole family uses for Graham. At first, I hated that the nickname stuck. But it was fitting, because when Graham was a baby, taking care of him really was a team effort and he was always with me, Jameson, or Jules during the first year of his life—our little buddy who we carted around with us everywhere we went, making it work with our various school and work schedules.

It takes me about half an hour with the laser measure to record each room's dimensions, and while I work, my mind is reeling with the possibilities of what we can do to transform this family room into the perfect first-floor living space for Drew's mom.

As it always happens when I create a new floor plan, I picture the possible layouts and different design ideas spin in my brain until a fully formed image comes to the forefront. And then I know exactly which layout will work best —before I ever even sit down with my drafting software—

and just how it will look once I can have Jules work her magic.

I design the layout, Jules does the structural engineering and construction, and then I work with the client on the finishes and design. Our synergy means our system flows seamlessly and the results are always spectacular.

But I have the nagging feeling that we can't keep going at this pace. Jules works nearly 24/7, and I probably would too if I didn't have Graham. But even in the evenings, once he's in bed, I'm usually on the couch with my laptop, talking through different projects with Jules. But how long can we sustain this without burning out?

I make a mental note to circle back to Morgan's idea about partnering with different trade schools in the area so we can recruit female contractors directly out of their training programs. The possibility of building this business is not only exciting, it's necessary.

As I walk over to my bag, which I set on the couch under the window, I'm distracted by the view to the backyard. Drew is kneeling behind Graham, who has a football in his small hand. Drew's got his hand over Graham's and is pulling his arm back and snapping it forward, without letting go of the ball. My eyes fill with tears when I realize that my son's father is teaching him how to throw a football. It's a sight I never dared dream I'd see.

"How's it going?" Mrs. Jenkins's voice surprises me, and I spin to find her standing in the doorway watching me.

"Great. I just finished measuring everything. I think this space will be the perfect bedroom, and it'll be easy to convert the hall bath to a nice ensuite for you."

"I never thought my son would be a catastrophist, but

that's what this feels like," she says, folding her arms across her stomach.

"Do you not want this work done? Because I in no way want to infringe on this situation if you're not ready." I want to be transparent here, because even though Drew's right that these adjustments will be necessary if she's going to be able to continue living in this house long term, they probably don't need to happen quite yet.

"I just wish it wasn't necessary," she says as she walks across the room to stand next to me. "But in the long run, I know this will need to be done. He thinks I don't see how he worries," she says, and I follow her gaze out the window to her son. It takes me by surprise that she's speaking about this with me—a virtual stranger.

"Is he naturally a worrier?"

"No. I used to joke that he didn't have the good sense to worry. He was always so happy, such an optimist. It's been hard watching him be an adult so far away. I'm glad he's back home."

Me too, I almost say. "I bet," I manage instead.

"I never imagined this scene, though," she says as she watches Drew show Graham how to release the football.

Me either. "He's great with kids."

"He's great with *his son*," she says, turning to look at me. I can't hide my shocked reaction, but I clench my teeth together before my jaw falls open.

I try to speak, but all that comes out is a breathy sigh. Finally, I manage to ask, "H-how did you know?"

"Besides the way Drew looks at him? Graham is a carbon copy of him at that age. Even the way he speaks is the same. Reading on the couch with him was like getting to revisit my son's childhood." She pauses for a moment as her eyes fill with tears. "I'm not sure how we got here, but I'm sure glad we've arrived."

She reaches out a shaky hand, and I take it, knowing it's a gift that she's offering it—knowing there are a thousand different ways this conversation could have gone, and appreciating that she's welcoming me and Graham into her family without questioning how we got here.

I give her a gentle squeeze, and then she says, "Do you want to see pictures of Drew when he was younger, so you'll know what I mean?"

"I'd love to."

She crosses to the other side of the room and grabs a thick photo album off a shelf, returning to the couch and sitting. I take one more look at the backyard, where Graham is running and looking over his shoulder, waiting for Drew to throw him the ball. My heart hurts—both because of how this scene squeezes all my emotions until I feel like I'll burst, and also because of all the years Graham missed with Drew.

If I'm being honest, maybe also because him being back in my life is bittersweet—he's much more like the boy I adored in college than like the wild pro-hockey player the media makes him out to be. Maybe I bought into those rumors because I wanted them to be true, but in my heart of hearts, I knew Drew was a good person.

And he's been nothing but good to me since he's been back.

I sit next to Mrs. Jenkins while she flips through some old photos of Drew, and I see exactly what she means. Graham does look just like him.

"Oh, this one is my favorite," she laughs, showing me a

picture of Drew when he was probably Graham's age, sitting naked on the toilet, making a face like he's trying to poop.

I burst out laughing. "You must love showing this picture off any time Drew brings someone home."

"That would require him having ever brought a girl home."

"What?" I let out a nervous laugh. "He's never even had a girlfriend he brought home?"

"He always insisted that the first girl he brought home would be the woman he was going to marry."

That information hits me like a lead weight. "Well, I guess he's making an exception for the mother of his child. Do you mind if we don't mention this conversation to him when he comes in? Graham doesn't know yet, and I'd like for Drew and me to be able to talk to him first, and for you and Drew to have a chance to talk about all this without me and Graham around."

She looks at me like I just said the dumbest thing in the world, but then her face gets a far-away look. I'm about to ask if she's okay, when I hear a feminine voice call out "Ma?" from the front room.

Mrs. Jenkins's head snaps toward the door, then she grasps my hand where it sits on the photo album and gives me another little squeeze. "Don't mind Caitlyn," she says quietly. "She's prickly."

Ahhh, Drew's oldest sister. The one who he said is deeply unhappy, and therefore makes everyone else unhappy. Awesome.

"Back here," Mrs. Jenkins calls out, and when she goes to stand, she struggles a bit, so I give her my arm for support.

She's just reached a full standing position when Caitlyn

bursts through the open doorway and comes to a halting stop, eyeing me suspiciously. "Who are you?"

"My name's Audrey Flynn. I'm the architect Drew hired to draw up some plans for converting this space to a primary bedroom for your mom."

Her gaze narrows. *Shit.* I shouldn't have made it clear that I knew who she was even before meeting her. I should have acted like I knew nothing about their family.

"Hey, Caitlyn." Drew's voice comes from behind her, right as Graham runs in—narrowly squeezing his body between Caitlyn's and the door frame—and throws his arms around my legs.

"Mom! Drew taught me how to throw a football. Do you think I can play hockey *and* football? I'm really good at throwing!"

I give him a smile as I push his hair out of his eyes. The kid needs a haircut, but like most hockey players his age, he's perpetually growing it out.

"Sure, we can talk about that."

I watch as Caitlyn's head swings from me, over to Drew, who's looking at me and Graham like a love-sick fool. *Knock it off*, I say in my head, wishing I could somehow send that message telepathically. But he just continues staring at me with that devilish grin. If any adult in the room didn't know we'd just slept together, they probably do now.

"You're seeing someone with a kid, Drew?" Caitlyn's voice is accusatory at best, downright disgusted at worst.

I open my mouth to say that we're not dating, but Drew beats me to it, instead telling her, "It's none of your business, Caitlyn."

"Hey, Graham," Mrs. Jenkins says. "How about we go find another book to read while the adults have a conversation."

"Okay," Graham says and runs from the room, oblivious to the hostility lacing the atmosphere in here.

"Be nice, please," Mrs. Jenkins tells Caitlyn before she leaves.

Completely ignoring her mother's request, she focuses her dark eyes back on Drew. "You can't even take care of yourself or Mom. How the hell are you going to be there for someone with a kid?"

"Let me repeat myself so we're absolutely clear here," he says, his voice taking on an icy tone I've never heard before. He doesn't sound anything like himself. "It's. None. Of. Your. Business."

"Fine," she huffs, crossing her arms like a petulant child. "Just don't let this get in the way of your other obligations. Like, let's make sure you don't forget about tomorrow morning's appointment, like you forgot about the last one." Her snide tone and the reference to the appointment he almost missed turn my stomach to acid.

Drew's eyes slide over to me, and he gives a little shake of his head like he's trying to tell me it's not my fault he wasn't there for his mom.

But it is. I didn't ask him to come over and help me, but if he hadn't, then he'd have been there for his mom. *And you'd probably have gotten scarlet fever,* I remind myself.

Caitlyn's eyes narrow in on me. "Oh. My. God. You were with *her?*"

Drew's gaze snaps from me to Caitlyn.

"You didn't show up for Mom because you were too busy...what? Shacking up with some random chick?" She turns toward her brother, and she looks furious. "Of all the irresponsible, selfish things you could do, putting this puck bunny before your mom is probably the lowest."

I dig my nails into my palms, knowing it's not my place to get involved in their argument, and I watch as Drew's hands curl into fists too. He's clenching his teeth together so tightly I'm surprised he's able to speak, but his voice comes out clear and deathly serious. "If you ever speak about the mother of my child and my future wife that way again, you and I are done. For good. Understand?"

I'm pretty sure the air has been sucked from my lungs, or maybe from the whole room, because it's now deathly silent in here, like there's no air for sound waves to carry through. I might pass out, or throw up, I'm not sure which.

What the fuck is he saying? And why?

I can't breathe. I need some fresh air. I need to get out of here. I need to leave.

Chapter Twenty-Seven

DREW

Audrey tries to run past me and through the doorway, but when I reach out and grab her wrist, she spins back toward me. I can't read the look on her face—she looks mad, but that doesn't make sense. I just defended her to my sister, and finally admitted the depth of my feelings for her. What could she possibly be mad about?

"Not now, Drew," she says, then pulls out of my grip and shuts the door behind her on her way out. I can barely hear her talking to my mom and Graham over the pounding sound of fury in my ears.

"Who the fuck do you think you are?" I say to Caitlyn. She deflates a bit at the deadly low, focused tone, "barging in here and insulting Audrey like that."

Caitlyn rolls her eyes. "I was today years old when I learned that you're: A, a dad, and B, in love. I didn't even know Audrey existed."

"And how dare you call her a puck bunny. You really

think I'm going to bring some random girl to our childhood home? You think I'm introducing someone to Mom who I don't actually care about? When have you ever known me to do something like that?"

Caitlyn looks at me like she doesn't even know me. And it hits me then, like it should have so many times in the past... "Oh, you wouldn't know, would you? Because you've never taken the time to get to know me. Instead, you resented that you had to take care of me so much when I was a little kid who'd just lost a parent—"

"I'd just lost a parent, too, Drew. And I didn't even get a chance to grieve because, suddenly, I had all these additional responsibilities, like taking care of you and Missy every time Mom picked up a shift at the diner down the street after teaching all day. I didn't just lose my dad, I lost my childhood."

Oh, so we're finally talking about this, I guess.

"I get that *now*," I tell her. I'd always thought she resented having to take care of me; I never really thought about what she lost in the process. "But I was a little kid. I didn't have the emotional maturity to understand all of that. All I had was one less parent and a sister who suddenly hated me. And God forbid I actually be good at hockey—the thing I loved more than anything—and you did nothing but mock me for it and tell me it was a waste of time and money. It was like you hated me."

"I didn't hate *you*." Her eyes are sad, her lips are turned down at the corners, and I've never felt our seven-year age difference more than I do right now. "I hated that Mom had to keep spending money she didn't have so that you could play, while Missy and I had to go without things we wanted because you and hockey always took priority. I hated that I couldn't pursue the things I was interested in during high school, because I had to be available to take you to hockey practice. Did you ever wonder why I stopped playing basketball, the thing that *I* loved?"

"I thought you got cut?"

"No. I couldn't play because the varsity games were at night, and I needed to be around in case Mom needed me to help with you or Missy."

"Did Mom ask you to quit basketball?"

"No, but it needed to happen. I couldn't be in two places at once."

"But by your junior year, Missy was a freshman, and I would have been in, like, fourth grade. Missy could have watched me if Mom picked up a night shift."

"Missy wasn't old enough to drive you to your practices. Plus, she had cheerleading practice almost every night."

"I'm sorry you gave all that up," I tell her. I'm still not sure if she really needed to make that sacrifice, or if it's part of her martyr complex, but it's what she thought she needed to do for me and Missy.

"Someone had to get you to hockey." She rolls her eyes.

"Why didn't you talk to Mom about this when it was happening?"

"I did! She said hockey would pay off in the long run."

Of course she did. Mom has always been my biggest champion, willing to support me and stand up for me, no matter what. "Well, it did, didn't it?"

"*For you.*"

I bite my tongue so hard I taste blood. I will not let her bait me into this argument. I'm not doing all of this for my mom because I want credit, and that's how it will seem if I explain exactly how my success benefits our whole family.

When I don't reply, Caitlyn says, "Plus, thanks to hockey, you're never around."

"I literally moved back to Boston to help out, so *you* could go back to school to become a nurse practitioner. I spent all summer with Mom, but just like you and Missy, I need to show up for work now that the season has started, and my job requires that I travel. But when I'm not traveling, I'm around plenty."

"Yeah, well, for all the times you're not here, someone has to be around to help her." Caitlyn smothers Mom, then makes her feel guilty for all the time she spends here.

"Mom needs help, not hovering. And she doesn't need someone here 24/7. She will eventually, but not yet. How would you feel if Mom or Missy or I were *always* in your house, trying to be helpful, but making you feel bad about how much we were giving up to help?"

"I don't make Mom feel bad about helping her out!"

"Like you didn't make me feel bad when I was growing up?" I fold my arms across my chest and lean back against the door, and that's when I notice the photo album sitting open on the couch.

I can picture my mom sitting in here with Audrey, showing her pictures of me when I was younger. And there's no way Mom could miss how much Graham looks like I did at that age. I don't know why it didn't occur to me how obvious it would be to her? There's zero chance she didn't figure it out, and I wonder how she's feeling about this, and if Audrey knows that Mom knows?

"Are you telling me that Mom's been complaining that

I'm around too much?" Caitlyn asks the question begrudgingly, clearly upset at the idea that her help isn't appreciated.

"Nope, she's never said that. But I am telling you that if you ever really paid attention to her and how she's feeling, you'd know that she doesn't always need *or want* someone helping her. Let her do the things she can still do by herself, while she can still do them."

Caitlyn looks away, her face full of sadness. "There's nothing I can do to make her better. The only thing I can do is make her comfortable."

"Maybe try waiting until she asks for help, then, instead of always assuming she wants it."

"How do you even know this is how she's feeling?"

"Because I pay attention." I'm so tempted to suggest that she might want to try it if she's going to be a nurse practitioner, since listening to the patient seems like an important part of that job. But it would be a shitty thing to say to her when she just expressed the slightest amount of vulnerability, so I hold my tongue. "I need to go find Audrey and Graham."

"I still can't believe you're a dad." She shakes her head, sounding a bit in awe. It's a nice change from her normal caustic tone, so I keep my reply light as well.

"Yep, took me by surprise too."

I leave the family room, feeling like Caitlyn and I just made a little progress in our relationship. We didn't solve anything, but something about airing our grievances seems to have left us both a bit lighter.

I head down the hall to the small front living room, where my mom sits alone on the couch. "Where's Audrey?"

"She left in quite a rush. Did you really tell Caitlyn that

Audrey was the mother of your child and your future wife, or did I mishear you while I was eavesdropping?"

I can't tell how my mom is feeling about any of this, and I hate that—the way she sometimes seems just like herself and other times her expression is distant or vacant. Right now, though, I think she might be amused?

"Yeah, that's really what I said."

"Doesn't seem like she took it that well." A small smile plays on her lips, so I know she's teasing me.

"I know. I should never have blurted any of that out without at least talking to her about it first. Did Graham hear?"

"No, he was 'reading'"—she uses air quotes around the word—"to me, so he wasn't paying attention."

"You just found out you have another grandson, and you don't seem surprised by this information?" I don't ask if she's happy about this, because I want to let her express her own emotions.

"He's the spitting image of you when you were that age. So either you expected me to figure it out, or you didn't really think it through before bringing him over."

I take a seat on the chair that sits catty corner to the couch. "It didn't occur to me until I saw the photo album sitting out in the family room."

"I'm glad you brought him over. Would have liked it better if you'd told me ahead of time, but figuring it out on my own was its own kind of victory, I guess."

"We haven't told him yet."

"Yeah, Audrey mentioned that. So, how did this happen?"

"There's only one way it *can* happen, Mom." I give her a playful wink.

"I know there's no way you knew this whole time and kept it from me, so I guess my question really is: why didn't you know?"

I tell her the briefest version of the story possible, and she shakes her head, a small smile playing on her lips. "Your agent's little sister? You could find trouble inside a paper bag." It's something she said to me all the time growing up, and in some ways, I guess that's followed me into adulthood.

"I guess so."

"So before you opened your big mouth to Caitlyn, did Audrey have any idea you plan on marrying her…after only a few weeks back in her life?"

"Probably not. I initially told her that I had too much on my plate, and couldn't do a relationship. But every minute I spend with her, I'm more and more sure we're meant to be together." I glance out at the driveway and am disappointed that she's not sitting there in her SUV waiting for me.

"Drew, do you *love* her?"

The word catches me off guard. "I mean…" I don't know how to answer that question. It feels too early in our relationship to even ask it.

"Then *why in the world* would you announce that you're going to marry her?" Mom's voice is so exasperated I feel like I'm a little kid again.

"Because she's all I can think of, day in and day out. If I'm not playing hockey, I'm pretty much thinking about her— texting her, calling her, trying to find reasons to go see her. I want to be with her all the time."

"That's the infatuation stage of *any* new relationship, Drew. It's not the basis of marriage. You can't commit to a lifetime with someone based on that infatuation because, eventually, it will fade. There are a lot of tough times in life and in a marriage, and if anything less than love is at the foundation of the relationship, things will eventually start collapsing."

"I don't know what to do, then."

"Sure, you do," Mom says as she pulls a blanket off the back of the couch and spreads it across her lap. "You show her you're the type of person worth building that foundation with."

"C'mon, Audrey, answer the damn phone," I curse and bang my hand on the steering wheel. After Ubering back to my house, I hopped in my Jeep and headed to her. I've called her about ten times as I've driven from the Back Bay to the South End. Now I'm pulling onto her street, and she's still not answering.

I take the turn into the driveway that leads to the alley behind her house, and when I get to their back door, I see that her little SUV isn't there, just a big truck with *Our House* written across the side in white lettering. It must be Jules's truck, but it's not at all the vehicle I would have pictured her in.

I take Audrey's spot and barely pause to turn my car off before I'm out the door and up their back steps. Jules swings open the door before I even have a chance to knock, crosses her arms over her chest, leans against the doorframe, and says, "She isn't here, Drew."

"How do you know who I am?" I realize how ridiculous the question is as soon as it's out of my mouth. We've never officially met, but I've seen her at Jameson's and at the preseason game last week, so of course she's seen me too.

Jules just rolls her eyes. "Like I wouldn't know my own sister's baby daddy."

I hate that label and hate it even more when it's being applied to me. "Thanks for making me sound like nothing but a sperm donor."

"If it walks like a duck…"

"Hey, you do know that I didn't know about Graham, right?"

Her ordinarily angelic face goes hard, and her short fingernails dig into the fleece fabric of her sweatshirt where she squeezes her biceps. "I know that she called you twenty times to tell you, and if you'd valued her even the smallest amount as a person, as a friend, and as someone you'd slept with, you could have called her back."

I shove my fists into the front pockets of my jeans. "You're not wrong. And I'm trying to make it right."

"By freaking her the fuck out? If you knew anything about her, you'd know that she's the kind of person who needs time to adjust to big changes. Having you back in Boston, letting you meet Graham, having…whatever relationship you guys have…it's a huge amount of change within a few short weeks. You don't go and say you're going to marry her when you barely even know her!"

"Even if it's true?"

"Drew." It almost makes me laugh how much she sounds like Audrey when she says my name like that, all exasperated and sounding like she's about to reprimand me. "You can't know that after being back in her life for, what, three weeks?"

I shrug, because I have no idea how long it's been. It feels like just yesterday and forever ago that I saw her across the backyard. "All I know is that I want her in my life, and I want to be part of hers."

"Right, that's called dating, or even friendship." Jules looks at me like I'm missing a very important and obvious fact.

"Dating doesn't seem serious enough for our situation."

"Why?" Jules asks, right as the cold wind blows through the alley, kicking up leaves and banging together trash bins. Her whole body convulses with a shiver. She's the kind of tall and thin that means she probably gets cold easily. "Because you have a kid together?"

"Yeah. And because 'dating' is way too loose a term for what I want with her."

"Well, you may need to slow your roll a bit, because like I said, Audrey needs time to adjust to big changes. You want some advice?"

From the little Audrey's told me about her sister, I know there's no one in the world she's closer to. So if anyone can help me make this right, it's Jules. "Sure."

"Go home. Let her come to terms with this on her own."

That was not the advice I was hoping for.

"She can have until she gets home to come to terms with it, and then I want to talk to her. I'll wait for her in my car."

"That's a mistake," Jules says as she steps back into the kitchen and grabs the edge of the door. "But it's yours to make."

Chapter Twenty-Eight

DREW

It's only hours later—after I've had dinner delivered and eaten it in my car, called my mom to check on her, fielded texts from some of my teammates who are meeting up for beers, and watched an entire movie on my phone—that it occurs to me that Jules might have told Audrey I was waiting in my car. Audrey could just as easily have parked elsewhere and gone in the front door instead, where I would never have seen her.

Have I been sitting out here like a fool, and she's been inside this whole time?

I decide to test the theory, so I open my Jeep door and shut it quietly, then walk up the back steps. The door only has a transom window, but by standing on my tiptoes, I'm able to see through it, and sure enough, Audrey is sitting cross-legged on the couch, typing away on her laptop.

When my fist meets the door for a few quick knocks, she practically levitates out of her seat. Then she turns, and the look of annoyance on her face transforms to one of shock when she catches sight of me peering at her through the window.

She stands there, staring at me. Her face conveys the message that she wants me to leave, but when she mouths, "Go away," there's no doubt. I raise my hand like I'm going to knock on the window, and she shakes her head back and forth as she starts walking toward the door.

She cracks the door open, then plants her leg behind it like she's trying to stop me from coming in. As much as I want to push that door open and pull her into my arms, I know that's not what she wants right now.

"Talk to me, Audrey."

"I'm not ready to talk about this."

I take a deep breath through my nose, feeling my nostrils flare and my jaw tick as I grind my teeth together.

"I never want to force you to do anything you're not comfortable with. But..." I take another deep breath. "I'm kind of going crazy worrying about how badly I screwed things up. I didn't mean to spook you. I just...I know how strong my feelings are for you, and I don't want to hide them like I did when we were in college. I don't want you to doubt how I feel. I don't want you to question whether I'm in this." I think back to this afternoon, to how being inside her knocked my whole world off its axis. I've never been more sure of anything in my life.

"Okay..." The word is tentative. She chews on her lower lip and her hand immediately tracks to the necklace I notice she wears every day, her fingers pulling the small gold disk between them.

"You don't have to be in the same place I am with your

feelings," I tell her. "I know these last few weeks have been a lot, and you're probably still processing how you feel about this, and I'm fine with that. But Audrey"—I reach out, taking her free hand in mine—"I need to know what you want me to do about these feelings? Should I be hiding them from you, because you're not ready to know about them? I'm pretty sure that, back in college, not talking about our feelings was part of what led us into this mess in the first place."

"What I want you to do, Drew, is stop and fucking think for a moment instead of acting impulsively all the time. We talked about me not being ready to tell your family about Graham, and then you went and blurted it out to Caitlyn like we hadn't just had that conversation. Then, you *knew* I wasn't ready to talk about what just happened—Jules *told* you—and instead of going home and giving me space, you camped out in your car and waited for me to come home so you could corner me into this conversation. It's cute that you can just put your life on hold, sitting in your car for hours, eating takeout and watching a movie, just because suddenly you have these feelings that you don't know what to do with. But that's not my life. I don't get to put my life on hold like that to figure things out."

Shit. Jules was right. I stayed because I felt desperate to fix the situation right in the moment, even though things may have been better if we'd both taken a night to process. She told me Audrey needed time to adjust to the way things are changing, and I kept pushing.

"I don't want you to put your life on hold; I want you to *invite* me into it."

"Well, forcing your way in when I'm still trying to make sense of all of this isn't the right approach." Her voice has a high-pitched quality that seems tinged with panic. "How can you be so sure you want a lifetime with me when we've never even been on a date? We haven't even talked about what's happening between us. You said you couldn't do a relationship, and then you told me you were never going to get tired of being with me. You're sending huge mixed signals! And then you go and proclaim that you're going to marry me in front of your sister, when you've never said anything even remotely like that to me? How the hell did you get here from there?"

"I don't know, it just happened."

Her lips twist at the corner in a look of uncertainty, and then she sighs. "That's kind of your whole personality, right?"

All of the noise of city life recedes as I block out everything around me—a skill I'm usually only able to employ while playing hockey—to focus on those words and the underlying current of sarcasm lacing its way through them.

That's kind of your whole personality... What does that even mean?

"Are you saying that '*I don't know, it just happened*' is my whole personality?" When a slight tilt of her head and a raised eyebrow are her only response, I continue. "Like you don't think that I think things through before I do them? And don't take responsibility for my actions?"

She looks away, but her fingers continue working the gold disk on her necklace. I wish I could see what was on that thing. "Can we just...maybe forget I said that?"

I run my hand across the brim of my Rebels hat, pulling it down on my forehead. I can't remember the last time I was nervous around a woman, but maybe what I'm feeling isn't nerves—it's anxiety. I hate that all I can think about in this moment is that her low opinion of me and my past could prevent us from having a future.

"It's not exactly the kind of thing one forgets."

"Drew." Instead of the normal reprimand, my name comes off her lips like a plea.

"Yes?"

"Please, try to see this whole situation from my perspective. For years, I watched as your hockey career took off, and the photos of you at parties and restaurant openings and on dates popped up in the media. The wild nights out with the guys, the women who followed you around, the antics between you and your teammates, all the fights and the time in the penalty box…it doesn't exactly scream 'reliable guy.'"

I try to see it through her eyes: the years of partying in Vancouver, and then the years of fighting in Colorado. It occurs to me that I never told her what happened there, why things went sideways between me and my teammates, and how it affected my game and my personal life. She doesn't know how often I came home to Boston to see my family. She doesn't know it's been years since I had the type of wild party night she's imagining. Because I haven't told her. It's like my mom said…I need to *show* her.

Sure, I've done a couple of small things, like taking care of her when she's sick, or taking her and Graham out for cookies. But she doesn't actually know that I'm capable of being the person she needs me to be. She doesn't see what we could build together.

"If your picture of who I am now is based on who I was years ago, you're not giving me a fair chance. I'm not expecting you to be the twenty-one-year-old I first flirted with, or any iteration of yourself except who you are right now, in this moment. That's all."

"This isn't about not understanding who you are now, Drew." She crosses her arms and sighs in frustration. "But you just found out you had a kid, for Christ's sake! We haven't even told Graham that you're his dad yet. We have no idea how he's going to react to that, or what impact it'll have on him and on us. So yeah, the chemistry between us is amazing, but that doesn't mean we need to play house right away. It's like suddenly, out of the blue, you want the wife and the kid to come home to."

"No, it's like suddenly I want *you and Graham*. You're not some faceless family in some domestic fantasy I'm living in." How do I explain this to her? "I feel like…when you're not around, I can't breathe…and when you are, I can."

"There're more than your feelings that we need to consider here, Drew. Like Graham and what he wants. Plus, a relationship, especially a marriage, needs to be based on more than just wanting to be with the other person."

As she pauses to take a breath, I consider how similar her words are to my mom's earlier.

"You've only seen the fun times: the hockey practices where you get to skate with Graham, taking him out for cookies afterward, or throwing the football around in your mom's backyard. You haven't lived through a tantrum, or the changing tastes of a five-year old who never wants to eat what you make for dinner, or the heartbreak when a friend tells him he doesn't want to be his friend anymore. You call when you're on the road, and stop by my office when you're in town so you can give me amazing orgasms, but you haven't had to be part of all the mundane shit, like grocery shopping and folding laundry. Real family life is so much more complex, and also less exciting, than the moments you've participated in. You don't decide you want to start a family with someone just because you've seen a couple clips from the highlight reel."

I take in her pink cheeks and the way her body is practically vibrating with all her emotions. "You're right."

"Being part of my and Graham's life means seeing the messy parts too. And it means sticking around when things get ugly."

"I know. I hear everything you're saying." It's in this moment that I have absolute clarity about what I want: Audrey and Graham. I didn't think I was ready for a serious relationship, or for a kid. But now that I've gotten a taste of what that could be like, now that the possibility of Audrey and Graham being part of my life is right in front of me, I'm terrified of losing them.

"So, where do we go from here?" she asks, her body relaxing as she lets go of some of the frustration from a few moments before.

"Well, since I haven't seen all this *real family life* you're talking about, should I move in right now, or wait until tomorrow?"

Her eyes widen, and then I can tell she realizes I'm joking. The laugh that bursts out of her is exactly what I was hoping for, but then her face grows serious again, and she says, "It's not something to joke about."

"I know, I just needed to see you smile. For real, though, let me prove to you that you and Graham are what I really want, and that I deserve you both. Let me be here for you in the good times, and through all the mundane shit, and when things get hard."

I watch her trying not to let down her guard, trying to hold everything in. Finally, she says, "I don't think you're ready for all that."

I've never been more ready for anything in my life. "I look forward to proving you wrong."

"Sure," she says quietly as she looks up at the sky. "Goodnight, Drew."

She closes the door slowly, like she thinks I'm going to stop her. But I realize she needs time to process all of this, and I need time to figure out my game plan. Because there's no way I'm not giving this relationship everything I've got.

Chapter Twenty-Nine

AUDREY

When I push open the door from the basement into our kitchen, Jules spins around in surprise, almost spilling her bowl of soup down the front of the *Our House* sweatshirt she's wearing with her dirty work jeans. She comes home a bit early on Wednesdays so I can make it to my dance class.

She takes one look at my face, and asks, "What's wrong?"

I'd been downstairs printing the revisions for the Livingston plans before leaving for my class, but walking up those basement stairs has all kinds of memories washing through me.

I bite my lower lip, which I know is a nervous habit, but I still can't seem to stop myself. "Long story."

She glances over at Graham, who's engrossed in an episode of his favorite show that I told him he could watch after he finished his dinner while I changed for dance. She looks back at me and points to the kitchen.

I follow her in there, but with our open floor plan, it's practically a part of the living room and not far from Graham. "What's going on?" she whispers. "Why are you being weird?"

"I'm not being weird. I just..." *am not any good at lying!* Why can't I think of anything to say to finish that sentence?

"What the hell, Audrey? You're scaring me." Jules's voice is approaching a normal speaking level.

"Keep your voice down," I hiss, glancing over at Graham, but he's entirely focused on Spiderman. When I glance back at her, she's set her soup on the counter and folded her arms across her chest.

"Then tell me what's going on, so I don't have to make a big deal out of it." She narrows her eyes at me.

"Fine, so those basement stairs hold...certain memories... of..."

"Oh my God," she groans. "Spit it out."

"A certain person, whose name I'm not going to say right now"—my eyes track over to Graham so she'll understand why—"and I...kind of..."

Jules snorts out a laugh, then drops her voice to a whisper. "Did you and Drew *do it* on those stairs?"

I can't tell if she's horrified or delighted.

"Sort of."

"How do you *sort of* have S-E-X with the father of your kid?" she whispers.

"I meant we were sort of on the steps. It was more like... up against the wall...on the landing at the bottom of the stairs?"

"You sure?" Her light brown eyebrows scrunch down toward her gray eyes. "Because you seem confused."

"Don't be an asshole. You know I hate talking about this stuff." It does make me wonder, though, why I had absolutely no issue keeping up with Drew's dirty talk on the phone that night. Something about him brings that out in me, I guess.

"Well, don't be such a prude and I won't have to be an asshole about it. So why can't you even walk down the stairs now?"

I can't think about yesterday without picturing it happening all over again—images of the way he kissed me like he owned me, how he held my ass as he drove himself into me, the deliciously full feeling of him sliding against my inner walls, the way my nipples dragged against his chest as his body moved... Heat flashes through me, and my mouth parts with a breathy sigh, and I can feel the dampness pooling against my underwear.

"Holy shit," Jules laughs as she watches me. "*This* is what happens when you think about it? Must have been some damn good sex."

"You have no idea," I say, and then when I see the look that flashes across her face, I instantly regret it.

"Truth."

I didn't mean it literally, but that's how she took it.

"Jules..." I say, starting to apologize, but she raises her hand to cut me off.

"Time to say goodnight to your mom, Graham!" she all but yells, as I give her my most apologetic look.

Graham jumps off the couch and comes running into the kitchen to give me hugs and kisses goodnight. As he does any night I go out, he makes me promise that I'll come give him more kisses when I get home—which I always do, and he always sleeps through.

"I won't be out late," I tell Jules when Graham heads back to the couch to finish his show. She nods in response, but she's doing that thing she sometimes does where she gets quiet and withdrawn. I can tell by the way she's tugging on the gold disk of her necklace and staring blankly out the window into the darkness that she isn't ready to talk. It's so opposite of her normal hold-nothing-back personality that it used to scare me when she got like this, but eventually I accepted that this is how she deals with her feelings. There's no point in pushing her when she's like this. I'll have to wait for her to be ready to talk.

―――

"Oh good, you're still alive." Danika's voice cuts through the music that's pumping throughout the studio, and I have to scan the dark space lit only by purple spotlights to find her. She's at the mobile cart that contains the sound system near the far wall.

"Yep, just barely survived," I call out. I head toward the long wall at the back of the room where we keep our bags and drop to the floor to remove my shoes and street clothes. I leave my sweatpants on, as I'll want them while we warm up, but I toss my sneakers and sweatshirt into my bag. And then Danika's platform boots appear right next to me, like they did last week when I'd crumpled to the floor. I'm still laughing at how I was half-way dying on the floor at her feet and she still told me, "this ain't no sleepover."

"I kept searching the obituaries, but your name wasn't there, so I figured you were okay," she says.

My laughter escapes so fast it comes out more like a cough. "Thank you for your concern."

"You recovered enough for this?" she asks.

I stand, and even if she wasn't wearing 7-inch platform boots, I'd still be looking up at her. "I think so."

"Good, because if whatever you had last week didn't kill you, tonight's workout probably will."

I tilt my chin up, acknowledging the challenge. "Looking forward to it."

And I am, because I am finally feeling recovered enough from my illness to do this. And even when it kicks my ass, pole dancing still makes me feel strong and badass like nothing else can. A few months ago when I started, I could barely hold myself up on the bar. Now I can do some impressive stuff, even if it does come with some bumps and bruises.

So when Danika puts her headset on, changes the music to something slower, and starts calling out directions, I approach the pole eagerly. I need to channel my inner-badass so I can deal with the complicated emotions I'm having about Drew and our relationship.

An hour later, I'm regretting all my life choices, but most especially whatever stupid bravado led me to think I could do this. Danika wasn't kidding about this workout being a killer. Tomorrow, the inside of my right thigh is going to be covered in bruises to match the ones already springing up on my left forearm from where it connected with the pole when my hand missed it. But you know what? I still did it—even though it was hard and, at times, painful. And that's exactly why I leave every week feeling so good about myself, knowing that I can overcome difficulty and pain and still come out on top.

"Good work today, ladies," Danika says. "And I expect you to practice at home before next week, because if you thought this was hard, you better prepare yourselves for seven days from now. It'll be easier if you practice what we learned today."

I groan internally, because there's no way I can practice at home unless I get a pole, and no way I could hide that from Jules. I've thought about installing one of the temporary ones in the basement playroom and claiming that it's a climbing pole for Graham, but I feel like she'd see right through that or catch me practicing on it.

I don't know what it is that prevents me from telling her about these classes—we really do tell each other everything—but for reasons I can't quite explain, this is something that I want to keep to myself.

Maybe I'm just waiting until I'm really good at it before I share, or maybe it's because I'm still buying into the stigma that pole dancing is just for strippers and, by my very nature, I'm a good girl who never does anything risqué. Well, except for the phone sex the other night, and actual sex in my office yesterday. But as long as I'm not around Drew, I'm the queen of good decisions.

I'm still pondering whether I should just break down and tell Jules about the class so that I can actually practice at home, when I walk out of the studio and am hit full-force by the chilly night air. The middle of October has brought unseasonably cold nighttime temperatures, and I rush toward the small parking lot two buildings down. I'm not paying attention to anyone around me, so I almost don't notice my name being called. It probably wouldn't have even registered if that same voice hadn't been saying my name, along with a lot of other nonsensical things, like how he couldn't live without me while he climaxed inside me yesterday.

I stop, my whole body going rigid, as I stand rooted on the sidewalk. *Shit.* As much as I'm conflicted about our situation, I crave Drew in a way I never have anyone else. I want to see him. I want him near me. But not here. Not steps from the dance studio with its bright neon sign.

I hear his soft footfalls behind me and am not surprised at all when his large hand clasps my shoulder. I want to melt right back into him, but my body seems to have a case of rigor mortis from the shock. What are the chances that he'd happen to be here, on the same city block, the minute I'm walking out of my class?

"Hey, where are you rushing off to?" he asks as he turns me to face him.

"I have to get home to Graham. Jules is watching him for me while I...run errands." I pause just long enough before saying "run errands" that I know it sounds like I was thinking something up.

Drew's eyes slide down my body, and my skin reacts as if he's sliding his hands along every curve, goosebumps following the path of his gaze as he takes in my sweats and sweatshirt, then my high-top sneakers. His eyes track right back up to my face, no doubt noticing how sweaty I am, my hair slicked back into a now-damp ponytail. "Errands, huh?"

"Yep." I use my elbow to push my bag behind my back, as if he won't notice the wide canvas straps over my shoulder.

"Are you sure"—his gaze flicks back to the neon *City Pole*

sign hanging above the door I just walked out of—"you weren't at your weekly dance class?"

Even the cold wind that whips through at that moment can't stop the full-on flush that creeps across my face. "I don't know what you're talking about," I say, even though I'm pretty sure he just watched me walk out of there, and the sign—with its electric blue pole and red high heel—leaves no room for interpretation.

He gives me his trademark smirk as his eyes continue to assess me. "I think you do. And I think you want to tell me about it, but you're not sure how I'll react."

"I think I just want you to mind your own business." I shove my hands into the pockets of my hoodie, wishing I could just melt into the sidewalk so we didn't have to have this conversation.

He steps in so close that I have to tilt my head up to see him. "You *are* my business, Audrey. And the sooner you accept that, the sooner we can move forward here."

I open my mouth to respond, but pause when I hear, "Jenkins," yelled at the top of some guy's lungs from behind me.

"Fuck," he mutters.

"What's wrong?" I ask, knowing this is about to get awkward.

"It's Colt. I'm meeting him for dinner."

"Shit." The word comes out on an exhale, and I look over my shoulder to see Colt barreling toward us. "Hey, Colt!" I call out, plastering a smile across my face and hoping that acting like my brother's best friend seeing me and Drew together isn't a big deal. And then I realize that it isn't, because I already told Jameson, who probably told Colt.

Colt pauses mid-step, clearly surprised to see me talking to Drew on the street. Then his face goes hard as he looks at Drew. Okay, so Jameson hasn't told him.

"Audrey," he says with a small nod as he stops next to us.

"Good to see you. Okay, gotta run. Jules is at home with Graham, and I told her I'd be back as soon as I finished my errands."

Colt's lips press together like he's trying to hide a smirk. "Tell her I said hi."

"Why? You trying to piss her off?" Jules and Colt have a tumultuous relationship, where he's always egging her on, trying to get a rise out of her. It was funny when she was a kid, but now it just annoys her, and by extension, everyone else.

"Always. We still doing Halloween, like usual? Or are we moving it to Jameson and Lauren's this year?"

"Hmmm, we haven't talked about it yet," I say, wondering why Jameson hasn't brought it up. Halloween is always the holiday he made the biggest deal out of. He loved to decorate the outside of our brownstone with enormous cobwebs and huge, fuzzy spiders. On the day itself, he'd usually stay home so he could sit on the front steps and pass out candy, while Jules and I took Graham out trick-or-treating.

Then a few years ago, Graham wanted to be Woody from *A Toy Story* for Halloween, and he insisted that Colt be Buzz Lightyear. Luckily, Colt's pretty much an overgrown kid and thought it was a great idea. And he's come trick-or-treating with us every year since.

"Okay," Colt says, "well, keep me posted." Then he turns to Drew. "You ready for dinner?"

"Yeah," he says, then glances at me. "Good seeing you."

"You too," I say, then head off down the street toward the parking lot, feeling like I dodged a bullet by not having to finish that conversation with Drew. For now.

And when I turn the corner, I glance over my shoulder, and Colt and Drew haven't moved an inch. Instead, they look like they're engaged in a pretty heated debate, which doesn't bode well for Drew if he's trying to build a good relationship with his new teammates.

Chapter Thirty

DREW

"Just let me explain when we get inside. It's cold as balls out here," I say to Colt when he finishes his inquisition about what part of 'stay away from Flynn's sisters' I didn't get.

"Never understood that phrase." He shakes his head, his sandy blonde hair blowing around in the breeze. "Are *your* balls cold? Because mine sure as hell aren't."

I snort out a laugh and shake my head. "Are these the ponderings that keep you up at night?" Colt's a good guy, but he can be kind of an oaf sometimes.

"Not exactly," he says, and starts walking toward the restaurant, which is only a few doors down from where I now know Audrey takes pole dancing classes. I can't fucking wait to hear more about that.

The restaurant is stuffy and warm when we come in from the cold, and I'm so busy taking off my jacket as the hostess leads us toward the back corner of the restaurant that I don't notice a table full of my teammates until we're right in front of them.

"What the hell are you all doing here?" I ask as I slide into the round booth next to my team captain.

"Colt said you needed relationship advice," Patrick Walsh says.

"Walshy seemed like the natural person to ask," Colt says when I glare at him. "Given that he's so happily married, he's making us all sick with how much he talks about his family." Walsh just smiles in response. His wife and kids are at every game, even the baby, and I've never known another player who is more into his family. So even though it annoys me that he opened his mouth about it, Colt was probably right about including Walsh in this conversation.

I'm about to flippantly ask if McCabe is here to give me relationship advice too. But then I remember he's my team captain and think better of it.

Impulse control…clearly still a developing skill. But I heard what Audrey said last night, and I'm going to work on being more intentional, both with my words and my actions.

"And everyone else?" I ask instead.

"I'm your fucking Captain, that's why I'm here," McCabe says. "I want to make sure that whatever's going on isn't going to fuck up your game."

"Dude, you have a baby at home. Could you just get one sentence out without swearing?" Walsh asks.

McCabe's legendary scowl crosses his face. "Fucking doubt it."

We all burst out laughing. Then Zach Reid adds, "I'm here because I've been in therapy for, like, a decade, so I'm a pro at dealing with emotions."

"Alright," I say. "But I wasn't planning on broadcasting this situation. Honestly, right now, the fewer people who know about it, the better."

"You didn't fucking get someone pregnant, did you?" McCabe asks.

When I pick up my water glass instead of answering right away, all heads swivel toward me. "It's kind of complicated."

"Nah," Colt says. "Either you did, or you didn't."

"I did, but—"

"Dude, you've only been back in Boston for, like, a month! How is this even possible? Or was this some chick in Colorado?" Zach asks.

From across the table, Walsh eyes me skeptically.

"First of all, she's not 'some chick.' So cut that shit out." I lift the water glass to my lips and take a sip, hoping that Colt doesn't lunge across the table and strangle me when I come clean. "There was a girl in college, and we got together right before I was drafted. I headed to Vancouver, and she didn't find out she was pregnant until after I was gone. I only discovered I'm a dad a few weeks ago."

"You. Fucking. Asshole." Each word comes out of Colt's mouth on an exhaled breath, low and deadly sounding. He's gripping the edge of the table with both hands, like he might flip it.

"I didn't know Audrey was pregnant," I say, holding my hands up in a gesture of surrender, "or I would have been there for her and Graham."

"Who's Audrey?" Zach asks.

"Flynn's little sister," McCabe says. Jameson isn't his agent, but he's been with the team for long enough that they probably played together at one point.

"Jameson Flynn?" Zach sounds worried. Jameson's got a reputation for ruthlessness, and I'm sure Zach is wondering what the fallout will be for me. When I nod, he asks, "Does he know?"

"He does now. Audrey initially didn't tell him, or anyone except for her sister, that I was the dad. But she told him, like, a week ago."

I can tell by the look on Colt's face that he's surprised Jameson knows, which means Jameson hasn't told him. And unless I'm reading too much into it, he looks a bit hurt not to be in the know.

"Why didn't she tell you?" Walsh asks.

"This is the part where I'm the asshole," I warn them, and Colt's eyes narrow. "She tried calling me, and I didn't call her back. She obviously could have told her brother and had him reach out to me about it, but she was afraid he'd ruin my career if he knew."

"Yep," Walsh agrees. "You're the asshole in that situation. So, how did you find out?"

I describe the scene at the fire a few weeks before.

"So you *were* watching her that night. It wasn't just my imagination!" Colt says, and I nod. "How is Audrey taking all this?"

"Well, that's the part I need advice on. Things between us are...actually really good. But she doesn't trust me to stick."

"To stick?" Walsh asks.

"Yeah. She's worried I'll leave her, either because Boston won't sign me again at the end of my contract, or just that I'll change my mind."

"There's not much you can do about the contract except

play to the best of your ability and show AJ that you're the kind of player she wants to keep around," McCabe says.

"And what kind of player is that?"

"Honest. Hardworking. Dependable." McCabe doesn't even have to think before listing these qualities off. "Your talent will continue to develop, but she also wants *good* men on this team."

"I can be all of those things."

"You *can be*, or you *are*?" McCabe's voice is no-nonsense, and I know that everything hinges on my answer.

"I'm honest and hardworking, and I'm working on being dependable."

He nods, and I assume that means my answer satisfies him. Colt's still eerily silent.

"So the part you *can* control," Walsh says, "is showing Audrey that you're committed to her and that nothing's going to change your mind."

"How do you know, in less than a month, that you're not going to change your mind?" Colt asks, and he sounds genuinely curious. It makes me wonder if there's never been anyone he's felt this way about.

"I'm not really sure how to explain it," I say, feeling a bit awkward getting all up in my feels with my teammates. But they're all looking at me like they want to know the answer to this question as well. "When I'm with her and Graham, everything feels right. I was really into her in college, but she hardly gave me the time of day. She had feelings I didn't know about, and same. It feels like we've just picked up right where we left off, only somehow, it's better. The chemistry is hotter than before, but I also legitimately just like spending time with her."

I think about coming to her house when she had cramps, and how relaxed I was when we were watching the movie and talking. Sure, it was great when things heated up, but that's not why I came over, and I was in no way expecting that to happen.

"Sounds legit," McCabe shrugs. "So what's the problem?"

"I accidentally told my sister, in front of Audrey, that Audrey was the mother of my child and my future wife."

"Shiiiiiiiit," Colt hisses out.

"Yeah, she stormed out of there so fast."

"What?" McCabe says. "I thought women loved shit like that?"

"We'd sort of agreed we weren't going to tell my family about Graham yet. And she thinks that my feelings for her are just because everything between us is new and the shine hasn't worn off. I don't know how to change her mind."

"That's easy," Colt says. "You just gotta shower her with gifts so she knows you're always thinking about her."

"And show up for her whenever she needs you," McCabe says. "But, like, not so much she thinks you're a stalker."

"If she likes you," Zach says, "she's going to want to spend time with you. Just don't smother her."

Walsh shakes his head. "You guys are idiots."

"Oh yeah, family man? Then do share all your wisdom," Colt mocks.

"No two women are alike, so you can't treat her like she's anyone else. You need to know what *she* wants out of a relationship." Walsh looks at me, pausing until I meet his eyes. "She's a single mom, and she's been doing this by herself for years. So either she's happy on her own, or she wants a partner and hasn't found the right person yet. Which is it?"

"Ugh…"

"If you don't even know what she wants, how can you be the person she needs you to be?" he asks me.

"Well, shit," Colt mutters. "Walshy's dropping some truth bombs tonight."

"She wants a partner," I say more confidently. "Someone who can share the load of parenting. But she also wants to be seen as more than someone's mom."

"You mean she wants sex," McCabe says, his voice certain.

"I think she wants to feel desired," I clarify.

"Are you making her feel that way?" Colt all but growls.

"I know she's like a little sister to you, so I'm just going to leave it at: I'm giving her what she needs in that department."

His jaw ticks as he grinds his teeth together, but he looks away.

"Okay, so the sexual part of the relationship is taken care of," Walsh says. "So how are you showing up for her in other ways? How are you showing her that you're dependable—the kind of guy she can build a life with?"

I tell them about volunteering with Graham's team and taking them out for cookies afterward, coming over when she didn't feel good, and taking her to the pharmacy when she was sick.

"Oh good." Walsh rolls his eyes when I'm done. "So you've done, like, three nice things for her, when it's convenient for you, in at least as many weeks? Stellar start, dude."

"I've also been on the road and sick myself in that time." I don't mention my mom and the time I'm spending with her because then I'd have to explain that situation, and I don't want to derail the conversation. I think Walsh can legitimately offer me some good advice when it comes to Audrey.

"When you're married, you don't just get to show up when you feel like it. You're there together every day. And if it's a good relationship"—Walsh looks at Zach—"no one feels smothered."

"Could have fooled me," he mutters as he spins his Rebels cap backward, using both hands to position the bill behind his head.

"Sounds like there's a story there," Colt says.

"We're here to dissect Drew's love life, not mine," Zach grumbles. I sense that, unlike Colt, he's the type of person who likes to keep the details of his private life private.

"Okay, if you yahoos are done talking about how to *not* have a relationship, maybe we can talk about how to build a good relationship here?"

Everyone stares back at him.

"So," Walsh continues, "I think half the issue is that you're too used to pulling women based on your good looks and the fact that you're a hockey player. You don't know what it means to actually *work* for a woman's attention."

I look at Walsh, who is not even close to the best-looking guy on the team, but has an insanely hot wife who seems incredibly happy, and beautiful children.

"You need to show her that you'll be there for her, no matter what," he continues. "And, if you ask me, the secret to a solid relationship is that you need to complement each other. Whatever she's lacking or whatever her weaknesses, you gotta make up for those. And same for her. You gotta balance each other out."

I consider what he's saying, trying to imagine how I could be that person for Audrey. I think about how hard she's worked to get where she is, what a wonderful mom she is to Graham, how close she is to her siblings.

"What if she doesn't have weaknesses?" I ask.

"We all have weaknesses," Zach says. "And if she isn't showing you hers, she doesn't trust you."

"I think we already established that," I mutter, as the rest of my teammates say, "Damnnnnn."

"So there's your answer, then." Walsh looks at me like it's so obvious.

"What's my answer?"

"Show up for her. Give her reasons to trust you, to reveal her weaknesses so you can make up for them. Be the one to show her what unconditional love looks like."

Chapter Thirty-One

AUDREY

The way Drew practically swaggers off the ice at the end of Graham's hockey practice has me clenching my thighs together.

For the last hour and a half, I've sat in these stands, trying not to marvel at how a two-hundred-pound man who's over six feet tall can look so fucking graceful on thin blades gliding across the ice. He shouldn't be able to move like that —to pivot all that weight and speed so quickly, to stretch and bend like his body is elastic, or handle a tiny puck with enough finesse that he can slap it into whatever corner of the goal he claims he's sending it to.

I've always enjoyed hockey, but watching Drew play is something else. And watching him share his love of the sport as he shows our kid how to play is a next-level turn-on.

Drew's hand is on Graham's shoulder as they step off the ice, then Graham looks up at Drew and says something. Drew nods, then peels off toward his bag. Jameson follows him, and the two chat as they take off their skates. I'm trying to judge if the conversation is more friendly than the last time I saw them together, but my attention is drawn back to Graham as he rushes up to me.

"Mom," he whisper-hisses, loud enough for the whole rink to hear.

"Yeah, Bud?" I take the sweaty helmet he hands me and drop it into his unzipped bag.

"Drew has a surprise for me. He said he wants to give it to me before tomorrow night's game. We're going to that, right?"

"The home opener? Yeah, definitely." Now that Graham's so into hockey, I'm super thankful that Jameson got us season tickets.

"So can he give it to me tonight?" Graham asks as he takes off his jersey and starts unstrapping his pads.

"Sure, I guess so."

"Can we meet him outside? He said he left it in his car because he didn't want anyone else to see and get jealous."

I glance around and notice how many pairs of eyes are trained on Jameson and Drew. The moms who used to show up for these freezing cold practices in sweats suddenly look like they're ready to go out for the night—full faces of makeup and everything. I noticed the shift when Jameson started coaching, but it's amplified now that Drew is here too. Even the dads are looking at the former and current NHL players like they're a tad starstruck.

"Alright," I say as I continue packing away each piece of Graham's gear as he strips it off. Drew ambles over as Graham takes off his skates, and even though I'm standing on the first elevated level of seats, I still have to tilt my head up a bit to look him in the eye.

"Hey." How does one word manage to carry so much meaning? Or am I imagining the heat behind the word, and the effort it's taking to hold his emotion in?

A few nights ago, he swore he was going to prove to me he was ready for a relationship, and last night when I saw him outside the dance studio, I could have burned up with the heated look in his eyes. It's impossible to tell if his feelings for me are purely sexual, or if there's truly more there, because whenever I'm around him, I, too, can't resist the pull of attraction. But does that mean that's all there is? Figuring out my feelings for him, and his for me, is fucking confusing.

"Hey," I reply, but the word comes out breathy and full of the longing I'm feeling now that he's standing in front of me.

He leans in a bit closer, and I can picture everyone in the rink staring at us. I'm almost positive that's what is happening behind me. "Meet me at my Jeep?"

"Sure," I say, and he gives me a satisfied smile as he turns to leave. It has me picturing the way he looked at me when we had sex on the stairs the other day.

"Mom?" Graham asks right as Drew walks away and my brother walks up. "Why do you have that funny look on your face?" He asks the question so earnestly that Jameson coughs out a laugh. After watching my and Drew's interaction, I'm sure he knows exactly what's up.

"Yeah, Audrey," Jameson says, his voice unusually playful. "Why's your face all flushed?"

"It's not."

"Does your mom always look like this when she talks to

Drew?" he asks Graham. Okay, now I may actually throttle him.

"I don't know," Graham says with a tilt of his head. "Maybe?"

"Do you think she has a little crush on him?" Jameson asks.

I think back to how much Jules and I teased him when he first reconnected with Lauren, back when he was trying to pretend like he didn't have feelings for her, but doing things like secretly remodeling her house, connecting her with Alessandra Jones and the Rebels, and finding her the perfect nanny for her kids so she could go back to work, all the while letting her believe he wasn't involved.

And knowing how much shit we gave him through that is the only thing that saves me from strangling him right now.

"So, we need to get going," I say to no one in particular. Graham reaches down to lift his hockey bag onto his shoulder, and I give Jameson my best death glare. He just smirks in response. "Are we doing Halloween this year?" I ask, hoping that I can stem the tide of our previous conversation by bringing up his favorite holiday.

"Ugh, yeah. Lauren and I have been meaning to talk to you about that," he says. "Can we do it at our house this year? There are some other neighborhood kids that want the girls to trick-or-treat with them."

Graham looks up at me, and for a moment, I panic, thinking he'll want to trick-or-treat from our house, because it's what we've always done, and that he'll be disappointed if his uncle, aunt, and cousins aren't there. But his eyes get big and hopeful, and he says, "Can we?"

"Sure." We chat preliminary plans as we walk out of the

rink, and when we step outside, Jameson takes one look at Drew, who's leaning casually against the front of his Jeep and clearly waiting for us, and says quietly, "He better be treating you right."

I give him a nod, but don't trust myself to talk about this in front of Graham yet.

Jameson says, "I'll wait for Graham at my car, okay?" and I tell him I'll bring him right over. Graham's spending the night at their house again. There's no school tomorrow due to a faculty professional development day, so he'll stay with the twins and their nanny.

Jameson heads toward his car, and I walk over to Drew while Graham runs ahead, his bag banging against him until I'm half-convinced he's going to fall over. Drew squats down on his heels and I try not to notice the curve of his muscular thighs, but they're the size of tree trunks and hard to miss. The two of them exchange a few words that I can't hear, and when I get over to them, Drew takes Graham's bag from his shoulder and sets it on the ground, then opens the front side door of his Jeep, leans across to the far side of the car, and grabs something.

He hands Graham a neatly folded piece of fabric, and when our son shakes it open, it's a small version of Drew's jersey. The Rebels logo is on the front, and when Graham turns it around to look at the back, JENKINS is clearly spelled out above the number 12.

"Is this for me to wear to the game tomorrow?" Graham asks, the excitement making his voice shake. I feel like if I were to speak right now, my voice would shake for an entirely different reason.

Drew's eyes flick to mine, watching me swallow down my

emotions, then move back to Graham. "Yeah, if you want to wear it. But if you want to keep wearing your uncle Jameson's," he says, and I didn't realize he'd noticed that detail at the pre-season game we were at, "that's okay. I just thought you might want one from me, too."

"I'm going to put it on right now!"

As Graham slides the jersey over his head, my eyes meet Drew's, and then I have to look away. I keep my emotions tamped down, because for Graham's sake, I need to pretend like this is just his hockey coach giving him his jersey—rather than what it really is: Drew claiming Graham as his own.

He's very clearly saying that Graham should be wearing his last name, not Flynn, across his back. But we haven't told Graham yet, so Graham has no idea how or why this would be so significant.

We need to talk about how we're going to tell him, but every time we're together, we end up letting the attraction get the best of us—and maybe that's part of the problem here. We have some important decisions to make about how to move forward, but we're not making them because we're letting our hormones take over.

"Do you think Uncle Jameson will let me sleep in it?" Graham asks, looking up at me. Behind him, Drew scrunches his eyebrows together in confusion, probably wondering why Graham is sleeping at Jameson's.

"I think you should take it off before bed so it's not a wrinkled mess, and then put it back on for the game tomorrow night. You want to keep it nice, right?"

"Yeah," he says, then turns and wraps his arms around

Drew's thighs, giving him a huge hug and thanking him for the jersey.

"Alright," I say, "let's grab your backpack with your stuff, and I'll walk you over to Uncle Jameson's car."

Drew picks up the hockey bag from the pavement and follows behind us as we move two cars down to where mine is parked. There, he sets the hockey bag in my trunk and hands Drew his Spider-Man themed backpack, then he closes the hatch and leans against my car as he watches me walk over to Jameson. After I've safely deposited Graham in his backseat and given him hugs and kisses goodbye, I return to my car to find Drew waiting for me.

"Does this mean you're home alone tonight?" Drew asks, his smooth voice tinged with hope.

"No, I'm going out with the girls."

"All night?"

I know exactly what will happen if I invite him over after I get back from having drinks with my friends. And even though my thighs are already clenching together to quell the ache between them, it's not a good idea. "Yep."

"Alright. Well, I have something for you too," he says, producing a gift bag from behind his back. He must have grabbed it from his car while I was dropping off Graham with Jameson.

I take the bag tentatively, wondering why he would feel the need to get me a gift. The first thing I pull out is an envelope, and when I slide the card out, there's a handwritten note inside.

I read it, then look up at Drew, confused. "You got me a personal shopper?"

"Yeah, I use this service for grocery shopping and other

errands that I don't have time for. It's a flat-rate per month, so you should use them as much as you want."

"But...I've always grocery shopped myself and run my own errands. Why would I need someone else to do that for me?"

"Because you're a single mom, though not for long, if I have anything to say about it"—my breath hitches at his blatant statement of intent—"and you have better things to do with your time. If you were married, there'd be someone else around to split the load with. You haven't had that."

"I have Jules."

"Yeah, well, I know how much you hate asking people for help, so I'm guessing you still do a lot of...everything, yourself," he says. My teeth sink into my lower lip as I try to hide my smile. He knows me better than I realized, and he's come up with a very thoughtful way to make my life easier. "I wanted you to have this option too, so you don't have to feel like you're asking people for favors."

"My and Jules's agreement is that I grocery shop, and she cooks. This feels like cheating."

"Do you want me to hire a personal chef?"

The question is asked so earnestly that a laugh bursts out of me. "No, Jules loves to cook. It's her stress relief. I think it would feel like a punishment if that was taken away from her."

"Do you feel the same way about shopping?"

"Definitely not." I loathe grocery shopping and errands, in general, which is why I ran out of ibuprofen before my period earlier this month.

"Good, so then put the personal shopper to use. Whatever you need—clothes, food, a pharmacy run—she can take care of it for you. And there's something else in there," he says, leaning an arm out and planting his hand on the frame of my SUV, right beside my head. He leans in close, and heat flashes through me as my whole body responds to his proximity.

I glance down into the bag and remove the piece of tissue paper stuffed in the top. And as I pull out a larger version of the same jersey he gave Graham, I wonder how I didn't anticipate this. I hold the jersey bunched in my hand, the letters of his last name rippling in the crumpled fabric but visible just the same.

With a deep breath, I think about how many times I've worn my brother's jersey. "I appreciate the thought, but the only name I wear on my back is my own."

He leans in so close his lips graze my earlobe and the sparks of desire shoot straight through me. "Don't worry, baby, one day my last name *will* be yours."

"Holy shit," Morgan says, the words rolling out slowly as she fans herself with the drink menu. I have a feeling it's Drew's words and not this stuffy bar or the multiple drinks the birthday girl has had that have her feeling the heat. "What did you say?"

"I don't even know. I think I stuttered out something about needing to come meet all of you?" I can't even think about the low rumble of laughter just under his breath as he shut my car door after I got in without my entire core clenching up in response. He knows exactly what effect he has on me.

Lauren looks at me, her blue eyes wide. "You are a fool."

"Geez," I tell my future sister-in-law. "Don't hold anything back."

She tucks her red hair back behind her ears, and then rests her elbow on the table and props her chin up on her hand. "No, really. I'm thinking about how hard I fought against my attraction to Jameson, and how confusing it was trying to figure out what his intentions were and if he was a relationship kind of guy or if he was just looking for a friends-with-benefits situation. And here you have Drew *very directly* claiming that he wants you, wants to raise your kid together, wants to marry you one day…and you're still fighting this because…?"

"Because…" The word trails off as I try to think of how to explain my hesitation. "What's it all based on? He's been back in my life for a few weeks. How can he know this is what he wants?"

"You've heard of the phrase 'love at first sight,' right?" Morgan asks.

"But we've known each other since college."

"Correction," Jules says, rolling her eyes. "You knew each other in college, and he's fully admitted to having feelings for you back then. Fast forward six years, and you have a kid together, and he *still* has those feelings, but now they're amplified by spending time with you and Graham. Yeah," she says, sweeping her hand through the air in front of her, like she's shooing away my objections, "maybe it's premature to jump from there to forever. But that doesn't mean those feelings aren't real."

"Okay…and also, I'm scared," I admit quietly.

Morgan flags down the waiter as he passes our table. "We're going to need another round over here!"

"What, exactly, are you scared of?" Lauren asks.

"Besides getting my heart broken?" The rhetorical question comes out saltier than I'd planned, but the next words are raw and honest. "I'm afraid that if Drew and I get involved—"

"You're already involved," Jules interjects, but I keep going.

"—and things don't work out with us, then not only will I get hurt, but so will Graham. He doesn't even know that Drew is his dad yet. And if we tell him, and then Drew and I are dating…I don't want him picturing us as a happy little family if it's not going to happen."

"Why do you think it's not going to happen?" Morgan asks.

"Because men leave. Even when they tell you they love you, sometimes they still leave."

"Like your dad and Scott?" Lauren asks. I don't even remember if I've ever told her about Scott, or if she's just heard about it from Jameson.

"Who's Scott?" Morgan asks.

I give her the quick rundown of how long we dated, and how he was like a father figure to Graham, and how much it hurt when he broke up with me and walked right out of my and Graham's life. "I don't think I could watch that happen again, especially not with Graham's real dad."

"So, are you just planning to never date again?" Jules asks. The question is flippant, but her tone isn't. I stare at her, trying to determine if this is a legitimate question. "Because if you *ever* date again, there's the possibility this could happen."

"I think the next time I date someone, I'll wait to introduce them to Graham."

"You did wait with Scott," she reminds me. "You guys were together for over six months before you introduced them."

"And then a year and a half later, he was gone." It still hurts when I remember how I'd take Graham for walks in the stroller, and every time he saw a white Subaru, he'd point at it and say, "Scott car?" or how he'd periodically look at me and ask, "Where Scott?" At least now, he hardly remembers him. But those first months after Scott left were especially painful and, unfortunately, I still remember it all.

"I know this isn't what you want to hear," Lauren says. "But that could happen with anyone. It could happen whether you're dating, or even when you're married." I watch her look away and I know she's thinking of her late husband. "You can't control other people's feelings."

"Yeah, but I do feel like I need to do everything within my power to protect Graham's."

"Do you think Graham is better off by you sacrificing your own happiness?" Morgan asks. "Because it kind of seems like you're choosing to push Drew away because maybe down the road he *might* hurt you or Graham. But… what if he doesn't?"

What if he does? is on the tip of my tongue, but I hold it there, because my friends are right. Part of getting involved with *anyone* new is opening yourself up to the possibility that they might hurt you.

"Everything just feels more intense, I think, because Drew is Graham's dad."

"Are you planning to tell Graham soon?" Lauren asks.

"I'm halfway afraid one of us is going to slip up and say something. Especially since all the adults in his life know at this point."

"I know, and so do most of Drew's family. He's got a grandmother, aunts, and cousins who he's never met. We need to tell him soon; we just haven't talked yet about how we're going to do that."

Jules snickers, and we all turn toward her. Her eyes widen. "What?"

"What the hell was that?" Lauren asks with a laugh.

"I was just"—she glances at me apologetically—"thinking that if Audrey didn't bang him every time she saw him, they could talk about this."

"Jules!" I burst out. "What the hell? We had sex once!" Suddenly, the tables around us get quiet, and I realize how loudly I just proclaimed this fact. And my cheeks practically burst into flames when it occurs to me that half of them are probably trying to figure out if it was Jules and me who had sex, or if I'm talking about myself and someone else.

We all laugh at the awkwardness of the sudden quiet, which breaks the tension and has conversations starting up again at other tables. "So…" Morgan leans in. "Was it hot?"

"I'm not describing our sexual relationship," I say, releasing a whoosh of a breath. "But…yes."

"Girl, you *so* deserve this!" Lauren says as she reaches over and squeezes my shoulder. "I'll spare you the details, given that you're related to my fiancé, but suffice it to say that a good sex life makes just about everything better."

"Ewww." Jules cringes.

"It's not like you didn't know they have sex," I say and roll my eyes at what a role reversal this is. Normally, I'm the one who has a hard time talking about sex.

"I get it," Lauren says. "This is what it's like when Sierra talks about her sex life in front of Jackson." Two of Lauren's best friends are now related, since Sierra married Jackson's little brother, Beau. "Which is why I won't tell you how fucking unbelievable my sex life is now."

"*Lauren.*" Jules groans her name out like it's two long syllables, and then covers her ears. "Please, stop."

Lauren laughs lightly, a satisfied smile plastered on her face. "Okay, I promise, no details."

As the waiter returns with our drinks, we toast Morgan. She's turning twenty-six, and even though I'm only two years older, our lives feel very different. The weight of being a single mom has…aged me?

I don't know how to explain it, except to say that for Graham's entire life, I've felt like my load was so heavy I might drop it at any moment. But the fear of everything shattering caused me to hold on tighter, push through even harder. Now that Drew is back in my life, it's the first time in years I've felt like maybe I can rest—maybe I can *breathe—*without having to worry about everything falling apart.

And that, in and of itself, feels like a reason to give him a chance.

Chapter Thirty-Two

DREW

"You really don't have to help me like this," my mom says, and I pause with one hand on her elbow and one on her lower back. I don't want to be overbearing, but at the same time, she seems less steady on her feet today than is normal. I don't know if it's because her doctor's appointment and her physical therapy appointment were back-to-back today and she's tired, or if maybe taking her to her favorite bookstore and out to lunch was just too much. But something's different.

"Let me get the door for you, at least," I say, stepping in front of her to unlock the door and push it open. I step through it so she can follow, and because if she trips coming over the raised threshold, I want to be in front of her to catch her.

"I'm fine," she says, trying to shoo me away once she's inside. She turns and shuts the door behind her, and she seems more at ease now that she's back in her home. I try not to spend too much time imagining how scary the world and the future must feel when you're a Parkinson's patient. My mom doesn't let herself go down that path of negativity, so I won't let my mind go there either. I know that depression is a serious side effect of this disease, but we've been lucky so far. "Why don't you go get a little more work done outside before the sun goes down?"

I glance out the window at the backyard, thinking about how much I could accomplish in the next hour or two. At the same time, I'm a little worried about leaving her, given how she's been presenting this afternoon. Unsteady. Distracted.

"How about I set up a chair with some blankets for you and you can read out there?"

"You don't think it's too cold?" she asks.

"We were just outside, so what do you think? Is it too cold for you?"

I think about all the hours my mom spent in frigid hockey rinks during my lifetime, all the days we built snow forts outside during the winter. It's a brisk fall day, but it's nothing like the temperatures this hardy New England woman is used to. But that's not what bothers me. It's how frequently she's unable to make up her own mind about things, or how she second guesses herself, that's hard to watch.

"We can try and see," she says after pondering it for a moment.

"Alright. Want me to make you some tea or something?"

"Sure," she agrees, and I wonder if it's only because she wants me to feel useful. "That would be nice."

While the tea steeps, I head outside and set up one of the chairs on the deck. I drag it into the sunshine so she'll get some warmth, and I pull the cushions out of the big storage bin. Mom comes out with her tea, a book, and a blanket slung over her arm, and gets herself situated in the chair.

Meanwhile, I drag the tools out from where I've stored them in the shed, and I get to work. I've cut exactly one piece of wood trim when Mom starts offering me what my sisters and I like to call her "helpful suggestions." Normally, this kind of nit picking would drive me crazy, but I'm so relieved that she seems sharp and astute that I just agree with everything she says. *Cut a little more off that piece*...sure (I pretend to make another pass with the miter saw). *You need to move that ladder over a bit*...will do (I move it an inch). *You should paint that blue, so it matches the house*...great idea (I already got the paint in that exact color).

I'm standing under the tree, admiring my handiwork, thinking all that's left to do is paint, when Mom scares the shit out of me by stepping right up beside me. I was so lost in thought, thinking about Graham and whether he'll like this little surprise, that I didn't even hear her approach.

"Missy and the boys are going to stop by," she says after I finish clutching my chest from the shock. "I wasn't sure if you wanted to put all this away first?"

I understand the opportunity she's giving me to keep this project a secret. "Thanks for the heads up. How much time do I have?"

"'Bout fifteen minutes." Mom watches me pack up the saw and the wood, and finally she asks, "Are you going to tell Missy about Audrey and Graham?"

"Caitlyn didn't tell her?"

"Not that I know of. But what do I know?"

"Audrey and I haven't told Graham yet, so I don't want

Ryan and Finn to know they have a cousin yet either. I want to bring them both over so everyone can get to know them, but it's hard if everyone knows Graham's my kid except for him. So I really need to talk to Audrey about it first and figure out how we want to handle this together."

"I'm proud of you. You know that, right?"

"In general?" I ask. "Or about this, specifically?"

"Both. I'm proud of how you've worked through tough situations, and I'm happy you've found the right team for you. But also, I'm proud of how you're managing this. A lot of men wouldn't have handled this as well as you have, especially since you didn't know about Graham from the beginning."

"I wish I had," I say, shoving my hands in the back pocket of my jeans. "At the same time, what would twenty-two-year-old me have been like as a father? How would I have played hockey in Vancouver if Audrey and Graham were here? Maybe..." I look up at the deep blue sky with orange streaks above the trees from the setting sun. "I don't know. Maybe it happened this way for a reason. Audrey would never have left Boston—"

"Are you sure?" Mom asks.

"She's so close with Jameson and Jules, her siblings. They all basically raised Graham together. She and Jules own a company together, and it's doing so well—they're just getting started."

"Why do you sound sad about that?"

"I'm thrilled for her," I say, as Mom and I start walking across the lawn toward the back deck. "She and Jules have worked really damn hard to make this happen. But the reality is, there's still a reasonable chance I won't end up playing for Boston next year, and there's no way she's leaving."

"She said that?" My mom's question literally stops me in my tracks, so she turns to face me. "Or did you assume?"

"I mean…why would she leave all that behind?"

Mom stares at me, but doesn't respond, then she shakes her head and turns toward the house.

"What?" I call out as I take a few steps to catch up to her.

"Has it ever occurred to you that maybe, if she feels the same way about you that you do about her, she'd move so your family could stay together?"

I actually had never considered that possibility…not because it isn't what I want, but because I didn't dare hope that it would be possible. She's still so tentative about our relationship.

"She's used the fact that I might have to leave Boston after this season as a reason for us *not* to have a relationship, Mom. So I'm not really sure she'd consider moving."

"Maybe because you haven't asked her if she would?" Mom's voice is so hopeful. "You can't expect her to consider it if you don't offer it up."

"Hmmm." She might be right. Or that might freak her the fuck out. I feel like I started off a little too intense for her, and maybe I need to dial it back a bit. That said, I don't want her to doubt my feelings. So it's quite a conundrum.

"What if—"

"Hey, anyone home?" Missy's voice carries through the house and out the door to the deck, which I'd left cracked open.

"We're out here!" I call to her, giving Mom a look that says, *We'll have to finish this conversation later.*

"You can't stop! You have to keep drawing until you die!" Ryan's peals of laughter ring out as he watches me draw what's probably my thirtieth Uno card in a row. Meanwhile, he and Finn have about five cards each.

"It's not fair," I make my voice intentionally whiny, playing up the completely lopsided rules my nephews have set because they're finding it hysterical that I'm losing so badly. "If adults have to draw until they get a card they can play, you should too. Why is there a three-card limit when you guys draw?"

"Our hands are too small to hold that many cards," Finn says, his face so solemn I think he might actually believe himself. Really, they just want to win, and I'm the unbeatable Uno king of our family. But with rules like this, I'm definitely going to lose.

I chuckle as I draw, and then play a Draw 4 card on Finn. "Hope your little hand can hold at least four more cards. And the color is now green."

Ryan cackles away next to his brother, until Finn plays a reverse, making it my turn again, and then I hit Ryan with a Draw 2 card. Now Finn's laughing, and they're feeding off each other's energy and getting themselves all wound up.

"Drew," Missy says, her voice stern, "it's almost bedtime for these two. You weren't supposed to get them all wound up."

"I'm playing a *card game* with them," I say, but I wink at the boys, which just throws them into another round of giggles. "They're the ones getting each other wound up."

"It's not our fault you're so funny," Ryan says as he rolls around on the floor near the coffee table.

"I think we might need to wrap this game up," Missy says. "Dad's on his way over to get you two and bring you home for bedtime."

"No way!" Finn says. "We have to beat Uncle Drew!"

I look at my hand, and even though there are a lot of cards, I'm still pretty sure I could beat them if I'm smart about it. But we'd be here for another half hour, at least. "Nah," I say, trying to sound defeated, "I think you already won. Look at all these cards. There's no way you aren't going to beat me."

"So you're just going to forfeit?" Finn asks.

"What's forfeit mean?" Ryan asks.

"It means I know I can't win, so I'm giving up," I tell him as I reach over and ruffle his hair.

"But what about your twenty-year winning streak?" he asks. At four, he only started playing my favorite card game this year, but he's watched Finn play for a couple of years, and my winning streak is legendary in this family.

"Guess everyone has to lose once in a while," I tell him.

"Alright, boys," Missy says. "Get your shoes on. Dad will be here in just a minute."

"Aren't you coming home, too?" Finn asks.

"Yeah," Missy says, lifting the glass to her lips and taking a sip. "I'm just going to finish my wine, and then I'll walk home." Perks of living only a few doors down, I guess.

Once the boys leave, Missy turns toward me. "Okay, spill it."

I'm just opening the fridge, but I pause and turn toward

her. "What?" I can guess what she's talking about, but I want to make sure.

"I've been waiting for you to bring up the whole *I have a kid* thing all night, and you're like a freaking vault."

"Caitlyn told you, I take it?"

"Yeah, but she didn't give me any details. What the hell? How have you not said anything about this?"

I reach into the fridge and swipe a beer off the door. "I didn't want to say anything about it in front of the boys."

"Why not?"

"Because Graham doesn't know I'm his dad yet."

"Okay," Missy says, pulling out a seat at the kitchen table for Mom, then taking the seat next to her. "I'm going to need you to rewind and tell me this whole story. Because I'm assuming it's a good one."

I sit and nurse my beer as I catch Missy up on the past few weeks, and when I get to the part about what I told Caitlyn, she says, "I can't believe you freaking did that!"

"What part can't you believe?"

"I can't believe that the first time you indicated how strong your feelings were was to your *sister*, who you don't even like, and not to Audrey!"

"I see whose side you're on," I tease.

"I'm not on anyone's side," she says. "I just want you guys to end up together, and if you keep doing stupid shit like that, it's not going to happen. Just *show* her she matters to you instead of telling her. Trust me, that's what every woman wants."

"I'm working on it," I assure her. "And I'm hoping you can meet her soon."

Chapter Thirty-Three

AUDREY

I don't know how I already forgot what it feels like to watch Drew play—the thrill and the terror that volley back and forth leave me exhausted, like I've run a marathon even though all I've done for the past forty-five minutes is squeeze Lauren's hand so hard I worry she's going to be bruised tomorrow.

Graham is sitting on the other side of Jameson, who's explaining all the technicalities of the game to him, blissfully unaware of my turmoil. Instead, he's thrilled each time Drew comes off the ice and glances up, giving him a nod.

But right now, I feel like I might have a heart attack, because Drew is only about ten feet from our seats when he passes the puck to one of the wingers and is slammed into the boards by Colorado's captain. Words are exchanged, Drew pushes Leland Alistair away from him and tries to skate off, and Alistair follows him across the ice.

"What the fuck?" I mutter.

"Didn't they used to be teammates?" Jules asks, as confused by this behavior as I am.

"Yeah," I say. "He hasn't really talked much about his time in Colorado. But we all know they weren't the best years of his career."

"It was bad," Lauren says quietly as she leans over. "I don't know all the details, but there was something between the two of them that involved Alistair's wife." I don't know what she sees on my face when she says this, but she quickly follows it up with, "But it wasn't Drew's fault."

I always think of the Rebels as Jameson's thing. Sometimes it's easy to forget that Lauren works for the team and is good friends with the general manager, AJ. While a lot of people would try to leverage that job for social capital, Lauren's always been so understated about it.

"How do you know it wasn't his fault?" I ask.

"Because he told AJ everything."

Everything...from his point of view. But there are always two sides to every story. And he's going to tell his GM the story in a way that paints him in the best possible light. Could he have actually had an affair with his teammate's wife?

I take a deep breath and remind myself that just because my mind is going to the worst possible scenario, that doesn't mean it's what happened. And it doesn't track with the kind of person Drew has shown me he is. I release my breath, trying to expel any negative thoughts.

The ref blows the whistle, and Drew lines up for the face-off, then Alistair skates into the circle opposite him. He sets his skates forward and puts his blade on the ice, and though we can't hear what he's saying, it's clear that he's chirping at Drew.

Drew sets his own blade on the ice, and the ref holds the puck above their sticks, but before he can drop it, Alistair raises his stick between Drew's legs and pulls forward so that the blade connects with the back of Drew's knee, making his leg buckle as his leg is pulled out from under him by Alistair's stick. He ends up on the ice and the whistle is blown, but the entire rink erupts into chaos as Boston players fight with Colorado players in retribution for Alistair's offense.

Drew's up on his feet, gloves off in a matter of a second, but the refs are already on Alistair and sending him to the penalty box. As fighting is a standard part of hockey, normally they'll let the players get into it. It's almost like they anticipated this and were already planning to prevent the fight.

Drew looks like he wants to kill someone as he skates back toward the bench, but right before he gets there, he looks up and we lock eyes. I don't know what to make of the smirk that crosses his face, until he pulls at the jersey where it's stretched over his chest pads. I told him I wouldn't be wearing his jersey, and there's no way he didn't notice when he saw me before the game started, so why he waited until near the end of the first period to make a point of it is beyond me.

I went for more of the Wives and Girlfriends look tonight. I'm wearing a pair of navy-blue skinny pants that hug the curves Drew says he loves so much, a fitted white long-sleeve t-shirt with a deep V-neck, and a gray-blue blazer that matches the Rebels' blue. I was entirely happy with this outfit, except now a chill runs through me and I wish I'd worn something warmer.

Less than a minute later, the buzzer sounds to mark the end of the first period, and Drew glances up one more time as he heads to the hallway that will lead back to the locker rooms.

"What the hell just happened between Drew and the Colorado guy?" Jules asks Jameson. I lean forward to hear his response, but he gives us a curt shake of his head, like he's saying, *Not here.*

"Excuse me, miss?" I hear as someone taps my shoulder from behind. I turn to find a guy probably about my age in Rebels sweats and a sweatshirt with a lanyard around his neck.

"Yeah?"

"Uh, Drew Jenkins thought you looked cold and asked me to give you this." He hands me a black parka with a big white Rebels logo embroidered on the back. If I thought wearing his jersey would be noticeable, this would be like wearing a flashing neon sign—because this is very clearly a player's jacket.

I'm momentarily paralyzed. If I accept the jacket, I'm sending him the message that I'm his, and I'm okay with everyone knowing it. If I don't accept it, it's one more time I'm rebuffing him when he's clearly trying. The second option feels petty. I *do* want Drew and me to end up together; I just want it to happen in a measured and thoughtful way. I want him to choose me because he can't live without me, not just because we have a kid together.

"Tell him..." I swallow, as I reach out my hand to accept the offered jacket. "Tell him I said thanks."

I slide my arms into the warm jacket, feeling incredibly conflicted about wearing something that is so obviously his while in this arena. It feels so personal, like he's claiming me as his in a public way, and I'm not certain I'm ready for that.

Leaning back against my seat, I hope that between the hood and the seat back, no one will be able to see the big Rebels logo. Then I sweep my hair over one shoulder, trying to cover the place over my chest where Drew's last name and number are embroidered.

But ten minutes later, when the players return for the next period, Drew looks up at me, and there's no mistaking the look on his face when he sees me in his jacket. It says, *You're mine.*

AUDREY:
Sorry I left the game with your jacket. It's cold out. I'll make sure to get it back to you before you leave on Sunday.

I glance at my phone, noting that Drew hasn't replied yet, then I look over at Jules where she sits next to me on the couch. She's on her laptop, getting some supply ordering taken care of. She's a total night owl, so I know she's spending her Friday night doing this so she doesn't have to do it in the morning.

"Did you decide when you're headed back to Maine?" I ask.

"I think I'm going up next week. We're doing the kitchen cabinet install next Monday and Tuesday, and I want to be there for that. I'll probably head up on Sunday, and just stay for a couple nights."

"Are you regretting taking on this project yet?" I tease. I'd warned Jules that a project renovating a historical home on the coast of Maine was going to be more trouble than it was worth. All of our other projects so far have been local in the Boston area, and the distance and her need to be there to see that things are being done properly mean she's got to go up there frequently.

"Nah," she says. "I don't mind the drive, and this is going to be such an amazing property to add to our portfolio."

I glance back at my phone when another text from Drew comes in.

DREW:
Game's over.

AUDREY:
I know, I watched the end at home. Congrats! That was an amazing goal at the end!

DREW:
Thanks. I'm going to shower and then come over.

AUDREY:
You're really not going out to celebrate with your team?

DREW:
I'd rather see you.

AUDREY:
It's late, Drew. And I really need to sleep.

What I *really* need is for him to go make nice with his teammates so that the team bonds with him, and management wants to keep him around for another contract.

DREW:

That's fine, I need to sleep too.

"What is that face you're making?" Jules laughs. "It's like smiling skepticism?"

I tell her about Drew's texts. "They're having a stellar start to this season, and he should be spending time with his teammates after this win."

"Audrey." She says my name so sternly my back stiffens. I feel like I'm a little kid again and in trouble. "A professional hockey player who just scored the winning goal in the home opener wants to come over and spend time with you rather than going out and celebrating. What the hell is wrong with you that you'd say no to that?"

I press my lips between my teeth. "I just know how important it is that he gets off on the right foot with this team. I still don't know what happened in Colorado, but I don't want him to have that experience here. And…"

"Don't even think it," Jules says, her voice low and hard, warning me off my train of thought.

"You don't know what I'm thinking."

"Of course I do. You're questioning why he'd rather spend time with you than go out and have a hundred women fighting for his attention."

"Okay…maybe you *do* know what I'm thinking." I'm not sure how she always seems to know what's going on in my head, whereas I've never had to really consider what she's thinking because her lack of filter means every thought comes out of her mouth.

"You're gorgeous and kind and a great mom to his kid. He's been nothing but clear about wanting a relationship with you. Don't let your own insecurities get in the way of your happiness."

I take a deep breath, knowing she's right. Knowing that I'm letting my past—my dad ditching us, Drew not responding to my calls years ago, Scott leaving me and Graham after we'd already started talking about marriage—get in the way of my future.

AUDREY:
Okay. Come over whenever you're done.

"Alright, I told him to come over."

"Good," she says. "I guess that's my cue to relocate to my bedroom."

"He's still got to shower and stuff. It's not like he's going to be here any minute."

"I bet he will be. I bet he already has a car waiting for him, and he'll be here in less than half an hour."

Sure enough, Jules is right. It's not even thirty minutes later when Drew is knocking on my front door.

He's in his game day suit, and I literally feel like I can't breathe as I look at the perfectly tailored navy blue pants and jacket, with the crisp white shirt unbuttoned at the collar. His brown hair is still damp at the ends, like he got dressed after his shower and left the arena as fast as he could. Good thing my place in the South End isn't far from where they play.

"You're…" I don't even know what words I intend to follow that up with. Here? Sweet? Gorgeous?

He watches me, a smile tugging up one corner of his lips as I struggle for words. "You need me to finish that sentence for you?"

I lean against the door frame. "Go ahead and try."

"…so crazy about you that I couldn't take my eyes off you during the game?" He takes a step closer, his toes meeting the threshold of the door, and even though I'm a step above him, I still have to look up to see him now that he's so close. "…unable to stand the thought of not seeing you again tonight?" He wraps one arm around my waist and tugs my body against his. "…looking forward to falling asleep with you in my arms?"

Stomach fluttering incessantly, I rest my forehead against the base of his neck, inhaling his clean, masculine scent. It would be so easy to let go, to throw caution to the wind, and let him sweep me off my feet. But I'm too pragmatic for that. I need to know there's a solid foundation under us first, and I need to not be afraid to fall.

"You're really determined, aren't you?" I murmur against his shirt.

He raises his hand, sliding his palm along my neck until he cups my jaw in his hand. The sensation has me practically moaning against his palm. Then he tilts my chin up so I'm looking at him, and it's a struggle not to get lost in the depths of those big brown eyes.

"I'm determined not to hide how I feel, Audrey. I know I fucked up in the past. I know I missed out on the baby years and raising Graham with you. I know you're scared, and I know you've been hurt, and I know you're not going to give me your heart easily. But I'm here until you're ready, however long that takes."

Chapter Thirty-Four

DREW

When I wake up, I'm overly warm. I can tell it's still dark even with my eyes closed, but it isn't until I feel movement in bed with me that I remember where I am. When my eyes drift open, Audrey's hair is in my face, the light citrus scent wafting up around me. She's either dreaming or just moving around in her sleep, but either way, she's unintentionally pressing her ass against me, and my dick is springing to attention.

I want to wrap my arm around her waist and pull her tighter against me, then shower her with kisses until she wakes up. But my bladder has different ideas, thanks to the cup of tea she made me last night when I was a little too keyed up coming off a win to go straight to bed, no matter how much I'd insisted that I could go right to sleep with her. It had been sweet torture to wrap her in my arms but not make anything about the experience sexual—but that was what she needed from me. Now, however, my body is reacting to being in bed with her, and so I need to get up.

When I return from the bathroom, she's rolled over and is facing my side of the bed. I slide in between the sheets, and she reaches over, stroking my face. In the darkness, I can barely tell she has her eyes open.

"You're not leaving yet, are you?"

"No, my alarm's set for 6 a.m. We have another hour before I need to go." Do I need to leave that early for practice? No. But I do need to leave before Graham wakes up, because we don't want to confuse him. Last night, we decided that he needs to know as soon as possible. But it needs to be an intentional conversation, not because he wakes up to find me in bed with his mom.

"Good," she says, then reaches her arm around my neck and pulls me to her. When her lips meet mine, the kiss is soft and tentative, so different from the hungry, almost desperate way we clawed at each other in her office the other day. But when she parts her lips with a breathy sigh, and pulls my lower lip between her teeth, it's like even though I want to take it slow with her, I can't.

I press forward into her, rolling her onto her back as I prop myself up on my elbow to deepen the kiss. She gives it right back to me, wrapping her leg around my hips and pulling herself onto her side, lining our lower bodies up so that her center is pressed right against the quickly hardening length of my cock.

Her sighs quickly transform into breathy moans, and her hand slips from my neck, trailing along the muscles of my chest and abdomen, until she's dipping her fingers into my boxer briefs. She trails her fingertips along the inside of the waistband, where she runs them back and forth over the muscles of my lower abdomen, but she doesn't explore farther as she continues to kiss me.

It turns out she doesn't need to, because my cock springs to life, pushing up into her touch, and as soon as she feels the smooth head brush against her skin, she lets out a groan and slides her fingers down, gripping my shaft in her warm hand. The feel of her skin sliding against mine as she works her hand up and down has me reaching for my boxers and pushing them down my legs. But of course, getting them over my thighs is a two-handed job, so Audrey pushes me back onto the mattress, saying, "Allow me."

As she kneels on the bed in nothing but a t-shirt, her long brown hair messy from sleep, and my boxers now in her hands as she gazes down at me, I feel a tightening in my chest.

"I want you so badly—"

Her lips turn up at the corners with a little smirk and she interrupts me to say, "I can see that."

"I want all of you, Audrey. Not just your body. I want your days, and your nights. I want the good times and the messy, difficult bits too. I want to be the one to be there for you when you need a shoulder to lean on. I want to be there for Graham as he grows up. And I don't want to wait any longer. I know it will take time for you to fully trust me"—I reach out, sweeping her hair off her shoulder and gripping the back of her neck—"but I'm not going anywhere. I'm always going to be here for you. We're going to figure out how to make this work, forever."

She closes her eyes and takes a deep breath, then opens them again. "I know."

"What do you know?" I ask, searching those pretty blue eyes that light me up.

"I know that you're in this for the long haul. I know you want to make the past right by being there for me and Graham in the future. And I know that I'm being difficult, needing time to adjust to the idea that your feelings for me are genuine and not just part of you trying to fix your mistakes from the past."

"Is that what you think?" I ask, using my thumb to tilt her chin back up when she looks down. "Look at me, Audrey."

Her eyes track back to my face. "I'm always going to be here for you. Not just because I think you're unbelievably beautiful and because you're the mother of my child and because I always want to get you naked. I'm here for you because I *want* to be part of your whole life. Because you're the kindest, smartest woman I know. Because you make me want to be the kind of guy who deserves someone like you."

There are tears in her eyes, but I hold her face steady, refusing to let her look away. She needs to know how serious I am about her. Most importantly, though, she needs to believe that *she's* worth it. Because what I'm coming to realize is that, with the exception of her brother, every other man in her life has let her down, made her feel like she wasn't worth staying for. Including me. But I'm not going to let her down again.

I sit up and pull her face to mine, kissing her lips gently. Then she pulls back, looking me straight in the eye, and admits, "I'm scared."

"I know."

"The last person I gave my heart to left me. He broke my heart, and he broke Graham's too."

"Audrey, your worth is not determined by his inability to value precious things. He was obviously an idiot. But you know what? I'm not. I see what I have here, and there's no way I'm ever walking away. So, you're stuck with me."

She leans forward, resting her forehead against mine. "Good."

I pull her onto my lap, her legs straddling me, so she's sitting right on my cock. "I'm going to take care of you in every way I know how. Starting with satisfying all your needs in bed."

Her chest shakes with inaudible laughter.

"Lose the shirt."

Eyes widening, her voice gets a playful tone when she says, "Yes, sir."

I don't think she means it the way my dick wants to take that comment, but it has me pressing up into her so that I slide along her wet seam. "Careful princess, or I'm going to start getting a lot more demanding just to hear you say that again."

She pulls the shirt off and leans back just enough that I can let my eyes roam over her breasts and down her stomach. This time, she doesn't try to hide from me, and it feels like a million miles of progress have been made.

"God, Audrey, the things your body makes me want to do to you..."

"Tell me," she says, and moves her hips forward so she's sliding along my shaft.

I cup her full breasts in my hands and slide my thumbs over her nipples, watching the way her eyes close halfway as a result. She tilts her head back and presses her chest forward, bringing one of her nipples to my mouth and running it over my lips. I can't help but open for her, and I trail my tongue around and then over the hard peak before I suck her fully into my mouth, holding her breast there as I tease her nipple with my tongue. Her hands grip my shoulders as her hips move in tempo with my tongue, and she hisses out a sound of pleasure that has the need coursing through my veins harder than before.

I let her breast go, resting my hands behind me so I'm leaning back slightly as I look up at her. "You want me to tell you what I want to do to you? Everything. Starting with, I want to slip inside you right now and watch you ride my cock while these perfect tits bounce in my face."

She rises on her knees on either side of me, reaches between us to line me up with her entrance, and then slowly sinks down onto me, sighing as I slide into her. "So fucking full," she whispers as she pauses.

"C'mon, baby," I say, hoping to encourage her to keep going. "I know you can take all of me."

She squeezes her eyes closed. "This isn't all of you?"

I let out a low laugh. "No. But you took all of me the other day, so I know you can do it again." This angle is different, deeper, which is why she feels so full. So I reach my thumb between us, gently stroking her clit until she's rocking her hips, sliding up and then sinking down, taking more of me until eventually she's fully seated with me inside her. I hold her hips down, filling her completely. "Stay there for a second."

"What's wrong, Drew?" she teases. "Is this too much for you?"

"No, but I could easily make it too much for you, and I don't want to hurt you by going too fast." My hands caress from her hips, up her sides, cupping her breasts as I lean forward and run my tongue over one nipple, then the other. Then I let my hands continue under her armpits and around to her shoulder blades, and then down her back to her ass. I grip each cheek in a hand, and say, "You have the most delectable ass. I can't wait to fuck you from behind so I can see it spread out before me as I enter you."

She exhales sharply as her hips start to move of their own accord, and she doesn't complain when I bottom out. Instead, she holds my shoulders tighter and rides me like it's what she was built to do. Watching her take the lead and take all of me like this is the sexiest thing I've ever seen. "That's right," I tell her. "Use me. Tell me what you need."

"I need you to talk to me," she says breathily.

Oh, I can do that. "Do you want me to tell you how all I can think about is spanking this ass?"

"Yes." The word is a hiss, and I'm not sure if it's confirmation or an invitation, but I take it as both. I pull my hand back a few inches and give her a playful slap on her ass, and she grunts, then takes me harder and faster, so I do it again, but a little harder. Her grunt is louder this time, and I soothe my hand over the place I slapped while I watch her bouncing up and down on me and noting the thin sheen of sweat covering her skin.

I move my hands to her hips to help her lift and lower herself, then I say, "Or do you want me to talk about how I will never, ever get enough of your tits?" I lean forward and suck one of her nipples into my mouth again, and her groan is so loud I have to pull back and look up at her. "Quiet, princess, or you'll wake our kid."

She bites her lower lip into her mouth, so I keep talking. "There is nothing sexier than the way you're taking me right now, bouncing up and down on my cock, your breasts in my face." I lean forward and suck the other nipple into my mouth, and she groans again, but is quieter about it this time. "Lean back," I say, and she does what I ask, resting her hands behind her and leaning back on them. I hold her hips in place so I'm fully seated inside her. "Now move your legs so they're behind my back."

She laughs lightly. "I'm not sure I'm that flexible."

"I'll wait."

Rolling her eyes at me, she slides one knee up, and then stretches the leg out so her foot is flat on the bed behind me, and her knee is up around my armpit, and then does the same with her other leg. The angle has me even deeper inside her, and she squeezes me from within, making it impossible for me not to move. A gentle rocking of my own hips, and my hands moving her hips, sets the pace. And then I lean forward to where her breasts are pointing straight up at me from the way her back is arched, and I bury my face between them. "You're fucking amazing, you know that, right?"

When she doesn't respond, I look up at her, increasing the pace and watching her face intently. I can tell she's getting close by the short pants escaping her lips. It only takes another minute or two for her eyes to widen. "You close?"

"Yes," she pants.

I bring her down on me hard, holding her there. She squirms, wanting to feel me sliding along her inner walls.

"Why are you stopping?"

"Because I want something from you before I make you come."

"Oh yeah?" she asks, as she brings one of her hands from behind her and slides it between us to circle her clit.

"If you think I'm letting you come before you give me what I want, you're so wrong," I tell her.

"What is it you want?" She tilts her chin up as she continues touching herself, wearing a look that borders on defiance.

"I want you to dance for me."

"What?" The word comes out with an incredulous laugh. "Now?"

"No, not now. But when I get back from this road trip, I want to see what you're learning in this class."

"I don't even have a pole to practice on," she says.

"You will when I get back."

"And where will that be?" I can tell the thought turns her on by the way her hips start to move. I let her take the lead, giving her what she wants.

"In my bedroom."

Another laugh bursts out of her. "Drew, what will people think if you have a pole installed in your bedroom?"

"Since there'll never be anyone in there but you, no one else will have an opinion. Not that it would matter if they did, anyway."

"You're ridiculous," she says, sinking down on to me harder and faster than before.

"I'm deadly serious. So are you agreeing, or are we stopping this right here?"

"You wouldn't," she says, eyes widening. Her reaction almost makes me laugh.

I pull her down on me rough and hard, hitting deep inside her so that her eyes roll back in her head. "Baby, there's nothing in the world I want more than to see you fall apart on my cock. But I want that promise first, or it's not going to happen."

"I can just make myself come," she says.

"You could, but it would be a sad replacement for coming with me deep inside you, and you know it."

"Fine," she sighs. "Now finish me off."

"With pleasure," I say, lifting her off me and setting her on the bed next to me.

"What the fuck, Drew?" she whispers, but it comes out more like a whine.

Instead of answering, I get on my knees, guiding her body around so she's on all fours in front of me. "I told you I wanted to see this ass when I came inside you."

I enter her swiftly, and she pushes back into me, her pelvis hitting my hip bones. Leaning forward, I run my hands under her breast, tweaking her nipples between my fingers as she pushes back into me over and over. "Now touch yourself," I tell her.

In the quickly lightening room, I watch her bring her hand up to her mouth, then she reaches between her legs. And as she strokes herself, I feel her gripping me tighter from inside, and I know her orgasm is close. I pinch her again and she mewls out in pleasure, and then her soft grunts punctuate the silence as she slams herself back onto me repeatedly. And once she's done coming, I reach forward, gripping her throat in my hand. "This pussy is mine," I growl. "All of you is mine."

"Yes," she says, and she looks over her shoulder at me as her hand slips farther back and lightly grips my balls. "And you're mine."

As I spill myself inside her, that's the only word left in my vocabulary: *Mine*. Over and over, on repeat. Mine.

Chapter Thirty-Five

AUDREY

"You brought hot chocolate?" Graham's squeal matches the energy he's had ever since he woke up and I told him we were going apple picking with Drew this afternoon.

Drew and I had talked a bit this morning about the best way to tell him who his father is, and we decided that it might be easiest if we were out doing something that felt family-like. Drew suggested apple picking, because he wanted to take Graham to the farm his family had always gone to as a kid anyway. Given that the location was meaningful to Drew, and we'd be able to find enough open space for the conversation, it felt like the right place. And now feels like the right time.

"Yep," Drew confirms, as he pulls the paper cup back toward him before Graham, who is jumping around in his enthusiasm, can grab it with his outstretched hand and spill it. "It's still a little too hot."

I glance over at Drew, who's balancing two larger takeout cups of hot chocolate in his other large hand. But all I can think of is the way that hand felt as he slapped my ass while deep inside me early this morning and, suddenly, I just want to be alone with him again. I wish he could spend the night again tonight, but I already know he can't because their plane leaves early tomorrow morning for their first series of road games.

"Where'd you get this?" I ask instead.

"I made it."

"You...what now?" In my mind, I imagine Drew in his kitchen—not that I know what it looks like yet—with several packets of hot cocoa.

"I made it. It's a family recipe. I hope you like peppermint and Fluff."

"What's Fluff?" Graham asks.

Drew's face transforms first into shock, and then to horror. "What's Fluff???" He looks from Graham over to me. "You haven't taught"—he pauses so quickly I think he must have just caught himself before saying *our son*—"Graham what Fluff is? What kind of mother are you?"

I laugh. "The kind who's not trying to give her kid a sugar high by adding even more sugar to something that's already sweet."

"That's an outrage!" Drew says, mock horror in his voice as he turns and sets the to-go mugs on the kitchen counter. He squats so he's at eye level with Graham. "Okay, so Fluff is this marshmallow spread, and it makes lots of things better. Like hot chocolate, and also peanut butter. If you've never had a peanut butter and Fluff sandwich, we're going to have to fix that immediately!"

He reaches into his back pocket and pulls out his phone.

"C'mere, I'll show you a picture of it. And when your mom puts in her grocery order this week, she can get some for you." He glances up at me, and his face is so playful that for a moment I feel like I have two kids—until he drops his voice low and says, "Right, Mama?"

Holy. Shit. Never in a million years did I think I'd ever find it hot for a grown man to call me Mama, but somehow when Drew says it in that smooth, deep voice of his, it makes me instantly want to jump him. And as he studies my response, I can tell he knows exactly what that word just did to me.

Drew looks up Fluff and shows Graham the picture on his phone.

"Do you think my hot chocolate is cool enough to drink yet?" Graham asks. "I want to taste the Fluff."

"I don't know that you'll be able to taste it, specifically," Drew says. "It's more that it will make it sweeter and creamier."

I pick up Graham's drink and take a sip, determining that it's not too hot for him. "Wow," I say to Drew as I hand Graham his cup. "What's in that? It's delicious."

"Family secret," he says with a shrug. "I can't tell you unless you marry into my family."

"Mom's never been married," Graham says, as he holds the warm cup between both palms and looks up at us.

"Easily fixed," Drew says, giving me a wink.

"I know!" Graham says, his whole face lighting up. "You two can get married. Then Mom won't be all alone."

"I'm not all alone," I tell him as I reach out and brush my fingers across his cheek. "I've got you."

"But you could have Drew, too," Graham says, shrugging

like it's the most obvious thing in the world. I love his wide-eyed innocence.

Drew keeps his lips pressed together, but there's no doubt he's laughing.

"That's not exactly how getting married works," I tell him, then give Drew a look that I hope communicates how awkward it is that he just opened up this conversation.

"How does it work?"

"You know what," Drew says, "I'll explain it to you later. Right now, we need to get going before all the apples get picked."

When we head out the door behind Graham, I reach over to pinch Drew's side, and I'm disappointed to find nothing but chiseled muscle—there's barely anything to grab onto. In response, Drew snakes his arm around my back and pulls me close, then whispers, "That was your turn," in my ear. He gives me a devilish smile, and I roll my eyes.

"Do *not* pinch me back."

He drops his voice even lower. "Or what?"

"Try it and find out." I give him a little wink as I saunter over to my SUV and grab Graham's booster seat.

Once it's settled in the back seat of Drew's Jeep and Graham is all buckled in, I give him his cup of cocoa and a warning about not spilling it.

"It's a Jeep," Drew says. "If he spills, I'll hose it out."

I take a look at the interior, which is much more luxurious than I realized the last time I was in here. Then again, the only thing my illness-addled brain retained from that night was the way it felt to be in Drew's arms. "You can hose this out?"

"Yep. It's part of the allure of having a Jeep."

"Why? Do you get it very dirty?"

"In the summers, I generally leave the top off unless it's raining, so yeah, it can get pretty dirty."

"Hey…" Graham says from the back seat. "Why do you have rubber ducks lined up across the front?" I glance back at him to see his nose scrunched up like he's trying to figure out why a grown man has plastic ducks along the dashboard in his car. It's a fair question, and I vaguely remember asking something similar the night he took me for the strep test.

"It's a Jeep thing," Drew tells him. "It's called 'Getting Ducked.' When you see another Jeep, like in a parking lot or something, you leave a rubber duck on the windshield or the driver's side mirror. And when someone sees my Jeep, they leave me a rubber duck."

"Do you *have* to leave a duck if you see another Jeep?"

"No, it's more like if you see one that's just like yours, or one you really like."

"Do people know you're famous when they leave a duck on your Jeep?" Graham asks, and I watch Drew's cheeks pull up and his throat bob as he tries not to laugh.

"I'm not really that famous," he says as he backs out of the space and heads down the alley to the street. "I'm just lucky that I get to play hockey for a living."

"Everyone at my school knows who you are," Graham insists, and it's the first time he's mentioned this to me. It makes me wonder what he's told his classmates—not that he knows anything particularly newsworthy to tell them. But he will soon, and one of the things that's worried me most about telling him is trying to figure out how he'll process this, and what his life and our life will be like when he finds out this hockey player he looks up to is actually his dad.

"That's what happens when you play a sport professionally. There're good things and bad things about it," Drew tells him.

Graham looks like he might ask a question, but then nods solemnly, glancing back at the plastic ducks lined up on the dashboard. "Did you know that ducks can communicate with each other before they're even hatched?"

I glance at Drew, who's focused on the road but whose cheeks are definitely turned up in a smile now. "I didn't. Who do they communicate with?"

"The baby ducks in the other eggs. They can all talk to each other and that's how they know when to hatch, and then they all hatch at the same time."

"For real?" Drew asks.

"Yeah. I saw it in a video about ducks."

"He's a little obsessed with birds," I tell Drew as he comes to a stop at a stoplight.

"Do you want one of these ducks?" he asks, nodding toward the row of plastic ducks.

"Yes!"

"Which one?"

"Ummmm…." Graham pauses as his eyes move across the row. "Could I have the police officer duck?"

"Sure," Drew says, reaching over and plucking it out of the row, then reaching behind him to hand it to Graham. "But only if you tell me more about ducks."

I groan internally as I press my head back into the headrest and close my eyes. He has no idea the floodgates he just opened.

"Well, because of where their eyes are, on the side of their heads, they can see in almost a full circle around them…"

"Stop fucking pinching me," I hiss at Drew. "At this rate, my ass is going to be covered in bruises."

"Good." The sight of him with those aviator sunglasses, a backward Rebels hat holding his wavy hair back, and a sexy half-smile dawning on his face, does funny things to my chest. Being with Drew feels like letting my heart grow in ways I didn't know were possible, especially when I watch him lift our son onto his shoulders so he can reach apples high up in the tree, like he was doing just a minute ago.

"Why in the world is that good?"

"It'll give you a reason to think of me while I'm gone."

I hate that he leaves tomorrow for a seven-day West Coast road trip. "I won't need any more reasons to think of you, trust me."

His eyes flick over to Graham, who's running ahead on the path to the next orchard with a different type of apple than the one we've been picking. Drew's hand presses into my lower back as he pulls me into his side and drops a kiss on the top of my head. "Also, good. And just to make sure you have lots of reasons to think of me while I'm away, I'm sending you a little care package."

He releases me, then calls to Graham to slow down and wait for us at the picnic table that's just come into view. Beyond it, a valley of trees interspersed with fields and houses, spreads out before us.

I want to ask him about that care package, but I get the sense that he's asking Graham to stop for a reason. "Are you going to tell him now?"

"Yeah, if you're okay with that."

"I'm nervous about how he's going to take this," I say, hating the way my stomach feels like an open pit.

"Me too. But he needs to know, and not telling him because it makes *us* uncomfortable isn't fair."

We're quickly approaching Graham where he's standing on the seat of the picnic table, taking in the view. "He's going to have so many questions about why I didn't tell him who his dad was if I knew all along."

"Maybe," Drew says. "Or maybe he'll just accept it. He's only five. He's not going to think about it the same way we are."

"True, but he'll have questions, eventually."

"And when he does, we can answer him."

And while I know he's right, I also know my kid, and I'm afraid he's going to throw us a curveball we aren't expecting.

Which is sort of what happens, because when Drew says to Graham, "Your mom and I have something we want to talk to you about," our son holds his half-eaten apple in two hands and looks at Drew like he knows exactly what he's going to say.

"Okay," Graham says.

"So, you know how your family is just you and your mom?"

"Yeah, it was. Until you came back."

Drew's eyes flick to mine, but my face is frozen in a mask of surprise.

"What do you mean, Graham?" I finally spit out.

"I saw the picture at Drew's mom's house," Graham says, as if we know what he's talking about.

"What picture?" Drew asks.

"The one I thought was a picture of me. But your mom said it was you when you were my age. So I knew you were my dad."

"Wait," Drew says, then coughs out a laugh. "You saw a picture of me when I was your age and decided I must be your dad?"

"Yep. It's like how Ivy looks just like Lauren when she was little, right, Mom?"

A couple of months ago, Lauren was showing us some photos of her and Paige when they were little. Graham was amazed at how Lauren, at three years old, looked exactly like her daughter, Ivy, looks now. We'd explained that sometimes kids look just like one of their parents at the same age. I guess it isn't a huge leap that he'd see how much he looks like Drew and jump to the same conclusion.

"Yeah, I guess it is," I say. "So how are you feeling about Drew being your dad?"

Our son takes a bite of his apple and chews it with his eyes scrunched up like he's deep in thought. Then he looks at Drew and says, "I'm glad it's you."

He looks between the two of us, and instead of asking any questions about how this happened, how Drew didn't know or how he eventually found out, Graham says, "So, are you guys getting married?"

It's the second time in as many hours that he's mentioned this idea.

"You don't just get married because you have a child together," I tell Graham. "It's a bit more complicated than that."

"Why *do* you get married, then?" Graham asks.

"Well, when you love each other very much and you want to spend the rest of your life with that person, then you get married," I tell him, feeling Drew's eyes on me.

Graham's big brown eyes are wide, and his face is curious when he says, "And you don't love each other enough to spend the rest of your lives together?"

Why do kids always have to ask the hard questions?

Drew pulls at the neck of the t-shirt he's wearing under his flannel and looks at me like he doesn't want to say the wrong thing. "I think that it takes time to make those kinds of big life decisions, and your mom and I need more time before we can decide."

I'm trying to figure out if he's come to that realization himself, even after telling Caitlyn he was going to marry me, or if he's saying it on my behalf so that I don't have to be the one standing in the way of something Graham obviously wants to happen.

"We're just taking things slow, Bud," I tell Graham. "We need to figure out what this whole family thing looks like. For a long time, it was just you and me, and it's only fair to give Drew time to adjust to being part of our family, and for us to adjust to him, too."

"Okay," Graham says and lifts his little shoulders in a shrug. "Can we go find more apples now?"

Drew and I glance at each other, both of us obviously bewildered by how this conversation went.

"Sure," I say, thinking there's no way we got off that easy after I've been building this up in my mind for so long.

But as Graham runs down the path ahead of us, holding

his half-eaten apple, Drew slings his arm over my shoulder and pulls me to his side as we walk. Then he says, "I'm not just going to marry you someday, Audrey. I'm going to marry you someday *soon*."

Chapter Thirty-Six

AUDREY

JULES:
Where are you?

AUDREY:
I'm almost home, why?

I just dropped Graham off at a friend's house for his first kindergarten playdate, and I'm almost back to our place —it's not like Jules didn't know I was taking him over there today.

JULES:
Did you forget about brunch?

Shit. Earlier this week, when the mom of one of Graham's friends reached out about a Sunday morning playdate, I suggested to Jules that we should host a girls' brunch. She must have made those plans, but she didn't tell me about them. Or, I don't think she did?

> **AUDREY:**
> Yep. I sure did. I'll be home in a minute.

> **JULES:**
> Also, you got a package...

We get a lot of deliveries, which means this one is standing out to her for some reason. And then it hits me: Drew said a package would be coming my way today.

> **AUDREY:**
> Okay?

> **JULES:**
> Let's just say I recognize the packaging and I have questions.

I have no idea what she's talking about, but I'm pulling onto our street when her message comes through, so I don't bother replying. Instead, I hop out of my car after I've parked and take the steps two at a time. When I come in the back door, Jules and Lauren are standing at the kitchen table, inspecting a black mailing box.

Lauren takes a sip of what appears to be a mimosa to hide her smile.

"What's going on?" I ask. They're acting unusually strange.

"You got a package," Jules says.

"Yeah, you mentioned. Why are you looking at me like that?"

"Why don't you come open it?"

"Drew said he was sending me something, but that I should open it alone."

"I'll bet he did," Lauren mutters, and she and Jules break into what can only be described as uncontrollable giggles.

"Are you guys drunk?"

"Nope," Jules says, then looks at Lauren. "She really doesn't know."

"What don't I know?" I ask, my voice raising slightly.

"What's in the package?"

"How would I know? I haven't opened it yet." I look between them, suspicion making my eyes narrow. "Why do you both seem like you already know what's in there? Did you open it before I came back?"

"Hey," Morgan calls out, and we all turn toward the open front door. Apparently, everyone I know has the code to the keypad on our front door now. "What's going on?" She looks between all of us, and then at the black box sitting on the table. Suddenly, she looks a bit embarrassed.

"You know what's in that box, too, don't you?" I ask her. Why am I the only one who is so clueless? My mind is spinning, trying to think of what Drew could have sent that all three of them would immediately recognize.

Morgan's eyes sweep back and forth between all of us, and she makes a face like she's trying to smile, but her teeth are clenched together, which makes Jules laugh. "Am I supposed to say yes, or no?"

"How do *you* know what Drew sent me?"

"Drew sent that?" she asks with a laugh. "That's not what I was expecting you to say."

"Alright. Now I freaking have to know, right now."

Jules hands me a pair of scissors as I approach the box, and that's when I notice that the box has an embossed black-on-black diamond pattern—it's super subtle, but distinct—the type of pattern you'd remember if you'd seen it before.

It's the kind of box where the front flap pulls out, so I turn it on its side and slide the blade through the tape at the seam, then set it down flat and lift the front. Inside, there's black tissue paper with a crisp white envelope sitting on top. I open it and read it out loud. "To hold you over until I get back from this trip. Drew."

I look up and all three of them are very clearly holding in laughter. *What the actual fuck is happening?* I have a feeling that whatever's in here, I'm going to be embarrassed about it, so I start to close the lid.

Jules's hand shoots out and grips my wrist. "No way. You have to open it now! You can't just leave us hanging like this. We need to know what's inside."

"It seems like you already do?"

"I mean, we know what's in there, but not *what's in there.*"

"That makes no sense," I say with a shake of my head.

"Just open the damn package, Audrey!" Lauren is clearly exasperated. "We obviously all know what comes in that particular box, so you're about to be initiated into this club."

"I didn't know we had a club," Morgan says as she pulls her hair back into a ponytail.

"We didn't, until now," Lauren says, then focuses her eyes back on me. "Open it."

I tear the gold foil sticker off the black tissue paper and lift out a smaller box, probably about ten inches long and five inches square, surrounded in bubble wrap. It's not until I've unwrapped it and am lifting the last layer off that I can tell exactly what it is. I feel my whole face flush, until I'm sure I'm beet red. Because pictured on the outside of the box is an enormous and *very* realistic dildo, balls and all.

"Ohhh," Jules says. "That's a good one."

My mouth drops open as I look up at all three of them, who are now openly laughing at my discomfort. I drop it into the bigger box and slam the lid down. "Beyond how fucking embarrassing this is," I say in a rush, "I'm trying to wrap my mind around the fact that you've all seen this box before."

"It's from the leading online retailer for...you know...sex toys," Morgan says. "They have discreet but distinctive packaging. I think it's intended that *you* know what's just arrived, but no one else will know."

"Well, fail on both accounts, then!" I practically yell. Then I turn to my sister. "And what do you mean, *oh, that's a good one*? Do you have this already?"

Jules bites the corner of her lip, just like I do when I'm nervous. "I mean, yeah. It's not my go-to, but I do have it. That suction cup at the bottom makes it great for the shower."

My mouth drops open. The shower? "Not your go-to? Like, you have others?"

"Why do you sound so shocked?" Lauren asks, coming to Jules's defense.

"Am I the only one without a vibrator collection?" I ask, horrified at the thought that at twenty-eight I'm apparently the grandma of the group—or at least when it comes to my own self-care.

They all just kind of shrug, and then my eyes narrow in on Lauren. "Okay, the rest of us are single. But why do you... need these?"

She takes a sip of her mimosa and says, "Your brother travels a lot."

"Aaaaaand"—Jules says loudly—"that's all the info we need."

"I can't believe that you all have been holding out on me! I've been single for the past *four years*." I look at my sister, since Lauren and Morgan haven't been in my life that long. "And you didn't once think to tell me what I was missing out on?"

"I mean, I kind of assumed you knew what a vibrator was," Jules laughs as she reaches out for two more champagne flutes on the counter behind her.

"Knowing they exist and knowing that everyone is already using them feel like two very different things in this instance."

"Well then," Morgan says, "you're about to have a whole new kind of sexual awakening."

"I feel like we need to toast to that!" She hands me and Morgan each a flute, and then the three of them hold theirs up while Jules laughs and says, "To Audrey's vagina!"

I shake my head, but I'm laughing as I raise my glass. And I already can't wait to tell Drew this story when he calls after his game tonight. I hope he doesn't care that the first thing they do is take that box out and start commenting on the size of that realistic dildo and speculating whether Drew's is really eight inches long, or if that's just wishful thinking.

I neither confirm nor deny their theories.

When the video call comes in, I'm already in bed, waiting to talk to him.

"Hey," I say. "Good game. I'm sorry about the outcome." The Rebels lost earlier tonight in Arizona, and it was a close game. Drew and the rest of the team played well, but Arizona played better. It's their first loss of the season, and not how you want to start a series of away games.

"Thanks," Drew says, holding the phone in front of him as he walks farther into his hotel room. He's still wearing his game day suit, this time a dark grey with a blue shirt under it. I'd seen the video footage of the players' arrival at the game on the team's social media feed, and I'm not going to lie, I was thrilled that Drew was the best dressed of the bunch. I mean, Colt's always been the fashion icon of the team, but lately, it doesn't feel like he's trying to hold up that reputation as much.

"You doing okay?" I ask.

"Better now that I'm talking to you." He sets the phone down, and I imagine it's propped up against the TV because of the way it's tilted up at him and because I see the big king-size bed behind him. He slides his arms out of his jacket and sets it carefully on the end of the bed.

"I got your note, by the way," I tell him.

"Which one?"

"There's more than one?" I ask, and Drew gives me a shrug like, *Who knows?* "It was stuck to my laptop and said *I hope you have a good day. I can't wait to see you in a week.*"

"Not that either of us is counting, though," he says as he unbuttons his dress shirt.

"Oh, I'm counting, alright. I need you back here. I already miss you." It feels both foreign and freeing to be so honest with him, but he's never been anything but honest with me and he deserves that in return.

"I miss you too," he says, a soft smile curling his lips as he looks at me.

"I love your shirt, by the way," I tell him as he slips it off his shoulders.

"Thanks," he says, tugging at the sleeves to get them down over his muscular arms. "I got it specifically because it reminded me of a certain someone's eyes."

I glance at myself at the corner of my screen. He's right, it's almost the exact color blue of my eyes.

"Did your personal shopper pick it out?" I tease.

"She did, actually. I sent her a picture of you, told her I wanted something that matched your eyes, and she came back with this shirt."

"Why do you have a picture of me?"

"Because I found the one on the Our House social media feed," he says as he unbuckles his belt, and I know exactly which one he means because it's the one Morgan posted after our lunch when I told her she could take over our social media. "I think you're at a restaurant? Anyway, it's a beautiful photo of you, with your bright eyes and your flushed cheeks. I can't even look at it without getting hard." He drops his pants and stands in front of me in his briefs, and I don't miss the way his body is already reacting.

I shift beneath the covers and the cotton sheets graze along my nipples, sending spasming need through my body. Watching Drew undress while he tells me he can't even look at a picture of me without getting hard has me extremely turned on.

"Oh yeah?" I ask, my voice coming out breathy and needy. "Do you look at that photo often?"

"Every fucking hour."

"Must be *hard* to deal with the consequences of that, no? I mean, what do you do when you can't fix that problem right away? Just suffer through it?"

"Thinking about you is hardly suffering."

"Just seems like you could use some help getting rid of that"—I nod my chin toward my phone as I watch the bulge in his underwear grow—"problem."

Drew's shoulders shake with a low laugh as he pulls his briefs down. "You mean *this* problem?" he asks as he palms himself and slides his hand along his length.

Suddenly, my mouth is dry, my lips parched. So I lick them and stutter out a "Yes."

He swipes his phone off the dresser and carries it over to the bed, and I miss the sight of his body but love the close-up of his face. He looks like he skipped shaving today, and it suits him.

"What do you propose we do about it, with you in Boston and me half-way across the country?"

"I have a few ideas. You see, I received a package today—"

"And you didn't lead with this info?" Drew's voice is full of mock outrage.

I tell him about opening the package with my sister and friends, and his chest shakes with laughter as he settles into his sheets. "Whoops."

"Hey, as long as you don't mind that they're speculating about the size of your dick…"

He lifts one shoulder and gives me a little smirk. "Let them wonder."

I pull the toy out from beneath the sheets, where it's been waiting for his call, and hold it up for him to see. I'd washed it and charged it earlier so it'd be ready for this moment, and I honestly found it a bit hard not to take it for a test drive before talking to him.

As if he can read my mind, Drew takes one look at it and asks, "Did you test it out yet?"

"No, I wanted to wait until we talked."

"You know it's for you to use whenever you want, right? As much as I know I'm going to love watching you use that thing, I bought it for your pleasure, not mine."

"Yes, and while I appreciate that, I still wanted this to be a you and me thing."

"Audrey, *everything* is a you and me thing. If you were using that and I wasn't on the phone with you, would you be thinking about me?"

"Of course," I say as I take my free hand and explore the tip of the vibrator. It does feel surprisingly realistic.

"Good. Because there's never a time that I'm jerking myself off that I'm not thinking of you, and there never will be."

"Good," I say right back to him. I don't know how we got so serious so quickly, but I'm done fighting it.

"Why are you still hiding under those covers?" he asks. I can see the upper half of his body, so quid pro quo, I push the blankets down to my stomach. He sucks in a breath and then sighs. "You really do have perfect tits, you know?"

Lying on my side, facing him, they're falling forward and look even bigger than normal.

"Do I?" I ask, taking the head of the vibrator and running it around one of my nipples.

"Holy shit, Audrey," he says, his words escaping like trapped air hissing out between his lips. "Do that again, but turn it on."

I do as he suggests, and as the vibrations move through my nipple, it's like someone's connected it to my core. My hips curl forward, my pussy clenching with need, so I push the sheets down and bring the vibrator to my clit. "Oh crap," I say, the words slipping out the minute the vibrations hit that sensitive spot.

On the other end of the phone, Drew's stroking himself and sending words of encouragement my way. "That's right," he says, watching intently as I circle the vibrator over and around my clit, "get yourself good and ready."

I bring my other hand to my breast, squeezing it gently and pinching my nipple between my fingers. My hips find a rhythm as they move against the vibrations, and it doesn't take long before I can feel an orgasm coming on. My body is tense and my back arches, my toes curling as my breath comes in soft pants.

"Alright, beautiful," Drew says, and my pussy clenches in response. "Let's see you fuck yourself with that thing."

I'm so close to coming, I can't speak, so I lift my top leg, setting my foot behind my bottom leg. I run the fat head of the vibrator through the slickness that coats my entrance, back and forth, ever so slowly, while Drew hisses out a long "Yes."

I slide it in an inch, letting my body adjust to the size, because it really is as big as Drew. And then I pull it out a bit and slide it in a little more, and the combination of being so full and the vibrations moving through my muscles have me immediately clenching around it.

"Hit the button again so it's thrusting inside you," Drew says, but I don't know if I can take any more pleasure. I'm so full, and this is so much. "Now."

My eyes snap to his, and I give him a lazy smile. "Yes, sir."

He legit growls in response, the low sound reverberating across the video in a way that has me wishing he was here physically. I'm always wanting him with me lately.

When I press the button at the base, the vibrator lengthens even farther, then contracts, over and over. It feels enough like Drew that I relax into the sensation, letting it pull me toward the edge of my orgasm.

"What are you thinking about?" Drew asks, and I open my eyes to look at him. He's a model of physical perfection as he lies there jerking himself off, watching me with this sex toy filling me up.

"How amazing this feels, but how I wish it was you instead."

"Honey, if I was there, you'd already be on orgasm number two. Maybe three."

The laugh shakes my abdomen, and with the vibrator thrusting inside me at the same time, my whole body convulses.

"That's a good girl," Drew says. "Now touch yourself."

"Drew, the feeling is already so intense."

"Audrey, I need to see you run your fingers over that gorgeous swollen clit while you fuck that perfect pussy of yours, because I need you to come. *Right. Fucking. Now.*" He grunts those last words out through gritted teeth, and that's when I see how close he is. How every muscle in his abdomen is contracted, how he's biting his bottom lip with a look that borders on pain as he holds himself off until I come.

So I reach down and slide my finger over the ball of nerves, and my muscles clench deep inside, a fast contracting and releasing that has my knees curling up—and as I do, the vibrator slides along the top edge of my inner wall, hitting the perfect place.

"Fuck yes," Drew grunts out, and it's followed by a guttural sound. But I barely hear him orgasming through the pleasure that's erupting inside me as I come harder than I've ever been able to make myself come, the waves of sensation rolling through me for what feels like forever as I ride out my pleasure.

When I finally pull the vibrator out of me and hit the button to turn it off, I open my eyes to find Drew watching me, a shit-eating grin on his face. "That was so fucking hot. But my God, are you loud."

"Shh," I tell him. "Or I'll replace you with this thing."

"Fucking say that again, and I'll tie you to the bed and make you come so many times you beg me to stop." There's a dangerous and determined glint in his eyes.

"That sounds like a challenge." I raise my eyebrow as I repeat, "Shhh…or I'll replace you with this thing."

"Challenge accepted," Drew says, a mischievous glint in his eyes. "Don't make plans the night I come back."

Chapter Thirty-Seven

DREW

"That's bullshit!" I spit the word at the referee's face.

I was on a breakaway, advancing quickly toward Vegas's goal, when my former teammate and one of Leland Alistair's closest friends, Pierre Eckhart, who also got traded at the end of the season, tripped me from behind.

"Watch yourself," the ref says, and I pause to take a deep breath, knowing how close I am to stepping over the line. I'm not the captain, and it's not my place to argue this call.

Walsh skates up behind me, hooks his arm around my shoulders, and grits out, "Keep your fucking mouth shut and let McCabe do the talking."

He's right, and I know I can't let my temper get the best of me. I take another deep breath and remind myself how lucky I am not to be playing with assholes like Eckhart and Alistair anymore.

On my other side, McCabe skates up and asks the ref about the penalty. They're giving me a penalty shot, but it means Eckhart won't have to serve his penalty. I think his trip was dirty enough to have been a game misconduct, and they should've given him some time in the sin bin, but I'll just have to make the most of this.

As I stand at center ice, I analyze their goalie. Pierce is a big guy. He'll catch anything down low, so I know everyone will expect me to take it top shelf. But as I take the puck toward the goal, a different plan formulates in my mind. I skate toward him until I'm just about at the crease, then I fake shooting to the right, and Pierce butterflies to block the shot. But instead, I spin back around and slip the puck into the opening on the left, directly behind his right skate. The buzzer sounds and I skate back to the bench amid the cheers of my teammates, but before I get there, I turn toward the Las Vegas bench and my eyes meet Eckhart's.

As he glares at me, I nod my chin at him and call out, "Thanks!"

From the look he sends my way in return, I know this isn't over.

It's in the middle of the third period when Eckhart takes his next shot at me, bringing the toe of his stick up to spear me directly below my ribs, where I don't have any pads to protect me. I hit the ice on my knees, the intense pain radiating through my diaphragm and up into my chest. But as the ref closest to me goes to grab Eckhart, all hell breaks loose on the ice. So many punches are being thrown that the refs back away, and I watch as Eckhart drops his gloves and skates toward me.

I hop up onto my skates just as he gets to me, and his fist would connect with my face, except I duck and jab him in the gut with my gloved fist as he flies by me. As I turn, I see

Zach behind me and he's grabbing Eckhart's extended arm by his fist, and pulling him forward, using his own weight against him so he lands on the ice on his stomach. Eckhart goes sliding across the rink toward the center line, and the refs are able to break up the fight.

AUDREY:
Funny, I don't remember ordering three containers of Fluff when I put my grocery order in with your personal shopper.

DREW:
Just looking out for my little man.

AUDREY:
And exactly how much Fluff do you think the kid is going to eat?

DREW:
You'd be surprised how fast it goes!

AUDREY:
You're his dad, not his fun uncle. Don't be a bad influence when his mom says no to too much sugar, Drew.

DREW:
Part of being a dad is helping to find ways around Mom's rules.

AUDREY:
Sounds like a good way to start a fight.

DREW:
Just think how much fun we'll have making up, though.

AUDREY:

"I thought I told you no fighting." AJ's voice comes from behind me in the locker room, and I set my phone down and turn to face her, even though I'm wearing nothing but a towel wrapped around my waist.

She doesn't give a shit if we're half-naked. This is her team, and she's going to come in here whenever she damn pleases—as she should. She keeps her eyes trained above shoulder level, but other than that, it's just like any other GM in the league coming into the locker room.

"I didn't fight." It's a childish thing to say, but I feel like it's important to establish the facts here. "I defended myself after being attacked."

"Don't be a smartass, Jenkins. You threw the first punch in that situation." AJ's hands are in the pockets of her trousers, like she's trying to pretend she knows how to be casual. But her ramrod straight spine and the hard line of her jaw indicate otherwise.

"I'm really not being a smartass," I tell her. Over AJ's shoulder, Colt is silently mouthing "Owwwwww," like I'm in trouble and he's an overgrown child teasing me about it. I look back at AJ. "But it wasn't fighting, it was roughing. And you told me that you didn't want me spending all my time in the penalty box this season. So far, I've been in there *once*."

Tonight's two-minute penalty for roughing, thanks to the gloves-on gut punch I gave Eckhart as he skated past me, had no effect on the team. Everyone else on the ice except for Zach Reid and the goalies got major penalties and Eckhart was ejected for being the instigator within the last five minutes of the game. It was a shitshow, but it absolutely was *not* my fault.

She doesn't say anything, just tilts her chin as she assesses my face. "Did you say or do something tonight to set Eckhart off?" She's keeping her voice quiet, and with the rowdiness of my teammates still celebrating our win, I doubt anyone can hear us.

"No. Just like I didn't say anything at the home opener to set off Alistair. This is just how these guys are."

"Toward you."

"Yep, toward me." No point in denying this. Eckhart isn't known for acting like that, and Colorado didn't make Alistair captain because he treats all of his teammates the way he treated me. There's bad blood and, apparently, no amount of time or distance is going to dissolve that.

"So long as you didn't do anything to antagonize him, I don't have a problem with you defending yourself. That was a low blow, what he did out there, just like with Alistair last week. At least you weren't hurt."

I don't mention the huge bruise I know I'm going to have on my abdomen. The team doctor checked me out for any signs of internal bruising or bleeding, and she thinks I'm clear but wants a follow-up every day we're on the road. I'm sure AJ already knows that.

"Just out of curiosity, why are you so adamant about me not fighting? I mean, you brought Zack Reid and me into your office and basically told him he might need to fight more, but you don't want me to fight?"

"I want every player on this team to do what's best *for the team*. In Zach's case, I needed to know he would step up and defend his teammates if needed. In your case, I didn't take over your contract to have you spend all your time in the penalty box like you were doing in Colorado. You have too much talent to waste your playing time sitting in there. You were halfway to throwing away your career with your last team. I want to see you be successful here."

She turns to leave, then stops and turns back around. "And Drew, I know you have the potential to do great things here. Make sure you keep your mind on the game. It would be easy to get distracted in a new city, with new people. Just…stay focused, okay?"

My throat bobs as I swallow, wondering what she knows. She and Lauren are close friends, but I can't see Lauren telling her about me and Audrey—both because she doesn't seem like a gossip, and because she knows that we're trying to keep this relationship quiet. What's growing between Audrey and me is still new, and we've got a kid who doesn't need any unwarranted attention. So I'm not sure what AJ knows, or thinks she knows. Maybe she's just speaking in generalities?

"Of course," I say, and give her a definitive nod before she turns and makes her way through the crowd of half-naked men and right through the door to the coaches' office.

"What was that all about?" Colts asks as he saunters up, still unshowered, in nothing but his compression shorts. For an older player, he's in impeccable shape—there's no soft midsection or an ounce of unnecessary weight on him.

"Nothing."

"Don't be like that, dude. What was that all about?"

"AJ was just reminding me that she isn't paying me to spend time in the penalty box, is all."

"Wasn't that your first time in there all season?" he asks.

"Yep. It was just a friendly reminder to stay focused," I say, because that's how I'm choosing to take it. There were no veiled threats, no undue pressure. Just a reminder that I'm here to do a job, and to not let my focus waver.

"She know about Audrey and Graham?" He asks the question quietly, because even though he, Walsh, McCabe, and Reid all know, I don't think they've told anyone else.

"Don't think so. And it should probably stay that way for a while longer."

"Noted. You coming out with us tonight? Or running back to the hotel to call your girlfriend?" He teases that last word out so he sounds like a second grader on the playground.

"Definitely headed back to call Audrey." There's no way in hell I'm missing the opportunity to talk to her, and it's already past 10 p.m. here, so with the hour time difference, if I don't call her soon, she'll be asleep.

"So whipped."

"Given that she's like a sister to you, isn't that what you'd want to see right now?"

"Good answer." Colt gives me one of those aggressive pats on the shoulder as he walks by, headed toward the showers. I dress quickly so I can say goodbye to my teammates and catch a cab back to the hotel, praying that Audrey's still awake when I call tonight.

Chapter Thirty-Eight

AUDREY

"What do you mean, you're taking Graham for the night?" I ask my brother.

Jameson's deep voice carries over the phone. "I mean that Drew talked to Lauren and asked her if there was any way we could watch Graham tonight so that he could have you all to himself."

"I hate that you know exactly what that means," I tell him. But he travels a lot as an agent, and I know he and Lauren have an active, healthy sex life. So I'm sure he can imagine how we'll be spending our time tonight, after a week of not seeing each other.

"Let's pretend I don't, because I don't want to think about that. Like, ever." His voice is so disgusted that it makes me laugh.

"So you'll be here in an hour?"

"Yeah, and Drew wants me to tell you to pack a bag for yourself, too."

I reach into my back pocket and take out the note I found this morning in my makeup drawer in my bathroom. *Can't wait to see you tonight!*

When I first started receiving these daily notes, I thought maybe he set them up around my house before he left for his trip. But then the new ones started appearing each day in places I would have seen them before, like the refrigerator. So then I assumed he must have given them to Jules to place around the house. Except, she left for Maine two days ago, and I got a message yesterday and another one today. Which means she must have put Graham in charge of them while she's gone? The thought of our son putting little notes around the house from his dad to me has tears filling my eyes...the good kind, which is funny because I'm not a big crier.

"Uhh, okay," I say slowly, wondering what, specifically, I'm packing for. I'll have to ask Drew, though, because there's no way I'm asking Jameson. "You seem surprisingly okay with this."

"If he treats you well and is there for Graham, then I'm happy for you. But if he steps out of line even a tiny bit, I'll fucking kill him, and he knows it."

"How does he know that?"

"Because we've talked."

"Stop interfering, Jameson."

"I'm not interfering."

"Okay, stop overstepping then. You're not my dad. And even if you were, I'm a grown-ass woman and don't need you stepping in to protect me. Drew and I can talk through things on our own."

On the other end of the line, Jameson grunts, "Fine."

"Okay, I'll have Graham ready in an hour. Thank you so much for taking him. Let me know if there's anything I can do to repay you for all the times you guys have watched him recently."

"I'm hoping to take Lauren away for a weekend, probably between Thanksgiving and Christmas. Maybe you can take the twins for the weekend?"

"Absolutely." Lauren and Jameson almost never ask me to watch the twins, but they take Graham all the time, so it's the least I can do.

When we hang up, I text Drew to find out what I should pack.

DREW:

Nothing. I plan to have you naked all night.

AUDREY:

Am I staying at your place, or are we going somewhere else?

DREW:

My place. For real, wear comfy clothes— we're staying in. Maybe bring a toothbrush and face wash? I don't know. What do girls need to spend the night somewhere?

AUDREY:

Has a girl never spent the night at your place???

DREW:

Not sure how you want me to respond to that?

AUDREY:

Are you for real? Like, have you never had a girlfriend?

> **DREW:**
> I've dated, but any spending the night was more of an unplanned thing. I guess I've never had a serious relationship. I've certainly never wanted to spend every free moment with anyone, until you.

> **AUDREY:**
> So what am I? Like a test to see if you like having a girlfriend?

> **DREW:**
> Pretty sure I've made it clear that you're my future wife. But sure, you can call yourself my girlfriend if you need to put a label on this.

The mostly empty take-out containers litter the coffee table, and the candles Drew lit when I arrived are burning low. I sit back against the bottom of the couch and rub my stomach.

"Why did you let me eat so much?" I groan, looking around the space.

Drew's condo isn't at all what I expected. Instead of being all wood and metal and glass like I'd envisioned, it's homey and cozy. The couch that serves as a divider between his living and dining room is a beautiful shade of off-white. Two brown leather chairs face the couch on the other side of the big, wooden coffee table, which is currently decorated with candles, two placemats, and the remnants of the dinner that arrived right as I did. There's a TV hanging above the fireplace, but it's one of those framed TVs that shows artwork when it's turned off, so it doesn't look like a TV at all.

I could live in a place like this. I don't know where the thought comes from. Except for college, I've lived in one house all my life. I thought I'd be raising Graham in that house, too. But somehow, Drew's place already feels like home.

"I mean, with the sounds you were making each time you tried something new," Drew says, drawing my eyes back to him, "I felt like I had to keep feeding you different things. You were *obviously* enjoying it."

"Oh yeah? What kind of sounds was I making?"

"Let's just say that it sounded an awful lot like a sexual experience."

My cheeks heat. "No, it didn't!"

He huffs out a laugh. "It really did. And I quite enjoyed it, so please don't be embarrassed now. You *should* enjoy food as much as sex, when it's that good." He reaches out and smooths a piece of hair off my face, tucking it behind my ear. His fingers slide through my hair to the back of my head, and he pulls me toward him, dropping a kiss on my forehead. "God, I missed you."

I melt into his touch. "Missed you too."

I'm about to roll onto my knees from my sitting position so I can get a better angle to kiss him, when the shrill ringing of my phone cuts through the low music Drew has on in the background.

"Shit, sorry," I say, grabbing for my purse where it sits on the couch cushion behind Drew. "Let me just make sure this isn't Jameson or Lauren."

I fish my phone out of my bag and am horrified when Karl's name is flashing on the screen, and even more horrified when Drew clearly sees it.

"Why's he still calling you, Audrey?"

"I don't know." I shrug. *Ring.* "I stopped returning his texts and answering his calls over a month ago." Right when Drew came back into the picture.

"You haven't told him you're seeing someone?" There's a hard edge to his voice as he narrows his eyes at me.

"No." *Ring.* The grating sound makes my whole body tense up. "I just stopped responding."

"Are you trying to keep that door open, just in case?"

Ring. "What? No!"

Drew holds his hand out, obviously intending to answer my phone. For a half-second, I hesitate, but then I realize there's no reason not to let him. I'm not going back to sleeping with Karl, ever.

"He's a colleague. Be cordial, at least," I say as I hand him the phone.

"Hello?" His tone is annoyed.

"Oh, sorry," I hear Karl's voice. Drew doesn't have the phone pressed against his ear, like he wants me to hear the conversation. "I think I have the wrong number."

"No, I think you have the right number."

"Oh. Is this Audrey's phone?"

"Yeah."

"Who's this?" Karl asks.

"Her future husband. So do me a favor and lose her fucking number."

He ends the call before Karl has a chance to respond. I should probably be bothered, but I can't find it in me to be—because if that was a girl he used to sleep with when he needed to scratch an itch and she'd been calling him regularly for the last month and he hadn't told her to go to hell, I'd want to do the same.

"Anyone else going to be calling in the future that I should know about?" he asks, eyebrow quirked. "Because it'd probably be easier for everyone if we just block their numbers now."

I roll my eyes. "No, you jealous caveman. No one else is going to be calling."

"Good."

"Is there anyone I should be worried about calling you?"

Drew huffs out another laugh. "I just moved back to Boston, and I think I made it perfectly clear that I haven't so much as looked at or talked to another woman since I first saw you again."

"What about on the road? There must be other women you've hooked up with, in various cities, who still have your number?"

"Nah, I only communicated with women via social media DMs, and I've blocked every single one of them and closed my DMs down. You have absolutely nothing to worry about." He sets my phone on the table and reaches his hand to my neck, slipping his fingers under my hair. "But I'm happy to keep reassuring you as often as you need."

I close my eyes as he pulls me forward, just enough to drop another kiss on my forehead. I hate feeling insecure and needy, and I look forward to the day that I'm so sure of his feelings that I don't need reassurances. But I'm not there yet, and I'm glad he understands that.

"Thank you." I swallow roughly. "I'm not normally a jealous person, but I've seen the way some professional athletes act when they're on the road, and I hate to think of all the temptations out there."

"First of all, no woman is, or could ever be, as tempting as you. And second, the women these guys hook up with on the road are looking for someone who's *available*, which I'm not. And aside from going out for a post-game dessert with a few of the married guys"—Drew lets out another little chuckle—"and Zach Reid, it's not like I've even gone out after a game."

"Why is Zach not going out looking for women on these trips?" I ask curiously.

"He's a serious relationship-only kind of guy, I guess. Just like me." Drew winks at me when I glance up at him.

"Just like you *now*."

"*Now* is the only version of me that matters, because it's the one you're stuck with. Forever." He sweeps his hands under me and lifts me from where I sit next to him between the coffee table and couch, depositing me on his lap like I weigh nothing.

I absorb that word as my fingertips trace the line of his cheekbones. I never imagined Drew could be this wonderful, or that being with him would make me feel so complete. "Forever, huh?"

"Yes." He leans in so his lips brush mine, and then he says, "Forever."

My lips part for him involuntarily—my body knows exactly what I need from him. And he kisses me back like he knows exactly what I need, too. Which is why I'm shocked when he pulls back and says, "Hang on, I want to show you something."

Chapter Thirty-Nine

DREW

"I really did think you were joking," she says as she stands in the doorway to my bedroom. Her eyes focus on the pole set up in the corner, then she looks over at me, skepticism written across her face.

"We had a deal." I slide my arm around her waist and pull her to me. Her back rests against my chest, and my breath carries over her hair when I say, "And I plan to collect."

She steps away from me, walking straight over to the pole. Did I have to buy a new dresser and rearrange my whole room in order to accommodate this pole? Yes. But as she grips it in one hand, leaning back and pulling on it like she's testing whether it's sturdy or not, I realize I'd do it again in a heartbeat.

"I've literally never danced for anyone before. Even my sister and friends don't know that I take pole dancing lessons."

"If not for the performance aspect, why do you take

lessons?"

"I wanted to do something fun and empowering that would also be a good workout."

I take a seat on the end of my bed, facing her. She's holding on to the pole with one hand, her arm fully extended, and her ankles crossed near the base. She's fully covered in her leggings and sweatshirt, but just the thought of her in fewer clothes has my dick stirring.

She takes a few quick steps and a small leap, then hooks one leg around the pole while bending her other leg so that her feet meet behind her. She spins around the pole a few times, so graceful and light.

Once her feet are back on solid ground, she looks at me over her shoulder and the wink she gives me has me up on my feet and closing the distance between us.

When she turns to face me, I back her right into the pole so that she's pressed up between it and me. My fingers glide along her hips and under the hem of her sweatshirt until I find the soft skin of her abdomen, and I tip my face down and inhale her scent—the honey and citrus smell I've come to love.

I can't imagine not having her in my life. I love every single thing about this woman.

"What's wrong?" she asks. That's when I realize that I'm completely frozen in place, like a rigid statue pressed up against her.

"Nothing," I say, giving my head a little shake to clear it as I step back to give myself a little breathing room. I could get lost in her so deep that I'd never find my way back...and that doesn't scare me as much as it probably should.

She tilts her head back along the pole so she's looking up

at me, and the delicate column of her neck is begging for me to kiss it. She gazes up at my face, and I see the concern and the lust swirling together in those bright blue eyes. Then she brings a hand up to my cheek, cupping one side of my jaw. "Drew, what's wrong?"

I press my lips together between my teeth, then say, "Nothing's wrong, I promise."

"Then why did you just get that look on your face, like you were panicking?"

Beneath her sweatshirt, I press my hands into her sides, holding her tightly. "I just had a second…where I was kind of overcome by the realization of how much I love you. I already knew I couldn't see myself with anyone else, ever. I already knew I wanted to spend the rest of my life with you. But…" In this moment, words seem to be failing me. "But this is the first time I've ever felt completely overwhelmed with how much I care about you."

Her lips curve up in a smile, and I know she's not ready to say those words back to me, and that's fine. I don't want her to say them until she's ready. But I want her to feel secure in knowing what my feelings are.

She slides her hand from my jaw to the back of my neck, pulling me toward her. And when her lips meet mine, the kiss is languid, like she's drawing this kiss out to savor the moment. I return her kiss, but when her throaty moan reverberates against my mouth, I can't hold back. My hands slide up her sides as I lift the sweatshirt over her head.

Beneath it, she's wearing a sexy black lace bodysuit, and when I kneel in front of her and drag her leggings down, I realize she's not wearing anything under it. In fact, I'm not sure it's a bodysuit after all—it seems more like lingerie.

I remain on my knees, my fingers toying with the edges of the lace fabric where they rest above her hipbones. As I slide my thumbs under the seams, her body shakes with a shudder that matches the look of longing on her face. I spin her around so she's facing the pole and I press her back forward while telling her to hold on.

With her hands clasped on the pole above her head and her back arched so her ass is in my face, the blood rushes to my cock so fast I'm practically dizzy. The lace of the thong runs between that peach of an ass, and I want to sink my teeth into her so badly my mouth waters.

Instead, I pepper kisses up the back of one thigh, across the slope of her cheeks, and then down the other thigh. And when she moans, pressing herself back toward me farther, I drag my hands from where they're gripping her legs just above her knees, and slide them along her inner thighs until my thumbs meet at her entrance.

She tilts her hips backward and up, trying to make contact with my thumbs, and instead of letting her, I place one hand on her ass and slide my other hand forward, slipping my fingers under the front of the bodysuit to find her clit.

She moans again, so damn eager for my fingers. I pull the thin scrap of lace fabric to the side to fully expose her to me, then bring my fingers back to coat them in her arousal before sliding them forward and rubbing them over her clit. Her hips move, trying to increase the friction, and I bring my tongue to her entrance as I move my fingers faster.

My cock is pressing against the zipper of my jeans so hard it's almost painful, and the noises coming out of Audrey's mouth are only making the situation in my pants worse. I pull my fingers from her clit and use them to adjust the bodysuit back in place, then my hand that's on her ass gives her a little slap. "Dance for me."

"Drew!" She spins around to face me. "You can't just stop like that."

"I can, actually," I say as I stand.

She steps toward me, her hand cupping my cock through my jeans. "How would you feel if I had you halfway to coming and stopped?" She's gripping me in her hand, her thumb sliding over the head of me, but I can barely feel it because the damn zipper's in the way. As much as I want to throw her on the bed and bury myself in her eager little cunt, I'm playing the long game here.

Bringing my hands to her breasts, I run my thumbs over the stiff peaks of her nipples, and in response, she closes her eyes and sighs. "Dance for me, and then I'll make you come so hard, you'll still feel me in your dreams."

She lets out a deep sigh. "Drew, the thought of having my body on display like that—"

"Has me about to unload in my pants," I finish for her. "There is nothing about your body that I don't love." I trail my hands from her breasts down her sides and grip her hips as I drop to my knees for her. Pressing kisses across her soft stomach through the sheer lacy fabric, I trail my lips down between her legs, where I press my tongue to her clit while I move my hands down to grip the backs of her strong thighs. "You are fucking perfect," I say, sitting back on my heels and looking up at her. "And I'm going to worship your body after I see what you can do on this pole."

She gives me a playful roll of her eyes. "I'm not very good."

"Let me be the judge of that."

"You have a lot of experience judging people's pole dancing abilities?"

My laugh is practically a snort. She's so cute when she's jealous. "No. I've never seen anyone pole dance before."

"Not even at a strip club?"

"You might find this surprising," I tell her, "but I've only been to a strip club once, for a bachelor party. And no, there was no pole dancing."

"Well, I'm glad the bar is low, at least," she says, biting her lip.

"Audrey." The word is sharp, and she looks down at me, her bright eyes assessing me from behind those dark, thick lashes. "There is no bar. I'm not comparing you to anyone else, and never will. You're it for me."

Her shoulders relax as she sighs out, "Fine. But I need my phone."

"I'll be right back," I say, as I rush to my feet before she changes her mind. I grab her phone off the coffee table where I left it, and bring it back to the room, where I find her running her hands along the pole like she's testing it out.

She opens an app and music fills the space. I unbutton and unzip my jeans before taking a seat at the end of my bed, because the pressure in there is actually painful. I'm not sure how long I can even watch her before I'll need to have her, but whatever this mental block is about her feeling comfortable with me seeing her body, we need to move through that.

Gripping the pole, she swings around again, with one leg out and one leg around the pole, and then she pushes both arms off the pole and sweeps a leg through so she's doing some sort of a V sit as she spins.

At the bottom of the pole, she places her feet on the ground, takes a few steps around as she grabs hold high on the pole with both hands, and then bends her inside leg around the pole so she's gripping it with the back of her thigh and inside of her knee. As she spins, she slides her inside arm down the pole and extends it out in front of her, holding the pole between her ribcage and the inside of her arm, and as she kicks her outside leg out and back, she extends her outside arm behind her and glides through the air gracefully as she circles that pole.

Seeing her like this, so strong, powerful, and sexy, is pushing the limits of what I can stand without touching her. I know she's not done, but I'm done waiting.

As I stand and stalk toward her, our eyes meet. She finishes her spin around the pole, and as I get to her, she spreads her legs open in a V in front of her, wrapping them around my waist and grinding herself over my cock.

Letting go of the pole, she wraps her arms around my neck, and I back her into the long piece of metal, hoping it's sturdy enough for both our weight. She hisses as her back meets the cold pole, but I thrust up against her, giving her the friction she wants as I move against her.

My hands are at her shoulders as I drag the delicate straps of her body suit down, and she carefully pulls one arm out at a time, freeing her breasts to me. My mouth and hands are on them instantly, sucking and rubbing those pretty pink nipples in a way that has her grinding herself against me almost frantically. She's so sensitive, and if the breathy sighs leaving her mouth are any indication, she's worked up already and I haven't even touched her.

"Put your feet on the floor."

"So bossy," she says, but she unwraps her legs from my waist and does as I ask. I pull the bodysuit down her abdomen and over her hips, letting it drop to the ground.

"Now spread your legs." She slides her feet apart, keeping her back along the pole for balance. I bring my tongue to her center, smiling against her when I find her drenched. "You're always so ready for me. Tell me what you want."

She runs her tongue along her lips. "I want you to make me come so hard I'll still feel it in my dreams."

"Look at you, repeating my words back to me like such a smartass."

She smirks down at me, and I bring two fingers up, slipping into her fast and hard. Her head falls back against the pole as she hisses out, "Yes."

When I lean forward, pulling her clit between my lips with gentle sucks, she moans out my name, and I'm certain I've never heard or seen anything sexier. I fuck her hard with my fingers, and don't let up on her clit, so that I have her on the edge quickly. "Fuck yes, Drew. Don't stop."

I reach up with my free hand and tweak her nipple between my fingers, and she lets out a guttural groan, and then her hips are bearing down on my fingers over and over. I flick and swirl my tongue over her clit, picking up the speed and intensity until she's practically screaming, "Drew, yes, fuck yes!" as she comes all over my fingers.

"You're so fucking needy for me. I want you to see what I do to you," I say as I stand, holding my two fingers in front of her face until she opens her eyes.

She's breathing hard, short bursts escaping her lips as she rests back against the pole, and she gives me a lazy smile before she takes my hand and sucks those fingers into her mouth. "Now fuck me, Drew. I need to feel you inside me."

I sweep her into my arms so fast I don't think she even registers what's happening until I set her on my bed. Standing beside her, I drop my jeans and boxers, and then reach over, taking her wrists and bringing them above her head. She watches me intently as I grab a coiled necktie off my nightstand.

"Recognize this?" I ask as it unfurls above her head. It's the one I wore with the shirt that matches her eyes. She nods, saying nothing but looking up at me with trust in her gaze. I'm glad we've established that, at least.

I loop a leg over her and bring my other knee up to the bed so that I'm straddling her. "You remember what you said, right?"

She swallows, recognition dawning on her face before she looks at me coyly and says, "What did I say?"

"That you'd replace me with your vibrator."

"Hmmm." The sound rattles around in the back of her throat. "I seem to remember something along those lines. And I think, in response, you threatened to tie me up and provide me with endless orgasms?"

"You're about to regret those words."

"Drew, I mean this as respectfully as possible." Her lips curve into a smile when she says, "Shut up and make me come again."

I lean forward and loop the tie around her wrists a few times before tying it off. Then I take the long tail of the fabric and tie it around the post that connects my headboard to the bed frame.

When I look down at her, she's licking her lips as she stares at my cock where it rests right between her breasts.

"I hope you remember that request, because I'm about to disrespect the fuck out of you. Open that mouth, beautiful."

She does as I ask, and I lean forward farther, gripping the top of the headboard above me with one hand while I hold her wrists against the bed with the other, and then I angle my hips down so the tip of my cock brushes against her parted lips. Circling her tongue around me, she opens, and I push inside. I'm careful not to go too deep, as it would be easy to make her gag at this angle, and that's not my goal. I just want to be good and wet for what I've got planned next.

She closes her lips around me, sucking me into her mouth as she runs her tongue along the bottom of my shaft while the top presses into the roof of her mouth. I thrust into her with relatively shallow pumps, until she moans again, and I'm so turned on that the vibrations have me about to come down the back of her throat. When I pull out quickly, she looks up at me in surprise.

I scoot back a bit so my cock rests in the crevice between her breasts, and then I bring my hands to them, cupping each side and pressing them together around my length. I look at her to make sure she's okay with me using her body like this, and she gives me a nod. As I start to move, I run my thumbs over her nipples, and she grunts out a "Yes" in response.

I watch her watching me fuck her perfect tits this way. Under me, her legs fall open and her hips are moving. "Drew, I need you inside me. Or I need you to let me touch myself."

"Your hands are staying tied up." I run my thumbs across her nipples faster than before, and she bites her lip through a moan. She's sexy as fuck, with her dark hair spread out around her and her hands tied up on my pillow. "Tonight's about *me* making you come until you beg me to stop."

Releasing her breasts, I reposition myself so I'm between her legs, which are spread wide apart and waiting for me. And then I bring my face to her again, and I don't hold back. My tongue flicks over her clit fast and hard, and when I sink my fingers into her and curl them toward her abdomen, she rides my fingers and chases that second orgasm until she's chanting my name. "I need you inside me, Drew," she says on a breath, her eyes earnest as I feel her muscles starting to contract around my fingers.

"I will be." I lift my head to tell her. "Most likely for orgasm four or five."

She falls apart at that moment, her hips coming up off the bed to meet my fingers. I'm gentler with her as she rides the waves of that orgasm, and when she's done, she practically dissolves into the bed.

"Holy shit," she says, and a contented sigh leaves her lips. "How do you do that to me?"

"What?"

"Make me come in, like, three minutes."

"Three minutes seems like a long time. I bet we can do better than that."

"Drew..." She says my name in that warning tone I enjoy too much.

"I like it so much better when you're screaming my name."

"Was I?"

"Honey, I haven't even met my neighbors yet, but I'm confident they know my name now."

Her cheeks flush. "I guess you'd better stop giving me such great orgasms, then."

"I'll tear up the floor and install soundproof insulation if needed, because there's no way in hell I'm not delivering these orgasms regularly."

I trail my fingers along her abdomen, then I push off the bed and prop myself up on my elbow beside her so I'm looking down at her. "So how many more orgasms do you think I'm going to get out of you before you're begging me to stop. Because I'm pretty sure I could do this all night."

"Oh my God, Drew, no. I need you inside me and then *maybe* I can give you one more. But that's all I've got in me."

"No way, Mama," I tell her, watching that same shiver of desire snake through her that I saw when I used that term the day before my road trip. "I'm not fucking you until you give me *at least* one more orgasm first."

Her face is a mask of defiance when she says, "Make me."

And so I do, two more times, just to prove a point. And right before she climaxes the last time, she's begging me to fill her, whimpering and writhing beneath me, and I can't hold back any longer. I'm so keyed up after giving her four orgasms that there's nothing gentle about the way I fuck her, but if the way she screams my name as she comes is any indication, she doesn't want gentle anyway.

She falls asleep in my arms before I can even clean her up, and as I watch her sleep, it occurs to me that I'm going to need to get some soundproof insulation for the walls too, and maybe a soundproof door. Because once I convince her and Graham to move in here, we're going to need our privacy in the bedroom—my girl does not know how to be quiet.

Chapter Forty

AUDREY

When I pad into Drew's kitchen in the morning, he's standing at the big marble island in nothing but a pair of sweatpants. I don't know how long he's been up, but he's got a mug of coffee in one hand and a stack of papers he's sorting through with the other. When he sees me, he sets the page in his hand down on top of the pile.

"What's that?" I ask, nodding to the pile of papers.

"Nothing."

"It's obviously not nothing," I say, keeping my voice light as I take in the guilty look on his face. "But I'm the one in your space, so if it's none of my business, or you don't want to talk about it, you can just say so."

He licks his lips and sets his coffee cup on top of the stack of papers. Then he sighs. "It's just medical bills."

"For your mom?" I come around the island and run my hand over his back.

"Yeah. I'm responsible for all the bills and stuff."

"I'm not trying to pry, but what do you mean by responsible?" I glance up at him, and he looks at me affectionately.

"I don't want to hide things from you, Audrey. But talking about money is so…I don't know…taboo, I guess."

He lifts me by my hips and sets me on the counter, and when the cold marble meets the backs of my bare thighs, goosebumps erupt all over my skin. I'm wearing one of Drew's Rebels t-shirts and nothing else. He steps up between my legs.

"You don't have to talk about it," I say, cupping his face in both my hands and kissing the flat bridge of his nose. "But if you want to, I'm always here."

"That's the thing," he says, and I draw back to see him better. "I want you to always be here. I want you in my kitchen in the mornings, and in my bed at night. I want to eat dinner with you and Graham right there." He nods his chin at the dining room table that runs parallel to the massive island I'm sitting on. "And I want to curl up on the couch with you and watch TV together after Graham goes to bed."

My breath hitches. I spent the night for the first time last night, and he's talking about me and Graham moving in?

"But there's so much you don't know about me and my life," Drew continues, brow furrowing, "and so much I don't know about you and your life. And I know it'll take time to get to that point, for you to be ready—but I don't want to hide things from you and slow-roll it just for the sake of taking it slow."

"You don't have to hide things, Drew." I run my thumbs across his cheeks, loving the scratchiness of his early morning face. "And in case I didn't make it clear before you left, I'm all in. Especially now that we've told Graham. I thought I'd want to take this slow for his sake, but he's clearly on board with us being together, and...this is what I want. Am I ready to move in tomorrow? No. But do I see that in our future? Yes."

He squeezes his fingertips into my hips and pulls me up against him. "I am so fucking impatient. I want you with me, always. I want to be the kind of man who deserves to marry you, and who deserves to be Graham's dad. I want *everything* with you."

How did I get so lucky with this man? How did I sleep with the irresponsible playboy he was six years ago, and wind up with the grown-up version of him who wants to be a husband and a father?

"You already are that kind of man, Drew. Every day, you're showing me more and more who you really are."

He trails kisses along my hairline, then past my ear and along my jaw. "And I'm going to keep showing you, until you let me put a ring on that finger. And then I'm going to start putting more babies in you, and showing you how good I am with the newborn stage too, until we've built our whole family."

"Oh yeah?" I laugh, not hating the idea of giving Graham some siblings as long as Drew is the father. "And how many babies are you planning on giving me?"

"At least a hockey team's worth." He nips my neck playfully with his teeth.

"You want SIX kids? Like hell that's happening." I push his face away from my neck and give him a death glare as he laughs.

"Okay, maybe, one or two more?"

I smack his shoulder. "You said six just so that I'd say yes to fewer, didn't you?"

"Guilty. But hey, I missed seeing you have our first child. I missed the baby and toddler years with Graham. I missed out on so much, and I want to be there for everything this time around—the ultrasounds, the baby shower, choosing baby names, the birth. And I want to watch Graham become the best big brother to those babies too…"

I want all of that too, and I want it with him. "Okay, one or two more, then. And, I'm looking forward to seeing you experience all of that, and getting to go through it with you."

He wraps his arms around my lower back, holding me to him. "I fucking love you."

I nuzzle my face into his neck, loving the closeness—not just physical, but the emotional connection we have, too. "Always the romantic."

"I mean, I could have said 'I love making you scream my name.' Which is what I plan to do as soon as I tell you about these medical bills." He pats his hand on the pile of papers beside me.

"Drew, I'm exhausted. Not only did you keep me up half the night—"

"You didn't seem to be complaining while I was giving you orgasm after orgasm."

"—but then you woke me up early this morning for *more* sex!" Am I really complaining about this man taking care of me in ways I didn't even know I needed to be taken care of? *No.*

I thought sex was an itch I needed to scratch every once in a while when I got tired of taking care of my own needs. I had no idea what it could be like when I was with a man who loved me and loved bringing me pleasure.

"Listen, we get Graham back in"—he glances at the clock on the oven—"like, two hours. And there's no way I'm not coming inside you at least one more time before then. We can call it practice."

I burst out laughing, and he looks at me like I'm crazy.

"Practice? Like, for what? Having more kids?"

"Yeah, because the minute you're ready, we're doing that again," he says. My heart squeezes in my chest. He's so ready for the next step that it makes me feel like I could be ready, too. "But stop trying to distract me with talk about sex, because I have important stuff to talk to you about regarding my mom's health care."

That blasts me right out of my love-infused stupor. Drew's mom is wonderful, and the thought of her having a degenerative disease like Parkinson's is heartbreaking—and I've only known her for a couple of weeks. I can't imagine how it weighs on Drew, Missy, and Caitlyn.

"Okay. What's going on?" I ask.

He updates me on the course of his mom's treatment, a bit of which he'd already told me when we talked about the need to remodel the first floor of her house. "All the doctor's visits and treatments are expensive, and I manage it all." I try not to shudder at the thought of all those visits to hospitals, because this is his future, and that means it's mine too. But watching another terrible disease take another mother away from her kids, like cancer did for mine, has my eyes filling with tears. "Hey..." he says, cupping my face. "What's wrong?"

"I'm so sorry. This isn't about me. I don't know why I'm crying."

He gently strokes the tears off my cheeks with his fingers. "I didn't even think about what you'd told me about your mom and all those doctor visits and hospital stays. Is that what this is about? I'm so sorry."

"No, I just...I know what the journey through a terrible disease is like. And I hate that you're going to have to go through that with your mom."

He kisses the top of my head and runs a hand up and down my back. "Parkinson's isn't deadly, but I'm not going to pretend that it's going to be easy. There will be more doctor's appointments, and more hospital visits. In the long run, there will be live-in nurses and home health aides. I'm committed to giving her the best possible care that's available, no matter the cost. But the end isn't going to be pretty."

"I hate this for you."

"I hate this for *us*. Because we're going to have to be there for her together. The good news is, she still has a lot of good days ahead of her."

"I'm sorry about the crying," I tell him as I use my fingertips to wipe away any leftover tears. "It's just that, knowing what this disease is like in general, and then imaging how it's going to impact your mom specifically, felt like very different things. I know I've only met her once, but I adored her and so did Graham. I hate to think he's finally going to have a grandparent in his life, and she's so wonderful, and then he's going to lose her."

"We all lose our grandparents eventually," Drew reminds me. "I think the best we can do is to make sure he gets many happy years with her." I nod up at him, knowing he's right.

"Which is why, after you go get Graham at Jameson's, and I sit here and pay all these medical bills, we're going to go to my mom's for Sunday dinner."

"My family usually does Sunday dinner together," I tell him, though lately it seems like it's been less frequent. Tonight, for example, we aren't all getting together because Jameson and Lauren are meeting up with one of her brothers and his wife who are in town for the weekend. "But, we can probably switch off—go to my family some weekends and yours others?"

"I'd like that," he says. "Normally, Missy does it at her house now, but she's going to cook at my mom's tonight. Given that Graham's been there before, and knowing that this whole experience of meeting aunts and uncles and cousins he didn't know he had is probably going to be overwhelming, it seemed best to have it at my mom's, where it's familiar for him."

"You sure made a lot of plans *before* asking me." I raise an eyebrow.

He squeezes the back of my neck as he brushes a kiss across my forehead, and his touch—both supportive and loving—instantly relaxes me. "No, I made sure these plans were *possible* before asking you. Now I can tell Missy it's a yes. Right?"

"Yeah. Is it crazy that I'm nervous about meeting your whole family?"

"No, but you better let me help with those nerves, anyway. I know exactly how relaxed you get after you're done screaming my name..."

"Can I go up?" Graham asks when Drew shows him the treehouse in the backyard at his mom's house. The exterior walls are freshly painted a deep blue-gray that matches the house, but I don't know how old the structure actually is. The wood at the base of it isn't fresh, except for a few added supports.

"Of course," Drew says. "That's what it's here for."

"Are you sure it's safe?" I ask him.

"I had a structural engineer check it out, just to make sure," he tells me.

"You know a structural engineer?"

"I know your sister," he says, "and she stopped by the other day on her way out to that house in Wellesley that you guys are working on. She gave it her seal of approval."

"How did you coordinate all this—the notes and the treehouse—with Jules?"

He gives me a wink. "I have my ways." Then he turns to Graham. "Are we going in?"

"Yes!" Graham yells as he runs toward the tree. He grabs hold of the rope ladder and climbs up, and Drew follows behind him.

"You know," Drew's mom says from behind me, and I turn in surprise. She'd been up on the deck a moment ago, and I didn't even hear her come down the steps. "He's been working on that thing every single time he's been over here for the past few weeks."

My heart feels like it expands in my chest. There are so many reasons I adore Drew, but watching him grow into being a dad makes me love him even more.

Love? The realization that I just used that word, even though it was only in my own thoughts, rips through me. I love Drew. I love the way he shows up for me and the way he takes care of my body. I love the way he tells me how he's feeling, and makes me feel things I didn't know were possible. And maybe, most of all, I love watching him with our kid—how patient and kind he is, how he wants Graham to feel loved.

"He built it?" I croak out the words through the lump in my throat. Based on the gray color of the wood at the base, I assumed the treehouse had been here for many years.

"No, it's the one his dad built for him when he was little. Watching him fix it up and make it like new again for his own son—" Her voice breaks, and she stops speaking, instead swallowing hard as her eyes fill with tears. I wrap an arm around her shoulder, and we stand there for a moment, listening to the sound of Drew and Graham's conversation, which we can barely hear, flowing from the treehouse while we both try not to cry.

"I got so lucky with him," I tell her. "Graham is the best thing that ever happened to me, but having Drew in our lives and watching him get to experience fatherhood…it's more than I ever hoped for."

"I think it's the last thing he expected, and probably the best thing that ever happened to him, too."

"Hey, Ma?" Missy's voice rings out behind us. She was inside getting dinner started when we got here, so we got a chance to meet her. But her husband and boys haven't arrived yet. I appreciate that Graham is getting a little time here with Drew first, before the rest of the family descends.

I can't wait for him to meet his cousins, but I also don't know if he's going to be overwhelmed by all these new people in his life. Graham seems to take things in stride though, probably because five-year-olds don't have the capacity to complicate things like adults do. I know I need to stop projecting my own worries onto him because he seems fine.

Mrs. Jenkins turns toward Missy. "Yeah, honey?"

"Can you help me with the sauce?" her daughter calls from the sliding glass door. "It seems like it's missing something."

"Sure, I'll be right there." She turns back to me. "Thank you for coming over today. I know that meeting a whole new family is going to be a lot for you and Graham, but we're really excited to have you guys here."

"Thank *you* for welcoming us like you have," I say, returning her soft smile.

When she heads inside, I take a seat on the stairs leading up to the deck. I love listening to Drew and Graham as they hang out together in the playhouse. They're talking about Spider-Man, Graham's favorite superhero, when the sliding glass door opens behind me and Mrs. Jenkins pads across the deck to take a seat next to me.

But when I glance over, I find Caitlyn sitting there instead. I'm sure I don't do a good job of masking my surprise, because she says, "I'm sorry, didn't mean to scare you."

"I just thought you were your mom, is all." I don't really know what to say to her after our last interaction, where she called me a Puck Bunny and chastised Drew for being late to his mom's appointment because he was with me.

"I owe you an apology," she says, and that shocks the shit out of me. From the way Drew talks about her, an apology was the last thing I expected. "I'm sorry I made the assumptions I did when we met."

"It's okay. I showed up out of nowhere. You don't know me." I pause, wondering if I should hold back the next thought in my head, but it's out of my mouth before I can stop it. "And to be perfectly honest, I don't think you really know your brother, either."

It's probably not my place to say this to her. But, if she's going to be my sister-in-law someday, I want to make it perfectly clear that I'm not going to tolerate her treating Drew like she has been. He deserves better than that, especially because he's a wonderful son who goes above and beyond for his mom, and he clearly has a good relationship with Missy. I don't think he's the problem here.

She sighs. "You're probably right. Which is sad, because I practically raised him after our dad died."

"I know how hard that is," I tell her, and she looks at me, seemingly taken aback.

"You do?"

"Yeah. My mom died when I was fourteen, and my dad left when I was fifteen. I helped raise my sister, who's three years younger than me."

"Helped who?" she asks.

"My brother. He used to play for the Rebels, but retired when my dad left so that he could be there for me and Jules. He got guardianship of us, but it was me who did most of the day-to-day stuff because he was so busy building his career as a sports agent. He's Drew's agent, actually."

"Wait, Jameson Flynn is your brother?"

"Yep."

"And he gave up his hockey career to raise you and your sister?"

"Yeah."

"Does he…" It's like she can't find the right words. "How does he feel about that?"

"He doesn't really talk about it, but my future sister-in-law says that he told her he's never regretted his decision for a second."

"Are you and your sister close?" she asks, propping her elbow on her knee and resting her chin on her fist.

"She's my best friend. I was supposed to go to Georgetown for college. It was where I'd dreamed of going since I was little. I got in, but the thought of leaving her, of missing those high school years, was unfathomable. After my parents were both gone, Jules and Jameson were all I had. I didn't want to miss out on any of the milestones. So I went to BU instead."

"Where you met Drew…"

"Yeah." I nod.

"How did he not know about Graham?" she asks, but her tone holds no judgment.

"He'd moved to Vancouver before I found out, and there were some missed phone calls and miscommunication." If she wants to know more than that, she can ask Drew herself.

"And then…?"

"I ran into him at my brother's house when he first moved back to Boston. He met Graham, and it was pretty obvious whose kid he was."

"I'm still having trouble wrapping my mind around the idea of Drew being a dad," she says, her eyes flicking from me to the treehouse where laughter has just erupted again.

"Well, he's a pretty great one, if I do say so myself."

She opens her mouth to respond, but that's when the side gate opens and two boisterous boys run toward us, both of them carrying several plastic action figures in their hands. When they approach us, Caitlyn introduces me to Missy's husband, Rusty, and their boys, Ryan and Finn.

Then Drew's walking across the lawn with his hand on Graham's back, and tears fill my eyes as I watch my son meet his cousins for the first time. And when my eyes meet Drew's, and I see the tears in his eyes too, mine start to fall down my face. I wipe them away through my smiles, and when Drew comes over and wraps his arm around my shoulders, I snuggle into his side, wondering how I could possibly be any happier.

Chapter Forty-One

DREW

We're crowded together in the hallway outside the locker room, waiting to take the walk to the ice. I'm absorbing the sound of the music and the cheering crowd when Zach nudges my shoulder. "I forgot to ask you after our home opener how it feels to play in your hometown."

"It's pretty fucking amazing, actually," I say, thinking about how tonight my whole family is here, and so is Audrey's. It feels a million times better than playing for a faceless crowd in another city.

"Is she here?"

I assume he means Audrey. "Yeah. Every game."

"And your kid?"

"He's here too. She usually takes him home after the second period so she can get him in bed."

"Is that where you rush off to after every home game?" he asks.

I nod, thinking about how I already can't wait to see her

later tonight. I want to add her to the Wives List, and I want her and Graham waiting for me in the Family Room at the end of the game—provided he can stay up that late—but I have to talk to her and see if she's ready for that.

"Sweet."

If I didn't know Zach as well as I do, I'd think the guy must be a stoner or something. He's so Zen about everything, on and off the ice. I take a deep breath, trying to channel some of his calm, because for some reason, I'm really keyed up today. We're 6-1-1 so far this season, so we're off to a good start. I'm playing well. My coach is happy with me, and I haven't been in the sin bin once since that talk with AJ, so I assume she's happy too. But there's something there, some current of electricity right under my skin, making me feel almost jumpy.

"You good?" Zach asks, watching me carefully.

"Yeah. Just taking it all in."

"You sure?"

"I'm fine." The words come out with more of an edge than I'd intended. What the fuck is wrong with me? I take a breath, and say more convincingly, "Really."

We make the walk down the hallway, each of us reaching out and touching the Rebels logo painted on the wall. The music and the sound of the crowd are practically deafening as we approach the rink, and I let the energy settle into my bones. At least one goal, and no penalties. That's my job tonight.

I take to the ice, letting my skates glide across the smooth surface while the lights and music flash around me. And as we line up for the national anthem, I glance over to where I know Audrey's standing, and my breath is absolutely stolen from my lungs.

She's wearing my jersey.

She's got my last name on her back.

And as she looks down at me, an enormous smile plastered across her beautiful face, I know she's mine. I have to make it work in Boston. I need to be able to stay and play here. There's no way I'm uprooting her and Graham, taking her away from the company she started with her sister, or taking Graham away from the small, private elementary school he's so happy at. It has to be Boston or nowhere.

A small knot of anxiety winds itself around my stomach as I stand there with my helmet in one hand and the other over my heart, listening to the national anthem with my eyes locked on Audrey.

"You sure you're okay, man?" Zach asks when the music stops and the lights come up.

"Never been better." And it's true, which is why it's hard to rationalize the pit in my stomach.

We're sixteen minutes into the first period when I score my first goal, and four minutes into the second period when I score my second. We're leading 4-1 and the guys are insisting tonight's the night for me to score a third goal.

"Last time you played against us," McCabe reminds me, "you scored a hat trick. Colt's never forgotten that. The least you can do is to do it again, this time *for* us."

"No pressure," Walsh says, his eyes focused on the ice, waiting for our line change.

When it comes, we absolutely explode onto the ice, and I skate hard and fast toward Washington's net, where one of their defensemen currently has the puck behind the goal. He sends it along the boards, trying to get it to the left winger, and I reach for it with my stick, managing to bat it over to Walsh, but crashing shoulder first into the boards. It hurts like a motherfucker, but I shake it off, jumping to my feet and advancing toward their net.

I don't even have the puck when one of Washington's defenders pushes me for absolutely no reason. I try to channel Zach's inner calm as the asshole follows me, talking shit about how I won't score again. And when I turn to receive the puck from McCabe, who sends it across the ice in front of the goal, the asshole from Washington checks me.

Before I even have time to pick myself up, the refs blow the whistle and give him some time in the penalty box for roughing. I force myself to shake it off, knowing that not responding was exactly what AJ wanted, but the booing from the crowd lets me know they were hoping for a different response.

They're not paying your salary or signing your next contract, I remind myself.

I line up to take the face-off, determined to win it and make this power play count. A third goal before the end of this period will feel so much better than punching that asshole in the face.

But at the end of the two minutes, we haven't scored, though we're still up by three, and I should feel good about that. The allure of a hat trick, and getting it done in front of my son, hangs heavy in front of me as I sit the bench, taking a drink of water before our next line change.

There's such a thing as focusing too hard on a single outcome, and I know I'm straddling that line. Being determined to be the one to score, rather than being determined to pass to the player in the best position to score, has resulted in many a hockey player losing an important shot for their team.

I don't want to be that person. But man, do I want that hat trick.

My chance comes as I'm taking the puck across the blue line into the attacking zone, but one of Washington's defenders is advancing too quickly, and Walsh is open, so I pass the puck to him and start to skate past the defender. We've practiced this move a hundred times, where Walsh passes to McCabe, who then saucers the puck all the way across the ice to me instead, and as I surge forward to get in place to receive it, another Washington player comes out of nowhere and hits me from behind. The hit sends me sliding across the ice, right into the goalpost, knocking the net off its moorings.

I don't even stop to think, I just throw my gloves down as I jump up and come face-to-face with Henry Levine. We played together in college, and we've faced off against each other several times tonight. And I can tell by the look on his face that he didn't mean to hit me like that, but in my enraged state, it doesn't matter because he *did* hit me. I advance on him as he throws his gloves to the ice, and when I take my first swing, he blocks it with his shoulder pads and hits me right in the side where I'm unprotected. The pain flares through my rib, and I swing my other arm up and get his jaw with an undercut. His head snaps back, but he stays on his feet, and in that moment where we lock eyes but don't move, the refs move in and grab each of us.

And as I take my seat in the penalty box, I look across the ice for Audrey and Graham. Her head is bent, talking to him where he stands on his seat, so I can't sense if she's upset about the fight. It's part of hockey, but she knows about AJ's warning last week, and I'm sure she's not happy I just lost control of my emotions like that. Standing next to her, Jameson is shaking his head. He knows I just fucked up, but neither of us knows how bad.

I slide my arms into my suit coat and grab my phone from where it sits on the shelf of my locker. All I want at this moment is to go see Audrey. To forget about the penalty, the way my coach looked at me when I got back to the bench, and the way AJ was waiting for me at the door to the locker room at the end of the game to read me the fucking riot act. The shine was taken right off the hat trick I managed with my goal in the third period, and our team's seventh win of the season, because now all I can think about is that none of the good stuff matters if I don't get a handle on my "impulse control issues," as AJ called them. It's the same term Audrey used, which makes me wonder if there's some truth to it.

"AJ's pissed?" Zach asks from beside me before I even have a chance to unlock my phone.

"You think?" I'm pretty sure everyone inside the locker room knew exactly what happened outside that door, because the minute I walked in, the whole celebration came to a screeching halt. Finally, Colt screamed, "A fucking hat trick, man!" and my teammates pulled me into the center of their celebration. "She says I have 'impulse control issues.'"

"You ever talk to anyone about that?"

"Anyone like…a shrink or something?"

"Or like a sports psychologist?"

"Is that why you're so calm all the time?"

"No." Zach huffs out a laugh. "I'm calm because I've spent significant time and attention working on my capacity to keep my emotions in check. I meditate every day. I have strategies in place for dealing with my shit before it gets the better of me."

"What's that mean?"

"It means that the first time I ever got in a fight on the ice, I ended some kid's hockey career. We were thirteen. I've spent my whole life working to be better than I was in that moment."

"Was it your fault?"

"It was shit luck that he fell the way he did, but it wouldn't have happened if I hadn't punched him. It took two years before I could find a coach willing to have me on their team. I almost missed my shot at going pro because of a stupid, impulsive decision." Zach runs his hands through that sandy blonde hair, his square jaw set firmly. "I had to learn to be smarter than my emotions."

"That's why you never fight?"

"Part of it, yeah."

"What's the other part?" I ask as I gather the last of my stuff together out of my locker.

"That part won't help you." Zach just shakes his head. The guy is kind of mysterious—quiet and observant, and it makes me wonder if any of us *really* knows him. "If you want to focus on getting control of your emotions, I know a great therapist. I video call with her twice a week. I'm sure she'd talk to you if you want."

I nod, willing to give it a try. "Alright, send me her info. I gotta get going."

I hold my phone up to unlock it as I leave the locker room, but the screen is taken over with Caitlyn's name and an incoming call. As much as she's not the person I want to talk to right now, she never calls unless something's wrong.

"What's up?" I answer.

"Drew, Mom fell leaving the game. She was really disoriented, and they ended up taking her to the hospital via ambulance to have her checked out."

"What?" The word rips out of me so loudly that the friends and family members lingering in the hallway turn to stare. "Is she okay?"

"I think so, but we're waiting to see the doctor. It...would be great if you could come by. She'll want to see you."

"Of course I'm coming." She gives me the details as I rush out to my Jeep, thankful that it's a home game and I can get to her quickly, but then realizing that if it wasn't a home game, this wouldn't have happened. She'd have watched the game from the safety of her couch.

That guilt nags at me for the twenty minutes it takes me to get to the hospital and park, and when I find my sisters, they're sitting side by side in the ER room. It feels so empty without the bed.

"What's going on? Where's Mom?"

"They just took her for a CT scan," Caitlyn says. "Since she was disoriented after hitting her head, they want to make sure she doesn't have any swelling or bleeding in her brain."

"It was probably just the Parkinson's making her disoriented," Missy tries to reassure us. And she might be right—being disoriented because of the Parkinson's could be what caused the fall. Or being disoriented could be a result of the fall. And we won't know until the doctor reviews the images and comes to talk to us."

"It might be a while," Caitlyn tells me. "They have to put an IV in so they can inject the contrast, and normally they'd do it here. But she was really agitated when they were trying to place the IV, so they took her to imaging to do it. It'll take a while for the IV bag to empty into her veins, and then they can do the scans."

"Can we see her in the meantime?"

"I don't think so. I think the more people around, the more agitated she'll get."

"But it feels like one of us should be with her at least," I say.

My phone buzzes in my pocket, and I pull it out to see that Audrey's calling. *Shit.* In my rush to get here through the post-game traffic, I completely forgot to let her know what was going on.

"Hey," I say, pressing the phone to my ear as I walk out into the hallway.

"Everything okay?" she asks, concern evident in her sweet voice.

"I'm at the hospital. My mom fell leaving the game, and when Caitlyn called to tell me, I rushed straight here. I'm so sorry. I meant to call you on my way, but I was so distracted."

"Oh no! Is she okay?"

"I'm not sure. I haven't seen her yet…" I pause and take a deep breath as I lean against a wall. The adrenaline rush that had carried me here is over, and I'm crashing—emotionally and physically. Then I explain about the CT scan.

"Drew, I'm so sorry. What can I do?"

"I don't think there's anything to do. We just have to wait

and see what happens." I hate this part. I hate the waiting and the uncertainty. Unfortunately, that's what this disease brings. All I want to do is wrap myself in Audrey's arms, but I'd never ask her to come here. Not only because she's home with Graham, but also because I know how she feels about hospitals.

"Okay," she says. "You'll keep me posted?"

"Of course." I pause, taking a breath. "And Audrey?"

"Yeah?"

"I'm really sorry about tonight."

"What for?" she asks, sounding confused.

"For losing control of my emotions on the ice. I don't want you to think that it means I'm not serious about making sure my contract gets renewed, or that I'm not aware that I need to set an example for Graham."

"Fighting is part of hockey, Drew. No one expects that you'll *never* fight. I think AJ just wants to make sure you're not spending all your time in the penalty box. And you haven't been."

She's right, I haven't spent nearly as much time in the penalty box as was normal for me in Colorado. But still, I know AJ's not happy with me right now. "I know, but she's pissed about that fight."

"You're worried?"

"A little."

"It's going to be okay, Drew," she says, but she can't know that for sure.

"I hope so." I sigh, and we say our goodbyes before I return to the room to wait with my sisters.

It's probably half an hour later when there's a knock on the door, and then it swings open. We all look up, expecting a nurse or doctor to update us on my mom, and in strolls Audrey.

"What—what are you doing here?" I ask, as relief crashes over me just at the sight of her.

"Since you don't know how long you'll be here, I brought provisions." She holds out a plastic container of cookies, telling us Jules made them earlier today. And then she sets what appears to be one of those bags that hold four bottles of wine on a rolling table next to where the bed should be, and starts taking out reusable coffee mugs one by one. "It's hot caramel apple cider," she says, "because that's what I had on hand. I hope you guys like that? I didn't want to attempt hot chocolate now that I've had your secret family recipe."

Missy and Caitlyn look at me, and Missy laughs, saying, "We have a secret family recipe?"

"It's *very* top secret," I say, looking at my sisters. "Sorry, you two didn't make the cut."

"You made that whole thing up!" Audrey practically screeches.

"I do have a recipe, and I'm the only one who knows what it is, thus making it top secret. I did say that I'd tell you when you married me." I shrug, and then reach my hand out for a cup of her hot caramel apple cider.

"Well, now maybe I don't know if I *want* to marry you," she says, but her voice is teasing as she hands me the cup. "If you'd lie about a hot chocolate recipe, what else would you lie about?"

I pull her to me and my lips to her forehead, telling her, "I'm so glad you're here." She wraps an arm around me and gives me a squeeze, then looks up at me. "I would never have expected you to come. I know how much you hate hospitals."

"Drew, I'll happily sit in a hospital if it means being here to support you."

I drop my forehead to hers and breathe her in, the vanilla citrus scent that she seems to be infused with, as I try to absorb the love and the empathy she exudes.

My sisters start making gagging noises behind us, and I'm about to say something crude in response, when the door swings open and a nurse walks in.

"Everything's okay," she tells us. "But the doctor wants to keep your mom overnight for observation. You can see her, and then we're going to get her admitted."

Chapter Forty-Two

AUDREY

We're crowded together at the table in our kitchen, having a Friday night family dinner. Jules is heading back up to Maine this weekend, and so our normal Sunday night won't work. It's loud and rambunctious with four adults and three kids, and I love having my whole family together like this.

But Drew's empty seat next to me is putting a damper on things. He had a mid-week game in Tampa, so I haven't seen him in days, and he was supposed to be here already. I glance at my watch, and when I look up, I see him through the kitchen window as he walks up the back steps. His head is hung low, and he looks…not like himself.

Jules is at the counter, so she lets him in, and when Graham sees Drew, he runs across the kitchen and throws his arms around Drew's legs. Drew bends and picks him up, giving him a huge hug, but the way he squeezes his eyes closed like he's in pain has me worried. What the hell is wrong?

He carries Graham back to his seat, then slides into the chair next to me, leaning over and kissing me on the cheek. It's a chaste kiss, the kind you'd give a friend or a relative, but maybe it's just because we're in front of my whole family and it's his first time being here for a dinner with us?

I glance over at him and don't miss the purple circles beneath his eyes. He looks like he hasn't slept in a week. Lauren offers him the serving platter of pasta, which we'd made because he has a game tomorrow. One of the things I'd forgotten from when Jameson used to play is how much damn pasta hockey players eat when they're carb loading the night before a game.

I watch him eat a few bites here and there as his eyes scan the table, but it feels like he's somewhere else. So I slide my arm along the back of the chair and lean my head on his shoulder, looking up at him as I whisper, "Everything okay?"

"Not now, Audrey."

It takes everything I have not to respond—not to whip my head up and look him dead in the eye and tell him not to take that tone with me. There's obviously something going on, and he clearly doesn't want to talk about it in front of my family. I just wish he'd given me a heads up.

Across the table, Jameson's eyes flit from Drew to me, and he does not look happy.

When we're done eating, Graham is chasing Ivy and Iris around the living room while Lauren and Jameson take care of the dishes. Jules excuses herself and heads to the bathroom, so I turn in my chair to face Drew. His hand drops from where he's been playing with my hair while staring off into space.

"What's going on?" I ask him quietly.

"I can't talk about it right now."

"I haven't seen you in days, and you show up here and act like a totally different person, and I'm supposed to...what? Pretend like everything's fine?"

"Maybe I should go." My stomach drops at the despondency in his voice.

"Drew," I say, grabbing his forearm where it's now folded across his chest. "What the fuck?"

"There's just a lot going on right now, Audrey. And I can't talk about it with everyone around."

I think back to last weekend and how happy Drew was to have me at the hospital with him when his mom fell. And how earlier this week, before he left for Tampa, Graham and I went with him to visit his mom when she came home from the hospital. We'd felt like a family, and Graham clearly loved getting to spend time with his grandmother.

I know Drew's worried about her, and even the Apple Watch with the fall detection feature that he got her isn't taking that worry away. But this is more than that.

"Is something going on with the team?"

He stands quickly, and his chair scraping along the terracotta tiles makes a screeching sound that has all heads turning his way. "Sorry, I have to head out," he says as I sit there in stunned silence, staring up at him. But he doesn't even look at me. He gives Graham a hug goodbye, asks Lauren to tell Jules that dinner was delicious, nods at Jameson, and then heads out the door. Jameson is hot on his heels, and even though he slams the door behind him, we can hear their raised voices.

I glance at the living room, wanting to see if Graham has noticed any of this going down, but he's playing with the twins, blissfully unaware. So I cross the kitchen to where Lauren stands near the sink. "What the hell is happening?" she whispers.

"I don't know, but I have a feeling Jameson does." I watch as my brother shoves his hands deep into his pants pockets, exhaling a deep breath that crystalizes in the icy air while he watches Drew drive off. He doesn't turn to come back in immediately, but when he finally does, he looks up at us watching him through the window, and his shoulders slump.

"What the hell was that all about?" I ask as soon as he steps back inside.

"I hate to say this, but as his agent, I really can't tell you. You need to talk to Drew about it."

"Hard to do when he just left without telling me what's wrong or even saying goodbye." There's a bitterness in my voice that I don't like. I hate this feeling of us not communicating, of him saying that he loves me and wants forever with me, and then turning around and icing me out like this. This isn't how relationships are supposed to work.

"Maybe..." Jameson pauses, then looks between me and Lauren. "Maybe you should go after him. I don't think this is the kind of thing that you should wait on."

"I have to see if Jules can watch Graham."

"Just go," he says. "If she has other plans, one of us can stay."

The look of concern on Lauren's face has me worried. "Sometimes," she says, "we need to bury our pride and step up to fight for the relationship when the other person can't. I don't know what's going on, but Drew obviously isn't in a position to fight for you guys right now. *So you need to.*"

Next to her, Jameson nods in agreement, so I nod back. They have the best, strongest relationship I've ever seen. This is probably an area where they have some experience, so I need to trust that their advice is right. Because even though I don't know what's going on with Drew, I know that what we have is worth fighting for.

He's been the one fighting for us all along, so maybe now it's my turn.

AUDREY:

I'm at your door. Can you buzz me in, please?

I wait outside, standing at his door for a few minutes, and there's no response. But I know he's in there because I checked that his Jeep is parked in his spot behind his building, and I can see lights on through the top-floor windows.

I hit the button to call him, and I'm surprised that he answers on the first ring. "Hey."

"Did you see my text?"

"No, I just stepped out of the shower."

I couldn't have been more than five minutes behind him. How do guys shower so fast?

"Can you buzz me in?"

"You're here?"

"Yes. And it's freaking cold out here, so unlock the door,

please." I don't think he's going to refuse to let me in, but I play up the fact that I'm waiting in the cold, just in case.

"Hold on." I hear his footfalls as he walks through his otherwise silent condo, and then there's a buzz, followed by a click, and I push the ornate wood and glass door open. I've never been so glad to walk up four flights of stairs as I am now, because by the time I reach his door, I'm already warm again.

He's standing in his doorway when I approach the top landing, and he's in nothing but a towel.

"Do you have any idea how confused and embarrassed and frustrated I am right now? Drew, what the hell is going on?" I put my hand on his chest and push him back into his entryway, shutting the door behind me. I can tell he wants to talk to me, or he wouldn't have let me in so easily, but he also clearly doesn't know what to say. "Talk to me."

He folds his arms across his chest and leans back against the wall. "I'm just under a lot of pressure and trying to deal with it all. I've never had to consider anyone's feeling but my own before, and I fucked up at the game a few days ago, and I just feel like everything is imploding around me. I can't drag you both into that with me. I might just…need some space for a bit."

My stomach drops, and then anger flares through me. But I think about Lauren's words. He can't fight for us right now, but maybe what he needs to see more than anything is that I'm willing to.

"Hell no! You don't get to promise me forever—the marriage, the family, the house, everything—and then start to pull away because things are stressful. *We don't do that to each other.*"

He won't even look me in the eye as he just stares down at the floor.

"Drew, there are going to be hard times in our life and in our relationship, but we have to deal with them, and get through them, together."

He looks up at me then. His eyes are so full of anguish that it has me worried. "And what if we can't?"

"Why wouldn't we be able to?"

His nostrils flare, and then he says, "I'm being traded."

I stumble back a step into the wooden door behind me, but I'm glad to have it there because it might be all that's holding me up at this point. "What?"

"It's not definite, but it looks likely."

"Where?"

"Las Vegas."

How is this possible? He's only been back for a couple of months. "But you're having a great season. You're on the first line. You're staying out of the penalty box like AJ told you to. You got a goddamn hat trick in the last home game. Why would they trade you?"

"We need another goalie, and Vegas needs another center."

That's an odd trade, but it must make sense or AJ wouldn't be pursuing it. She doesn't seem like the kind of person to make any decision that isn't incredibly well thought out.

"When will you know for sure?" I ask, swallowing roughly.

"I don't know. A lot of times you don't even find out about this stuff until the day the trade happens. In this case, Jameson had a bit of a heads up and told me."

"When?"

His throat bobs, and there's nothing but guilt in his eyes.

"When, Drew?"

He tightens the towel around his waist as it starts to slip, then admits, "When I was in Tampa."

"You've known for *three days* and you're just telling me now, and only because I followed you home and demanded an explanation?" Now I understand why Jameson was yelling at him. He must have assumed Drew had already told me. "Why didn't you tell me when you found out?"

"Because I don't know what to say, okay!" Drew's voice cracks and his eyes fill with tears, and it's fucking heartbreaking to see him like this. "It's like someone handed me every amazing thing I could have ever wanted in life and now it's all being ripped away!"

"What's being ripped away?"

"You and Graham!"

"Why?" I pause as I take in the anguished look on his face. "Ohhh…" The word comes out slowly as the realization dawns. And then I step forward, drilling my finger into his chest with every question I ask. "You think you're being traded and so we're over? That after you forced your way into my life, showing me what a good father and good partner you are, practically demanding that I fall in love with you…you think what? That you're just going to walk away because you're being traded?"

He grabs my hand and holds it against his chest. "What choice is there, Audrey? I would never ask you and Graham to uproot your lives and move across the country."

I look up at him, and it hurts to have to ask the question. "Why not?"

Does he not want us to come with him? Or does he not think we would if he asked?

"Because you and Jules just started an amazing company, and Graham just started elementary school. Your whole family is here, and so is mine. Graham just met his grandma, aunts and uncle, and cousins. I would never uproot you from all that. Boston is your home."

My shoulders relax as I exhale, trying to calm my racing heart. I step closer to Drew and wrap my free arm around his waist, relishing the feel of his warm skin against my hand as it slides along his back.

"Did it ever occur to you to ask what I would want in this situation? Drew, how could Boston be home if you weren't with us?"

He bites his lower lip as he looks down at me. "Are you serious right now?"

"Why wouldn't I be?" I pull my hand from his and use it to cup his jaw. "Don't think for a second that you're getting rid of me that easily."

"Audrey." He drops his forehead to mine. "I'm not trying to get rid of you. The thought of losing you was *killing* me. I was trying to figure out how I could still make this still work while I was in Vegas and you were here—but the thought of being without you was physically painful. Even though I would just be doing it until the end of the season."

"What about your next contract?"

"There wouldn't be one. I've already decided it's Boston or nothing."

That has my head snapping back to look at him. "What? Why?"

"Because you and Graham are here. My family's here."

"Hockey families move, Drew. It's part of that life, and one that I accepted the minute I agreed to this relationship with you. I hope it can work out for you to stay in Boston, but our relationship isn't contingent on you playing here. If we have to make our home somewhere else, Graham and I would go with you. That's what family does."

For a moment, he's frozen, like he's trying to process what I just said—trying to make it make sense. Then, he wraps his arms around my back, pulling me to him as he brings his face down and ghosts his lips across the bridge of my nose. "What did I do to deserve you?"

"Everything. Every single thing you've done since you've been back in my life has made me fall more and more in love with you."

His head snaps back and his eyes widen as she stares down at me. Voice thick and words rough, he says, "Say it again."

"What? That I love you?"

"I'm never going to get tired of hearing that," he tells me, his breath warm as it caresses my skin. "In fact, I'm probably going to be needy as fuck, demanding that you say it all the time."

"I'll tell you as often as you need to hear it," I say with a light laugh. "But don't you *ever* try to push me away like that again. That's not what we do. Okay?"

"Promise." He leans down and takes my lips gently in his. The kiss is slow, and sensual, and as much as I want to let it lead to more, we have business to attend to first.

So I pull back, looking up at him, and ask, "Okay, so how are we going to deal with this?"

Chapter Forty-Three

DREW

We're standing in the hallway outside the locker room, waiting to make the walk to the ice. It feels like a hell of a lot more than a week ago that I stood here last, and I don't let myself consider the possibility that it could be the last time I do this in a Rebels jersey. Audrey and I decided, and Jameson agreed, that the only thing to do was to have the best damn game of my life. I need to be focused and in control. I need to show AJ that I'm the type of player this team needs.

"You good?" Zach asks.

And this time, my answer is honest. "I'm ready."

"Did Chloe help?"

Last night, after Audrey and I talked, I picked up the phone and made the call I'd been avoiding since Zach sent me the number of his sports psychologist. Her title really should be 'miracle worker,' though. I've never talked to anyone who was able to identify my fears and the ways in which I self-sabotage, and she managed it in a one-hour video call. She left me with some routines to try before tonight's game, all of which I ran through with total fidelity. And she also gave me some strategies to use in heated moments on the ice. I feel calm, and ready.

"She did. I wish I'd called her sooner."

"Keep talking to her," Zach encourages. "You'll be amazed."

I'm about to tell him I already am amazed, when a hand grips my shoulder from behind me, and I turn to find Jameson standing there. "I need you not to panic," he says, and instantly my blood is like ice.

"What happened?"

"Audrey and Graham were in an accident on the way here—"

Adrenaline floods my system, making me want to bolt out of here and go find them. "Are they okay?"

"They're at the hospital. Audrey's shaken up, but fine. Graham's hurt, but I'm not sure how badly. I'm on my way there, and I'll text you updates that you can check between periods."

"I'm coming with you!"

My teammates are turning to stare at us, but I couldn't care less.

"You *need* to play this game. I only told you because I didn't want you to look into the stands and worry about why they aren't here."

"If you think there's any way I could go out there and play right now, while Audrey and Graham are in the fucking hospital, you're insane. Give me two minutes to get this gear off while you explain to Wilcott that I'm not playing tonight."

Jameson grips my forearm as I turn toward the locker room, pulling me back toward him. He drops his voice low. "Are you absolutely sure this is what you want to do?"

"Without a doubt," I tell him, my voice clipped. I need to get out of here. Now.

I head into the locker room and am getting undressed so quickly that gear is flying everywhere, and I don't even care. Someone else is going to have to shove it all in my locker space because I don't have time. I've just pulled my sweats over my compression shorts, when the door swings open and AJ walks in.

"Why the hell aren't you on the ice, Jenkins?" Her voice has a hard, a demanding edge to it.

"My son was just in a car accident, and I need to get to the hospital to be with him and my wife."

AJ's eyebrows are practically touching her hairline. "Your...wife? And son?"

I sit to pull my sneakers on quickly and the words tumble out in a rush, "Well, future wife—I keep telling her I'm going to marry her, but I have to actually ask. And our son, who's hurt."

She presses her lips between her teeth and nods. "Okay. You should go."

My head snaps up. "Really?"

"Yeah. You should be with your family." She pauses as I stare back at her. "Why do you seem surprised?"

"Because I was treating tonight's game as my last shot to prove to you that you should keep me on the team. And by not playing..." I shrug as I stand and pull my hoodie over my head.

When I look up, AJ has her arms crossed over her chest.

"By not playing, you're showing me that you're exactly the type of trustworthy and dependable man I want on this team. I need another goalie"—she lifts one shoulder—"but Almatrov's save percentage could be better. And he's just come off the IR List, so who knows how well he'll play. Plus, the guy is kind of a douche. Wasn't sure I really wanted to add him to our team, and now I'm certain it wouldn't be the right trade. So, go. Be with the people who need you most."

My throat is tight as her words sink in. I'm staying. It's such a relief it makes my eyes water, but I don't really have time to process the emotions because I need to get to Audrey and Graham.

My GM turns and starts to walk out of the locker room.

"AJ," I call out, and she turns to face me. "Thank you."

"Go," she says. "Go be with your family. We're good."

As she walks through the door, headed back to the game, I grab my phone, wallet, and keys and am right on her heels. "I'm parked in the player's lot," I tell Jameson, who's waiting outside the locker room door. "I'll drive."

"Lauren's already got my car and is waiting right outside. Let's go."

I'm almost out of breath from how I sprinted into the ER after Lauren and Jameson dropped me at the doors before going to park, then demanded the hospital staff tell me where my son was and sprinted to his room.

I slow to a walk as I approach the open door, not sure what I'm going to find there. What I don't expect is Audrey sitting in a chair, while Graham sleeps in a hospital bed next to her. She turns when she hears me enter the room, but startles when she sees me.

"What are you doing here?" she whispers, tears streaming down her face. "You're supposed to be at your game." I shake my head.

"No, I'm supposed to be with my family."

"Drew…" Her voice is anguished. "How could you just leave the game like that? With everything on the line, you needed to be there."

I walk across the room toward her, and she stands to meet me. Taking her hands in mine, I pull her toward me and kiss her forehead. I want to wrap her tightly in my arms, I want to absorb her into me so she's always with me, I want to do everything I can to keep her and Graham safe, and in this moment, I feel like I've failed them.

"Staying was not even an option I considered. Because no matter what the choice is, no matter what I stand to lose, I'm always going to choose you. There's nothing that's more important to me—you and me and Graham, we're a family, and I'm always going to choose my family first."

She wraps her arms around me and pulls me to her. I don't know what to do except hold her to me as she sobs in my arms.

"Is he going to be okay?" I ask as nausea turns my stomach.

"Yeah, his arm is broken. No concussion or anything, though. They're giving him some medicine for the pain, which is probably why he's sleeping, and they want to do a few more tests to make sure everything else is okay."

Thank God. "Are *you* okay?"

"I…I'm just a little shook up. It all happened so fast. The

light turned green, and then as the taxi entered the intersection, a car came out of nowhere and T-boned us on the passenger side, where Graham was sitting. We're lucky the airbags all inflated, and it wasn't worse."

"I'm going to rent you a parking spot at the arena so you can drive yourself there from now on." Parking in Boston really is the worst part of living in the city, especially on game nights.

Audrey gives a little laugh in my arms. "Driving anywhere near there on a game night is a nightmare. That's why we always take a taxi."

"We'll figure out a better plan. I'll get you a driver for game nights. Someone with an impeccable driving record and an indestructible car who can be on call whenever you need them." That makes her smile, even with tears still glossing her eyes. Funny how she finds me amusing when I'm one hundred percent serious.

"You're making an awful lot of plans for someone who doesn't know if he's staying in Boston."

"For now, I'm staying." I tuck her hair behind her ear as she looks at me with confusion written across her face.

"Even though you left the game tonight?"

"Yeah, when I told AJ why I was leaving, apparently that confirmed for her that I was the kind of guy she wanted on her team."

"The kind who walks out of games?"

I think back to what McCabe said at dinner that night, about AJ wanting good men—honest, hardworking, dependable players.

"The kind you can depend on. And if my family couldn't depend on me in a situation like this, if I'd chosen my job over my family, I don't think that's the kind of person AJ wants on her team. She was one hundred percent supportive of me coming here."

A heavy breath leaves her, and she stretches up on her toes to kiss me. I'm so relieved she's okay, and that Graham will be too, that I practically melt into her arms.

"Ewwww, why are adults always kissing?" Graham asks, and Audrey's head snaps toward him, but I hold her to me.

"Because when you're in love with someone, that's one of the ways you show them how you feel," I say, my body relaxing a bit at seeing him awake.

"Like Uncle Jameson and Aunt Lauren? They're *always* kissing."

"We're not *always* kissing," Jameson says, striding into the room.

"Just most of the time?" Graham asks.

"Yep," Jameson confirms, as he slings his arm around Lauren and pulls her to him. "Most of the time."

"Excuse me," a nurse says from the door, and then she spots Graham awake in the bed. "Wow, you've certainly got a crowd here to see you, huh?"

"Yeah. This is my dad, Drew," he says, pointing at me, and I wonder if I'll always feel this sense of pride when Graham introduces me as his dad. "And my Uncle Jameson and my Aunt Lauren."

"Well, even though your family is here, I'm going to have to borrow you for a little while," she tells Graham, "because we need to do an ultrasound and make sure everything inside your body is okay. Alright, little man?"

"Can my mom come, too?" Graham asks.

"Of course," she says. "I'm going to need the rest of you to step out into the hallway so I can move this bed out and get Graham down to imaging."

My eyes and Audrey's lock, because it's then that we apparently both realize we were here in this very ER, while my mom was down in imaging, after the last home game. "Let's not make a habit of this, eh?" I kiss her nose, and she squeezes my hand, and even though I don't want to let go of her, I move out into the hallway with Jameson and Lauren.

As the nurse wheels him past, Graham waves at us with his good arm like he's on a float in a parade, and Audrey turns and mouths *"Love you"* to me as she passes.

"You made the right decision tonight," Jameson says once they're gone.

"I know." I appreciate his show of support, but this would have been the right choice even if he didn't agree with it… even if Audrey had been mad that I left the game…even if AJ hadn't decided it was a good reason to keep me on the team.

There's no world in which this *wasn't* the only choice.

Chapter Forty-Four

AUDREY & DREW

AUDREY

"That's the last of it," Colt says as he carries two boxes through the front door. They're balanced between his arms and held in place by his enormous hands on the bottom of the first box, and his chin on the top of the second. Behind him, Zach Reid and Ronan McCabe each have a box in their arms.

"I shut and locked the moving van," Zach says, nodding to the keys that sit on top of the box in his hands.

"Thanks so much," I say, grabbing the keys and hanging them on one of the hooks by the door. "Can you drop those two in Graham's bedroom?" I nod toward Colt's boxes. "And those two can go in my and Drew's room," I say, nodding toward Zach and Ronan, and thinking that it's a damn good thing Drew installed a temporary pole in his bedroom so we can take it down and put it back up whenever we want.

"For you, anything," Colt says and moves down the hall, followed by his teammates.

Behind me, the crowd in the kitchen is boisterous. I turn and head in there, loving the sound of our friends and family all coming together for our moving day. The kids are playing in the living room, and McCabe's daughter is asleep in her infant car seat on one of the chairs, completely unfazed by all the noise.

The adults are gathered around the island, helping themselves to all the brunch foods that Jules brought over for the occasion. Morgan and Paige are kicking back what has to be at least their third mimosa each, and Lauren's bemoaning the fact that she has to be responsible for toddlers.

"Have another drink," Jameson says, pushing the champagne bottle across the counter toward her. "I've got them."

Lauren laughs, and says, "You don't have to ask me twice."

When I come up next to Jules, she wraps her arm around my waist and rests her head on my shoulder.

Colt and the guys come up on the other side of her, grabbing plates and piling them with food.

"I'm going to be lonely without you," she says.

"I'm only going to be a few minutes away. And we work together. You'll see me all the time." I'm trying to remain upbeat for her sake, but the hardest part about deciding to move in with Drew was the thought of leaving Jules all alone. For years, it was the four of us—Jameson, Jules, me, and Graham—in our childhood home. And now Jules will be truly by herself for the first time in her life. Jameson and I are still close by, but I know it's not the same as having us in the house.

"I'll come over and torment you whenever you want," Colt adds, poking her in the side so she jumps up from where she's resting against me.

"Please, don't. I won't be *that* lonely," she says. "In fact, I'm changing the code for the doors just so you can't amble in whenever you feel like it."

"Pfft." The sound that escapes his mouth is part laugh, part scoff. The man lives to rile her up, and has ever since she was a gangly kid. "Like that would stop me."

"Hey," Drew says, his mouth close to my ear. I hadn't realized he relocated from the other side of the island, where he was chatting with his mom and sisters. "C'mere, I want to show you something."

He takes my hand, and I follow as he leads me to the door in the hallway that opens to the staircase up to the roof deck. He closes the door behind me and pushes me up against the wall, trapping me there with his hips as they press into me. When his mouth descends on mine, pulling my lower lip between his and nipping at it with his teeth, I laugh. "So this was just a ploy to manhandle me without our family and friends seeing?"

"There are entirely too many people here. We should have hired movers."

"Movers wouldn't have made sense," I remind him. We'd considered it, but given that the only furniture we were bringing was from Graham's bedroom, and the rest of our stuff easily fit in boxes, it made more sense to do it ourselves. "Besides, our family and friends *wanted* to be here with us. Everyone's thrilled. And I love seeing Graham surrounded by his whole family—yours and mine—and all these other friends who love us."

Three months ago, I couldn't have even envisioned a world where Drew's family and mine not only knew each other, but genuinely liked to spend time together. I couldn't have imagined all the love that constantly surrounds us now. It's the most perfectly unexpected gift, and I will be forever grateful.

"I do too," Drew says, dipping his head to run his nose along my jaw. "I just didn't realize that with you and Graham living here, and me always wanting to get you naked, there are going to be endless opportunities to practice my self-restraint. I don't want to traumatize my kid." He lets out a deep rumble of a laugh that's barely audible.

"Pretty sure that you having the opportunity to practice self-restraint, both on and off the ice, is a good thing. And while Graham will get our days, you will have all my nights," I assure him.

"Away games are going to be even harder now that I know what I'm missing at home," Drew says. It's not the first time he's mentioned this, as the team has another week-long road trip coming up in a few days.

"We'll manage," I tell him. "Like we always do."

"Can't wait for you to see what I picked out for this trip," he says with a grin. Every single time he's away for more than a night or two, a new black diamond-patterned box arrives for me. At least it gives us both something to look forward to while he's gone.

"We need to get back to our friends."

Glancing at the stairs, he says, "Okay," then opens the

door to the hallway, and when we exit, Colt glances over from where he stands at the island and smirks at us.

"Colt totally thinks we were just getting it on in the stairwell," I say to Drew as he exits behind me.

"Whatever. Let him think so," Drew says, then puts his hands on my hips, pulling me back against him as he dips his head toward my ear. "Because even though it didn't happen yet, I fully plan on fucking you on those stairs one of these days."

"Sounds...uncomfortable," I tease as I walk away toward the kitchen.

DREW

"What do you think of your new room?" Audrey asks Graham as I slip through the door from the hallway to his bedroom. His hair is still wet from his shower, and we've already gone through all the pre-bedtime rituals: brushing his teeth, picking out his pajamas, reading stories.

"It's bigger than my old room," he says as he climbs into his bed and settles himself, sitting up against his pillows.

"Sure is," she says. I'm trying to figure out how she's feeling about putting him to bed in a new house. She seems worried, but Graham seems totally fine. I don't know how the kid isn't exhausted.

After our friends and family left this afternoon, Audrey wanted a little time to get Graham's room ready—she said she was fine living amongst boxes for a bit, but wanted to make sure everything in Graham's room was unpacked so he'd feel right at home. I'd taken him over to the Esplanade—the park that runs along the Charles River in the Back Bay—and we'd thrown the football around, chased the ducks, walked all the way to the new park they just built, and then raced each other back. *I'm* exhausted just from keeping up with him.

"This room's really quiet, though," he says. "Dad, can you turn on the crickets?"

My throat tightens as the realization washes over me that he just called me Dad for the first time. He's referred to me as his dad when talking to other people before, but he's never addressed me that way. My eyes meet Audrey's, and she appears to be having the same thought.

"Sure." My voice comes out about an octave higher than usual. I turn to the dresser and hit the button for the white noise machine. It glows with a pale blue light, and the nighttime sound of crickets fills the air. "Is that better?"

"Yeah," he says, moving his pillow so it's flat on his bed, then laying down. "Can I have one more story?"

"Sure," Audrey says, "but just one."

"Will you stay too?" Graham asks me.

"Of course." I take a seat on the end of his bed, facing Audrey where she sits next to him so he can see the book as she reads to him. And as I watch them, I'm overcome with the exact same feeling I had in our kitchen earlier today. Gratitude. Complete and utter gratitude.

This could have gone so many other ways. If I hadn't been traded. Or if Audrey hadn't let me back into her life. Or if Graham hadn't adapted to the idea of us as a family. I could have missed out on this. And I'm so fucking grateful that we're here now, together—the family I always wanted eventually, and didn't even know I already had.

When we say goodnight to Graham, Audrey grabs the baby monitor off his dresser. She didn't use one anymore at their old house, but their bedrooms were right next to each other. Now that we're going to be sleeping down the hall, with a bedroom and bathroom between our room and his, I understand why she wants one. And it's a good thing she has it, because I'm about to pull her out of our condo entirely.

In the hallway, I nod my chin toward the door to the stairwell we hid in for a moment of quiet. "Earlier today, when I pulled you in there, I really did want to show you something."

"Does it involve sex on those stairs?" She gives me a little wink. "Because my back is sore from all the unpacking, and I really don't think my body can handle that right now."

"No, actually, that wasn't on the agenda."

She follows me up the stairs, and when I hit the lights and open the door to the roof deck, we step out to the amazing view.

Below us, the now bare branches of the trees along the grassy expanse of the Esplanade stretch along the muddy Charles River, so dark at night that it's perfectly black. On the other shore, the white dome of MIT's most prominent building is lit up, and the lights of the other Cambridge buildings make them glow.

"You hung lights?" Audrey asks, looking up and taking in the strands of string lights that hang from a center location on the brick wall behind us, and fan out to the tall posts I had installed along the low wall opposite. I wanted to make sure it added some ambiance, but didn't block the view. "It's so beautiful up here. I can totally picture us sitting on those couches"—she gestures to the two outdoor couches facing each other, which are currently covered for the winter—"on warm summer nights."

"We should get some of those outdoor heaters too, so we can enjoy this space even when it's cool," I say. I don't know what brought on today's amazing weather, but we got one of those freakishly warm winter days for our move. Even with the breeze tonight, I'm plenty warm in my sweatshirt, but any other year in early December, and this space might already be covered in snow.

I haven't spent much time up here by myself since buying the place, but I've tried to make it a space that Audrey, Graham, and I can enjoy together three seasons of the year.

"That would be perfect," she says as she turns toward me, and then gasps as her eyes land on the back of the roof deck. "Oh my god, Drew!"

She walks over to the planting boxes that I built along the back wall. "I wasn't expecting this."

"I wanted you to be able to have your rooftop garden here, too."

"I can't believe you even remembered that I have one," she says in awe.

She'd never taken me up to the roof deck space off her third floor, which I know used to be part of Jameson's now-vacant apartment. But she'd talked about how much she loved gardening up there in the summer.

"Believe it or not, I listen to everything you say." I shove my hands in my hoodie. "I'm not *only* thinking about getting you naked when you're around."

She trails her fingers over the two tiers of planters, with

their wood composite exterior and their lined plastic bins that I'm told will be perfect for the herbs and vegetables she grows. "I appreciate this so much."

I come up behind her, wrapping my arms around her abdomen. "I want to make sure you feel like this is your home too, not just that you and Graham are moving into my space."

"I already told you," she says, melting against me, "wherever you are feels like home."

"Well, I'll do whatever I can to make sure there's another Boston contract when mine's up at the end of the season, so that this can be our home for a while longer. Or if they do offer me another contract and you want to look for another place, we can do that, too. Whatever you want." I mean that last sentence with my whole heart. Whatever this woman wants, I will make it happen for her.

She tilts her head back against my chest and lifts her chin to trail kisses along my jawline. "I think we'll be very happy here, unless you really do want to start growing our family soon. And then, we may need a bigger place."

"Believe me, I can't wait to give you more babies." Just the thought has my whole body humming. "Whenever you're ready, you just tell me."

"Look at us," she says. "We had a child first, reconnected later, fell in love last. It's not the typical way of doing things, but I wouldn't change a single thing. I love where we've ended up. And even though I'm not quite ready to have more kids, believe me...when I am, you'll be the first to know."

She tugs on that gold disk of her necklace, the one I now know has a moon engraved on it.

"You do that when you're nervous," I say.

"Do what?" She looks up at me.

"You run that moon between your thumb and forefinger."

She huffs out a laugh. "Do I? Jules does the same thing. I didn't even realize I did, too."

"You have the same necklaces?"

"Yeah, they're from our mom. Mine has the moon, hers has the stars."

"What about the sun?"

"My mom had that one. We buried her with it." I hold her close to me, knowing there isn't anything I can do to take away that loss except to love her through it. "It's funny," she murmurs against my chest, "me being the moon and Jules being the stars."

"Why's that funny?" I ask.

"Because the moon is anchored to the Earth and can only reflect the light of other stars, whereas the stars shine on their own."

I tilt her chin up and look down at her. "Is that what you think? That you can only reflect the light of others?"

"I think…maybe that's what I thought, until you came back into my life. With you, I feel like I shine on my own."

My throat is tight and my eyes water. I didn't think there was anything she could have possibly said to make me love her more, and then she goes and says that.

"Audrey, you already shone plenty bright on your own. It's why I was attracted to you in the first place, because the love and beauty just radiate out of you. But if I make you feel like you don't have to hide that anymore, then that's perfect."

She brushes her lips against mine. "And I wasn't tugging on my necklace because I was nervous, it's because I was worried."

"What are you worried about?" I ask, wanting to ease any fears she might have.

"What if we wait to have kids, and find out we can't have any more?"

"Why in the world would you be worried about that?"

"I don't know, it happens."

"Audrey, we're a team. And if for any reason we have issues getting pregnant again, we'll deal with them—together—as they come."

"Okay," she says, and takes a deep breath. And then her hands move to my hips as she pulls me tight against her, "but maybe we should practice, just to make sure."

A rumble of laughter shakes my chest. "I think that's a phenomenal idea." I run my hand up her neck and hold her chin in place. "We'll probably need lots and lots of practice."

Epilogue
AUDREY & DREW

AUDREY

Five Months Later

"We're going to fully wrap up the project at your mom's house by the end of this coming week," I tell Drew as we trail behind Graham on the bike path along the Esplanade.

Between the cold weather and the months it took for Graham's broken arm to fully heal—during which he couldn't play hockey or do anything very physical—winter was rough. But now that the weather is nice, Drew has been bringing him here frequently, first to teach him how to ride his bike on his own, and now to practice.

I happened to come along the first time Drew let go of

Graham's bike and our son rode unassisted, and I managed to capture the whole moment on video. It feels like he's changing so fast these days, and I'm happy to be able to savor some of those milestones and to see him spending quality time with his dad.

On this particular Saturday afternoon, Graham is zipping ahead of us, then turning and riding back to us, on repeat as we walk behind him.

"I honestly think my mom is going to miss having everyone around all the time," Drew says.

We'd been so worried that she wouldn't be able to deal with the noise and the constant flux of people in and out of her house during the remodel we were doing on the first floor of her house, but somehow, she's not only adapted, but thrived. She adores Jules, who can do no wrong in her eyes. She's loved having me over there frequently checking on things. And she hasn't minded having the few other contractors in and out of her house.

"You know, that got me thinking," I say as Graham calls out to us and shows us how he can ride around in small circles without falling. We clap and Drew tells him what a good job he's doing. "Do you think she'd want to get involved in the local senior center? I'm sure she's a bit younger than most of the folks there, but she loves being around people. Maybe she could volunteer there or something?"

Drew glances over at me with that never-ending affection radiating from his face. I got so freaking lucky with this man.

"I think it's a great idea," he says. "Maybe we can look into the opportunity."

"I—" I bite my lip as he looks over at me. "I sort of already did."

He wraps his arm around my shoulder and squeezes me to him as we walk, then plants a kiss on the top of my hair. "Of course you did. And?"

"And they'd be happy to have her come in a couple times a week and help out. If she's interested."

"You should ask her," he says. Of all the wonderful things that have happened to me in the last seven months, gaining a bonus mom myself was the most unexpected. But Drew's mom has been nothing short of wonderful—supportive and loving without being overbearing. She's so much like I imagine my mom would have been if she'd lived to see me as a mother myself.

"I will," I tell him, knowing that we'll be seeing her in another hour or so. Our friends and family are all coming to our place to celebrate Drew—because not only did the Rebels offer him a new contract, it was a significant improvement over his old one. Obviously, trades or injuries are always possible in hockey, but it appears that he's going to be playing for the Rebels for the next six years. And that deserves a celebration.

We take the footbridge from the Esplanade over Storrow Drive once we reach BU's campus. We've been promising to show Graham the "BU Beach" since Drew first used the term a couple of months ago. We had to explain to our son that it's not a beach at all, but rather a grassy area behind Boston University's Marsh Plaza that borders the very busy Storrow Drive. But BU lore has it that if you sit on the grassy quad with the grassy knoll blocking the view of Storrow, the sound of the cars is reminiscent of waves.

The area is absolutely packed with college students when we arrive, because any time there's a nice day, people flock there for the sunshine and open space.

"So you guys used to study here?" Graham asks, looking around at the students in their shorts and t-shirts, spread out on blankets, a variety of music playing from portable speakers throughout the area. There's laughter and talking, a few students throwing around a frisbee, a group of people sitting together in a small circle playing harmonicas and singing. It's chaotic and busy, and not the kind of environment you'd imagine studying in.

"Well," Drew says, "not sure how much studying happened, but we met here a couple times, right at the end of the school year. Like right now"—he nods to all the students as we walk Graham's bike along a path through the grass—"all these people are getting ready for finals. Because at the end of the school year, you have a big test called a final in each class. Your mom helped me get ready for my final in my math class."

In reality, we got about as much studying done on the BU Beach as these students are doing now. Which is why we'd inevitably end up next door, in the library, where Drew would comment on how the coconut scent of my sunscreen was distracting him.

"Because she's the smart one?" Graham asks. I know he's just repeating Drew's words, but I hate the perception that his dad isn't smart enough.

I give Drew the *stop saying that shit* look over Graham's head. "Because while there's lots of things your dad is great at, I happen to be particularly good at math."

"Like me," he says. He's learning to add in kindergarten

and it's coming very easily. He's able to subtract, too, even though they haven't really started learning that yet.

"Like you," I confirm.

"And I'm good at hockey like Dad," Graham says, looking up with the same stars in his eyes that he had the first time Drew skated onto the rink at his practice. The fact that his dad is a professional hockey player has *not* gotten old for this kid.

"Very true," Drew says, reaching down and patting Graham's shoulder.

We walk down Bay State Road, showing Graham the brownstone that served as my dorm junior and senior year, and then the larger dorm that housed basically the whole hockey team a few blocks away. The fourth floor of that dorm wasn't officially the "hockey floor," but that's how we all referred to it.

By the time we're back to Beacon Street, a text from Jules comes in.

> JULES:
> I'm here with the food, so get your butts home.

After all the cleaning and prepping for the party this morning, we really needed to get Graham out for a while. I know Jules is happy to help, and that she's undoubtedly already got Colt and Jameson carrying dishes and trays of food into our place, but we also need to get back and help with the final touches.

Plus, it's hotter than I expected out here, and now I'm kind of a sweaty mess. "I'd love to grab a quick shower when we get back, before everyone else gets to our place," I tell Drew.

Drew looks at me over Graham's head and mouths, *Can I help?* and I widen my eyes in the *Stop it!* look I find myself giving him often. It's useless, though. I don't think he's ever going to stop wanting to get me alone and naked. And I find that I'm perfectly okay with that fact.

"Go ahead." He shrugs. "Graham and I can make sure everything's all set so you can shower, right, Bud?"

The two exchange a look I can't decipher, which seems to be happening more and more these days, almost like they have their own father-son language.

"Sure, Dad."

DREW

"Where's Audrey?" Jameson asks as he comes into the kitchen.

"Still getting ready," I say.

Across the island, Jules rolls her eyes as the buzzer rings again, signaling more people arriving, while her sister is still in our bedroom. I don't know what the big deal is. Audrey wants to look nice for our party, and it's not like we don't have everything under control out here.

"I'm going to check on her," Jules says, and heads down the hallway toward our bedroom. She stops to bend down and says something to Graham, who nods and gives her a little smile. Then she continues down the hall to our room.

Next to me, Colt's eyes track Jules before sliding back toward me. "So I'm stuck with you for six more years?"

"Like you're still going to be around in six years, old man." I elbow him in the side, and he doesn't even budge. He's a fucking brick wall, even in the back half of his thirties.

"Hey now," both Colt and Jameson growl, and I burst out laughing.

"Is that, like, the old man thing to say when you're called on your age?" I'm pretty sure Jameson's a couple of years older than Colt, but they're both still a lot older than me. At this point, Colt has been playing for Boston for going on two decades. I don't know how the man's knees still work.

"First of all," Jameson says, "you better cut that shit out if you want me to keep getting contracts for you." In addition to the contract with Boston, he recently negotiated my first big endorsement deal—and that alone will pay for any medical care my mom will need for the rest of her life. "And second, stop acting like a child. You're almost thirty."

I huff out a laugh. "I turned twenty-nine two weeks ago."

"It's so cute listening to you guys argue about your ages," Lauren teases as she walks up behind Jameson, circling her arms around his waist and squeezing. "I think it proves you're all just the same level of immature, so your ages don't really matter."

Jameson turns and bends his head, nipping at Lauren's ear so that she squeals and backs away, and he follows her.

And that's when Audrey emerges from the bedroom, with Jules trailing behind her. Her dark hair is down, the loose curls falling over her bare shoulders. Cheeks pink, her face is glowing, and those gorgeous full lips have a hint of gloss. She literally takes my breath away, over and over, all the freaking time.

She walks toward me, the black t-shirt material of her sundress hugging her curves, and the bottom flowing around her knees. The whole thing is held up with two tiny satin straps on her shoulders. Everything else going on around me fades away and I only see her. When she reaches me, she leans up on her toes to give me a quick kiss.

I must be getting much better at the whole self-restraint thing, because I don't run my hands along those seductive curves and slide my thumbs under the straps of her dress like I really want to. Instead, I wrap my arms around her waist, pulling her to me as I whisper, "You're so fucking beautiful."

She laughs lightly, and says, "Thanks." She's getting better at taking compliments.

Behind her, I watch Graham unzip his sweatshirt and toss it on the couch, and I know it's game time. "You'd better start saying hi to our guests," I suggest, as I kiss her forehead, and then guide her hips away from me so there's a sliver of space between us. I hate it when I'm not touching her, but I need her to stop focusing on me so she sees Graham.

"Alright," she agrees, and turns to start saying hello and thanking people for coming.

"How long do you think it'll take her to notice?" Jules asks quietly as she comes up next to me.

"No idea. But I probably should stick close to her, so I'm there when she *does* notice."

"Probably a good idea."

"I'll be shocked if someone doesn't accidentally spoil it." My money's on Caitlyn and her overly dramatic reactions to everything, but I don't say that to Jules because the two of them seem to get along well. Plus, my relationship with Caitlyn really is so much better than it was.

"Nah," she says. "Everyone's going to love it so much, they wouldn't dare ruin the surprise."

"You didn't tell Colt, did you?" I ask, watching Audrey chat with Missy and my mom.

"I told you I wouldn't tell anyone."

"Well, you do live with the man." I look for Graham, trying to make sure I'm still close enough to Audrey in case she sees him and his shirt.

Jules's laugh is a snort. "Not by choice. And it doesn't mean I swap secrets with him."

"I don't need to know anything about what you two are swapping–"

She slaps my arm hard and laughs, saying, "Ew, stop it. That's so gross."

"Let's just hope he knows how to keep it cool when he sees Graham's shirt." Colt's the biggest kid of them all, so maybe I should be more worried about his reaction than Caitlyn's.

"Your message in the group chat was *very* clear. You've got a surprise planned, and when people realize what it is, they need to not act suspicious. I'm sure most people have guessed." She nudges me in the side. "Go on, get your girl."

I don't know why I'm nervous as I come up behind Audrey, where she's now talking to her brother, but I am. I face two hundred-and fifty-pound giants who are trying to pummel me while I skate around the ice on literal knife blades, and it doesn't faze me. But give me a five-foot-six brunette with the brightest blue eyes who holds the key to all my future happiness, and suddenly I have fucking butterflies roaming around my stomach.

I scan the room, and Graham is walking around with his chest puffed out, like he wants people to start noticing his shirt. And they do. I see it in the way Lauren's hand flies to her mouth, her lips formed in a silent 'O.' I see it in the way Walsh shifts his baby to his other arm as he turns to look at me and nods in approval. I see it when Colt's eyes widen, and he looks over at Jules like he might murder her. I see it when my mom grips Missy's hand and her eyes fill with tears. I see it on the faces of every person who loves us as they realize what they are about to witness.

After another minute, the only people in the room who don't seem to know what's happening are Audrey and Jameson, because their heads are tucked together in conversation. When Graham looks at me, I give him a little nod and he walks toward Audrey.

The room has gotten quieter. The music still plays in the background, but people are so focused on Audrey that it's like they've forgotten to carry on the conversations they were having. So Graham's voice rings out when he says, "Hey, Mom, can you tie my shoe for me."

"Sure, Bud," she says as she turns and looks down at him. I'm only a step behind her when she gasps. I guess she finally noticed the *Dad wants to know if you'll marry him?* shirt Graham's been walking around the party wearing for the last five minutes.

She starts to turn, like she's looking for me, and the minute our eyes meet, I drop to one knee directly behind her, holding the ring box out in my hand. Her hand flies to her chest as her eyes fill with tears. This proposal is not unexpected—I've been saying for months that I'm going to marry her soon—but I guess the timing is.

"You may be wondering," I say while looking up at her, "why I'm proposing in a room full of people when I know what a private person you are, and how much you hate being the center of attention."

Her chest shakes with laughter as a small smile graces her lips. "Pretty much."

"The truth is, I couldn't imagine proposing without our friends and family being part of this moment. Many of the people in this room have been there for you and Graham since before I was in the picture. And everyone here helped get us to this point in one way or another.

"For years, I thought I wasn't ready to settle down, but now I realize that I just hadn't found the right person yet, because nothing about being with you and Graham feels like settling. There is no place I'd *ever* rather be than right next to you. You're the person I think about before I skate out for a game, the one I look for when I line up at center ice, the one I can't wait to get back to the hotel and call when I'm away." In the background, my teammates laugh because they're always giving me shit for rushing back to talk to her instead of going out.

"You welcoming me back into your life and letting me be a father is the most precious gift you could have possibly given me. And I want everything with you, the exciting moments and the mundane. I want the Stanley Cup championship celebration"—cheers go up around us because we're headed into the next round of the playoffs this week—"*and* I want to watch cartoons in our pajamas on Saturday mornings as a family. Because none of it, from the happiest moments to the most difficult, would mean anything if you weren't by my side.

"And when I finally watch you walk down the aisle to me, and when we grow our family, and when I'm too old to play hockey and you're exhausted from all our kids...we're still going to be surrounded by the people who are in this room right now."

There are tears streaming down Audrey's face, but I've never seen her smile quite so big. And as I stare up at her, she raises her eyebrows at me, but I'm too transfixed on her face to understand what she's trying to tell me.

"Were you...going to *ask* me something?" she says.

Around us, people's laughter fills the air, and Graham steps up beside me and uses his six-year-old whisper voice, which is only slightly below his yelling voice, to say, "I think you're supposed to say, 'Will you marry me?'"

I open the ring box. "Audrey Marie Flynn, will you marry me?"

She stares down into the box, to the big round diamond surrounded by smaller triangles of diamonds to make the shape of a sun. For a moment, she doesn't speak. And then she says, "Is that...?"

She understands the significance of me choosing a sun.

"Yes."

"Oh my goodness." She stands there, eyes focused on the ring box, completely mute.

"Were you...going to *answer* the question?" I tease.

"Say. Yes," Graham says in his stage whisper, and again, the room erupts in laughter.

"Yes. Without question, absolutely yes!"

I stand and take the ring out of the box, slipping it on her finger before she throws her arms around my neck. "I can't believe you got me a sun-shaped ring," she whispers.

"You are my sun, Audrey. You're the center of my whole universe, the star that Graham and I are lucky enough to orbit around. And you always will be."

She squeezes me tight, burying her face in the crevice between my shoulder and neck. "I love you so much."

"I love you too. Forever."

THE END

Want more Drew and Audrey? Get their bonus epilogue here.

Scan here for
Drew & Audrey's
Bonus Epilogue

Curious about Zach Reid? He has his own novella, THE TRADE UP, which you can download here.

Scan here for
The Trade Up
Novella

FAKE SHOT
Boston Rebels, Book 2

Colt & Jules

This steamy brother's best friend, fake dating story is coming soon!

Books by Julia Connors

FROZEN HEARTS SERIES

On the Edge
(Jackson & Nate's Story)

Out of Bounds
(Sierra & Beau's Story)

One Last Shot
(Petra & Aleksandr's Story)

One Little Favor
(Avery & Tom's Novella)

On the Line
(Lauren & Jameson's Story)

BOSTON REBELS SERIES

Center Ice
(Audrey & Drew's Story)

Fake Shot
(Jules & Colt's Story)

Acknowledgments

Each time I start a new book, I think the writing process will get easier. Somehow, it's always more difficult.

It is a privilege to have people in my corner supporting me through the entire process. It's a privilege to have people promoting this book before it's even released because of their genuine enthusiasm for my stories. It's a privilege to have a family that has carried everything for me while I finished this book. It is such a privilege to get to write THE END and know that there are people out there waiting for the book. And I don't take a single one of these things for granted!

I've been overwhelmed with the support readers have shown me for my Frozen Hearts series, and the way you all have enthusiastically waited for the first book in my Boston Rebels series. So this book is for you…

Melissa – There are no words. I genuinely can not put into words what your support, your feedback, your encouragement, and your tough love have meant to me. This book would not be what it is without you.

Casey – Your feedback on my book, and your hockey knowledge, have saved me more than once while writing this book. Thank you for always being willing to answer my questions and give feedback!

Kait – I'm not sure how I went through this whole "being an author" thing before finding you. Thank you for keeping me on track, picking up all the pieces I drop, giving feedback on this book, and just generally being amazing!

Autumn – Having you in my corner has been the best change. I can't wait to see what we do together in the future. Thank you!!!

Elizabeth – Thank you for being there for me through everything this crazy year has brought. I'm so glad we're in this together!

Sarah – You're a genius with naming everything for me: series, books, teams…thank you for sharing your talents with me!

Rhea – Thank you for all your help and feedback on the cover design for my books. I love getting to run ideas and thoughts by you, and the way you help me get what's in my head onto my actual covers. You're brilliant, and I can't wait to see what life holds for you!

And mostly, to *Mr. Connors* – I say this with every book, but it's only more and more true…I could not have done this without you. Thank you for supporting me in this journey while also gently reminding me that there's more to life than work and I need to find a better balance. You're not wrong.

Afterword

Thank you so much for reading! If you enjoyed the book, please consider leaving an honest review. Reader reviews mean so much to authors, and your time and feedback are appreciated.

Sign up for Julia's newsletter to stay up to date on the latest news and be the first to know about sales, audiobooks, and new releases!

www.juliaconnors.com/newsletter

About the Author

Julia Connors grew up on the warm and sunny West Coast, but her first decision as an adult was to trade her flip-flops for snow boots and move to Boston. She's been enjoying everything that New England has to offer for over two decades, and now that she's acclimated to the snowy winters and finally found all the places to get good sushi and tacos, she has zero regrets. You can usually find her in front of her computer, but when she stops writing she's most likely to be found outdoors, preferably with a pair of skis or snowshoes strapped to her feet in winter, or on a paddleboard in the summer.

goodreads.com/julia_connors
amazon.com/author/juliaconnors
instagram.com/juliaconnorsauthor
tiktok.com/@juliaconnorsauthor?
facebook.com/juliaconnorsauthor
pinterest.com/juliaconnorsauthor

Made in the USA
Coppell, TX
12 April 2024

31247740R00256